Books by B. V. Larson:

STAR FORCE SERIES
Swarm
Extinction
Rebellion
Conquest
Battle Station
Empire
Annihilation
Storm Assault
The Dead Sun
Outcast
Exile
Gauntlet
Demon Star

REBEL FLEET SERIES
Rebel Fleet
Orion Fleet
Alpha Fleet
Earth Fleet

Visit BVLarson.com for more information.

Jungle World

(Undying Mercenaries Series #19)

by

B. V. Larson

Undying Mercenaries Series:
Steel World
Dust World
Tech World
Machine World
Death World
Home World
Rogue World
Blood World
Dark World
Storm World
Armor World
Clone World
Glass World
Edge World
Green World
Ice World
City World
Sky World
Jungle World

Illustration © Tom Edwards
TomEdwardsDesign.com

Copyright © 2023 by Iron Tower Press.

This book is a work of fiction. Names, characters, places and incidents are either products of the author's imagination or used fictitiously. Any resemblance to actual events, locales or persons, living or dead, is entirely coincidental. All rights reserved. No part of this publication can be reproduced or transmitted in any form or by any means, without permission in writing from the author.

ISBN-13: 979-8375564050
BISAC: Fiction / Science Fiction / Military

"Remember: you will die."
—Roman proverb

-1-

When a man lives as long as I have and has suffered through many battles, wars, and outright deaths, he develops certain traditions. These traditions are designed to relieve stress, to reset one's mind, to change modes from that of conflict and stress to relaxation and normal living. Accordingly, when I got back home to Waycross, Georgia, I immediately began a lengthy and utterly lazy vacation.

For several long months, the world cooperated. I haunted the various eateries, bars, and pool halls of Waycross. I pestered any young lady who gave me a smile and a nod, and I generally enjoyed myself.

Months went by, and I soon tuned out all the nonsense coming from the online news streams. There were plenty of dark reports about border skirmishes with Rigel and strange, giant rocks flying out of deep space to strike a planet here or there. In fact, I was so determined to maintain my ostrich-with-his-head-in-the-sand attitude that I soon tuned out of every newsfeed, even those on my own tapper. Insulated and armored, I had a glorious time without a care in the world.

Then, one fateful autumn day when the leaves were just beginning to turn yellow, I received a message that I just couldn't ignore.

"This is Graves," it read. "I'm on my way down to your place. See you in the a.m."

I blinked at that, and a small amount of frothy bubbles from my shampooed head dribbled into my right eye due to my distraction. I was, in fact, taking a shower at that moment and just happened to be flicking through a few notices of interest on my tapper.

Squinting, I found I could hardly read the entire message. My forearm was just as covered in suds as the rest of me. But after spraying off the foam, I was able to see the truth. Graves had sent me a message indicating he was on his way down from Central.

My foggy mind leapt forward, and I realized this message must have come in last night. In fact, after checking the date and time, I figured out Graves had to be arriving soon. He'd said something about the a.m., which meant morning—and right now it was *definitely* morning.

My jaw sagged low in disbelief, and I muttered a multitude of curses. Spraying off the rest of my overly large person, I turned off the water, and that's when I heard the thumping.

Heavy, deep hollow-sounding bangs were reverberating through my domicile. Having a keen sense for these things, I was able to identify the source of the offending sound within moments—someone was hammering on my front door.

Climbing out of the shower, I grabbed the towel but didn't bother to dry myself off. The visitor seemed intent on invading my home in my most private moment. Being a man who wasn't much concerned by things like nudity or embarrassment, I walked across my stained carpet and threw open the door.

Graves was standing there on my sagging porch. His fist was raised up for yet another hammering. The look on his face could only be described as a scowl.

"Well, hello there, Primus," I said. "What can I do you for?"

Graves eyed me with a mixture of disapproval and disgust. "Get dressed, McGill," he said. "Then come out here and take a walk with me. We need to talk." With that, he turned around and marched out into the yard.

Grunting unhappily, I did as he asked. I had yet to have any breakfast, a proper shave or even finish relieving myself. I was annoyed to be accosted in this fashion by a superior officer when I was technically off-duty.

I had half a mind to make him wait until I was properly dressed and shined up. I considered pointing out to him I was demobilized, and that he would have to reactivate my contract to boss me around.

But I did none of these things. Graves wasn't exactly a friend, but he was a long-term acquaintance of mine. We'd gone through a lot together over the past four or five decades, and I knew that no amount of complaints or jackassery was going to affect the outcome of this situation. Accordingly, I pulled some clothes over my sticky, wet body, pulled on some boots—without even bothering about socks—and walked outside.

I gave myself a vigorous shake, spraying water droplets everywhere on the porch like a hound dog. Graves watched this performance from a safe distance and still looked disgusted.

"Didn't you get my message?" he asked.

"I surely did, sir. I just didn't expect you to be here this early."

Graves twisted up his face. "It's ten o'clock in the morning, McGill. That's not early."

"Well sir, I don't live by military time when I'm not on active duty. By the way, you wouldn't happen to have a contract approval in your back pocket, would you?"

"Hell, no. This visit is unofficial."

"Huh?" I said, thinking that over. I didn't like the sound of it. Sometimes, Graves was party to certain dark, unsafe activities. In fact, I'd gotten myself beaten to death multiple times and sentenced to a decade of nonexistence just last year. All that was just for the crime of having been associated with this man.

On my guard, I eyeballed him with suspicions of my own. My eyes narrowed, and I shook my head. "I don't know, sir… If this is unofficial, I don't think I want anything to do with it."

Graves gave me a cold glance in return. "You're involved with this McGill, whether you want to be or not. Now, I'm going to take a walk. If you don't want to know what's about to happen to you and your family, then you stay right here, finish your shower, have a beer and go back to bed. I don't really care. But, if you're interested in the nature of your fate, follow me."

With that cryptic comment, Graves turned around and walked away. He didn't stride out to the road where I suspected he'd parked a tram but instead headed across my weed-choked yard.

I didn't follow him immediately. I stood there on my porch, grumbling with my hands on my hips.

Graves walked into my toolshed and rummaged around for a bit. Finally, he came out again and headed for the woods. Oddly, he looked like a man who knew where he was going. This concerned me, as not that long ago, I'd made certain unsavory discoveries out in those forested, bog-filled regions. Normally, no one ever went out there except me or members of my family.

Mumbling fresh curses, I decided I had to follow him. Just in case, I pocketed a pistol and a combat knife. Neither one bulged too much in my pockets, the pistol being small and slim-barreled. It was one of those cheap alien brands that were only good for burning a hole in an unarmed and unsuspecting man.

Being long of leg, my stride widened, and I was able to catch up to him.

"Hey Primus," I called after him, "just where in the heck are we going?"

"You know where we're going, McGill."

I frowned at that. I knew of precisely two places in my parents' back-forty that were of extreme interest. One was an old barn to which I had taken many a person that needed killing—leaving the bodies there to rot away in the slimy bog. The second was an old Unification War bunker that Etta had discovered, which I had plundered only the year before.

I didn't want to see either one of these places again. I put up a good front and laughed heartily. "I'm sorry, sir," I said, "there's nothing out here but woodpeckers and water moccasins. Anybody who's told you different has been having you on."

"I know about the bunker, McGill," he said. "We talked about it. Remember?"

"Uh... oh yeah. Well, sir, there's not much to see. It's just a hole in the ground and a few rotten antiques. I did manage to get a pair of night vision goggles that work decently well. You want to see them? They're back in my shack."

"No," Graves said. He never turned his head to look at me, and he never shortened his stride. He just kept on plowing through the forested land, pushing aside branches now and then, so they snapped back and slapped me one in the face. I couldn't help but notice that he seemed to be well aware of the way. He definitely wasn't heading for the barn, but rather toward the area in which the bunker had been discovered.

That brought all kinds of fresh questions to my mind. "Sir, what's so important about my back property?"

Graves laughed, but there wasn't any humor in the sound. "You're finally interested, huh? Your lack of curiosity and the remoteness of this place is exactly why we decided to use it."

"We? Which 'we' are we talking about, sir?"

"Never mind. You don't want to know."

Reflecting to myself that he was probably right that I didn't want to know, I shut up about it, but I was still concerned. If Graves knew that the old bunker was out here, that meant he had to know what had been in it—which included some mighty strange things.

What was worse, I'd plundered the place and taken the sole item of interest—a disembodied talking brain in a jar. I'd removed this dubious trophy out to Dust World and left it there. I figured that when he learned about this... he might not be overjoyed.

Someone else might have confessed early, trying to mitigate the officer's anger—but I'm not a man who likes to reveal information ahead of time to anyone. In my experience, warning people about inevitable upcoming surprises, especially ones that were certain to be received poorly, often led those individuals to mistakenly blame poor old McGill for those unhappy feelings.

Accordingly, I talked about nonsense, pointing out various plants and animals of interest. The whole slog out into the swamp saw me chattering in a pointless, friendly manner to make myself seem as innocent and harmless as possible.

"Did you know some of these trees out here in this swamp are a thousand years old? It's true. I looked it up. Some of the oldest living plants on the entire North American continent are right here."

"Shut up, McGill," Graves said. "This is the spot, isn't it?"

"Uh…" I said, looking around as if I was baffled.

Graves frowned at me. "Where is the mound? I don't see it."

I swung my big head around, looking as ignorant as possible. After this display, I threw my hands high, and I threw them wide. "I don't even know what you're talking about, sir!"

Graves gave me a dark look. "You better not have come out here with a tractor and plowed the place over."

"That's just plain crazy-talk. I don't even know what you mean. I don't even…" While I was saying these nonsensical words and pretending that I was completely innocent and clueless, Graves beat about the bushes until he finally found the mound I'd hidden with a set of fresh bushes. I'd planted them here to disguise the hatch and keep unwanted eyes like his away.

"Ah, I get it," he said. "You camouflaged the entrance… Not bad—you covered the whole thing with soil, even the hatch. All right, here we go." He threw me a shovel he'd taken from our toolshed. "Start digging."

With a sheer lack of enthusiasm, I helped him dig up the bunker hatch. Soon he had it exposed, and he flung it wide open.

Dark earth crumbled and dribbled down into the black hole. The interior had that musty smell—the same rusted-out, old-fashioned hole-in-the ground smell that it had the last time I'd been out here.

Graves looked at me, and he smiled with half his mouth. "You've been out here hiding this place, haven't you?"

"What? I had no earthly idea, sir. No idea at all."

Graves gestured toward the yawning hole. "You first."

I heaved a sigh, tossed the shovel aside and climbed down the rusty steel rungs into the darkness. I flicked on a flashlight and looked around at the interior. It was pretty much the same as the last time I'd left it. Maybe a little wetter, a little colder, but essentially untouched.

Graves followed me down the ladder and stood on the wire deck at the bottom, looking around. "Where did the... oh, I get it. You stacked junk on top of the hatch to the second level, didn't you?"

"What sir? That's outright insane. I don't even know what the hell we're doing down here, and I'm damned sure I don't know what this place is. I think Etta used to play out here, though. She called it a hideout when she was little, but you know, I thought it was too dangerous, so..."

"Shut up," Graves said. He was tired of my lies, and next to my father, he was the hardest man I knew to fool with a line of horseshit. That was probably because he'd been listening to my particular brand for so many long years.

Graves began heaving and straining, pushing aside the various barrels and cartons I'd stacked on top of the hatch that led down to the second deck below us.

I acted as surprised and befuddled as I was able when he found the hatch to the second floor and heaved it open. It creaked, and the metal groaned. The hinges were unoiled and loud in the dark, confined space.

Graves led the way, and he soon disappeared down into the dark interior of the lower level.

I stood there at the top of the hatch, and I have to confess, certain unpleasant thoughts crossed my mind. For instance, if I simply threw that hatch closed, latched it, locked it, and chained it up—then maybe piled a few crates and cartons on top... Well, a man like me might be able to scuttle up that ladder, slam the hatch, and bury the whole bunker again.

The idea was captivating once it had crossed my devious mind. I would feel guilty, of course, but I knew myself. I knew I would fret for a while then soon forget about the whole thing.

That was a gift of mine, see. A power. Some people call it *compartmentalization*. It was a psychological advantage that gave me a third option in moments like this, one that ordinary people might never perceive.

For a more conventional soldier in the legions, when a superior officer gave you a direct order, you had two straightforward options. Number one, you obeyed immediately and without hesitation. Or two, you disobeyed and refused to follow the commands of your rightful superior.

The second option obviously had consequences. One could expect a flogging at the very least and possibly a demotion. All that was normal—the sort of thing that I'd experienced on any number of occasions in the past.

But, for a man such as myself—a personality type I've come to believe is rather rare and almost unique in this universe of ours—there was always a third option. That was to engineer the demise of the person giving you the command in the first place.

In short, I would be scot-free if I chose to trap Graves down here and let him rot in the dark. This bunker was in a dead spot, with no wireless connection to the grid. There were no communications, no electricity, water, food—nothing whatsoever to support life long-term. He would surely die within the span of a week, tops.

Then, I would have various choices to make. Since Graves and I were off the grid now, that meant that our minds weren't being recorded by our tappers and relayed to the data core. There was some short-term memory in the tapper units themselves, of course, but that could be erased by a little bit of unsubtle work with a sharp knife on your victim's forearm.

Essentially, I was in the position to either perm Graves by leaving him down there until he was nothing but a skeleton in a suit, or optionally, I could stage a shocking rediscovery of his body elsewhere.

On that happy day, he might turn up with a damaged tapper, an unrecorded mind, and essentially no memories of what had transpired. Best of all, I could do this hat trick at my leisure. It could come a week from now, a month from now—or maybe a decade on…

Now, any sane and normal person might be wondering to themselves why in the hell would I take it upon myself to abuse a good man such as Graves—one who definitely deserved better. It would be a callous and unforgivable act, that is for certain.

Well sir, the way I saw it Graves had brought this upon himself. He had come out here unofficially, without even the courtesy of activating my contract. He'd come to my home where my beloved family resided, and now he had involved me in the nefarious business of reviving ancient rebel ties to the distant past.

Sure, I knew Graves had been involved in the Unification Wars, but that wasn't my problem. I hadn't been there, my daddy hadn't, and as far as I knew, not even grandpappy McGill—rest his soul—had participated in those dark times.

The old rebel years were in the distant past. Even the oldsters avoided talking about those days.

But Graves was a man apart from the rest. He made old people look like kids. A century had gone by since this man had aged a day. He remembered things that everyone else had forgotten either on purpose or by edits to their minds.

What all this essentially meant was that Graves was a threat. He was a threat to me. He was a threat to my family. He was, in fact, a threat to everything I knew and held dear. That's why I didn't follow him down into that dark pit. He went down into the lower level of the bunker alone.

Instead, I stood at the top of the ladder and contemplated my options.

"McGill?" Graves called from under my feet. "Stop screwing around and get down here. What did you do to this door, man? By God, you're an idiot!"

I didn't answer. I just stood there, stared at that hatch, and considered my choices…

-2-

I made a fateful decision. It was a hard one to make because I liked Graves, I'd known and respected him for many, many years.

But he'd come out here uninvited and endangered me and mine. That just couldn't be tolerated—not in my book.

It was one thing when he ordered me on a suicide mission, or when he meted out a harsh but usually justified punishment. It was quite another when he involved my family, my father, my mother, my only daughter—innocents all of them—in something that was obviously not their doing.

You see, the real problem was that Hegemony was not a forgiving government entity. Just like the Galactics themselves, our true overlords, Hegemony officials took a very dim view of any rebellious behavior, seditious thoughts, or shenanigans in general.

I knew this myself, having been abused recently, simply due to the vaguest association with Graves and his secretive cause. Sure, I was sympathetic, and it might be nice to bring back the old Republic. Those were the good old days when Earth's nations stood independent, and men were comparatively free. But after I had been soundly punished for simply making a few on-grid queries about the matter, I knew there would be no mercy shown by the officials should they discover that Graves was out here in my swamp doing unacceptable things.

Therefore, I was acting out of an abundance of caution rather than malice or outrage. The long and the short of it was Graves had involved relative innocents that I cared about, and by doing so, he had forfeited any and all goodwill I had toward him personally.

The hatch clanged shut at my feet. I didn't even recall afterward having kicked it closed.

"McGill?"

This time, the shout had a different tone to it. Graves had finally perceived that his fate was in my hands, and that things were not going well. I wouldn't say that his voice was pleading or scared. I would definitely say, however, that he was now alarmed rather than contemptuous.

"McGill, open that hatch right now. That's an order."

"Sorry, sir," I said. "I just can't take the chance."

"What the fuck? What are you doing, McGill? You'd leave me down here in this dark hole to rot?"

"Not necessary, sir. You know how to off yourself. There are a dozen ways to do it, and you've probably tried them all."

Graves was silent for a moment. I took this time to walk to the ladder that led back up to sunshine, tweeting birds, fluttering yellow leaves, life, and happiness. All that good stuff was just above me. Soon, Graves would not be able to hear, smell or see any of it.

I put one foot on the bottom rung of the ladder.

Then Graves spoke again. He bellowed from down there under my heavy boots.

"McGill?" he said. "Wait a second. Let's talk."

I hesitated, even though in my heart of hearts, I knew I shouldn't. When you're going to murder someone, especially somebody you care about, somebody you respect and admire, it's best to do it quick and sudden-like.

I knew all that, but still I hesitated. "Talk away, sir," I said.

"All right—listen to me. I made a miscalculation. I shouldn't have done it, and I apologize for having come down to your home and treating you like you're one more recruit on my training field. That was an error."

My eyebrows shot up, and my eyeballs opened wide. Graves was admitting an error. This was an extremely rare event. Now mind you, he wasn't a man who was accustomed to making errors in the first place, but in my opinion, he was even less accustomed to admitting it when he did.

"Keep going, sir," I said.

"I—I mean, *we* left something down here, McGill. It was a mistake. It happened a long time ago, and it was done with the best of intentions, I assure you."

"A lot of people have died over this, sir, whatever the hell it is."

"I know that," he said. "Millions more died long before you were born over the same disagreement. But listen McGill, a long, long time ago, I was given responsibility for keeping alive an ember of hope for the future. I've been a poor steward of that hope. In fact, I think I let it die in myself."

I didn't rightly know what he was talking about. What's more, I didn't much care, but I let him talk with both my hands on that ladder and one foot on that bottom rung.

My eyes kept drifting up to the sunlight, the peeping of birds and the moving clouds. It all seemed far, far above. I wanted to get out of here and forget about the whole thing. Speaking of which, forgetting this was going to require a six pack—no, a twelve pack—of beer tonight and probably the next three nights in a row afterward.

"McGill, are you listening to me?"

I realized then Graves had been talking—prattling along and telling me something—but I hadn't really been listening. "I'm hanging on every word, sir."

"Well, like I said, this bunker was here long before your family came to own this land."

"I figured out that much, Primus."

"There are a lot of bunkers like this, hidden away in various remote locations. Many of them were discovered—but not all. I happen to know where a number of them are still hidden. Anyway, some years after your family bought this land and back when Turov sent some goons to your shack to get into a fight with you—"

"Ha-ha," I roared, laughing. "I remember that. I killed all three of them."

"Yes, you did," Graves continued, "and you got yourself killed in the bargain. Anyway, as you might remember, a full unit of troops was deployed here in this swamp back then. As a person who was intimately aware of the locations of various remote bunkers like this one, I realized that one of them was right here on your land."

"That was back during the Tech World campaign…" I said, thinking that over. "That makes more sense. Is that why you decided to come out here and stash some secret?"

"That's right. I knew you weren't going anywhere. Your family wasn't going anywhere. You were semi-friendly personnel, and I figured you would squat here on this land possibly for decades while you served the legions."

I thought that over, and I thought it was rather diabolical for a man like Graves. This was the sort of thing that Claver might have come up with—or maybe even me.

"All right, sir," I said. "I'm listening. Keep talking."

"Well, the rest should be obvious. We've got a man who's a long-term member of the legions and living on an isolated piece of land. This happens to be one of the rare spots on Earth that's still off the grid. What makes the whole equation perfect is this damned bunker down here. Where better on Heaven or Earth could we hide something we didn't want discovered by Hegemony?"

"Really, Primus, sir?" I asked. "You really had to choose my land for this? Without even telling me?"

Graves chuckled grimly. "You think I should have told you about it?" he asked. "Look how you're reacting now. You're ready to perm a career officer directly up the chain from you. May I remind you that's a serious offense, by the way?"

"Point taken, sir."

"All right. We made a choice. Possibly it was unfair, possibly it was ill-considered, but it doesn't matter now. It's decades old. We took certain individuals, let's call them 'lost souls', and we hid them here in this bunker a long, long time ago. Ever since then, we checked on them now and again. In fact, I get a message concerning the status of this bunker on my tapper every so many months on special days."

"Huh," I said. "Yeah, I remember you telling me that before…"

"Okay, now do you believe me?" Graves asked.

"Oh sure, sir. I believe you. I believed every word of it before you even spoke it. In fact, a lot of it fits and makes good sense. But that doesn't mean I can tolerate the threat you and this bunker full of illegal shit represent to me and mine."

"What?" Graves said, laughing. "Do you think Hegemony will quit hounding you just because I disappeared?"

"Uh…" I said, thinking that over. "No sir, probably not."

"McGill," he said, "my tapper isn't recording right now, but the data core knows where I went off the grid. It pinpointed this location, maybe an hour or two ago."

I thought about that, and I realized he was right. Like countless murderers who forgot their victim's tapper was always tracking their whereabouts, I hadn't considered that any investigator seeking information on the disappearance of one Primus Ryan Graves would inevitably come to my doorstep.

I laughed. "Sir, I have no intention of perming you!"

"What exactly is your plan then?"

"I just want you to forget any of this ever happened."

"Ah," Graves said. "Okay, I get it. Sure. You're going to let me die down here and then stage a recovery? Maybe throwing me out of an aircar into the Blue Mountains somewhere a week from now, right?"

"I don't know, sir. I was thinking more along the lines of dropping you in the middle of a forest fire, or a deep lake—something like that."

"Whatever," Graves said, disinterested. "That's not going to work either. I'm going to remember that I intended to come out here, and I'm going to find out that past-me actually *did* come out here and disappear. Don't you think that future-Graves is capable of putting together such a simple equation and coming up with the correct answer—which looks like a two-meter-tall ape? An ape who's well-known for violent outbursts and lying?"

I was frowning again. He had me. If I made him disappear, someone would trace his tapper right here to my doorstep.

Heaving a heavy sigh, I lifted my boot off the bottom rung of the ladder. I walked back to the hatch and kicked aside all the barrels and other crap I'd put on top of it.

Then I slid the bolt back and threw the hatch wide. I saw Graves looking up at me. Down there at the bottom of the second ladder, he stood with a gun in his hand. It was aimed squarely up into my face.

I gave him a healthy, welcoming grin. "There you are, sir," I said. "Sorry about the inconvenience. I'll be coming right down there now, so you can show me whatever the hell it is you want to show me."

Graves was in a poor mood after that. He was all surly and full of sour grapes, but he let me climb down the ladder. He kept his gun on me all the while I did it. At last, glaring and muttering about treason, insubordination, and conduct unbecoming... he finally shoved his pistol away angrily.

He pointed at one of the two doors that were at either end of the bunker on the second floor. It was the one that had a lot of red blinking lights and a heavily clamped shut doorway. "You tried to get into that vault, didn't you? And you failed with the codes?"

I nodded. "Yes sir, I'm afraid I did."

Then he pointed at the opposite end to the other door—the one I'd blasted open with a belcher when I hadn't been able to get in any other way.

"And you frigging destroyed the other...? I was a fool to put this stuff out here. I was a plain fool. I gave a hand grenade to a monkey and hoped for the best."

I nodded, putting my hands on my hips. I was unable to argue his point. He had indeed entrusted the wrong man with stewardship over his precious bunker.

"Uh, sir?" I said, having a thought. "Didn't you say once that you had an app, or something, on your tapper to monitor this place?"

Graves glared at me. "I didn't have an 'app', McGill. Don't you think the hogs back at Central would have found that?"

"Hmm... yeah, I guess so..."

We'd both been purged and generally abused during the Sky World campaign. Anything suspicious on our tappers would have been found by the investigators, I was sure of that much.

Graves sighed. "I haven't been able to get any reports for a long time. That's why I came down here in person, once I wasn't being constantly watched by Hegemony. You were essentially left in charge of this installation by default."

"See now... that was your biggest mistake," I commented.

"I'm beginning to see that. Well, let's see how bad it is." Graves marched away and grumbled curses. He headed to the blown-down door first, looking around inside the chamber in state of shock.

"They're dead?" he said. "They're *all* dead? What the hell is wrong with you, McGill? Did you kill all of them?"

Again, his pistol was out, and he was aiming it at me. He was furious this time, not just disgusted. He was angrier than when I'd threatened to perm him and leave him locked up down here in the dark.

I lifted my hands with my big fingers splayed wide. "Sir, as God is my witness, there were eight brains down here. Only one of them was alive when I broke in. Most were dead, dried-up little husks."

"One alive, huh? What'd you do with it?"

"Well sir, that's kind of a long story, see..."

Graves showed me his teeth, and his jaw jutted out so that his lower incisors were ahead of his uppers. He shoved his pistol into my face. "I should burn you down right here. Do you know how much damage you've done? You killed eight critical people. Eight irreplaceable people. People older than you or me!"

"Wait, wait, wait," I said. "Hold on a second, sir. I didn't *kill* any of them. Seven of them were dead when I got here, and one I actually rescued and saved."

"Where is that brain?"

"It's on Dust World," I admitted. That was a big confession.

Graves blinked a couple of times, but then he nodded slowly. "That's right, you do have a weird connection with the rebel colonists out there, don't you?"

It seemed rather strange to me that Graves would be calling someone else a rebel, but I let it pass. He walked over to the one missing jar on the shelf. He eyed the labels, and he did a little counting on his fingers. Then he turned back to me. "I know who you took. What do you know about her?"

"Not much," I said. "She's kind of a Karen... someone who likes to shout orders at everybody."

Graves let his mouth twitch. It was a tiny hint of a smile. "Yeah," he said, "that's her. I'm glad she's still alive." Then, he pushed past me and walked down toward the other door. He began fooling with it, typing in codes and such-like.

"Uh," I said. "Primus Graves, sir, could I ask exactly who these people are? Where did these brains come from?"

"Isn't it obvious, McGill?" he said. "They're people who disappeared a long, long time ago. They're important people—rebels, leaders. Essentially, they were members of the government who disagreed with Hegemony when it took over. In the eyes of an old-timer like me, they're our legitimate government to this day."

"Yeah but, uh... how did they get to be like... brains in jars with the eyeballs hanging off them? It's kind of nasty, you know?"

"You told me once," he said, "that you'd been far, far down below Central in the Vault of the Forgotten."

"That's right. It's a spooky place."

Graves nodded seriously. "We staged a jailbreak, freeing some of those forgotten souls. We saved them from purgatory, and we hid them down here in this bunker under your swamp."

"Wow," I said, "that's quite a story. When the hell did you do that?"

Graves shrugged. "Something like forty years ago, back when you were just a little splat-specialist."

"Okay..." I said, adding things all up in my head. "You must have figured I was just the sort of big ignorant clown you needed. I would probably sit here on this piece of swampy land for centuries, watch-dogging the people you wanted kept alive and on ice."

"That's right. Better in our vault than in Hegemony's."

I nodded, thinking it all over. It was not the sort of thing that I'd suspected Graves would have been capable of, but there had been occasional hints throughout my association with him which indicated he was not quite on the up-and-up when it came to being a member of Hegemony brass. Probably the biggest red flag of them all was the simple fact that Hegemony didn't trust him. He was among their best officers, but they had never allowed him to rise up in rank beyond primus. Looking at all this now, I was pretty sure they were right not to trust him.

Graves eventually managed to break his way into the locked and sealed door. Inside, he found nothing but eight more dead things dried-up in their jars.

"I don't understand," he said. "This life support system should have lasted a lot longer than this. The power is still on... What the hell went wrong?"

"Uh..." I said. "I don't rightly know, sir. I never did totally understand this place."

Graves ran his hands over various pipes, computers, control processors, and nutrient tanks. Eventually, he turned back to me. "I think the water was shut off," he said. "There's oxygen, power, nutrients—but no fresh water. All it takes, you know, for something to die is a few days without enough water."

"Huh..." I said. Suddenly, I had a dark, sinking feeling in the pit of my stomach, but it wouldn't benefit me in any way to explain these feelings to Graves, so I didn't.

He continued his work, muttering while he traced various pipes. He finally came back cursing. "It's definitely the water supply. It's down to a trickle. It must have just been enough to keep one pod alive. What could have happened? This is a frigging swamp. The water is virtually endless."

I lifted up a big finger and scratched the top of my head. I was feeling a little itchy. The truth was, I had a sneaking suspicion. "Just where, uh—where did those pipes lead to?"

Graves threw his arm off in a random direction. "Way across your swamp. There's an old barn and a well. We tapped into that well at the very bottom of it. There should be plenty of water. Certainly enough for all these fine minds to live indefinitely."

"Oh..." I said, thinking about what I'd done out there.

Something like a year or two back, during the Ice World campaign, I'd been trying to help my parents sell this land. In preparation for various inspections, we'd knocked down the old barn in question and filled in the well he was talking about. Could that have been the blocked water source?

"McGill?" Graves said. Suddenly, he was in my face again. "I see a guilty look on that dumbass face of yours." His pistol was out and poking into my chin. "Tell me what you did!"

"I didn't do *anything*, Mr. Primus, sir! I'd swear it on a stack of bibles *this* high."

He slapped my hand away, knocking imaginary bibles everywhere. "You did *something*," he said. "Something stupid, something destructive... Dammit, I was a fool. Imagine the insanity of thinking you were the best caretaker of our most precious leaders?"

"That's quite a stretch," I admitted.

His shoulders slumped in defeat. "All right... What's done is done. Let's get the hell out of here."

Graves and I climbed out of the bunker. We slammed the hatch closed. We covered it up with dirt and left it. As we headed back to my farm, I hoped to never see the place again.

-3-

On the trip back to Central I felt like I had to do all the talking. As a general rule, Graves had never been a man who was outgoing and boisterous, but today he was even worse than usual. I was down to talking about how sad I was when the last of the fireflies had faded away over the summer as we flew over what was known as Greater Virginia Sector. I could see the green blobs of the forest and the gray blobs of the cities out the window of the sky-train as we passed overhead.

Right about then, for some reason, Graves decided he'd had enough of my prattling. "You've got to shut the hell up, McGill," he said.

"Uh, yes sir. I surely do. Sometimes a man just doesn't know when enough is enough. Sometimes—"

"Shut up," he yelled, and I finally did shut up.

"Was there something else, sir? Something else you'd rather talk about?"

"You know there's nothing we can talk about right now, not on this sky-train. There are microphones everywhere. The AI is always listening, McGill. Don't forget that."

"Don't I know it sir, but it does seem like the AI in my house gets almost everything wrong that I say to it."

"That's true," he said, "but the AI works just fine when they want it to."

I looked at him, startled. That was a thought which hadn't enlightened my benighted mind previously. Was my parents' household AI really so terrible at voice interpretation? The truth was, Earth hadn't moved forward much over the last hundred years or so with that particular technology. If it worked sometimes better than others... was that entirely an accident? After all, people were certain to be more tightlipped in front of smart robots than they were in front of dumb ones, weren't they?

Squinting, I looked around myself. There were countless robots around these days. They usually didn't *look* like robots, of course. They didn't have any arms or legs—but they were always listening.

"There is something we can discuss," Graves said while I was sitting there having disturbing thoughts. "We need to talk about your new adjunct."

"My new...? Oh, you must mean Dickson."

"That's right. That's the one."

"Besides being a prick of a man with a sadistic streak as wide as a skunk's pinstripe, what's wrong with him, sir?" I asked.

"What's wrong with him is he doesn't exist."

"How's that again, Primus?"

"Just what I said. Adjunct Dickson doesn't exist. He never existed. We've been checking. He never was a Victrix man—not according to the official records. He was never in Legion Varus either, actually—at least not on an official basis."

I gaped at Graves, and he looked back at me. I could tell by his stony face that he wasn't joking. That was nothing unusual, as Graves pretty much never joked about anything.

"How is that possible, Primus?"

"The computers forgot about him. Therefore, it's best that we forget about him, too. As far as anyone's concerned, on our last deployment at Sky World you were down one adjunct. That's all you know."

"Oh... okay. But what about this next campaign, whenever that's happening? I'll need another man, won't I?"

"Indeed, you will. It's time for you to select someone you trust instead of a rando from another legion." While he said this, he gave me a few hard pokes in the ribs. That may not sound like much, especially as I was a bigger man than he was, but Graves had his own particular way of poking you with his finger.

He liked to use his knuckle, rather than a fingertip. A man's finger, bent over once, formed a very hard point of bone. Graves used this to ram up against my ribs, and somehow, he managed to make that hurt.

"Pick a man?" I said. "Like who?"

"Like, someone you trust from your own unit."

"Hmm," I said thinking it over. "One of my noncoms?"

"That would make sense. Just don't make it Carlos Ortiz. I couldn't take that idiot at any of our officer meetings."

"That won't happen, sir. Never on my watch."

"Good. See that it doesn't."

Graves shut up after that, and so did I. For my own part, I sat there thinking. I stewed a bit about who might become my new adjunct as well as wondering just where the hell Dickson had gone off to. As the second question was unanswerable, I stayed with the first.

After thinking it over for a bit, two names came to mind. One was Sargon. He was probably my most accomplished veteran, and he was really good at his job. He's been an excellent weaponeer before he'd been promoted to lead the weaponeer squad. More importantly, he was a man I trusted to commit heinous murder on command. If that wasn't loyalty, I didn't know what was.

The second name was Moller. Veteran Moller had been a fixture for well over a decade in 3rd Unit. She was almost as big, mean and unpleasant to gaze upon as old Sargon was himself.

Unable to come to any immediate decision, I turned to Graves. "What do you think about Moller, or maybe Sargon?" I asked.

"Hmm," he said, thinking over the two names. "I don't know if they're ready—and I don't know if either of them ever will be. But you know, the funny thing is, when you're an officer, you always think that everyone in your unit is a punk kid. Who would have thought you, James McGill, could ever become a decent officer?"

"Not me," I admitted.

"Right. Well, the decision is up to you, McGill. Veteran Sargon is senior. Veteran Moller probably has a little bit more of the typical officer temperament. I would probably go with her, especially after some of the recent insubordination reports that I've heard from your unit."

"Huh?" I asked, baffled for a moment, but then I understood what he was talking about. Old Sargon had murdered Dickson after my subtle command to do so, and he had served some time in the detention center for it.

That was a black mark on his record when it came to being elevated to the officer ranks. The other officers who had to approve such things never liked the idea of promoting a noncom frag-artist up into their own ranks.

Thinking that over I came up with an idea. I pointed a finger back at Graves, but I didn't dare to jab him with it. "Hold on a second," I said. "How could he have killed Dickson if Dickson didn't exist?"

Graves blinked once, then twice. He smiled with the right side of his face. "That is a good dodge," he said. "It's probably not going to get past the tribunal, but yeah, I've got to admit... that's a good dodge."

"Okay then, you've got my vote. I'll promote Sargon."

Graves shook his head. "No, it doesn't work like that. You've got to put in at least two names. Three is better. They won't let you make these decisions flat out. You're only allowed to make recommendations."

"Ah jeez, what's the point of even asking me then?" I grumbled. "All right, two names then, Sargon and Moller. Sargon as my first choice and Moller as my second. Those are my choices, sir."

Graves nodded. "All right. Your reasoning is sound, and I see no problem with it. I'll put my stamp on it and forward it to the tribunal."

"Where does it go from there?"

"It goes past Winslade's desk next. He's our tribune, after all, but that's sort of a formality. The main decision and the final choice will be made by everybody holding the primus rank when we get together as a group."

"As the lead primus of Legion Varus, aren't you the Grand Poohbah of that tribunal of primuses?"

"Sure—that's one way to put it."

"Great... but with that taken care of, why exactly am I following you up to Central?" Naturally, this wasn't the first time I'd asked this question on the long ride up from Georgia, but Graves had never bothered to answer it. He wasn't a man who loved questions.

"Something's happened," he said.

The big sky-train changed course. We were now spiraling down in a big loop that would eventually lead us to Central City. Various warning tones and orange-lit signs indicated we'd be on the ground in twenty minutes or less.

Graves looked around like he thought there was a robot listening in, and maybe there was. "It's about our planets in the Frontier Zone, McGill. Several of them have been hit by strikes from deep space."

"Deep space?" I asked. "Are you talking about something interstellar?"

"Absolutely," he said.

"What do you mean by strikes, sir? Are we talking about fusion, or antimatter, or..."

"None of those," he said. "Kinetic hits. Big, strange crystalline formations, kind of like comets but dark and deadly. We can't even see them coming. They fly out of a pitch-black sky with no color or emissions—barely any reflectivity. They strike planets, places like Storm World, Dark World—even Sky World. They've all been hit."

"Wow," I said, "what about Blood World?"

He nodded. "There, too. You know what's funny about it?" he asked. "Those craters. Remember all those craters on Blood World? Do you remember how when we first landed there long ago, we wondered who had bombed them so hard?"

I nodded with my mouth hanging open.

"There are fresh craters on Blood World now," Graves continued, "just like the old ones. Big divots the size of a small town, dug right into the surface of their world. If this keeps up, every planet in the province will look as pockmarked as our own moon."

"Nobody knows where these things are coming from?"

"We only know the general direction," he said. "They're coming from the rim of the galaxy—somewhere out past Rigel."

We glanced at each other, and I had to say I wasn't surprised. Those bears had been quiet for a long time.

We'd recently invaded Dark World and Sky World, kicking them out of the place. The Rigellians had fought a surprisingly weak fleet engagement at both locations. But now, many months later, they were finally making their counterstrike. It all made too much sense.

Rigel was on the move again.

-4-

We arrived at Central, a monstrous structure built of ballistic glass and puff-crete with crysteel bones. We landed on one of the little side shelves and walked inside.

After checking through security, I couldn't help but notice there was a lot of activity going on. Now mind you, with Central being my home planet's military headquarters, there was always something big going on—but today was different.

There were people everywhere. Squadrons of jogging troops rushed by with officers shouting and pointing in the hallways. I saw people from all kinds of different legion outfits. Germanica was there with their bull's head patches on their sleeves. A squad of Solstice men nearly ran me down. I even saw some boys from Teutoburg, and I hadn't seen them around in a long time.

"Hey, look at that," I said, slapping Graves on the shoulder.

He looked at me in irritation and followed my gesture. "So what?"

"Weren't those guys part of Tribune Deech's outfit?"

"No, McGill. She's an imperator now, and Teutoburg has been called back from garrison duty. Most of the legions have been."

"What the hell for?"

"If you'd been paying attention to what I was telling you on the sky-train, or the news reports in general, you'd know. There have been a lot of strange kinetic strikes. Essentially, big meteors are coming out of the dark and slamming into planets in the Frontier Zone."

"Oh yeah, you did mention that..."

"That's right. In your infinite wisdom, you suggested to Turov that she should nuke one of the main hives on Dark World. Well, guess what? Somebody else thought it was such a good idea they did it again."

"Another one of their big hives? It's gone?"

"That's right. Something like fifteen percent of the population of Vulbites has been wiped out. In fact, they decided they won't work for us any longer until we keep up our part of the bargain and deliver them the security we promised."

"Security... how the hell are we going to give them security from meteor showers?"

"That's what the brass wants to know. They're claiming it's all some kind of natural phenomenon and not part of our contract. But the Vulbites aren't buying it."

I shrugged. "I guess I wouldn't, either. Not if my cities were getting destroyed."

"Right."

"So... what's that mean? They're not working for us? No more starships? No more stardust armor for our troops?"

"Correct. We've got a massive work slowdown on our hands. That really alerted the brass. Fortunately, I managed to procure one of the suits already, and you still have your prototype. Now, all the upper officers in Varus have got a suit—all the way down to centurion-level."

"Wow, that's pretty good."

"It's not enough. I want every troop in a combat role to have one."

I followed him to the elevators and rode up with him. Twenty floors went by and then two hundred more. When we were up within a hundred floors and near the top of the apex of this giant military leadership pyramid, I noticed a change. We were starting to see a higher level of officers now, not just recruits, regulars, veterans, and specialists. The hallways were crammed with centurions, primuses—all kinds of officers.

Now, you have to keep in mind that most of the soldiers who were permanently stationed at Central were what a person would rightly call a hog, or in other words, a permanent member of Hegemony who was in the military branch of our home government. To any man from the legions, that meant they weren't real soldiers.

Hogs weren't starmen who went out and conquered planets for Earth. They were often lazy, half-incompetent and frequently overweight gentlemen who stayed at home and flew a desk. They rarely saw combat outside of a newsfeed from the frontlines.

Central was chock-full of such individuals—men who wore uniforms but who seemed not to know what they were really for. The higher you got up in this pyramid, the more of them you ran into, and the higher rank they were.

When we got up to around floor four hundred, everybody but me seemed to be a primus or above. In fact, I caught sight of one individual who surprised me. It was none other than Primus Bob.

I pointed a rude finger and gawked. "What the hell?" I said, "is that Primus Bob over there?"

Graves took a glance. "Of course it is."

"Why the hell is he wearing a Vulbite-made suit? I don't think I've ever seen that man lift a pen much less a rifle."

"You probably haven't, but he's a primus, and they're distributing gear by rank and seniority, not by need."

I have to confess a streak of foul cursing began—and it was all coming out of me. I would sooner give any recruit fresh off the training fields of Legion Varus a suit of stardust armor. Anyone who fought for a living deserved the protection more than Primus Bob did. After all, the entire point of the suit was to stop laser bolts, explosives, and good old-fashioned dumb bullets. Primus Bob was unlikely to encounter any of those. On the other hand, my troops were regularly killed by such things.

"Hey," I shouted, cupping my hands over my big mouth. "Hey, Bob!"

Primus Bob paused and glanced in our direction. He frowned, and I'm pretty sure he would have given me an admonishment if I wasn't standing there with Graves. He was the same rank as Graves—but that wasn't the real difficulty for

Primus Bob. I think, underneath, he was just a little afraid of old Graves.

Still frowning, Bob squinted in our direction and walked closer to us. "McGill?" he said. "I haven't seen you for nearly a year."

I shook my head. "Seven months and three days by my count, sir."

Primus Bob sneered. He didn't like me, and he'd never been anything but sour since the last time we'd met. On that fateful day in Drusus' office, Bob had been blown out of his socks by a pack of hardheaded hog guards. Drusus had ordered them to shoot anyone entering the room, and there had been some level of confusion when old Bob entered with a load of coffee and donuts…

The situation had been both unfortunate and embarrassing. What's worse, I suspected the final sounds old Bob had heard while he was dying on Drusus' fine carpet was my braying laughter.

"Hey," I said, poking Bob one in the belly. "That's a fine suit of armor—made with stardust, isn't it?"

"It certainly is, McGill. As you know all too well, the quartermasters of Earth aren't reserving such precious pieces of gear for your kind. Everyone of high rank at Central has been issued a suit like this one. They're all custom-made and custom-fitted."

Before he could go on, I poked him again. "Hey, if you had been wearing this suit when all those hogs shot you, why hell, I think you'd have lived through the day."

Bob glared at me. "I *am* alive, McGill."

"Yeah, yeah, but you know what I mean. You wouldn't have died on the carpet, squirming on your back and squealing."

Bob began to lift a stern finger. Despite Graves, I figured he was about to give me a piece of his mind.

But Graves stepped in. "We haven't got time for this, gentlemen. I'm sorry, Primus. Please excuse my rude centurion. I will discipline him, I assure you." Then, Graves brushed between the two of us and marched off.

I followed Graves, tossing a grin over my shoulder in Primus Bob's direction. The grin was not returned.

We eventually reached the headquarters floor for Legion Varus. Graves led me into the largest of the conference rooms, a chamber big enough to hold every Centurion and Primus in the entire outfit. As there were ten cohorts and ten units in each cohort, that put upwards of a hundred and twenty people in the room.

Not everyone was there yet, mind you, but most of them were. It was a full-on legion briefing. This revelation made me frown.

Now, I am an inattentive man. In fact, I could be downright *criminally* distracted at times, and I'd been punished for it on numerous occasions. However, I figured that even I would remember getting a summons to a full, all-hands-on-deck call from the Legion's brass—but I hadn't gotten any such orders.

I ran a finger over my arm, paging through countless ignored messages. Sure, there were a couple of red notices I was supposed to respond to. A few of them were even marked critical. Some came from our quartermaster, others from various self-important individuals in the command structure of my legion. But there was no mention at all of this meeting.

My eyes slid to Graves as he took his place up near the head of the table. Had he left me off the mailing list just so he could come down and check on his freaky bunker? Maybe forgetting to tell me about this briefing had been his excuse.

For Graves, this was impressive. He'd just about pulled a move, which was something he'd rarely done in the past.

Why had he changed his stripes at this late date? Why would he take it upon himself to get all tricky and circumvent standard procedures?

The only thing I could think of was he must have had a burning desire to go down to Georgia and pick me up in person. The only reason he'd have done that was to look inside that bunker…

"Huh…" I said to myself, heading for the snack tables. Graves had never even contacted me before coming down, except to privately text me once. Then, he'd just shown up.

Things were getting stranger and stranger around here, and I, for one, didn't want to get to the bottom of this mystery. I tried to put my thoughts onto a different, safer track.

Parking myself at the buffet, I was disappointed to see it was stacked with a crappy Euro-breakfast. There were a few scraps of thinly sliced meats, yogurts, some cheeses, bread, and a bagel or two... I sighed in disappointment because there was no bacon, no chicken-fried steaks, no omelets or gravy—no good solid fare. I gathered what little I could and washed it down with two cups of coffee.

Others in the group were snacking as well. Most of the Varus officers were wearing their dress blues, some were in fatigues, but there were a couple who were actually wearing Vulbite-made stardust armor. This made me happy, as I was comforted by the fact that not just the hogs had been issued these critical pieces of gear. At least a few real fighting troops would get their butts saved by the nearly impenetrable stuff.

"All rise!" Graves shouted. "Tribune on the deck!"

Everyone shuffled to their feet, putting down their drinks, wiping their faces and standing at attention.

A smug rooster of a man marched into the room. It was Tribune Winslade, and he was dressed head to toe in a shiny, brand new and unscuffed suit of Vulbite-made armor. I could tell he felt proud and fearless while wearing that suit. He'd always envied my gear, and I felt a pang to see him attired this way. For one thing, it was going to be nigh on impossible to intimidate him while he was wearing this stuff.

Oh well, such were the breaks. I guess I shouldn't have expected to keep that advantage forever.

"At ease, men," Winslade said. He tossed us a lazy salute, and we all relaxed—but we did not sit down. "Please, please..." he said. "Be seated. We shall begin the briefing." He made a fluttering gesture with his left hand in the direction of Primus Collins.

I hadn't really noticed her up until now, but I got the feeling she'd noticed me. Her eyes slid in my direction as she rose and walked to the front of the room. That was one of the problems of being a horndog—or in my case, an *infamous* horndog.

Over the years, I'd experienced intimacy with a significant percentage of the women in Legion Varus. This was a natural hazard of being trapped permanently in a young body and living a chaotic existence which included frequent death, revival, and lots more death. During our frequent deployments, the legion was inevitably deployed to remote locations, cutting us off from friends, family, and loved ones back home on Earth. Lots of people had had numerous affairs, and I certainly wasn't the only man who'd conquered the likes of Primus Collins.

Still, there was something odd in that glance she gave me. It wasn't friendly, but it was definitely personal.

This sort of thing was one of the reasons I tended to avoid the officer-type women—especially those who held superior rank to my own. In fact, the only other high-ranking officer I'd ever been intimate with was Galina Turov herself.

Fortunately, as Galina was an imperator and technically a hog, she wasn't present at this briefing. I was mighty glad Collins and Galina weren't in the same room together—not with Collins acting weird and tossing me strange glances. Galina would have picked up on that for sure.

Walking up to the front of the room, Collins lifted a tiny, egg-shaped remote in her hand and began waving it toward the largest wall of the conference room. The wall immediately lit up into a star-scape. What proceeded after that was predictable. She talked about our home Province 921, and the nearby Frontier Zone, which lay as a buffer between Earth and Rigel.

As we were technically at war with Rigel, she kicked things off with fleet dispositions and garrisoned worlds—all that stuff. I was immediately bored.

One would think that damned near a thousand empty lightyears would be enough room for everyone to get along—but you would have thought wrong. Thousands of star systems lay between Rigel and Earth, but that wasn't enough territory for our two fledgling interstellar powers on the rim of the Galactic Empire to play nice with one another. It was quite the opposite, in fact.

We'd fought several battles recently. Although things had cooled off since we'd invaded Dark World and Sky World, the war could break out hot again any day now. I had the feeling, watching Primus Collins as she detailed meteor strikes against places like Blood World and Dark World, that the war had indeed just kicked back into gear.

"The source of these mysterious assaults from the dark," she said, "has not yet been definitively determined. All we know is that rocks are flying out of deep space toward our planets in the region. Naturally, some suspect Rigel is involved. There are, however, counterarguments."

Several hands shot up. After a moment's hesitation, Primus Collins pointedly skipped over my hand, which was up higher than all the rest. Being the tallest man in the place, my vigorously waving fingers weren't easily ignored. They were, in fact, more akin to narrow flashlights flapping high in the air. Still, she didn't call on me.

"Centurion Manfred?" she asked. "Do you have a question?"

Manfred grinned at her with broken teeth. He was a man who was as broad and squatly built as I was tall. He pointed a fat hand in my direction.

"No, ma'am," he said. "I have no question—but I believe that Centurion McGill here has something to say."

Primus Collins twisted up her face. Manfred, among all the officers present, was probably the closest thing I had to a friend in the room.

"All right," she said. "What do you want, McGill?"

There it was, I thought to myself as I began to answer. She had a hint of a sneer in her voice, and I didn't understand that at all.

It couldn't be that she was pining away for me and wishing she was my girlfriend... it had been years since our fling on City World.

Besides that, it was obvious to me that she'd been spending time with Tribune Winslade lately. Hadn't he just pointedly given her the hand-control and directed her to carry out this briefing? If that wasn't favoritism, I didn't know what was.

With an effort, I pushed aside all this poisonous thinking and blurted out my question. "Primus Collins? Why do you keep hinting around that the attacks might not be from Rigel? It's obviously Rigel, isn't it? Who else would be doing this?"

Collins frowned at Winslade. Their eyes met, and Winslade gave a tiny nod. I didn't miss this. Quite a few other people present didn't either. He had just privately okayed something, something which they'd perhaps discussed earlier.

"McGill has put his finger upon an interesting point," she said. "I wasn't sure if I was going to go this far, as some of the intel I'm about to reveal is unconfirmed, but we've seen similar strikes hitting other worlds—other star systems close to Rigel. In fact, there's some evidence that they've been hitting Rigel itself."

There were a few gasps in the audience after this. The implications were huge. Could something, or someone, be throwing rocks not just at us but also at the bears? That was a significant change in the strategic situation. My hand shot up and began waggling again. Reluctantly, almost with a sigh, Primus Collins pointed at me.

"But wait a second, sir," I said. "These rocks are coming from the frontier, out past Rigel. That means they're coming from the outer rim of the Galaxy. They can't be from the Nairbs or the Galactics—none of the familiar species. They're all closer to the Core than we are."

She nodded. "Yes, exactly. If some entity is throwing rocks at us—and at Rigel—they're doing it from the other side of Rigel. They're attacking both of us, all of us, every inhabited planet in the area. In fact, our estimates indicate that if this is true, it's only a matter of time until Earth herself is struck."

There was some serious muttering going on after that.

"All right then," Winslade said, stepping into the conversation. He walked close to Primus Collins and held out a hand in her direction. She slapped the remote into his palm, and he smoothly turned toward the vast, glowing star map behind him.

"You've all got the gist of it now," he said. "No matter where these rocks are coming from, or who is throwing them, we're definitely stepping up our military involvement in the Frontier Zone."

He used the remote to make a large looping circle that encompassed hundreds of lightyears. It was a big region. It was a big region full of star systems—with some yet to be explored by Earth's forces.

"Just in case all these flying rocks are a prelude to an invasion of some kind—either from Rigel or some other unknown enemy—Legion Varus has been charged with advancing the interests of Earth. The brass has decided we aren't going to sit by idly waiting for these rocks to come flying in and smash against Machine World or Tech World or any of the other star systems and planets in our region of the galaxy. No, we're going to move proactively. We're going to move closer to Rigel, and we're going to invade a star system that is quite near the home world of the bears—quite near indeed…"

With a dramatic flourish, he lit up a small star that burned orange in the center of the projection. It was part of a binary star system, and when he highlighted it, the spectral data indicated it was a K-class.

"This 31 Orionis," he said. "This type of star is actually the most conducive to life and organic growth conditions of any other kind of star in the heavens. K-classes are even better than our own G-class, which is circled by old Mother Earth. Why would one say it's better? Because these stars tend to create what we call Super-Earths."

I glanced around the room at that point, and I couldn't help but notice that most of the troops looked bored. Manfred was fingering his tapper.

"What's a Super-Earth?" Winslade continued. "It's a planet even more suitable to life than Earth herself. Keep in mind it may not be better from the point of view of a given soldier in this conference chamber right now. It's from the point of view of the fecundity of life itself."

I frowned, wondering what the hell "fecundity" was, and if he was going to tell us, when he started talking again.

"A Super-Earth has a consistent list of traits. It's a planet that is always somewhat larger than Earth. A rocky world that is less dense but still retains a higher level of gravity than we're accustomed to. The world would also be wet and warm. Just think about it. Here on Earth, where is life the most plentiful? Why, in jungle climates, of course. Therefore, any world supporting large, primordial forests will boast a huge biomass."

I suppressed a yawn, and my eyes began wandering again. I investigated the snack table, but it was still laden with bland options. At last, my gaze fell on Primus Collins.

She happened to be staring back at me. We both startled a bit and snapped our eyes to the front of the room, where Winslade was still going strong.

"Ideally, the planet would have mountains that are lower and oceans that are less deep than ours. Certainly, the continents shouldn't be so huge as to have large dry deserts in the middle of them. All of these things are conducive to perfect, life-growing conditions."

My hand was up again, and so was Manfred's. Both of us were ignored. Winslade didn't even *consider* calling upon us. He was smarter about things like that than Primus Collins.

Instead, he pointed to Graves, who had bothered to lift just a single finger in a halfhearted gesture. "Yes, Primus Graves?"

"Sir," Graves said, "if both Rigel and Earth are under some kind of unknown attack, why are we considering assaulting a world that belongs to Rigel?"

Winslade's face screwed up. It wasn't quite a snarl. It was more of a pinched look of disgust. "Graves, I know you're a Boy Scout at heart," he said, "but this is war. Rigel and Earth have been in a state of war for quite some time now. Have we all forgotten the attack that blew up the Big Sky Project in its entirety? Have we further forgotten that the pieces of that wreckage fell and killed tens of millions here on Earth?"

Graves' face was stony. I thought for a moment he might mention that no one knew who had blown up the Big Sky Project, and therefore who was responsible, but he didn't. He simply stared.

Winslade cleared his throat. "In any case," he said. "It's not the job of Legion Varus or her officers to decide our targets. It's our job to receive our mission enthusiastically and execute it with professionalism. And so, back to the briefing."

He returned to his star maps. "Unsurprisingly, one of the Super-Earths I've been talking about is to be found here."

"Why's that, sir?" I blurted out.

Winslade glanced at me sourly, but he answered even though I'd spoken out of turn. "Because a K-class is the most conducive to the evolution of life. They tend to last much longer than even a G-class star, such as our own. That means there are many billions of years for life to grow and flourish. They also tend to put out a rather stable level of radiation, which prevents the star from either freezing or scorching planets in their vicinity. For sheer stability, therefore, a K-class star improves the odds of producing a true jewel of a world."

Graves raised his gauntlet, and Winslade flicked a finger at him.

"What's the significance of this planet—other than its likelihood to support life?"

"We've spotted frequent cargo deliveries made by ship and other means from this planet to Rigel."

My hand was up now and waggling with a dozen others. Winslade pointed toward Jenny Mills, a Centurion of our most attractive variety. "Yes, Centurion Mills?"

"Sir, are you saying that this world is supplying food to Rigel?"

"We suspect that it is. Either that, or possibly immigrant labor of some kind. We're not certain, but there's no doubt that there's a lot of trade with this planet. Whatever they're transferring to Rigel, we calculate that it must be of vital importance to them."

"So... are we going to just wipe it out, or what?" Jenny asked in a concerned tone.

"No, not exactly," he said. "We're going to capture it. Whatever is of value to Rigel, I'm sure will also be of value to Earth."

I was frowning now. I couldn't help myself. If you took away all the fancy talk, Winslade was talking about cutting off their food supply. That seemed mighty strange to me as Rigel hadn't been escalating the war for a long time, and if they weren't the ones throwing these big rocks at us from deep space, why shouldn't we sue for peace instead?

I thought about asking the question, but I didn't even bother. That wasn't how the hogs at Central operated. They tended to think in terms of strategic brinksmanship. They wanted to expand Earth's influence and reduce that of all rivals in the area.

It was a dangerous proposition, but who was I to judge? I was nothing but a lowly centurion.

The briefing went on and on after that. Lots of details were discussed. There were charts full of numbers, like gravity levels, types of gear that would be required, training regimens—that kind of thing.

I wasn't really listening anymore. I was thinking about several other details instead. One of them was Primus Collins and the odd glances she'd given me. The second was Graves, and the way he was behaving totally out of character.

Last but not least, I wondered what we would discover out there on 31 Orionis that Rigel so clearly depended upon.

-5-

After the meeting was finally over and done with, I sought out Tribune Winslade. He and I had never been friends, but at least we had a decent working relationship. Most of the time we got along. He made me wait until everybody else talked to him privately before he finally allowed me to step up close.

"What is it now, McGill?" he demanded. "Isn't it enough that you asked half the questions during the briefing?" Looking more arrogant than ever in his fine, black suit of armor, he crossed his skinny arms and looked at me flatly.

"First off, Tribune sir," I said, "let me congratulate you on being the recipient of that fine suit of armor."

"Yes, yes, McGill. At least you can stop whining about being the only one who wears one, the man who everybody's trying to steal from."

"That's right. I'm no longer the low man in the room with everybody trying to pull the clothes right off my back. But that's not why I'm pestering you today, sir."

"Then out with it. I'm busy."

"Sir, there's the small matter of my missing adjunct."

He blinked a few times and thoughtfully looked at his tapper. "Oh yes, your missing adjunct… that's an issue, isn't it?"

"That's right, sir," I said, "it surely is. As you are probably aware, I've been technically missing an adjunct for more than one entire campaign."

Winslade eyed me, and he seemed just a tad nervous. From his odd demeanor, I could tell that he knew Dickson's name was a word that could no longer be safely spoken. Officially, Dickson didn't exist and apparently *never had* existed.

"Just so…" Winslade said cautiously, "I guess it's only reasonable that you need a replacement man."

"That's right, sir, and I have a couple of names on my short list for promotion."

Winslade's eyebrows shot up. "Do you indeed? Let's hear them."

I threw out Sargon and then Moller. Winslade thought about it and then shook his head. "Negatory," he said.

"Uh…" I said. "No to which one?"

"Both of them. First of all, they'd have to bypass any kind of formal officer training. There's no time for them to train, and we're shipping out tomorrow."

"Lots of guys do that."

"No, they don't. Secondly, Veteran Sargon was recently involved in the abuse of an officer. In fact, he caused said officer's untimely death…"

I lifted a large finger and waggled it at him. He didn't seem to like this, but I didn't care. "Not so, sir. You're talking about an officer who doesn't exist anymore. Therefore, Sargon's crime does not exist."

Winslade shook his head slowly. "Think again, McGill. Just because one fact has been deleted from our minds doesn't mean *all* related events have been removed as well."

"Huh? That doesn't make any sense."

"Of course it does. If a computer forgets to pay your salary, would it also forget to bill you for the payment service? Hmm?"

He had me there. "Uh…" I said, pondering his twisted logic.

I knew that Hegemony sometimes operated like this. It was like when you wrecked your aircar, but they still kept sending you fines because you didn't register it. One would think that after such a loss, you would be relieved of all requirements to pay for the missing machine. But you would have thought wrong. That's not how the government operated at all. Every loophole had been caught and countered by some accountant in a dark room, long ago.

"Okay then," I said, "what's wrong with Veteran Moller?"

"Nothing," Winslade said, "but technically, she's served an insufficiency of hours in her current position."

"That's total bullshit, sir," I said. "Lots of people get bounced up in rank faster than that. She must have been a veteran for at least a decade now. How the hell is that not long enough?"

Winslade rolled his eyes at me. "You're right that she could be lifted in rank, but only with the express sponsorship of a high-level officer. Someone around the level of a tribune or an imperator."

"Well then, fine. Why don't you do it?"

He laughed at me. "I only have so much time and influence to spend, McGill. Worse, I'm short on favors to draw upon. There are numerous outstanding special requests already in the offing with the bureaucrats of Central. I'm not going to waste any political capital on your pet project."

I was beginning to get angry about Winslade's bullshit list of objections. After all, he had jumped two levels in rank long ago. Turov had done it on a whim, promoting him from adjunct to primus, where he had stayed for many long years.

"You mean to tell me," I asked him, "that just because Moller's not your buddy, she can't have a rank she deserves?"

Winslade shrugged. "Crudely put, but yes. I'm telling you exactly that. She's not my project, she's *your* project. You have exactly zero brownie points to spend here, McGill. In fact, at this very moment, you're losing what few points you might have had with me by complaining."

I was disgruntled and a little bit bitter, but I finally heaved a sigh. I knew when the bureaucracy had beaten me. "Good enough, sir. I need an adjunct. Who the hell is that going to be?"

"Hmm," he said. "I have quite a list of suggestions." He ran some of them by me, and I hated all of them. They were all pet projects, as he liked to put it, of other officers—men whose centurions had requested they be removed from their presence.

"These are all losers, sir," I said. "People that can't get along with anybody."

Winslade shrugged again. "Isn't that your strength?" he asked. "Melding in misfits that don't belong?"

I thought it over and even considered the idea of suggesting I should adopt a squid from our sister legion of Blood Worlders, but I didn't quite have the gumption to go through with it. I'd rather have a human officer. They were a lot easier to get along with and less likely to stab you in the back with a three-meter-long tentacle.

"Well?" Winslade said. I could tell he was becoming bored with the entire topic. "If you can't think of anyone, I'll simply assign you whoever's the most convenient—"

"Hold on, hold on," I said. I was wracking my brain now. Finally, at long last, a name from the past came to mind. "What about Clane?" I asked.

"Who?"

"Adjunct Clane. He's a Texas boy. I met him years back during the Edge World campaign."

"Clane…?" Winslade said, scrolling through a hundred names. "I don't see him on Varus's rosters. You're mistaken, McGill."

"No, no, sir. He was assigned to Fleet. He served on the lifters."

"What? He's a marine attached to a warship? I've got no pull with anyone in Fleet, McGill. None at all. Are you here purely to make things difficult for me today? I already have an entire legion to gather and a new ship to break in. Do you realize, Centurion, that we're a thousand troops short on this mission? I don't have any time for nonsense."

"You won't have to lift a finger, sir," I said. "I'll arrange it all. But if I can do it, would you approve moving an adjunct from the marines to join 3rd Unit?"

Winslade considered. Finally, he shrugged. "I suppose so, as long as this adjunct's current commander is willing, so am I."

"All right then, sir, we have a deal." I saluted him and left. Winslade seemed glad to get me out of his face.

As I marched off to the barracks to oversee the mustering of my unit, something Winslade had said struck through to me. He had mentioned a new ship. It occurred to me right about then, for the first time since I'd last been on deployment, that our ship *Dominus* had indeed been destroyed. Drusus had ordered it shot down to make one rather oversized Skay happy. The gambit had worked, but it had certainly left us with nothing to fly in.

That meant Legion Varus didn't have a home anymore. I had to wonder exactly what kind of ship Winslade had managed to wangle out of Central to replace *Dominus*. I hoped it wasn't going to be anything old, or cramped, or weird-looking. *Dominus* had been an excellent ship, and I was sad to think about her demise.

I forgot about it pretty quickly, however, as the matter was out of my hands, and I didn't give it another thought.

The next three days were spent gathering my troops together and working to locate Clane. We were given a cramped dormitory on a low-level floor inside Central. There, I summoned my two loyal adjuncts, Harris and Leeson.

Harris showed up first, and he was in as sour a mood as I'd ever seen him. "There you are, Centurion," he said, "proudly wearing one of those black suits of armor!"

He was right, of course. I was in my combat gear. After all, we were drilling, and it was best to get used to wearing what you were going to fight in before you shipped out.

"We're on a war footing, Adjunct," I told him. "Have you been issued a suit yet?"

Harris' face twisted up something awful. "No, I have not, and that's damned unfair. Have you taken a look around the upper decks of Central? You've got clowns running around serving coffee and donuts wearing full suits of impenetrable gear, and here I am issued nothing but a steel breastplate."

"I believe it's titanium alloy," I said. "But still, I take your point."

"Why the hell is it," Harris asked me, "that a serious upgrade to combat equipment is denied to a man who's about to go toe-to-toe fighting with Rigel or whoever? All the while, that same gear is handed out willy-nilly to every worthless piece of brass who's pushing around a desk upstairs?"

"You know the answer to that, Adjunct," I told him, "and you'd best stop complaining about it."

He sighed, sat down, and began working with me. As usual, I put him in charge of gathering the individuals who had strayed all around the planet. It was his job to pull them in, whatever it took to get them to the Mustering Hall within seventy-two hours.

"Speaking of slackers," he complained to me after several hours of work, "where the hell is Leeson at?"

"He assures me he'll be in soon."

Lots of troops filed in as time passed. Veteran Sargon and Veteran Moller were among them. They came and lingered around the officers' desk, glancing at me expectantly now and then. I didn't know what the hell they wanted, and I didn't much care. Finally, they wandered off, looking a little confused.

"Uh…" Harris said. "Sir…?"

"What is it, Harris?"

"I kind of thought you might want to have a little promotional ceremony right about now."

I looked up at him, and our eyes met. He nodded his head toward Moller and Sargon, who sat at a distant table talking.

"Promotional ceremony?" I asked.

"Yes sir, you know, I heard by the grapevine that one of those two is going to be your next adjunct."

"Ah, damn…" I slapped my forehead. "What, did some tech listen in on me?"

"No sir, no sir," he said. "I heard it from Graves."

"Shit…" I heaved a sigh. I had never officially announced that either one was a candidate, and here I was having to disappoint them both. They both deserved the actual rank, but the promotion had been denied. How the hell was I going to make this work?

Before I could even get up and walk over to the table to break the news to the two hopefuls, Adjunct Leeson strode in. He was wearing a black suit of Rigellian armor.

Harris stood tall. He pointed, and he howled. "What in the living hell? How did you score that armor, Leeson? You wanker! You cheater!"

Leeson marched toward us, and he was definitely swaggering. He had a huge grin on his face. "You've got to stop complaining so much, Harris," he said. "My face is starting to hurt from grinning too hard." Leeson was truly proud of himself.

"That is bullshit! Total bullshit!"

"No, it's not," Leeson said. "If anybody in this unit besides McGill here should get a suit of this armor, it would be me. I've got the second most hours logged as stand-in centurion."

"Yeah… but how the hell did you get it? Just from being the shortest man in the damn unit?"

Leeson shrugged and sniffed. "Well, they only made so many of any given size…"

Harris guffawed with laughter. "That's it! They gave it to you because you're short. Admit it."

"I admit to nothing."

I finally barked at the two of them and told them both to shut up. "All right, I have zero shits left to give today about any of this. Leeson, you start budgeting our gear and supplies. Harris, stick to the task of getting those stray men into this building. We leave in less than three days."

After they separated, I spoke to Leeson privately. "Hey, why don't you take that suit off until we're underway. It's just causing a ruckus."

He grumbled, but he went to his tiny, shared cabin and removed the suit. He tucked it away into a locker.

Going for a walk, I dodged all my troops and left Central entirely. I had to have a moment to think. Walking the streets of Central City, I contacted everyone I could think of that might help me to track down Adjunct Clane.

He was a man I'd once met on the battlefield at Edge World. Back then, I'd found him to be young, competent and friendly. I'd offered him a chance to join Legion Varus should he ever be inclined to do so, and he'd said he would like to do it.

Now was the time to see if he was as committed today as he had been on that distant planet at that distant time.

-6-

When I finally located Adjunct Clane, I found he'd been assigned to a battlecruiser as part of an anti-boarding marine platoon. He was, in fact, commanding that platoon. As far as combat experience went, he'd seen action over the years—but nothing like a Legion Varus man would have done.

I was surprised to see from his spotless records he was a lot older than I'd remembered. He had to be in his mid-thirties, maybe even upper-thirties, now. I shook my head at that. I was sure he was a tough man, a good fighter and in reasonable shape—but Legion Varus people simply weren't used to having old guys in our ranks.

I pressed ahead, sending an offer directly to Clane. He surprised me by answering affirmatively in less than an hour. He was willing to give it a try.

"The only thing is," he said, back to me out of my tapper, "you're going to have to get my ship's captain to agree, sir. He can be kind of, um… curmudgeonly."

I assured Clane there would be no problems. I told him I could talk a zebra out of his stripes. He wished me luck, and I made the fateful call.

"Hello, Captain Miggs, sir," I said.

Miggs was Fleet, and I was from an independent legion, so I didn't really have to call him *sir*, but I figured it was the polite thing to do.

Miggs gave me no sign that my attempt at friendliness was working. "What do you want, Varus?" he asked.

"Well sir, I've been talking to one Adjunct Clane—a man in your service."

"Forget it," Miggs said.

"Huh?" I said. "Forget what exactly, Captain?"

"Forget poaching one of my men, that's what. I'm more than satisfied with Clane's service. He's the best marine commander I've ever had. There's no way I'm going to give him up—not without a fight."

I shook my head. "I'm not here to fight you, Captain. I just want a good man at my side the next time Varus goes on deployment. I promised Clane a long time ago if I ever got the opportunity to invite him to Varus, he would be given a home in my unit."

"That's real sweet," Miggs said, "I'm sure you two are a match made in Heaven—but I don't care."

There was a tiny wisp of steam coming out of my ears by this time, but I kept on smiling. "Well Captain," I said, "if documents are signed and the request for a transfer is put through the proper channels, we could probably go around you and your permission, but I'd rather not do it that way."

Miggs smiled at me grimly. "That's a good thing, because you haven't got time to pull any of that bullshit."

"How's that?"

Miggs laughed at me. "McGill, I've done a couple of searches on you since you called here, and I've got to say you're just as dumb as everybody says you are, aren't you?"

Already, I was beginning to understand why Clane might want to escape the grasp of one Captain Miggs. This guy seemed like a five-star asshole. "How's that, Captain?" I asked.

"Because you're shipping out in about 48 hours. How the hell do you think you're going to get anybody to have a hearing over a contested transfer in that amount of time? Let me tell you how: It ain't happening—that's how."

He made a move, and I could tell he was bringing a big, old, fat finger down to cut off the connection.

"Whoa, whoa," I said. "Maybe we just got off on the wrong foot, here. Maybe I can offer you something that would change your mind."

Miggs hesitated. "Like what?"

"Oh, I don't know. All the usual things… like self-respect, personal pride, the knowledge that you've done the right thing, or maybe just a sense of loyalty to Earth. A man like Clane deserves to see the stars—and not just from the belly of a ship. He's a good officer, and his boots belong on alien soil. If he's still an adjunct after all this time, it can only mean he hasn't had enough combat experience."

Miggs shook his head. "These are pretty words, but they don't do anything for the bottom line."

I frowned and opened my mouth. I tried to voice a new objection, but it was too late. Miggs had cut off the feed.

"Damnation…" I said to myself. "What a tool."

Needing to think, I found a bar and bought myself some thinking-sauce. After four more, I found my mind was clearing up nicely.

I considered the grim possibility of taking a handoff from another unit, one of the rejects on Graves' list. After pondering for a time, I shook my head with vigor. Growling and scaring nearby patrons, I made a hard decision.

The last time around, I'd blindly traded Erin Barton to Victrix. Then I'd ended up with Dickson—the turd that wouldn't flush. The stink of that mistake was still figuratively in the air today, even though you couldn't find a trace of the man. I wasn't going to give up and go through all that again.

Standing suddenly, I slapped a skittering waiter-bot to pay with my tapper. Then I returned to Central, swaying only slightly as I marched with determination. Once there, I rode the elevators up to our overcrowded barracks.

The place was now half full of loud, boisterous troops. I scooted by the crowd and headed for the officer cubicles in the back. My real plan was simple enough, I was going to crash for the night and think about it some more in the morning.

If I wasn't going to get Clane, then I still had to come up with another name. I wracked my brain, but I couldn't come up with anything.

Finally, just as I was falling asleep, I heard a loud bang and some shouting. I drew a laser pistol and marched into the hallway. I wasn't in the mood for any nonsense.

Being Legion Varus men, you have to understand we're not the best-disciplined troops in the world. In fact, we're probably some of the worst-disciplined troops in the world. The men I commanded were rejects—tough, hard-fighting and hard-dying troops. Violent disagreements and even duels were common. That said, as an officer you had to put the fear of God into the rank and file now and then, or they just didn't listen.

To my surprise, the noises weren't coming from the bunks of the recruits that were lined up in stacks and rows near to the corridors. They weren't coming from the zone where the non-comms slept, either. No sir, they were coming from the tiny cabin set aside for my adjuncts.

That cabin was directly across from my cabin. I walked out my door and then threw the other one open. My jaw hung low as I saw that Leeson and Harris were facing off and howling at each other. Leeson had a knife in both hands. Harris was holding up a black suit of armor with one arm and fending off Leeson with the other.

"What in the living fuck…?" I growled, but the men ignored me.

By this time my non-comms, Moller and Sargon among them, had come to stand behind me and gape at the spectacle.

"What are you going to do, Centurion?" Sargon asked me. "Are you going to let them duel it out? They are the same rank, after all."

Sargon had a point. Normally if two soldiers of a given rank wanted to fight to the death, it was considered reasonable for their commander to just go ahead and let them do it. We had a "let them get it out of their system" attitude in Legion Varus.

But I shook my head. "Nope," I said. "I need them both. I need them both with their brains turned on."

I lifted my pistol, and I fired. The singing sound made both the men recoil in surprise. Harris dropped the black suit because I'd drawn a line across it. Smoking scorch marks were stitched across the chest plate. They looked like so many spot welds.

"Ah, dammit," Leeson said. He was upset about the scuffs.

Harris backed off, and Leeson dropped the knife. Leeson moved to cradle his precious armor. "You marked it all up, McGill," he complained.

"Give me that damned suit," I said. "Right now." Leeson did so reluctantly. "You two have got to be damned near eighty years old," I complained. "It's about time you act like it."

Confiscating the armor, I dragged it back to my cabin. I figured if there wasn't anything in the cabin for those two to fight over, they'd probably settle down for the night. I tossed it on the bunk opposite mine and threw myself onto my own bed a moment later.

Sensing that the show was over, the noncoms and other troops who had been peering from behind them melted away and went back to bed. Soon, most of us were snoring, and soon after that it was morning.

When I woke up, I found that my mind had somehow conjured up an idea. I contacted that crusty old bastard Captain Miggs, and I made him an offer—an offer he couldn't refuse.

He met me in the lobby before noon, and I handed him a bulky package. He took out the armor, shook it, and looked it over. He had the balls to complain about the scorch marks on the chest plate, but he accepted my gift.

"This is mighty considerate of you, McGill. I'm going to miss Clane. He's an excellent officer, but I can't refuse this. Do you realize with Dark World all wrecked, we may never see another suit of this stuff again?"

"Don't I know it," I said. "That is a rare and irreplaceable item, especially for a man of your stature."

Miggs glanced at me sourly. I don't think he liked these last words, as I was a man of unusual height, and he was a man of rather low stature. As it turned out, the suit was a tight fit for him, but all of these units were built with a little bit of stretch and wiggle room. He was able to get it on.

Happy as a cat in a cathouse, he turned and left. I glanced at my tapper and saw the promised permissions and signed documents pouring in. Miggs has signed off on the transfer orders just as he'd promised.

Marine Adjunct Clane had officially joined Legion Varus.

-7-

As evening fell the next day, the legion finally received the approval to head to the spaceport and ship out. Being only a lowly centurion, I didn't know much more than your average grunt about what transport we'd be flying on, what new module we were assigned to, or any other information about particulars.

When my cohort received orders to head down to the train stations underneath Central and head to the local spaceport, we were still in the dark as to basic details. Only one unusual command did come in, and it was from Graves.

"McGill," he told me, "I want you to separate your unit into two groups. All the irregulars, officers, and noncoms will go in group one. That group is to board a lifter bound for orbit. There, you will rendezvous with our new transport ship."

"Uh..." I said, responding to my tapper where Graves' craggy face was looking up at me. "But sir, we've got quite a number of fresh recruits here."

We'd had a significant number of defections since the Sky World campaign. I guess a lot of my boys hadn't enjoyed getting blown up just as they returned to Earth aboard *Dominus*.

"Good riddance," Graves said. "We don't need any more sour-grapes weaklings in this cohort anyway, but as I was saying, all the recruits will come up later as a second group."

I was about to ask the whys and the wherefores of this strange order, but Graves had already closed the channel.

I figured he was probably talking to other officers, and it was clear he had a lot to do. We were under a scrambled deployment order to invade 31 Orionis, a place Earth had never explored. I was sympathetic about all that, but I sure wished somebody was interested in feeding this dungeon-dwelling mushroom something besides horseshit.

As we all hustled out of the barracks and made our way down to the train stations underneath Central, there was an unusual level of bitching in the ranks.

"This is total bullshit, McGill," Harris insisted. "They've got something nasty planned, and I don't like the sound of it."

"That's right," Leeson said. "By the way, sir, could you see your way fit to give me back my suit of armor now that we're getting out of Central and all?"

This last bit caused me to wince. After all, I'd given away his armor, trading it for the new officer I needed. Some people, namely high-level members of the brass, would find that reasonable, even logical—but I knew Leeson wasn't going to feel that way.

Fortunately, I am a man born with an agile mind that was practically designed for moments like this. I came up with a lie almost instantly.

"I've got some bad news about your armor, Leeson," I told him.

Leeson's face went slack and then transformed into a rage. "Bad news? What the hell do you mean, bad news?"

Harris started laughing. "Bad news, as in you've been screwed to a puff-crete wall, Leeson."

"Shut the hell up," Leeson snarled at him. Then he turned back to me. "Come on, McGill, talk to me."

I conjured up a mournful face and shook my head ruefully. "I'm sorry, I really am, but I made a mistake."

"What kind of mistake? What the hell, man?"

"Well..." I said, giving him a pair of downcast eyes and a sad shake of my head. "You see, the mistake I made was bringing up the fight that you two had over the armor."

"What?" Leeson said. "That wasn't a fight. That was nothing."

"I know it was no big deal," I said, "but I happened to mention the argument in front of a few primus-level guys at lunch today—you've got to admit, it was a funny story."

Harris was listening in, and he hooted with laughter again. He liked any story which ended with someone else like Leeson or me getting screwed over. He was also a man gifted with the ability to know when a screwing was incoming.

Leeson, on the other hand, was glaring at both of us with his arms crossed.

"Unfortunately," I continued, "it appears that there were some higher-level officers, principally from Victrix, who never did get a suit of armor to fit them. I may have mentioned—just possibly, mind you—the rare extra-small size that you'd been issued, and that you were only an adjunct... so... well..."

"Oh, come on," Leeson yelled, "are you kidding me? Somebody went and put in a requisition order and stole my fricking armor? Is that what you're trying to tell me, McGill?"

"Yeah," I confessed. Even as I spoke this complicated and totally fabricated story, I was a mite proud of myself. Sure, Leeson was going to be upset. He'd be disgruntled and kicking rocks like a kid over this for months—possibly years—but the key to it was I'd dodged taking the blame.

Some other faceless prick from Victrix—that dude was the true villain. I'd always heard that reputable leaders claimed that when the blame stopped, it stopped right here, pointing to their own desks—but that lofty attitude was the polar opposite of mine. When I was in a leadership position, if the shit could be passed on in any way, shape, or form, it was passed on with extreme prejudice.

Leeson put on a little show after that. He went around kicking furniture, throwing his arms in the air, and marching in circles. He called me six kinds of a retard for having ever mentioned the suit to anyone.

All the while, Harris smiled and almost giggled at his misfortune.

On the other hand, my face worked hard to look as remorseful and contrite as possible. The important part was that none of Leeson's rage was being aimed at me, his rightful centurion.

In the overall scheme of things, it was probably better that Leeson didn't have a suit of armor that the other adjuncts in my unit didn't possess, anyway. That was only going to create jealousies and discord. For morale and cohesiveness, this situation was for the better. That was a large part of the reason why I traded away the armor in the first place. It was only going to cause trouble.

The entirety of 3rd Cohort piled aboard an underground express train at exactly 1607 hours. With all our gear, everyone looked like a pack mule. We were carrying every piece of equipment we may or may not need on this trip.

Knowing we were going to a hot jungle world, one might think we could've packed light. That we could leave behind all the parkas, space heaters, etc. Unfortunately, when it came to actual bulk, a hot humid climate took nearly as much space to prepare for as did a cold one.

That's because air conditioners are both heavy and power-hungry, even though they're more compact and effective than they had been in the old days. One could cool a whole room with a unit that was roughly the size of a six-pack of beer. But you still had to have generators, batteries, and other stuff to run them. As a result, every soldier aboard the train looked like a one-man band with a kazoo rammed up his butt.

Walking funny, we shuffled aboard, stowed our gear, and slouched on our seats. No sooner had we gotten our butts parked than the train set off with a lurch. Leaving the station underneath Central, we quickly flew out of a tunnel and into the open sky.

Trains in my time didn't always need tracks. In fact, they didn't always need ground of any kind. Often, they flew through the air like flying wingless snakes. This was normal for everyone aboard. Only a few of us even bothered to look out the window and see the sights of Central City.

Leeson was sitting toward the rear, his arms still crossed. He glared at any soldier who dared to approach him with a question. Reading his mood, at least the noncoms were smart enough to steer clear.

Harris came over and sat next to me during the flight. He grinned at me. "Sir?" he said. "What's this I hear about all the recruits being left behind? Do you know what's up?"

I eyeballed Harris. "Actually, I don't, but now that you put it that way, I'm starting to have my suspicions."

Harris' grin grew a little wider. "You think they're going to go up on a separate lifter? Huh? You think we're going to get a chance to skunk them all? I love that trick. I love that more than Halloween when high schoolers come to my door and need a good scaring."

Harris grinned at me, but I didn't grin back. I could remember long ago he'd enjoyed watching while I suffocated aboard a lifter on the way to Steel World.

Thinking over his idea, I shook my head. "No. I don't think that's it," I said. "I'm not exactly sure why the two groups were separated."

"Too bad," Harris said. "Well anyway, where's our third adjunct? Dickson, or whoever?"

"Dickson?" I said, frowning. "I don't recall that name."

Harris stared at me for a minute like I'd gone insane, but I continued to appear to be befuddled. Finally, he caught on.

"So... Dickson's disappeared, has he?"

"Who?" I asked, giving him a quizzical look.

"Okay, okay. I get it," Harris said. "He's a nonperson. We'll just forget about Dickson. I hated that guy, anyway."

"That makes two of us."

Harris kept probing, trying to get information about what our legion's plans were, but I was short on answers myself. Soon, we moved on to other topics like troop readiness, gear, and that sort of thing.

About fifteen minutes after we left the station under Central, we arrived at the spaceport. A lifter was there waiting for us. We boarded up, dragging all our gear with us. We sat on even less comfortable jump-seats with harnesses for straps and prepared for takeoff.

It didn't take long to lift off. Not ten minutes after the last man had boarded the lifter, the ramp was up, and we launched into space.

We began maneuvering to dock, but I still hadn't managed to get a glimpse of the new transport. I'd asked Natasha and Kivi to hack their way into the lifter's outer cameras, but nope—it was no-dice.

What was strange to my way of thinking was the docking process itself. Normally lifters were parked in a large landing bay that was sometimes even pressurized—but that wasn't the case today. Whatever passed for a Red Deck on this ship was different.

Our lifter inverted at the last minute, although that didn't bother us much because we were in null-G. The lifter sort of did a squat on the hull of the larger ship as we docked with it, and we finally halted.

"What the hell?" Leeson said. "What kind of trickery is this? First, they take my armor. Now, they've given us a shit transport. This better not be some little dinky battlecruiser."

"That's right," Harris said. "You remember the *Berlin*, Centurion? That thing was awful. We were sleeping on the decks."

"This is going to suck," Leeson said. "Mark my words. I'm sensing suckage, here."

"Shut up, both of you," I ordered. "We need morale riding high, not in the gutter."

Both of them stopped grumbling, but by their eyes, you could tell they weren't happy. News was flooding all over the cohort. Lots of the troops were grumbling.

Pretending I didn't notice or care, I led my unit down the ramps. We exited the lifter into a relatively narrow chute which allowed us to walk no more than four abreast. Essentially, it was just a large passageway that led into the ship.

Leeson reached out a gloved hand and scraped it along the walls as we walked down the ramps. "You see this? Look at this here. See all that flashing? All that loose, fresh metal? And over here, we've got burn marks. Those are spot-welds. All these signs indicate jerry-rigging, I'm sure of it. Whatever ship we're on, this isn't a real, professional transport. It's a refit."

"Ah, hell," Harris said. Obviously, he agreed with Leeson.

I ignored everyone and marched ahead. After all, there was nothing we could do. If we'd been assigned some dinky warship instead of a transport due to a budget crisis, well, we were just going to have to suck it up. All the complaining in the world wasn't going to fix it.

A man stood with his hands on his hips at the bottom of the chute. It was Primus Graves.

"About damned time you got yourselves down here," he said, "McGill, you're assigned to module number thirty-three. Go find it."

"Excuse me, Primus sir," I said, "but could I ask what the hell ship this is? I would think the time for secrecy is over and done with, right?"

Graves looked at me for a moment. "Yeah…" he nodded finally. "Yeah, I suppose you're right. This is *Scorpio*."

"Uh…" I said, "What exactly is *Scorpio*? I don't remember having heard of that ship before."

Graves smiled at me, and it wasn't a friendly smile. "You actually should recognize it, McGill. You captured this ship when we invaded the orbital factory at Dark World. Don't you remember?"

Gaping, I looked around. I took my helmet off and looked around some more.

Harris and Leeson were standing to my side, and both of them were gaping as well.

"Well, I'll be damned…" Harris said.

"I don't believe it…" Leeson said.

Then finally, I got it. "This is the battleship from Dark World? That big battlewagon, the titanium pig we captured?"

"One and the same," Graves said.

"Well…" Leeson said, "at least this thing's not going to be small. It can probably hold our entire legion at once."

"That it can," Primus Graves said. "To a large extent, McGill here is responsible for this exchange of shipping. He was instrumental in getting *Dominus* destroyed. He was also instrumental in capturing this vessel, which Fleet has refitted and renamed *Scorpio*. She's been heavily modified to carry troops, but she still has some big guns aboard, too. She's perfect for fast assault shuttle missions into deep space."

I thought about it, and I looked back at Graves instead of gawking at the decks. "But what about our Blood-Worlder legion, sir? What about—?"

Graves made a chopping motion with his hand in the air. "Forget about them. They're not coming with us—not on this trip. It's just Legion Varus and this battlewagon."

Leeson spoke up next. "But, sir, what if that's not enough firepower to take an entire planet?"

"Then," Graves said, "we'll have embarrassed ourselves, Legion Varus, and Earth itself."

With that, he waved us forward. We all marched by, leaving our new makeshift version of Red Deck and making our way through the winding passages to our assigned module.

-8-

It was only after we got to our module and settled in that Graves finally announced to the centurions why he'd divided each of the units into two groups. "Because *Scorpio* is not properly geared for our usual cold meet-and-greet for recruits, Varus command has decided to arrange a special event for all of our fresh-faced rookies—along with any stragglers who didn't manage to get to Central on time."

I frowned slightly, wondering what this special event might be. It probably wasn't going to be a happy event, at least not for the participants.

The cold meet-and-greet he was referring to amounted to a slaughter. In my particular case, I'd been left aboard a lifter as a fresh recruit, strapped into place. After the lifter had docked with the transport, the lights had gone out, and the air had begun hissing away—which turned the cabin into a freezing vacuum. We'd found ourselves trapped in our seats and unable to breathe.

Some of us had managed to cut our way loose and escape immediate death, but only a few had managed to make it to the airlocks. That was because the entire thing was rigged. Floating in null-G for the first time, we'd struggled with each other, and out of that first group, only I had been long enough of body to pry open an airlock door and escape. Everyone else had died or been marked for dead.

This time, however, it sounded like Graves had something different in mind.

Leaving my equipment behind in the module, I explored the ship. As I walked along the countless passages, I soon realized I was going to have to get used to marching in a somewhat hunched or at least neck-bent posture. This ship, after all, had been built for Rigellian bears, who were only about a meter tall. Although the ship was quite roomy for them given that the ceilings were close to two meters tall, that wasn't quite enough space for me.

I found it was annoying to have to dodge and weave my way down each passage—particularly in the case of passages that had pipes, wires and conduits running along the ceiling. Fortunately, as an overly tall man, I was used to this and fell into the habit of ducking easily. I only dinged my skull or scratched my scalp every once in a while.

Locating Graves' office at last, I found it was on what appeared to be the new equivalent of a Gold Deck. Really, it was an extended command deck built by the bears.

"What's the procedure, sir?" I asked Graves.

"Let's check the schedule..." he said. "Your recruits will be coming through the Gray Deck gateway posts at exactly 1600 hours later today. You or your designated instructor will greet them as they come through with a snap-rifle."

I blinked twice. "With a snap-rifle, sir? You mean like... one for each man or...?"

"Hell no, McGill. Turn your brain on. Don't you know how this works by now? You're going to shoot them as they come aboard."

"Uh..." I said, bemused, "so that's it, huh? Are we just going to gun 'em all down as they come through the gateway posts? What's that going to teach them?"

"How to die, how to improvise," Graves said. "How to expect the unexpected." He spoke without inflection, remorse, or even much emotion. Graves had always been a cold man. He'd seen it all.

I understood that it was Varus policy to make sure every recruit was killed shortly after joining the legion. This might sound harsh, but it served several purposes. For one thing, it taught them right off the bat that this was not a safe place. Further, they should expect pain and death and blast right out of their minds any feelings of depression, ideas about metaphysics, or any discombobulation in general after returning to life.

Men that died their first time while in the line of duty on an alien planet oftentimes had trouble adjusting to this new reality. We wanted to get that step over and done with before deployment.

The whole process served to, if nothing else, inform the fresh recruits that they had just joined the toughest, meanest, most unforgiving outfit in the service of Mother Earth. We were Legion Varus, an organization that was infamous for taking on missions none of the other legions wanted to bother with.

Another secondary benefit was the fact that after a long demobilization period, our troops sometimes came back out of prime physical condition. That was simply unacceptable to Legion Varus standards. We required physical excellence at all times. Accordingly, we tended to record the mental state of our troops pretty much continuously, but the physical state was retained at peak performance.

Bodily errors were instantly and conveniently edited out by the software. If a man had certain flaws in his makeup—such as too high of a BMI—a killing and a quick revive got rid of all that. This process was often referred to as "freshening" a man up or "recycling" him. It was generally considered a positive thing by legion brass.

Shrugging my shoulders, I accepted my instructions from Graves. I marked the time on my schedule and went back to the modules to spread the news. When I told my two adjuncts about it, Leeson didn't much care. He was still glum and grumbling about his lost suit of armor.

Harris, on the other hand, was overjoyed. "Can I volunteer for this duty, sir?"

"Yeah, sure." I shook my head, marveling at him. "You really do like to kill recruits whenever you can, don't you, Harris?"

"That I do, sir. But this—this is gonna be a special occasion."

"Why's that?"

He grinned at me, and he flicked up an image off his tapper. "Take a look at who didn't make it to the lifter on time."

I looked, and I saw a familiar face. It was the big, round, ugly mug of Specialist Carlos Ortiz.

"Carlos didn't make it?" I said. "I didn't even notice."

"How could you have missed that nasty pug of a man?" Leeson asked. At the thought of Carlos being shot down, he showed me the first glimmer of happiness I'd seen since I'd traded away his armor. "Harris, I want you to kill him just for me. In fact, I wouldn't mind volunteering to join in with my pistol."

"No, no, no," I said. "We're not going turn this into a shooting gallery. I'm going to be there to observe, but that's all. Harris can do the honors—one snap-rifle, and nothing else. You'll be up against thirty-odd recruits and stragglers."

"Wait a minute," Leeson said, snapping his fingers at me. "What about that, uh, that marine adjunct fellow? The new guy you were talking about."

My face drew a blank, but then I nodded. "Oh... Clane didn't have time to make the first lifter, did he? Maybe I should contact Graves and tell him to make a change. It seems unfair."

"Wait, wait," Harris said, lifting a hand. "Hold on a minute here, sir. Technically, Clane is a straggler. Let's not fool with the rules and make special exceptions just because he's a prissy-pants officer from Fleet."

I thought about it. It was rude, but it was playing the game by the rules that Graves had set out. Sure, Clane had just been transferred to Legion Varus, but if there was any time in which a man could be clearly schooled upon the nature of the legion he had just joined, it had to be at the very start.

"All right," I said. "Fine. I'll see you there at 1600 hours, Harris."

We went back to our assigned duties and before you knew it, four o'clock rolled around. Harris and I met up on Gray Deck, which was actually a decently roomy affair aboard *Scorpio*. I had to say that after having explored the ship a bit, it wasn't as nice, friendly and spacious as *Dominus* had been, but at least we were no longer sharing air vents with the Blood-Worlders. That meant there was a lot less stench in the air.

Scorpio was much more heavily armed and armored than any transport we'd ever been aboard. Even *Berlin*, a battlecruiser we'd captured some years earlier, was not as impressive as this monster of a ship. It was several kilometers long and almost a kilometer across. With its many decks and low-hung ceilings, it was like a small space-borne city inside.

Harris set himself up about twenty meters from the gateway posts. He was well back, lying on the floor and setting up a tripod for his snap-rifle on the deck plates. All the technicians that usually worked on Gray Deck seemed to be taking the day off.

I noticed they'd taken the time to wrap the gateway posts in steel to defend them from snap-rifle fire. What's more, the posts had been mounted using bolts. There was no way they were going to be knocked down or damaged during this exercise.

Harris was all grins and chuckles. He expertly set up his rifle, flipped up the sighting reticle and aimed it precisely between the posts.

"You're not going to give them a chance, are you, Harris?" I asked.

"Hell, no! Oh, I'll let them get a few steps in, just far enough to realize what's happening. If I plug them each just as they walk through those posts, pretty soon the pile of bodies will be too high. They'll trip, or they might even block my shots at the next man. You have to think these things through, sir."

I shook my head and stepped to one side where I couldn't easily be seen. From an alcove between two rows of lockers, I watched the proceedings.

At exactly 1600 hours, the gateway posts lit up. Using my body cams, I made a video of the entire thing. Less than thirty seconds after the posts flickered into life, our first customer arrived. It was a chunky young man who staggered as he walked.

No, that's not right. He wasn't staggering because that was his natural gait. He staggered because Harris had not let him step three steps into the room before he had plugged him right through the forehead.

I hadn't even heard the shot. A silencer? Had Harris affixed a silencer onto his snap-rifle? That seemed less fair than usual—even for him.

A slim girl walked through next. She made it far enough to lean down and check on the first guy, who was sprawled out dead on the deck.

Harris put several neat holes through her paper-thin spacer suit as well, and she flopped down hard.

After that, things got messy. Troops walked through, spotted the pile of bodies, and several of them had the wisdom to begin to run. Before they could take more than three or four steps, Harris shot them down, often with a burst of fire. Spinning around, blood spraying, they died moaning on the deck.

"That's seven in a row," I heard him crow to me. "Seven in a row and not a single miss yet!"

I twisted my lips up with mild disgust. Harris was enjoying himself entirely too much, if you asked me.

The eighth man was someone known to us. It was Carlos. Unlike all the others, he suspected something was up. Carlos had the intuition and self-preservation instincts of any large rodent. Accordingly, he came aboard running in a crouch.

The moment he saw the pile of sprawled bodies, the bloodstains, and heard the moaning of the dying, he scrambled on all fours off at an angle toward a row of lockers.

Harris cursed and fired a long spray of bullets. Each accelerated pellet rattled and punched holes in the lockers behind the gateway posts. Sparks showered everywhere, and from the way Carlos was dragging himself as he dove for cover, I figured he had to have caught a round or two—but he wasn't out yet.

Harris proceeded to hammer away at the corner of the lockers where Carlos had taken cover, keeping him ducking, but that tactic wouldn't last for long because more men were coming through now.

Two more recruits had come into the room, realized their danger, and began scrambling for shelter themselves. Harris had to turn his rifle back to them and put them down one after the other.

Carlos was a highly experienced soldier. He took that moment of distraction and used it to its fullest. He raced around behind the lockers and came out with something that looked like a power bar used for lifting and moving heavy gear. He charged at Harris from an oblique angle.

I nodded, folding my lips upward. I couldn't help but feel impressed. Carlos was indeed showing his superior training and knowledge. He'd always been a fighter.

In the end, he almost got Harris, but not quite. Harris rolled onto his back, no longer lying in a prone position but rather sitting up, aiming his rifle at the charging, enraged specialist.

He put a spray of rounds into Carlos's chest at close range, and that was that. Carlos wheezed his last, bleeding on the deck, while Harris went back to nailing recruits who continued to come through the gateway posts.

Something, however, had changed. There was another individual standing there in the midst of the carnage. He gaped at the situation in astonishment.

Unlike all the others we had encountered so far, this mysterious soldier was wearing a suit of black Rigellian armor.

-9-

Harris finished off Carlos and got back into position to gun down the last of the troops coming through the posts. Our latest customer, in fine stardust armor, used those few seconds to assess the situation and react to it.

The armored guy didn't move the way Carlos had. He hadn't lived with us for years, always suspecting some kind of evil skullduggery was afoot. That said, the new man moved fast enough. He danced back through the gateway posts and disappeared.

Harris chased him with a stream of accelerated pellets, firing a dozen rounds. Although several of these sparked and flashed on the runner's armor, they didn't bring him down. They simply couldn't penetrate the armor, which was exactly why everyone wanted a suit so badly.

"Centurion!" Harris shouted out to me. "I call foul!"

Harris was upset, and I could tell why. This was not the way today's agenda was supposed to go. He was supposed to gun down every one of these men, teaching them a lesson. They were destined to experience their first revival and proceed with their training.

I shrugged and splayed my hands. "No one's broken the rules so far," I told him.

"What are you talking about? That man ran right back through the posts. What's more, he was wearing a suit of armor that I don't even have."

"Yeah," I said, "deal with it. You're the one who volunteered for this duty."

Harris grumbled, and he cursed something awful. All his good mood and elation, borne out by easy killing, had evaporated. Now, Harris took up his weapon with a new level of seriousness. He put his rifle to his cheek, set it up carefully on the tripod again, and aimed precisely at head-level. I knew he planned to put down whoever stepped through next with an instant headshot. He was determined not to let another man get away.

For nearly two minutes, no one stepped through those gateway posts.

"He chickened," Harris shouted to me. "You saw that, didn't you? He chickened, whoever that guy was. You should write him up. He should face danger proudly and bravely."

I smirked, knowing Harris rarely faced danger with pride or bravery unless he was forced to.

After the third minute had passed, we began to relax. Even I was willing to believe the rest of the troops had lost heart. None of them would be fool enough to walk aboard *Scorpio* today. They were probably all sending texts to their mommas, begging for lawyer money or filing grievances with some bored official.

But then suddenly, the black armored fellow charged through. Harris immediately fired three crisp shots right at head-level. They sparked and spanged off the raised arm of the soldier. He'd held up his arm to guard his face. Although he wasn't wearing a helmet, this was enough to stop Harris's sharpshooting from taking him out immediately.

The man charged onto Gray Deck, covering his face and moving directly toward Harris. Behind him, a squad of seven more recruits wearing nothing but their papery jumpsuits poured in. They split off to each side, three to the right and four to the left. They spread wide and came around, clearly planning to flank Harris.

Adjunct Harris was no fresh-faced rookie, however. He showed professionalism and demonstrated what a smooth killer he was. Realizing he was wasting ammo on the armored man, he thumbed his snap-rifle to full-auto and hosed down the four on the left, bringing them down. Then he swiveled, nailing the three on the right. All of them were murdered before they could reach him.

The charging man in the armor, however, ran straight up the middle, and he made it to Harris.

Harris bounced up onto his feet, knowing that his gun wasn't going to win this fight. This was going to be decided hand-to-hand.

Using the butt of his rifle, Harris smashed the man's defending arm away, revealing his face. Then I knew the truth. It was none other than Adjunct Clane.

I should have suspected as much, as this was exactly the reason I'd chosen Clane in the first place. Having met with him on the battlefield many years ago, I'd been impressed with the young man. That's why I offered him a spot in my service.

Clane drew a combat knife and slashed, chopping Harris' rifle in half. Harris dropped his weapon and pulled out his own knife.

"That's not fair," Harris shouted, pointing at the knife in Clane's hand. "He's armed. None of these men are supposed to be armed!"

I shrugged with disinterest. Harris was an expert with a knife, even if he wasn't wearing armor. If anyone could deal with it, he could.

The two men sparred, trading punches and thrusts. It was clear to me that Harris was both stronger and more deadly than Clane, but Clane could passively block Harris' fist and knife with his armor. This gave Clane a significant advantage.

In fact, he took the unprecedented step of grabbing ahold of Harris' blade when it jabbed for his face, gripping it with a gauntlet that couldn't be cut. At the same time, he stabbed Harris and drove his blade into the other man's neck.

Wheezing in shock, Harris staggered a little, but he managed to wrench the knife out of Clane's hand and drive it, with both fists wrapped around the hilt, straight into Clane's face.

Both of them were mortally wounded. I came and stood over them while they shivered on the deck.

"Gentlemen," I said, "that was frigging amazing! I want to commend both of you on a well-fought battle."

Then, I clapped my big hands together. I kept clapping until the light went out of their eyes at last, and they slumped on the deck stone dead.

The day was rather peaceful after that, at least from my point of view. I went back to my module and waited at my desk. I was fairly certain there were going to be some complaints registered by various participants in today's exercise.

Sure enough, less than an hour later, the first man who arrived was Carlos.

"Specialist Ortiz!" I said, greeting him in a hearty tone. I stood and offered him a hand to shake. "I'm glad to see you back from the dead—but you know, you really should take a shower after a revive. Your hair is all slimy."

Carlos glared at me in a fury. "You know what, McGill?" he said. "You have a problem with hate."

"Hate?" I said, then I laughed. "I think you're the one who's hating on people today."

"Did you set all that up just to kill me? Just for laughs? Because from my point of view, that's what this looks like."

I shook my head and smiled. "Nah. That would be funny—but everyone is getting the same treatment."

I showed him some vids of other units nailing their recruits and stragglers. Carlos didn't seem happy, but at least he stopped blaming me for singling him out.

Carlos turned around and staggered away, muttering words like cuck, bullshit, and piss-goblins. He left my office in a huff.

I smiled and shook my head, taking all his sour grapes in the best possible light. After all, he had good reason to feel cheated, but I knew he would get over it. Anyone who couldn't get over a bad death such as he had experienced today had long since quit Legion Varus.

Next up, some twenty minutes later, one disgruntled-looking Adjunct Harris arrived.

"What the fuck was that?" he demanded, "who issued that man armor that none of us adjuncts are allowed to have?"

I shrugged. "I don't know. Maybe Fleet marines have better quartermasters than we do. Maybe all the adjuncts get them where he comes from."

After I explained the man was Adjunct Clane, and he was a marine transfer from Fleet, Harris was less pissed off. He was still angry, mind you, but he wasn't *insanely* angry.

"Well then, how come this adjunct didn't get his suit stolen from him like Leeson?"

My face went blank, as I didn't have an answer for that one. I didn't want to talk about it, as I didn't want my lie uncovered, so I played dumb.

Eventually, Harris left grumbling and complaining about how unfair everything had been today. That was Harris for you. He got to shoot down thirty unarmed men in an ambush, yet he still had the balls to say that he had been treated unfairly. Go figure.

The last man to accost me in my office that afternoon was one Adjunct Clane. I was happy to see he looked a decade younger than he had been earlier today.

"Hey there," I said, standing up and grinning. "Welcome to Varus."

I offered him a hand to shake, but he looked at it like it was a bag of dicks.

After a moment of bemusement and indecisiveness, he reached out his own hand with a sigh and shook mine. That was a good sign from my point of view. Sure, he was angry about our little surprise and probably in the mood to complain, but he was already taking steps to get over all that.

"Centurion McGill," he said, "Adjunct Clane reporting for duty, sir."

"At ease, soldier. Take a load off."

I offered him the only other chair in my tiny office, and he took it. I broke out two plastic cups and poured some nondescript clear liquid full of alcohol into both of them. I passed one across to Clane.

He looked at it dubiously, sniffed it, and then downed it in one gulp. When he was done coughing, he looked back up at me. His eyes were somewhat red, and there was some sticky, drippy fluids in his hair. Why was it none of these men took a shower after revival? It just didn't make sense to me.

"Centurion McGill, sir," he said, "that had to be the most fucked-up thing I've ever participated in."

I laughed good-naturedly. "It was nothing special for Legion Varus," I said. "Doesn't your outfit kill all its newest recruits as fast as possible?"

Clane looked at me like I was crazy and shook his head. "No, we certainly don't, sir."

"So, you coddle your marines, huh? Well, that's not how we operate here in Varus. We don't have time to tuck anyone into bed with a blanket and a bottle. Remember, this legion doesn't do things like escort princesses across their castles on some safe planet. No, sir. Legion Varus is for fighting men. We're a rough-and-tumble crew. We like to get that point across to our new recruits as quickly as possible."

"Well sir, I think you've succeeded today. But I'm not a new recruit. Why was I included in this exercise?"

I shrugged. "That was somewhat accidental, I have to admit. Keep in mind, the fact that you were included made sure that Harris, my instructor on today's training course, died as well."

Clane huffed. "Instructor, huh? That's what you call him?"

"That's right. He was instructing the recruits on the process of getting their first revive."

"Yeah, but—"

"Listen, Adjunct," I said, "this isn't what you're used to. I get that. But you're going to have to buck-up immediately if you're going to make it as an officer in my unit. You have to realize we've got a different culture here. You cannot allow yourself—no, *I* cannot allow *you* to demonstrate any level of fear, bitterness, or reluctance to enter combat."

Clane stared at me, surprised. "I wasn't saying I was afraid, sir."

"Maybe not, but that's how it sounds to me. That's how it's going to sound to every trooper in this unit."

Clane stared at the deck for a bit, and he finally heaved a sigh. He raised his eyes again and met mine dead on. "All right, sir. You won't hear anything about this again. Not from me."

"Good."

"But sir, there's another thing. Where do I pick up my armor?"

"Uh…" I said, thinking that over. "We're going to have to figure that out…"

-10-

I went down to Blue Deck later that evening to check on Clane's armor. I found that it wasn't there, and this worried me. Frowning all the way down the long passages and still occasionally bumping my head into the low ceiling, I found my way to the quartermaster's office. There, I caught the man in the actual act of holding up a suit of black armor and shaking it out to admire it.

"Centurion?" I barked.

He startled and turned to look at me over his shoulder. It was at that point that I recognized him. The Legion Varus quartermaster, at least the one from my cohort, was a man I'd had dealings with back a couple of campaigns ago. He had a pencil-thin mustache and a bureaucratic air about him that was unshakable.

"Ah," he said, "Centurion McGill, what can I do for you?"

"You can stop trying on that suit, for one thing."

He frowned and pointedly gestured at the black armor suit I was wearing. "You can't possibly be claiming this as yours, McGill," he said. "There's no way it would fit you, and you're already wearing your suit."

"That's right," I said. "That's not what I'm saying. My man Adjunct Clane died in a training exercise not two hours ago. That suit is his."

The quartermaster jutted out his chin and lifted his eyebrows, considering the armor. He appeared to examine it closely. Finally, he shook his head.

"There's no insignia here," he said. "No mark of rank, no name. I believe you must be mistaken."

"No, I'm not," I said, marching closer and putting my fists on my hips.

"You realize, McGill, that I also possess the rank of centurion?" the quartermaster asked primly. "If this man Clane of yours is only an adjunct, he shouldn't be issued armor before I am."

"Wrong," I said, flipping up a big finger for him to look at. Unlike most fingers raised while making a point, mine was a middle finger. The quartermaster frowned upon seeing this. "Clane is in the combat arms—in my unit. I'm not going to have him dying on the battlefield just because you stole his armor."

"I'm not stealing anything," the quartermaster said huffily. "This is going into the 'lost and found' box until its owner has been identified properly." He turned around and began stuffing the suit into a locker.

That was a mistake. You don't turn your back on an angry Varus man—certainly not a man like myself. I took three meter-long steps and loomed up close behind him. My combat knife was in my hand, and a moment later it was at his throat. The quartermaster froze.

"This is an assault, McGill," he complained.

"No, it's not. It's a duel. We're the same rank. We're not currently in a combat zone of operations. You know as well as I do that duels are nothing but a shrug of the shoulders to the brass."

"This will not stand," he said. "I'll file a complaint and take it to the top."

I laughed at that. "You've got to be kidding me. Who do you think has more friends in high places? Huh?"

The quartermaster considered that. He and most others in the legion of any significant rank knew that I had close connections and ties with no less than Primus Graves, who was second in command of the legion, Tribune Winslade, who was in full command, and even above that, Imperator Turov and Consul Drusus himself.

He sighed, and his shoulders slumped. Taking the hint, I backed off some. He threw the armor at me. I caught it with one hand and put the knife away with the other.

"That's mighty considerate of you," I told him. "In fact, I'm impressed. I'll tell you what, Quartermaster...if another suit comes along without an owner, I'll deliver it to you personally."

The man grumbled, and he didn't meet my eye, but he also seemed mollified. I exited and marched out of the lower decks. Ten minutes later, I presented the suit to Clane. This was met with a harsh cry of a rage.

Apparently, Harris had returned from the dead as well.

"Centurion, sir," he said, "may I have a private word with you?"

Beckoning, I led him into my office. He came in and slammed the door.

"Sir," Harris said, "you've got to be shitting me! That man Clane is keeping a stardust suit? First-off, I was passed over when Leeson got one. Then the next one Clane uses to kill me. If anything, I should have it."

I shrugged helplessly. "He came in with it, Harris. Nobody in Legion Varus issued it to him."

"This is the worst sort of horseshit. I can't frigging believe it. First Leeson and now Clane... I'm like nobody around here. I'm like invisible."

"I only wish that were true," I told him. "At this point, I kind of wish none of you guys had been issued a suit. It's caused nothing but trouble all the way up and down the ranks. Now get out of my office, Adjunct.

He marched out and slammed the door again. I had half a mind to go after him, but I didn't. I knew there wasn't any point. Harris had displayed a bad attitude on the first day I'd met him, and nothing had changed in the decades since.

He was an excellent fighter when it came down to it in the trenches, but he was no model soldier under normal circumstances. In short, he was just the sort of man who belonged in Legion Varus—an outfit made up of misfits and social rejects with violent tendencies. No wonder we were always given the worst missions to perform.

As to the nature of the mission we were on today, I had things to consider. What were we going to find when we made it out there to this jungle planet? I had no idea, but I was sure it wasn't going to be pleasant.

A few days passed after that, and they were blissfully uneventful. All my recruits were revived and returned to our module with their tails between their legs. We began a harsh training regimen, physically and mentally beating down the recruits before slowly building them back up. They had all been screened and selected for their fitness to serve, and after a death and a revive, even the greenest recruit was in excellent health.

It was their minds that needed the most work. They'd yet to ripen into what would be considered worthy for a legionnaire.

After two weeks of practicing on gun ranges, we'd managed to teach them to lineup, salute and handle their equipment properly. At that point word came down from Gold Deck that there would be a ship-wide training exercise tomorrow morning.

Graves himself delivered the news. Every large spacious wall aboard *Scorpio* showed his craggy face. It was enough to make a man wince and squint.

"Recruits," he said, "normally, Legion Varus is gifted with a ship that has what we call a Green Deck—a large expanse of park-like land. Green Decks are designed for military exercise, R&R and shooting practice. Unfortunately, although we do have plans to turn one of *Scorpio's* larger cargo holds into just such a facility, we've not been given the time or the budget to perform this miracle. Still, we'd prefer to have a serious combat exercise involving at least our green recruits before we deploy onto a new planet."

Graves took this moment to pull up a diagram of the big ship and her maze of passageways. He had a smile on his face as if he was about to deliver good news. "Your top officers have been working on this problem. You will not be disappointed, recruits. Tomorrow at 0700, all of the corridors on the main decks are to be sealed off from the rest of the ship. Every recruit aboard will be armed with a snap-rifle and a combat knife and let loose into these rat-tunnels—that's when the fun begins."

He was outright smiling now. Looking around at my men, I saw the expression of every recruit was faltering—switching over from concern to shock and dismay.

"Anyone of higher rank is advised to stay out of these corridors," Graves continued, "as it's going to be a free-for-all match starting at 0705. The exercise will end promptly at 0800 hours, whether there's anyone left alive or not. Please note that disqualification and execution will result for any combatant found hiding, either from the exercise itself or someplace in the ship that is off-limits. Gold Deck, Blue Deck, Red Deck—they're all off-limits. All the other main, heavily traveled decks are open, but remember recruits, you must stick to passageways not the chambers. If you're not a recruit and don't like getting caught in crossfire, I recommend you stay in your module or at your assigned post. Graves out."

Leeson came swaggering up to me shortly after this announcement. He whistled loudly. "Can you believe that horse hockey?" he asked me. "What kind of training is that? What are those boys going to learn by running around in their skivvies playing hide and seek?"

"That's right," Harris added, joining the conversation. "That's not a proper exercise. I bet they're all going to try to hide in the bathroom and claim they have the shits or something."

I ignored them, as they were both probably irritated that they weren't going to be allowed to shoot any recruits personally. For my own part, I was somewhat relieved. I didn't have to plan out, participate in, or judge the contest. All I had to do was relax in my office until it was over. Now, if you ask me, that's an officer's dream scenario when it comes to having an all-recruit training exercise.

The day dragged on after that. The entire unit ate dinner together, and we had a good time razzing the recruits about their probable death early the next morning. Everyone of higher rank hooted and jeered. The recruits, who had already been gunned down by Harris at least once, looked kind of green around the gills.

That evening I got a surprise text on my tapper. It was from a person I actually didn't mind hearing from most of the time—Imperator Galina Turov. I answered promptly with a video call. She accepted, opening a channel immediately.

"James?" she said. "What have you been up to on this mission so far?"

I blinked a few times and considered telling her about all my ornery adjuncts and their bitter complaints about who got to wear armor—but I passed on the idea. Instead, I grinned hugely. "Why sir, I've been completely and totally bored on this ship. I've done nothing but watch cartoons and play video games on my tapper every night. It's a sad state of affairs. I don't know what it is with young people in the legion these days... I can't even get them to accept my challenge to a friendly game of chess."

This, of course, was a sheer lie. I never played chess. In fact, I didn't even know how.

Galina smiled slightly. She liked my lies. They sounded good to her ears.

"Well," she said, "it just so happens that I'm aboard *Scorpio* right now. I've been sent out to oversee Winslade's progress. In case there are any diplomatic issues to be handled, I've been assigned to manage that part of this mission."

I blinked three times, but I managed to keep my grin in place. When it came to diplomacy, Winslade was—it was true—an abomination. That said, one of the few people I thought was probably worse at the job was Imperator Galina Turov.

But as Hegemony had rarely considered competency when handing out any high-level task, I was neither surprised nor overly concerned.

"I'm sure Tribune Winslade will be glad to have the help, sir," I said.

"He hates the oversight," she said, "but I'm bored as well. Would you be willing to—shall we say—take a small tour of the ship with me this evening?"

My grin was back. "I surely would be glad to escort you to any chamber, hold or passageway you might be interested in inspecting, sir."

That was it. I had myself a date. That was just the way Galina and I had gotten on over the years. We may not see each other for months or even a year, but that old flame always seemed to come back. Mostly, it came back whenever she was in the mood.

With no further urging from her, I considered pulling on my dress-blues—but I tossed them aside. Just in case, I kept my stardust armor on, even though I'd been wearing it all day. After combing my hair with my fingers, I hustled through a labyrinth of narrow passageways to what passed for Gold Deck on *Scorpio*.

Galina was waiting for me. The door to her cabin was open, and I stepped inside. Closing the door behind me, I was disappointed to see she was fully dressed in an appropriate, if somewhat overly tight, uniform.

"Uh," I said, looking at her, "are we really going to inspect something?"

"Yes," she said. "Follow me."

I followed along behind her. She led me out of her cabin and into the labyrinth of passageways. She took me to one of the support decks, where the ceiling was even lower than usual. Being a woman of slight stature, she could walk upright, unhindered. I, however, looked like the Hunchback of Notre Dame shuffling along in her wake.

At least I was given the opportunity to admire her hindquarters. Long ago, Galina had been revived in a remarkable state of youth and beauty. She'd never updated her body-scans since she'd joined the legions. So even though she was actually older than I was—something along the lines of my parent's age—she didn't look like it. She looked like one of the nineteen-year-old recruits we'd just brought aboard.

It was only when we moved on to another deck, an even darker, emptier region of this vast battlewagon, that I began to become concerned.

"Hey… uh… Imperator?" I said. "What the heck is going on, exactly?"

She didn't answer. She didn't even look back at me over her slim shoulders.

My dim bulb of a brain began to send danger signals to the rest of me. I stopped looking at Turov's butt and tried to take in the larger situation.

Half an hour ago, I hadn't even known Galina was aboard *Scorpio*. Out of the blue, she'd given me an obvious booty-call. Being a man of simple tastes, I'd been instantly taken in and raced to her side.

Now, however, my mind was filling up with questions. Just why was she here? Just where was she taking me? And the biggest question of all… why had Galina, after months of not even bothering to contact me, suddenly decided to strike things up in such a dramatic and immediate fashion? Sure, she was a woman who blew hot and cold like a Rocky Mountain rainstorm, but this was unusual, even for her.

-11-

When the passages narrowed further, the pipes started dripping. The air was kind of steamy down here, and the lights were flickering in spots. At that point, I halted.

"Galina," I said, "you're going to have to talk to me if you want me to take another step."

Slowly, she turned around. She still had that strange smile on her face. It was frozen there.

"James, just a little farther on now," she said, as if she was speaking to a child—which she sort of was. "I want you to come along and meet someone."

"Who, exactly?" I demanded, not budging.

Galina's eyes strayed down to my belt. I had worn my combat knife and my service pistol. She was armed the same way, but both of us knew that even if she got the drop on me and drew first, there was no way she was going to win a fair fight.

Her smile widened a bit farther. To me, the expression looked just a mite strained.

"Let me assure you, there's no danger," she said. "You have nothing to fear. Just come along to this little meeting. We'll have a discussion, and then we can enjoy the rest of our evening together."

I knew exactly what she meant by that. She was trying to lure me in with a promise of sex—and to her credit, it was working.

"Nope," I said, finally rejecting her offer. "I'm not going to do it. I'm standing right here until you tell me what the hell's going on."

She pursed her lips, but she didn't look angry. She looked thoughtful.

"All right," she said, sighing at last. She slipped her hand away from her pistol, and I did the same. She hadn't dared draw on me or order me to do anything. She knew that just wasn't going to work. "All right you stubborn jackass, I'll tell you. A certain person who is known to both of us has requested a meeting. She says she has some important information. She also says, unfortunately, that she won't talk just to me. She's demanded that you be present as well."

"Uh…" I said, thinking that over. "She? She who?"

Galina's mouth cinched up into a tight little pink butthole. I could tell I was pissing her off something awful, but she hid her anger well.

"Abigail Claver," she said at last. "That's who we're going to meet."

I blinked a couple times. Then, I breathed a sigh of relief. "Miss Claver? That makes sense. So now the Clavers are haunting you, too? What bullshit did she feed you? You know you can't trust that snake of a woman. She's as twisted and sneaky as you are yourself."

"Thanks so much for that charming comparison, James. Now, if you'll follow me, we'll find out what this is about."

She walked away down the steamy corridor, and I considered doing a U-turn and marching right the hell out of there. I really did. If there was one person in Heaven or Hell who was trickier and less trustworthy than Galina Turov, it had to be Abigail Claver.

Sighing, I let my curiosity get the better of me. I followed Galina deeper into the bowels of the battleship. At last, we came to a cabin that had probably been originally designed for some Rigellian engineer who'd been trapped down here doing maintenance.

Galina rapped her knuckles on the steel door, right between two of the biggest boilers I'd ever seen.

No one answered right off, so we stood looking around and waiting. I wasn't sure what was in these boilers. I wasn't sure what their purpose was, but the place was hot, humid and faintly disgusting.

Galina reached up to rap again, but the door swung open with a groaning creak of metal on metal. Sure enough, Abigail Claver stood there. She smiled at me and ignored Galina entirely.

"James?" she said. "It's so good to see you again."

"I wish I could say the same, lady, but right now... I'm a bit concerned. What's with this clandestine meeting down here in the bilge?"

"Well," Abigail said, "as you probably know, I'm not exactly an honored guest aboard this ship. In fact, everyone in Legion Varus probably has orders to shoot me on sight."

"That's exactly true," Galina said, glaring at the other woman. There'd never been any love lost between these two, and today, things looked hotter than ever. Galina was jealous of Abigail, with fairly good reason. After all, Abigail was flirty, and she had been intimate with me now and then in the past.

The Clavers were a race of clones. They'd started out as a single man who had gotten ahold of illegal revival machine technology and made countless copies of himself. Over the years, he'd varied these copies to become more numerous and dangerous. Abigail was the only known living member of the Claver clan who was female. This gave her a special high stature in my eyes, but Galina didn't share my perspective there at all.

Abigail frowned at us. "Are you two willing to listen and hear me out?"

"That's why we're here," Galina said. "Now, talk."

"I've come here to warn you. You're on a mission that you shouldn't be pursuing at all."

"What do you know about our mission?" Galina demanded. Her hand slid to the butt of her laser pistol, and her eyes narrowed like those of a pissed cat.

"I know that you're headed for 31 Orionis, a star near Rigel. There's a planet there that others might call a super-earth—a big, warm, wet world full of lush growth. Further, I know Earth shouldn't attack this world. You're only going to cause yourselves more trouble in the long run."

"Earth's government doesn't see it that way," Galina snapped.

"Obviously not," Abigail said, twisting her lips. Then she turned to me, and she made big eyes. "James?" she said. "I know you'll always listen to reason. Earth is kicking Rigel while she's down, but that's a mistake. There's another enemy, a bigger enemy that you'll have to face alone if Rigel falls."

"Huh?" I said, befuddled by the reference. "What enemy?"

"Trust me. They're out there, and you don't want to know any more about them than you already do."

Galina heaved a sigh. "Is that all you have, Abigail? No offers to help us, or trade with us, or anything like that?"

"I came to warn you… to warn Legion Varus… and to warn the captain of this ship. I'm not here to make a deal with you."

Galina's eyes widened. "You've talked to others? You've talked to Captain Merton?"

"Yes, of course. Merton was accommodating. He didn't require me to hide down here amongst the boilers with a thousand steamy pipes."

Galina was showing her teeth now. I knew that was a bad sign.

"Listen to me, James," Abigail said. She reached out a hand, placing it over mine. She was making eyes at me again, and I was a sucker for that.

Apparently, at that moment, Galina decided she'd had enough. She drew her pistol smoothly. "Miss Claver, I thank you for your time and for your message. Right now, on behalf of Hegemony and all of Earth, I regret to inform you that we're rejecting your advice and sending you back home. Thank you so much for coming."

After this little speech, she shot Abigail down before the woman could say another word.

"What did you do that for?" I said, leaning down on one knee and checking Abigail's vitals. She was stone dead.

"Quit pawing at her. She did her job. She gave her message, and we gave our response in return. All I did was send her home. Shove her out an airlock and be done with her."

Grumbling and more than a little bit irritated, I did as Galina ordered.

She kept her pistol out, and she waved it near me but didn't point it directly at me. That was a good thing for her because I was in a bad mood now, and I might have taken such a deadly threat the wrong way.

We found a handy chute that led out to the external ports on the big ship, and I fired Abigail's body right out of *Scorpio*'s belly into open space. There, it burned up in a flash of incandescent radiation.

On our way back to the more civilized portions of the big ship, I didn't say a word to Galina. After all, she'd brought me up to her cabin under false pretenses, and then she'd marched me down into what looked like a death trap. She'd followed up all this charming behavior by murdering Abigail in front of me. To me, this seemed inexcusably rude.

We came to a fork in our path—a spot where we had to either go up levels or down levels. Galina's cabin was located high up on Gold Deck. Mine was down low in the belly of the ship, in the modules reserved for the ground troops.

"James?" she said softly.

I turned around, slowly facing her. At least there weren't steam vents hitting us in the face anymore. We were in a brightly lit corridor amidships.

"What now?" I asked. "Do you want me to stuff myself into an airlock, too?"

"Such bitter complaining…" she said. "How can you like that woman so much? She's a witch."

This made me blink a couple of times. After all, in my personally developed hierarchy of snakes and witches, Abigail Claver and Galina Turov were at pretty damn near the same rung.

Galina was looking at me like she expected me to say something, but my mind was a blank. What did she want now?

Then, all of a sudden, I had it. She wanted me to answer her question. Of course, she didn't want me to answer it *honestly*.

No woman wanted that. She wanted me to tell her how much better she was than Abigail.

Fortunately, although my brain works as slowly as molasses in winter most of the time, I was gifted with natural instincts when it came to charming women. I always seemed to know what they wanted me to say.

Accordingly, I blew out a big puff of air. "I'm not thirsting for Abigail Claver," I told her. "That woman is a rat. A rodent, just like you said. I know that."

"Well then, why are you acting so butt-hurt?"

"Because you brought me here under false pretenses," I said. "You called me up. You flirted with me. I raced to your side, and what did you do? You led me down to the lower decks, to some steamy pit to interview Abigail."

"So, that's it? You're upset that I tricked you?"

"That's right. Skullduggery and murder, that isn't what I had in mind when I came up here to see you."

Galina looked down, studying the deck. "The last time I saw you was at your house in Georgia," she said. "That was a nice time."

"I'm glad you liked it," I said. "I liked it, too."

We both stood there for a moment. Galina was looking shy, but I wasn't fooled. There was nothing shy about Galina Turov. Finally, she sighed.

"Would you like to accompany me back up to my cabin?" she asked. "Just to see if we can get ourselves into a better mood?"

I smiled at last, and this time the smile was for real. I leaned down and gave her a gentle kiss. She responded, and the night was sealed.

We headed up to her cabin, had a drink to relax ourselves, and then we made a night of it. Sure, I knew this woman was evil. She might shoot me and stuff me into an airlock by morning, just as we'd done with Abigail. But when a man lives and dies as often as I have, you learn to take opportunities when they're offered.

After Galina went to sleep, I lay there beside her, wondering for a bit… I was thinking about Abigail's warning.

Was she right? Was Earth really making a mistake by flying out to 31 Orionis? What exactly was this threat that Rigel was dealing with? What would Earth not want to face?

I guessed I'd have to wait until we reached 31 Orionis to find out.

-12-

The next morning, I overslept. I'd meant to get out of Galina's cabin to sneak across the ship and have breakfast with my troops, but I figured I would just have to apologize for having missed it.

Galina shooed me out of her cabin into the passageways at around seven. "You'd better hurry," she said, and she slammed the door.

I thought I'd heard her lock her door and yep, sure enough, it was locked. I frowned at that.

Walking through Gold Deck, things looked normal enough, but once I got down into the main ship's passages, I began to become concerned. The lights were looking weird. There were red glowing double arrows on the floor everywhere.

What the hell was that all about? And then, I heard a fateful announcement come in over the PA system.

"All right, recruits…" said the voice of Primus Graves, "this is your chance to live and learn—or die and learn even harder."

Suddenly, I stopped walking. My eyes flew wide, and my mouth gaped.

"Oh shit," I said aloud.

All of a sudden, in a flood of memories, I realized that there was a live-fire exercise scheduled this morning. All *Scorpio's* main passages were free game for the recruits who were supposed to be gunning for one another over the next hour.

"Remember the rules," Graves said. "For the next fifty-five minutes, no one will be allowed into or out of the ship's main passageway system. It'll be every recruit for himself. Fight well troops, and remember, your officers are watching."

My eyes drifted up to the pinpoint cameras that were embedded in the ceilings of every passageway.

"Oh shit..." I said again. Was Graves watching me right now... timing this just perfectly to screw with me?

"Hiding and whimpering in some corner is not going to cut it if you want to gain rank and become regulars," Graves went on. "So, get in there and mix it up. Our hearts and minds are with all of you. Good luck."

The PA system cut out, and there was a buzzing sound. Yellow flashing emergency lights began to spin all over the ship, just to add a little flavor, I guessed. I heard thumping feet behind me, and I turned around to see a recruit racing up to me with a snap-rifle in his hands. He raised it up, aimed it at my chest, but then hesitated.

"You're an officer?" he asked.

"That's right, boy. Move right along. I'm just one of the umpires watching the show."

Befuddled, the kid trotted by, and I let him go.

I realized right then I was in a bit of trouble. Fortunately, I was still wearing my black suit of armor. I wasn't about to leave it in Galina's apartment, but I had neglected to bring a helmet, and I was armed with nothing more dangerous than my pistol and a knife. This was going to be one hell of a long hour to get through.

I ambled along in the wake of the recruit, wondering just what my first move was going to be. I kind of figured I'd head down to the modules and try to get somebody to let me into the one assigned to 3rd Unit. The problem with that, I realized, was that it was a long ways off.

Before I'd gone a hundred paces down the passageway, the recruit I'd spoken with got nailed. He'd been trotting along the passages, running lightly just like a light trooper was supposed to, but he wasn't paying quite enough attention.

As he got to the end of an intersection, there was a ripping sound of automatic fire. He spun around, did a little flip, and then face-planted himself on the deck. He shivered there, torn-up by something like thirty rounds.

Seeing that caused me to do a U-turn. I went back up to Gold Deck again and rattled the doorlatch. I was locked out of the whole deck, so I tried my tapper to see if I could get Galina to answer, but it was no dice.

Had they blocked tapper-traffic from the passages to the main decks? It looked like they had to me. I supposed that was only fair. You wouldn't want officers leaning on the scales a bit for favored troops. It would be too easy to pass intel to the men in battle who were running around killing each other on the decks.

Not being a man who was easily dissuaded, I hammered my fist on the Gold Deck door anyway, but no one came to open it. Cursing, I wished I had stolen Galina's Galactic Key. That would have gotten me right through this thing, pronto. But I hadn't thought of it, and it was too late now.

Walking the passages at random, I occasionally heard fire ripping out, along with screams and thumping feet. Each time I heard this, I turned in whatever direction led me away from the action.

Sure, I could have waded in and shot a few of these guys myself, but it wouldn't have been right. I was an officer, I was experienced, and I was wearing heavy armor. None of that matched the rules of this game, so I did my best to remain a noncombatant until I came walking around a corner and ran into three recruits who were all crouched and whispering together. I didn't know any of them. They were from a different cohort and a different unit. They gaped up at me, however, whipping up their rifles and aiming in my direction.

One of them turned his rifle toward the ceiling almost immediately. "It's a centurion," he said.

"So what?" said a second. "He might be here to kill us anyway. The third man—a man after my own heart—didn't say a word. He just opened fire.

I employed my only reasonable move, which was something I'd seen Clane do when faced by Harris' snap-rifle while he wore no helmet. I put my arm up in front of my face.

Dozens of rounds splattered all over my chest and arms, but none of them snuck past and got me in the face.

I marched forward, snatched the rifle out of the recruit's hands and then bashed him one with it. He was laid out on the deck cold-cocked. The other two men scrambled away out of my reach, and it seemed like their butts had suddenly grown legs they were able to skitter away so fast.

"What's this all about Centurion?" asked one of them. "What's the deal?"

"The deal is you boys are cheating," I said. "This is supposed to be an individual exercise. I'm here as an umpire to put a stop to it." This, of course, was another lie, but it sounded pretty good even to my own ears.

The two men looked at each other panting and then one shot the other down. That was it. The last man standing ran off.

Tossing the rifle aside, so I wouldn't be recognized as a combatant, I continued on my way.

Now, one might say that I had just interfered in this exercise, and I'd unfairly advantaged or disadvantaged various troops. This was sort of true, but in Legion Varus, none of that really mattered during an exercise because it's not a legalistic experience. It's more of a holistic one—meaning that we wanted troops to learn how to deal with the random fluctuations, and sudden unexpected events that always occurred on the battlefield. We wanted them to pay a horrible price, to feel death, pain and agony—as well as to experience betrayal and regret. This could only serve to toughen them all up for when events were real.

Maneuvering carefully. I made it down to my module's main door by hook or by crook. Feeling a wave of relief, I hammered on the door. There was a metallic ringing sound as my gauntleted fists struck the steel. Eventually, someone heard me and came to investigate. It was a specialist, and he looked befuddled and clueless.

I pointed over his shoulder toward my lazy-assed adjuncts, who I could see were drinking beers and watching the live vid feeds of the action going on all around the ship. Reluctantly, the specialist approached the officers and told them that I was at the door.

I couldn't hear any of this mind you. I could only see it through the porthole of thick bulletproof glass that allowed a very limited view of the module's interior.

Harris was the first to approach with Leeson in his wake. They did lots of expressive double-takes. They pointed and appeared to be hooting with laughter. I glowered through the porthole in their direction. I made some frantic motions indicating they should open the door. Harris dared to pretend he couldn't understand me. He pointed to his ears and put one ear up against the glass as if trying to hear through the porthole itself.

I had half a mind to burn a hole right through the glass and through his skull, but I didn't think I could do it with just a laser pistol.

Meanwhile, standing behind him, Leeson tapped at his tapper. When he was done, he finally held it up to the glass so I could read what he had written in large text, *GRAVES SAYS NO*.

Those three words caused me to grit my teeth. I could see it all now. Graves had never been happy about my relationship with Galina Turov. He saw it as inappropriate from the beginning to the end. If my overnight stay at her cabin resulted in my discomfort, that would make him all the happier.

Leeson and Harris walked away from the door, belly-laughing. Adjunct Clane, my new supporting officer came up to the porthole next. I had half a mind to insist that he open the door. I figured he might just do it. In fact, I typed out the message, *OPEN DOOR* on my tapper.

Would he dare disobey a direct order from his centurion? Probably not.

But then… as Clane looked on with concern, I erased the message and sighed.

Graves was a primus. I was a centurion. By all the rules, I would be in the wrong ordering him to discount orders given by a superior officer.

So, I sighed, sucked it up, and walked away from the module. I was just going to have to last for fifty-five more minutes.

-13-

I checked my tapper and figured out I had nineteen minutes to go. That might not sound like a long time, but maybe that's because you haven't tried trotting around for nineteen minutes with about a thousand teenagers taking potshots at you. In fact, I hadn't even finished flipping off Leeson and Harris through the portal before a couple of rounds spanged off my armor.

Ducking my head and taking off, I escaped into a side passage after being shot in the ass perhaps ten or twenty times.

Checking my tapper again, I frowned. Tappers were supposed to be disabled in the exercise, but mine was actually working—perhaps because I was an officer and therefore not officially part of this fiasco. I wasn't sure why I could access the ship's grid, but facts were facts.

Without compunction or hesitation, I promptly began to cheat. It was necessary, because there was some serious gunfire off to my left and my right. There was essentially nowhere to run. I had to get an edge.

Tapping into the ship's security cameras, I narrowed things down on my current location and took a look at what was going on up around the next corner.

There, I saw a young female recruit hunkered down in a doorway with nothing wider than a door jamb to provide cover. She wasn't fighting so much as spraying rounds from her snap-rifle down the corridor first in one direction then the other. It was nothing more than panicky suppressive fire.

Considering her situation, I had to nod in approval. I mean, wouldn't it stand to reason that if there was gunfire going on, you would run away from it? Anyone trying to survive this ordeal was likely to flee from the noise.

As further testimony to her success, I saw no less than three bodies lying in the corridor. I wasn't sure if she'd shot them all, but she sure as shit was the last one alive at the moment.

Widening my search, I discovered a group approaching on her six. A pair of recruits were sidling up in a side passage. I recognized these two—they were the survivors that I'd met earlier. The one I'd clocked with a rifle butt, wiped at a trickle of blood that ran down his temple, but they were still teaming up and still cheating.

"That's dirty pool," I muttered to myself.

They seemed to be aware of her position, which of course she'd given away by rattling off rounds in random directions. These two were aggressive. They were on the hunt. They knew where she was, and they meant to take her out. I had to admire their style.

Scanning the area, camera by camera, I did see evidence that most of the recruits in the area were already dead or incapacitated. Some still flopped on the deck, groaning. They were of no harm or use to anyone.

We were getting down to that dirty, sudden-death finish these exercises usually ended with. People could get real mean and animal-like when the end was near. I guess it was only natural.

Edging up to the corner of the next angle in the passageway, I dared to stick my hand out. I waved my black glove around a little bit.

"Hey... hey, you," I whispered.

The response was quick and predictable. My fingers did a little dance, and it wasn't from wiggling them. She must have put fifty rounds down that passageway, nailing me in the glove several times. It actually stung a bit, but nothing penetrated. I snatched my hand back, and when she stopped firing, I dared to speak again.

"Hey, settle down," I said. "I'm one of the referees and an officer.

"Fuck off," she said. Again, I nodded in approval. Hers was the appropriate response.

Just to prove my point, I then exposed an overly large leg with a size thirteen boot at the bottom of it. Predictably, she lit that up, but I held it out there gritting my teeth and letting the pellets spang and rattle—hoping none of the ricochets could by chance bounce up and catch me one in the face. I would have deserved it at this point, but I didn't want to eat a bullet all the same.

Finally, she stopped firing. "Who are you?" she yelled.

"I told you. I'm an officer, and I'm a referee."

"Why are you bothering me?" she demanded. "Are you trying to get me killed?"

"Nope. Quite the opposite. I just wanted to let you know there's a couple of cheaters on your six right now."

I was watching her on my tapper using the security cameras. I had spooked her good. Now, she was swinging her rifle this way and that, aiming at my exposed black armored leg one second and aiming her rifle down the passageway the other direction the next second. She was freaking out, and I'd given her good reason to do so. She was breathing hard and in an outright panic.

"I'm just telling you because those two boys coming the other way have teamed-up," I said. "That seems unfair to me, so I'm giving you a warning."

"How do I know you're not bullshitting me? How do I know you're not the one trying to put me out?"

"Well," I said, "first of all, because I've got stardust armor on. They don't issue that to just any random grunt. Secondly, I haven't made a move on you. I didn't try to come around the corner and fire even a single round—but still, it's your call. I'd recommend you keep your gun trained the other way. Keep checking my way, occasionally, too, but when those two clowns poke their noses around the corner, open up and put them down."

Several seconds went by, during which I heard a bit of confused cursing, muttering and panting, the girl was having a downright panic attack, and I couldn't blame her for it.

She wasn't given much more time to think things over. The teamed recruits were already making their move. Maybe they'd heard us talking, or maybe everything was just chance. I didn't know which it was, as I'd been watching the girl on the cameras and not those two scoundrels.

One of them dashed across at the intersection. I was betting on the little lady who was already hammering away at him with her snap-rifle. She fired a long, stitching streak of rounds down the corridor. None of them seemed to strike home however, and now, they had her boxed-in. The corners of the passages gave them cover to shoot around, and she had two targets to deal with.

Remembering her training, she threw herself prone on the deck to reduce her exposure and steady her aim.

The cheaters were whispering and signaling to each other, and when they came—I have to give them credit—they came both at once, and they came all-out.

The two boys edged around the corner and took aim—one from the left, and one from the right. My lucky little lady, however, wasn't going down without a fight. She had the drop on the man on the left, and she lit him up. Her fire came in low and accurate and took him out before he could get off a shot.

Now, against experienced troops, this would normally have been her last successful moment. The second man should have taken the opportunity to aim, fire and put her down.

He actually did fire, but his aim was off due to being surprised, and the girl's position paid off. His rounds sprayed right over her head. I think the fact he'd seen his buddy get nailed had spooked him. He'd miscalculated, or maybe he just squinched up his eyes, gritted his teeth and fired away blindly around the corner. Whatever the case, he missed her and was back out of sight, hugging the wall and pissing himself.

"You got Bobby, you little bitch," I heard him yell.

"Get the fuck out of my corridor, or I'll kill you both," the feisty girl shouted back.

It was all quiet for about thirty seconds after that. Then I heard a tapping sound—the ring of boots on metal. They seemed to be dying away. Had Bobby's best buddy in the world run off? I couldn't help myself, I checked my tapper, and the security cameras told the truth. The sneaky bastard was still there, up against that corridor wall and waiting. His snap-rifle was in his hands, and he was gripping it tightly. His finger lovingly caressed the trigger. That boy wanted revenge.

"Hey," I hissed. "Hey, girl, he's still there."

The recruit I'd been sponsoring for the last several minutes froze. She'd just been climbing to her feet, probably to go check on the status of her two victims. Hearing my words however, she threw herself prone on the deck again.

Maybe the ambusher had heard the whole thing. He chose that moment to make his move. He didn't jump across the corridor. He didn't step in and stand there and blaze away from the hip. No, he put his arms around the corner chicken-style, holding onto that snap-rifle and firing it down the corridor with only his hands, fingers and part of his arm exposed.

A roman candle's worth of sparks flashed and banged all over the corridor. The metal walls were hit and scored a hundred times or more.

Taking careful aim, the girl on the deck fired off her own steady stream of projectiles in return. It was a hard shot, but she struck the man's hand, arm and snap-rifle itself, tearing them apart.

Yelling, he fell back on the deck. The girl scrambled to her feet, raced forward, aimed down and pretty much executed him right there on the floor. He was helpless. His hands and arms were all floppy, torn up by a dozen rounds from her snap-rifle. She put a dozen more into his chest, and it was over.

It was all quiet after that. She prodded both bodies, stole some ammo, and then marched back to her half-assed defensive position.

Now, right then I knew what I should do. I should withdraw. The girl was saved. She had fought a fair battle against unfair opponents, and she'd won. Maybe I'd helped her a bit too much, in retrospect, but what was done was done. It was time for me to move on.

But...I didn't.

I considered teaching her a lesson... Graves might have done so, coming around the corner and shooting her down.

That would put the fear of God, officers, and Legion Varus into her brain nice and permanent-like.

I knew that's what Graves would have done, but I didn't have the heart to. Instead, I just stood around the corner, not moving.

Less than a minute later, she came nosing around the corner, and my big black gloved hand grabbed the barrel of her snap-rifle. She let loose with a chattering spray of rounds, but they all hit the roof and bounced down the corridor behind me harmlessly.

Being far larger and stronger than she was, I ripped the weapon out of her hands. That's when I noticed she was hurt. There had to be six or seven bloody holes in the girl.

Damn, she was a tough one—still on her feet, and still fighting. I guess nothing vital had been hit, at least not vital enough to kill her instantly. That was the strange thing about the human body. Sometimes, one shot could put a man down. Other times, a dozen didn't do the trick.

She sat back down on the deck, going partly limp. She laid down shortly afterwards, her hair spreading out around her head like a halo. That's when I noticed that despite the sweat, the blood, and a few tear-streaked lines under eyes, she was pretty—young and pretty.

She was also in the middle of dying one of her very first deaths.

I dropped the rifle, put my hands on my knees and bent to look down over her. "Hey," I said. "You did really good work here. I'm impressed."

"Who are you?" she managed to wheeze out.

"I'm Centurion James McGill," I told her. "3rd Cohort, 3rd Unit. Who are you?"

"Tessie," she said, but her voice was getting quieter. Her eyes were glazing over a bit too, and she was talking more slowly with every word. "I'm Tessie—3rd Cohort, 8th Unit."

"Nice to meet you, Tessie," I said, smiling.

I reached down to shake her hand, but she didn't reach a hand back up to meet mine. She was already as dead as it gets.

-14-

About fifteen minutes later, after I'd watched Tessie die on her back in a pool of blood, I returned to my module. The door was open, and not one of my three adjuncts was in evidence.

I hulked in through the doorway, and there must have been a grim expression on my face, because nobody met my eyes or got in my way. That was a good basic principle to follow in any man's legion, especially when it's Legion Varus, and you're talking about the centurion of your own personal unit.

They studied their shoes, polished chrome, worked on their kits, loaded magazines—pretty much anything and everything they could possibly do. No one dared address me or ask me how my day had been.

I eventually found Clane in the back of the gear locker. I startled him with my appearance in the doorway. "Clane?" I barked.

He jumped, turned around and faked a smile. "Oh, hey, there you are Centurion. Mighty sorry we couldn't help you out back there during the exercise. Glad to see you didn't catch one in the face."

I didn't answer immediately. My eyes slid around from side-to-side looking for my other adjuncts. Could all three be hiding back here?

"Where are Harris and Leeson?" I asked.

Clane shrugged and spread his hands wide. "I'm not quite sure, sir. They stepped out the minute the exercise ended.

Didn't you see them—maybe pass them by on the way down here?"

"No, I sure as shit didn't," I said.

Clane shook his head helplessly. "Well, I guess I can't help you. Maybe you could check by tracing their tappers or something."

I gave him a sour look. If Leeson and Harris were actually trying to dodge me, they were plenty smart enough to use a jammer or even wrap their wrists up in metallic tape. Anything to avoid being located until the heat was off.

I considered yelling at Clane for a bit, but then I passed on the idea. After all, he was in a tough spot. He had to worry about me, and he also had to worry about the two other adjuncts. If he played favorites, either helping me out or helping them out, he'd be called a kiss ass or a traitor. There was no winning in this situation for him, so I just nodded, turned around sourly and walked out.

To my surprise, Harris and Leeson were just stepping in the door about that time. I figured I was going to have to dig them out of the laundry deck or something.

"Hey, sir," Harris said, making the first attempt at mollifying my obvious bad mood. "Leeson and I just went down to the PX, you know, and we spent some of our hard-earned credits to buy you this here bottle for a job well done."

He handed me a bottle of brandy. It wasn't a *glass* bottle, mind you. They didn't really allow those on ships. It was plastic, but it was real brandy, imported up from Earth.

I eyeballed it sourly, but I took the plastic jug, twisting off the cap. I took a slug and handed it back to Harris, who took a swig himself.

Leeson made the next attempt to tame their angry gorilla of a superior officer. "Hey…" he said. "Did you know we were kind of watching you?"

I looked at him suddenly, and he gave me a hopeful smile.

"That's right," he said. "We were all tapped into the security cameras, pretty much everybody on board was. Now, I'm quite certain that not everyone was watching the drama that was playing out with you and that girl in the hallway—

way down around Module 68 or so—but of course, we had a natural interest. We were rootin' for you two."

"That's right," Harris said. He waggled the bottle back at me, but I refused it.

I still hadn't said a word to these two hooligans, and I hadn't yet decided their fate. I think they knew that, so they were working overtime to make me happy.

"That had to be a hard lesson for all those recruits," Leeson said. "You were in big-dog style. You didn't shoot anybody, not a single recruit that we saw, but you did help that one girl put down those two goons who were sneaking up on her."

"…seemed outright unfair," Harris said, "two buddies working in cahoots to kill one little girl huddling in a hallway."

"Totally unfair," Leeson agreed.

They were both full of shit, of course, and I knew it. But I let them keep talking.

"Hey," Leeson said. "You know what else I did? I went and looked her up for you. Here's her info."

He flicked his tapper, aiming whatever was on his screen toward mine. My tapper automatically caught the message, and I lifted my arm to look at it. A blue button had the word 'Accept' printed on it with the word 'Cancel' next to that.

Thinking it over for a moment, I finally tapped the blue 'Accept' and that was that. I had Tessie's info on my tapper. Of course, I could have looked her up myself, but Leeson was just trying to kiss ass. He probably knew I was lazy and that I might never have gotten around to doing the search.

Leeson and Harris were both giving me hopeful grins at this point. Harris waggled the bottle of brandy at me again. I sucked in a deep breath and walked past the two of them, brushing them with my shoulders as I went by.

"0600 tomorrow," I said. "Special exercises. You two are in the lead." Then I walked out.

As I left, I heard Leeson say, "Ah, hell," and that put a smile on my face.

Walking the echoing passageway, I managed to calm myself down. I was still a bit mad at my adjuncts for locking me out of my own module and laughing at me through the portal. I was a bit mad at Graves too, for having not made an exception for me.

The corridors were full of blue jump-suited bio orderlies and robots. They were picking up bodies all over the place. Now and then, I saw specialists from the quartermaster's armory, cursing and muttering. They'd been given the unhappy duty of finding every dropped snap-rifle and extra magazine. Apparently, they weren't enjoying picking these items up off the deck and transporting them back to an armory somewhere.

Before I even knew where I was going, I found myself arriving at Blue Deck. Now, just why the hell had I wandered down here?

I lifted my tapper, spotting Tessie's info, and I knew the answer. Something about that girl had captivated me.

As any number of women could attest, this is easily done. I'm a sucker for a genuinely attractive, feminine shape and a spunky attitude. One might even say it was my greatest weakness.

I hesitated for perhaps five seconds with my big glove hovering over my arm. Finally, I tapped the button and did a trace.

Tessie came up—her photo, her info, all sorts of stuff about her, but most importantly where she was in the revival queue. She was about a thousand down. That would be quite a wait. Probably, she wouldn't make it out of the oven until tomorrow, as most of the recruits aboard the battleship had died before she did, and so she had to be at the back of the line.

Oh well. There wasn't going to be any chance meeting today, engineered or otherwise, so I left Blue Deck and considered heading up to Gold Deck.

I ultimately rejected that idea as well. I needed a break, so I headed for Lavender Deck. Lavender Deck was midrange on the stack, under Blue Deck and Gold, but above Red Deck and Gray. It was normally reserved for the most important of personnel.

Centurions were right on the dividing line when it came to these things. Usually, civilians and only the highest-ranked officers, such as a primus, tribune, or above, were allowed to set foot on Lavender. Those rules relaxed when there wasn't any VIP presence aboard the vessel, however. These rules had eased even more on *Scorpio,* since the ship had a really crappy Lavender Deck.

This one, unlike the sumptuous accommodations that had been aboard *Dominus,* was decidedly lacking in luxury. There was only one restaurant rather than six. There was no theater, no park-like walkways, and only a few shops occupied by bored patrons and even more bored workers.

I consulted my tapper again, and my finger rose to hover over my rolodex file of interesting individuals. Unsurprisingly, every one of these prospective companions was female. I gave the Rolodex a spin and up popped another likely candidate for my attentions: Galina Turov.

I smiled. After all, I'd just spent a nice night with the girl, and even if she was a conniving, scheming, treacherous snake of a woman, she was also the most steady girlfriend I've ever had.

My finger almost went down, almost made contact and almost placed a call to her, when to my surprise, my tapper lit up. As if responding to my thoughts someone was calling me one second before I could call them.

Unfortunately, instead of Galina or Tessie, I got a rude surprise. It was none other than the craggy, unsmiling face of Primus Graves.

"McGill?" he said. "You're wanted in my office, pronto. Don't take any detours this time."

I opened my mouth to respond, but I didn't get out a word. This was partly because I was surprised in the first place, but mostly because Graves had cut off the channel so abruptly I didn't get the chance.

"What the shit is this?" I said to myself.

Sighing, I left all thoughts of rest, relaxation and entertainment behind. I took a nice, brisk walk back to Gold Deck and headed for Primus Graves' office. Arriving there, I found the place strangely empty.

"McGill?" he shouted from behind me. I turned and saw him farther on down the passageway. He beckoned for me to approach. He seemed to be standing outside a large conference room, the largest on the ship.

"Come on," he said. "You're late."

With a heavy heart. I followed him down the passageway and stepped inside. It seemed like every primus aboard *Scorpio* was there, having a meeting of some kind. Notably missing were the highest-level officers. Tribune Winslade, Imperator Galina Turov and Captain Merton were all absent. That meant this meeting was the worst kind, a bunch of middle-managers brewing-up trouble.

"Uh..." I said, looking around. "To what do I owe this honor, sirs?"

I was, in fact, the lowest ranked individual in the room. That was a bad place to be, especially when you were a man who was guilty of as many crimes as I was. What's more, I was concerned to see that every one of these gentleman had a black stardust suit of armor on, the same as I did. There wasn't going to be any intimidation or overpowering of the brass today. They were all just as well-geared as I was.

In the past, I'd used my stardust armor to throw my balls around and bully people, but I could tell in an instant none of that was going to fly today.

No one answered my question, as they were all very busy talking to each other. Meekly, I walked in and took the one spot at the table that was unoccupied. I sat there, faking a smile and looking around with an expression on my face contrived to indicate I was as dumb as a bag of hammers.

The group buzzed among themselves, but finally they quieted. Numerous cold glances flew down the conference table in my direction. Graves finally took a seat at the head of the table, clasping his hands together in front of him and regarding me.

"McGill," he said, "this group has convened because it has come to our attention that certain inappropriate and possibly dangerous activities have been taking place aboard this ship over recent days."

My jaw sagged low. I began to think over my last few days. What had I done? There was always something... but I couldn't quite...

Then, I latched onto it. Surely, they were upset about how I'd been running around the halls with the recruits. I wasn't quite sure how that could have endangered anyone above the lowest of the low ranks, but as Graves was pretty much a straight-arrow, Eagle Scout of a man, I figured he hadn't appreciated any of my shenanigans.

"Oh…" I said, laughing and slapping an overly large hand on the table. "About that, sir. No harm done. Hardly anyone extra died. In fact, I think it was probably good for every recruit I came in contact with. Don't you think?"

Graves stared at me coldly and sternly. "I don't know what the hell you're talking about," he said, "and I'm pretty sure I don't want to know."

"Uh…" I said, thinking that over. "Didn't you tell my adjuncts that I couldn't go back into the module from the corridors during this morning's exercise?"

Graves frowned at me. "This morning—what? Oh, the recruit thing… No, I didn't talk to your adjuncts at all, McGill. Start making sense, man. We're talking about a serious breach of protocol aboard this ship. We keep closer tabs these days on anyone who teleports on and off a legion vessel."

I was blinking now and totally confused. I was also somewhat relieved, of course. He seemed to be unaware and uncaring about the fact I'd participated in a forbidden exercise. That whole business of cheating heavily in favor of one little lady—that was all water under the bridge.

If there's one thing that a slippery and forever-guilty man such as myself learns early in life, it's to shut up when you catch a break. Many a fool might blurt out all kinds of red flags concerning his own guilt, but I instinctively closed my mouth and kept it clamped shut.

Graves stared at me for a moment. "Well, do you have anything to say for yourself?"

"I just don't know rightly what to say, sir," I shrugged. "I really don't know what this is all about."

"Ignorance…? You're going to play that card, are you? This is one of your scripted moves, isn't it, McGill? After fifty years, I'm onto you, Centurion."

"Uh… has it really been that long, sir?"

"Yes, almost."

"Well sir, when a man doesn't know what's up, he shouldn't talk out of turn. That's my motto. So yes, I'm as dumb as a fence post regarding whatever it is you're talking about, and that's a fact."

The assembled officers smirked, rolled their eyes, and a few even chuckled. Others appeared sour and distrustful. I supposed it all depended on their personalities, and their level of experience with one James McGill.

"All right," Graves said. "I'll play your dirty little game. Let me refresh your memory, on the 26th of last month…"

"The 26th, sir?"

"Yes," he said. "That's what I just said. Please pay attention, McGill. On the 26th, your tapper was located close to two other tappers, one of which should not have been aboard this ship. This occurred on the boiler deck, down near engineering. Am I ringing the bells in your head yet, Centurion?"

To be perfectly honest, he wasn't ringing any bells. Not one. My mind was a blank. I stared at him. I gaped. I didn't even blink, while I thought it over for a few minutes.

The 26th... that had been a week or two ago. For me, a week's time was like a century. I like to live in the here and now—but finally, at long last, I caught on, and I whooped aloud.

"Oh!" I said. "You're talking about when I went down below decks with Turov, right?"

Graves nodded. "That's right, McGill. You were with Imperator Turov and one other. We need you to identify that other person and state your purpose for being on that deck at the time."

Looking around the crowd again, I didn't see a welcoming eye in the bunch. I was beginning to catch on at last. Somehow, they had detected the presence of Abigail Claver aboard *Scorpio*. Galina, and I had met with her down there, and then Galina had shot her, and we'd tossed the body out an airlock.

Obviously, that move hadn't been slick enough to slip past Graves and whatever new tech he had for tracing everyone aboard this battleship. I thought that over, and I didn't like the taste. After all, I didn't want to implicate myself, Abigail or

Galina in any way, shape, or form—but at the same time, if I pretended I didn't know what they're talking about, or I made up some bizarre story, I would only cast more suspicion upon myself.

Thinking it over, I considered telling them the truth, but I quickly rejected the idea. "Well, now..." I said, looking down and rolling my head side-to-side. I was endeavoring, in my ham-handed way, to look as guilty and sheepish as possible. "I know how it is when something socially embarrassing happens aboard this ship. Far too often, I seem to be at the center of the storm. Call it a character flaw if you will. It's just part of who I am... I guess."

"McGill?" Graves interrupted. "Just what the hell are you talking about?"

"I'm telling you, sir. I'm confessing straight-up, right now. Don't stop a man when he's in the middle of a confession. Any prosecuting lawyer would tell you that."

He twisted his lips up into a sour expression, but he waved for me to continue.

"Well, you see, sirs... Galina Turov has been a close friend of mine for many years."

Primus Collins snorted at that point. My eyes slipped to hers as did Graves'. She, of all the people present, was another woman I'd actually had intimate contact with some years ago. Apparently, she was still keenly mindful of that fact, and she didn't appreciate my lifelong penchant for horndoggery.

My eyes left Primus Collins, and I went back to my bullshit story, which was a tangled web I had to weave with style. "You see, sirs, sometimes certain ladies have... well, shall we say unusual tastes..."

The whole group blinked at that. Nobody knew what the hell I was talking about.

"Could you elaborate please, McGill?"

"Well, I don't like to be the kind of guy to kiss and tell, you see, but Galina... well, you know... I try to be enough for her, sir, but she has appetites. All of us do. Don't you fellows try to pretend you're high and mighty!"

I opened my mouth to say more, but Graves lifted his gloved hand to stop me. He gave me a flat stare. "McGill... Are you trying to tell me that you and Imperator Turov met with another person on that deck for some kind of illicit moment of intimacy?"

I pointed a big finger at him. "That's a really nice way of putting things. I'm going to have to remember that."

Primus Collins snorted again. This time, she did it with such force that she blew her own bangs up out of her face. I wasn't sure if she was disgusted or disbelieving. I supposed it was probably a mixture of both, but I didn't much care anyways.

My eyes were on Graves. What did he believe?

After several moments of staring at me, he balled up a fist and hammered it once on the table like a gavel. "That's it," he said. "We're arresting McGill. Throw him in the brig. Get Turov in here, and Winslade next. We're going to get to the bottom of this if we have to get Consul Drusus himself out here."

I began sputtering and complaining, but I didn't resist arrest. I let a pack of soft-handed, primus-ranked gentleman lead me out of the place.

Down at the brig, some bigger, tougher brutes took over. I was deposited in a cell without any further ceremony.

Thinking over my testimony, I decided that I'd probably done the right thing. Sure, I'd lied and made up an embarrassing story about Galina., but how mad could she get? After all, I'd been covering for her.

What's more, I was pretty sure that Graves couldn't pin anything on me about meeting with Abigail, who was widely considered a traitor against Earth. In the end, that's what really mattered in these situations.

-15-

Some hours later, I was snoring on a hard bunk when Graves showed up. He kicked me in the ribs and my eyes fluttered open.

Rolling over, I smiled up at him. "Oh, hi there Primus. Is it morning already?"

"Get the hell off that bunk, McGill," he said.

I followed after Graves, massaging my ribs. One sad thing about today's events was that I had been stripped of my black armor. That was a terrible thing for any infantry man. I felt damned near naked without it.

"Uh..." I said, "Primus Graves, sir, is there any way you might see fit to give me back my armor? I don't want to lose track of that."

He turned around and glared at me.

"You're in trouble, McGill."

"How's that?"

"You lied to the tribunal."

"I did?" I said innocently, wondering which of my many fabrications he'd finally caught on to. I did my best to appear dumbfounded.

"That's right. We not only took your armor, we also went through your tapper's records with a fine-toothed comb. Would you like to guess what we found?"

My blood ran cold for just a second. It could have been damned near anything. I shook my head and yawned, faking complete disinterest.

"We found *nothing*, McGill, but that wasn't the end of the search," Graves continued. "You see, I think you forgot about the cloud."

I blinked at him. "The what, sir?"

"You know, the backup of your tapper and your mind. Your system does continuous updates to the central data core. You know that, right?"

"Yes, sir. I surely do. It's a wonderful form of modern technology."

"That it is, McGill. What you forgot is that it doesn't just backup your engrams for later revivals."

"It doesn't?" I asked, beginning to frown just a little around the edges.

"It does more than that," he said. "It also backs up your locations, your body-cam files—*everything*."

We stared at each other for a couple of long seconds. Then I became alarmed. "Uh, my body-cam files?"

"That's right, McGill. Guess what we discovered when we investigated and lifted those out of the data core?"

"You went and did all that just for me?"

"Yes, I did all that just for you. I smelled a two-meter-tall rat, and I figured out who it was. Can you guess what we found, McGill?

"Uh," I said. "I hope nothing embarrassing…"

"I found that you and Galina Turov met with Abigail Claver. That's a forbidden personal contact, Centurion."

I blinked a few times. I was pretty sure I'd deleted all that stuff. Could it be somehow that my tapper had backed it all up on the cloud somewhere? And it had stayed there?

Shit… There was always some damned recovery folder. *Shit!*

After seeing my alarmed look, Graves smiled a little. I was feeling pain, and he knew it. He nodded his head. "There you go. Now you know what's going on. You lied to the tribunal, and so did Turov. Now Tribune Winslade is back in charge of this legion. He's been cleared of all charges because he wasn't involved."

"Excuse me a minute, sir," I said to Graves. "Just how did you come to be running this show? I mean, this investigation…"

He looked at me sourly. "We had an intrusion aboard *Scorpio*. This is a highly sensitive and secretive mission. I was contacted by Praetor Drusus and ordered to look into the matter."

"Praetor Drusus? Don't you mean Consul Drusus?"

He waved his hand around. "That's just a temporary rank, but yes, I mean the consul."

"Okay, okay," I said. "Well, it looks like you've got the whole thing wrapped up. Congratulations."

Graves gave me another one of those cold, thin smiles. It was a predatory expression.

"Now, we're getting somewhere," he said. "You and Turov met with someone who is essentially a non-person as far as Earth is concerned. I'm going to take that as an admission of involvement."

"You mean Abigail Claver right…?"

"Yes, of course. Just talking to her is a crime."

I shook my head, and I sighed. "Don't I know it, sir. I tried to tell the imperator, but what can I do? She orders me around like I'm her private butler or something."

Graves nodded to me. "So, now you're changing your tune, huh? … throwing her under the bus. Is that it?"

"No, no, sir. Not at all. I'm just saying that if you want any more information, you should be talking to the imperator herself."

"I plan to do that—Winslade and I both will participate in the interrogation. Come on, we've got a meeting in ten."

I was given one of those soft papery prison jumpsuits made of orange cloth. I shuffled along in Graves' shadow as he led the way back up to Gold Deck.

As I walked, I kept checking my tapper. I'd sent a few messages to Tessie, but she hadn't answered. She probably wasn't out of the oven yet. I wondered if I'd be dead by the time she was revived. That would be just my luck. Sometimes, things just weren't meant to be. The timing wasn't always right.

When we got up to Gold Deck, I sighed, grunted, and took a seat at yet another long, boring conference table.

Graves had me gravity-bolted to the chair, and he left with his guards in tow. I was unarmed, sleepy, bored, and a little bit hungry. I tried to stretch out on two or three of the chairs at the same time, but it was hard to do when you were chained-up.

Before I could make a comfortable bed for myself, the door slid open again. When I struggled to get into an upright position, one of the chairs went flopping over on the floor.

"Trying to escape McGill?" Tribune Winslade asked.

"No, sir. I was just trying to get a little shut-eye."

"Of course," he said sourly.

He walked in, and a couple of guards came in behind him. Marching along in the rear of the procession was one Imperator Galina Turov. She wasn't in chains—not yet—but she was looking as pissed-off as a wet skunk.

They sat Galina down opposite me, and she went right into a tirade. "You're not going to get away with this Winslade, she said. "I know what you're after."

"Oh, do you now?" he asked.

"Yes. You're angling for my job next. That's what this is all about, but it won't work."

"Sirs…?" I said, attempting to stand. The gravity-bolt pulled me partway down again. "It seems like you two have a lot to talk about. I'm feeling like a third wheel, here, so I think it'd be best if I got out of your hair and went on back down to my module."

"You're not going anywhere, Centurion," Winslade said.

I flopped back down reluctantly. I was already hoping they'd just get this over with. I had half a mind to request that they either flog me, or execute me, or something. I was damnably bored.

Worse, I knew that Tessie would be coming out of the oven any hour now. Opportunities were sliding on by as these two alley cats wasted my day.

Winslade and Galina went back and forth for a while. Winslade displayed videos that had been taken from my point of view, depicting the two of us talking to Abigail Claver. Fortunately, and to my surprise, there was no sound. I'd like to pretend that I'd arranged that on purpose, but I really hadn't. I'd probably just muted it at some point and forgotten to turn the mic back on again.

While Winslade interrogated Galina, and she snarled back at him, my mind drifted off to Tessie. Now, why the heck was I so interested in that young lady? I'm not even sure... Sometimes, a person just catches another person's eye. They just hit you right, and you can't get them out of your head all day long.

Naturally, I knew that she was far too low-ranked and young in the head for me. She was a mean fighter—sure—and a resourceful girl. We'd had a sort of a moment out there in the corridors while she was fighting for her life, but as far as regulations went, any intimate contact between two individuals that are more than two steps apart in rank was frowned upon. It wasn't outright actionable and against regulations, mind you, but still it was frowned upon.

Now, in this particular instance, Tessie wasn't under my direct command. That would also have been a red flag for anybody auditing the situation, but in the modern legions, fraternization was expected and common. This went up and down the chain of command.

I guess it was unavoidable. When you had males and females trapped together on a ship for months—and deployed for months or even years at some remote location—you had to expect things were going to happen. In my case, they often did. Sometimes I thought Legion Varus was like a giant dorm party in space.

"McGill...? McGill!"

"Huh?"

Galina was talking to me, I realized. I startled awake, but I had absolutely no idea what she'd said. In fact, I hadn't been paying attention at all for like the last ten minutes.

"Consul Drusus is on his way to this conference room right now," she told me.

I looked at Winslade for confirmation, and he stared back nodding that narrow head of his.

"The consul? Here? He's coming here?"

"That's what I said, McGill," Galina said. "I can't believe you're not listening. You really need to be listening to this."

"It's hard for me…"

"Well, listen closely *now*. He's come through the gateway posts. He's coming to this conference room, and he's going to interview us individually. You're to be interviewed first."

"I guess that makes sense," I said, "as I'm the only one who's chained down at the moment. That might change, though!" I laughed a bit, but they both twisted up their lips in disgust.

"You've been secured to prevent any unseemly violence, McGill," Winslade said. "Now, if you don't mind, Imperator, I'll take my leave." He got up and headed for the door.

I could tell he didn't want to be caught in the neighborhood with a couple of traitors when Drusus walked in.

He was always a man who walked away quickly, but today he was mincing along like there was no tomorrow. He was gone in a flash.

Galina moved next. She walked toward the doors.

"Hey!" I said. "You're just going to leave me here alone, are you?"

"I sure as hell am, and I certainly hope that you'll behave yourself." She made expressive eyes at me, but I had no idea what that meant. None whatsoever.

"Sure…" I said, "but why do you think Drusus wants to talk to me first?"

"Probably," she said in a weird tone of voice, "because he doesn't think you'll have anything interesting to say."

She made those spooky eyes at me again. I think she was trying to give me a hint about something, but I wasn't catching on.

Finally, I shrugged. "Okay, whatever."

Galina walked out in a huff, and I waited around for several more minutes. I considered trying to stretch out on those business chairs again, but it just wasn't going to work out. I gave up on that idea and just slumped sitting up as comfortably as possible. I dozed in my chair as I waited for the consul of all Earth—currently, the highest ranked individual in all of humanity.

Drusus finally stepped inside, alone. The doors shut behind him, and he walked around to the opposite side of the conference table. He frowned at me and shook his head. "McGill, what are you mixed up in this time?"

"Well, I thought at first, you know, that these two ladies—I don't know. They seemed like they wanted to have a good time down there on that boiler deck. It was nice and private, you see, kind of like a steam bath. You know how girls are always feeling cold…"

Drusus thumped a medium-sized fist on the table. The computer brought up a wavering question mark, not knowing what his gesture was supposed to mean. Most, if not all, desks and conference tables were essentially computers these days, and when you pounded your fist on them, they were always confused.

"Stop bullshitting me, McGill," he said. "You owe me."

"I do?"

"Yes, you definitely do. Remember that raft of crimes you were convicted of? And then pardoned for, last year?"

"Oh, yeah… that stuff. That was all just a big misunderstanding, sir."

"Sure it was, McGill, sure it was. Now, before I talk to Turov, I want you to tell me what the hell's going on, and let's not have any more of these misunderstandings of yours."

I thought that over, and I felt my loyalties were somewhat torn. Finally, I decided to come clean and tell him a chunk of the truth.

"It's just not all that big of a deal, sir," I said. "You know, the Clavers, they're always trying to sell something. They're always trying to make a deal. They're always trying to tell us to do this, or not do that. Usually, it's because they've got some kind of business deal going on—this time, it's probably a deal that's hanging on the whole war thing."

"The war thing, McGill?" Drusus asked.

"Yeah, you know, profiteering, making a buck… They sell stuff to Rigel, they sell stuff to Earth. They trade back and forth. You know, they're out there to make a buck. When we get involved somewhere that might interfere with one of their operations, they complain. That's all it was about. Abigail Claver was lodging a complaint."

Drusus frowned, and he did a little bit of pacing. It seemed like he was taking me somewhat seriously.

"Okay," he said. "I can believe that. That sort of thing has come up before, but what in particular do the Clavers want us to avoid doing?"

"Well sir, Abigail said something about it being unwise for us to go out to this organic planet that we're on the way to right now."

"Really? They knew about that?" he asked. "They knew our destination?"

I shrugged. "Well, they were able to intercept this ship and get aboard her. They must've known something."

"Yes, right... they had to have the course, the triangulation. That's so startling. It's amazing what a little bit of money will do. For every actual traitor aboard this ship, McGill, there are probably ten others who would take a bribe and do the same. Often, that little tidbit of information they may pass along for a payout does as much damage as a sabotage effort."

I thought that over, and I figured it was probably true. "That's not me, sir. I wasn't paid a dime."

"I know. I know you weren't. We watch your bank records closely."

That was a startling admission, but I let it slide. Drusus began to pace around, and I watched him.

"So," he said, "Abigail came out to tell you not to attack 31 Orionis?"

"That's right, sir. She surely did."

"And who arranged this meeting?"

I hesitated then. Galina, of course, had done the arrangements. "Uh, I don't know exactly how that happened, sir," I lied. "You see, I was brought into it under false pretenses. Honest to God, I walked in thinking that I was going to get, you know, a little private meeting with a lady and her friend."

Drusus rolled his eyes at me, but he didn't say anything.

"So..." I continued, "unfortunately... it turned into this boring negotiation instead. After it was done, Galina shot

Abigail down and had me stuff her into an airlock. It just took a few minutes. It wasn't that big of a deal."

Again, Drusus hammered his fist on the conference table. Again, the blue question mark came up and shivered. "It *is* a big deal, McGill. No one is supposed to know this ship is out here. No one's supposed to know where it's traveling to. No one—most of all—is supposed to be able to teleport aboard a battleship in warp and have a private little conversation with the top officer aboard."

I reached up a single finger and scratched my chin. I hadn't shaved since my last revive, and it was getting a mite itchy.

"Right, sir. Right," I said. "I get where you're coming from."

"Okay then. I don't think I'm getting any more out of you. Dismissed, McGill."

I stood up the best I could with one arm still attached to the gravity-bolt.

"Hey, uh… Consul Drusus, sir? What about my arrest and all that? Am I reinstated to my duties?"

"Yes. Yes, you are. Get out of here."

A pair of burly, hog-like navy pukes came in after that. They freed me and sent me out walking and whistling on my way.

My first thought was of Tessie, but I decided she'd have to wait. I headed straight to the quartermaster's deck. I figured I needed to reclaim my armor before that boy got any more ideas.

Sure enough, when I got there, he had my gigantic black stardust armor on his front desk.

"Sign here, please," he said.

I signed, and then I hauled the suit up over my shoulder. It was quite a bit of weight when you put it all together on one collarbone.

"Not trying to steal this one, huh?" I asked him.

He glowered at me. "There's no way this would fit, McGill."

"Yeah, I guess that's true."

I laughed as I marched out.

-16-

All the while Galina, Winslade and Consul Drusus were up on Gold Deck having a catfight, I spent my time much more wisely. First off, I found some food and a dozen beers. Then I went looking for Tessie.

A few minutes after my personnel-search alert went off, indicating she'd been revived, I just happened to be hanging around outside Blue Deck's main exit. Of course, about a dozen other sad-sack recruits walked through those sterile doors before she did, but none of those clowns interested me.

A few of them were from my cohort. One guy attempted to strike up a conversation, so I gave him a hearty handshake and a big grin. After a few moments of banter, I slapped him one on the back, making him cough and stagger. Then, he scooted along back to his module to rest-up for next time.

At long last, Tessie stepped out of the Blue Deck doors. She looked bewildered, befuddled and a bit freaked out. It was only her second death—I knew, because I checked her records.

"Hey," I said as she walked out in the hallway. "Don't I know you from somewhere?"

She stared, she blinked, but she didn't smile. She just nodded.

"This is so weird," she said. "Centurion, I…"

"Hey, take it easy. Pretty soon, dying and coming back will be just like waking up in the morning."

Tessie gave a little shudder. "I hope not. You're creeping me out right now. The last thing I saw as I was dying was you looking down at me."

"Well… I hope there's no permanent bad associations made there."

She thought about that for several long seconds. At last, she shook her head. "No, I guess there isn't. There shouldn't be. I'm feeling better each minute… I bet you won't be creeping me out by tomorrow."

She started walking again, and I fell in step alongside her.

"How long have you been in the legions, sir?" she asked. "How many times have you died and come back like this?"

"Oh, I don't know…" I said. "A dozen… or maybe it's more honest to say two dozen."

"Two dozen deaths…" she said, shaking her head in disbelief.

Naturally, I was lying my ass off. In truth, it was probably more than three or four hundred times that I'd died, but it wouldn't do to talk to her about that.

"You look like you could use some food and drink," I told her.

She looked up at me, and she blinked a few times.

"I'm buying," I said, and I gave her a smile.

"Oh… yeah, that does sound good."

She followed me to a bar and grill down on Lavender Deck—in fact, the only such joint we had on Lavender Deck—and she put some good food and drink into her empty guts. One weird thing about revivals was that when you came out you were one hundred percent empty. Normally, human beings are never completely empty. We're always half-digesting something or other. But not when you get revived. At that point, your guts are so clean inside, it's a special kind of weird.

We talked for a while about the exercise and the legions and where she'd come from back on Earth. She seemed to be a smart girl who gotten caught-up in big loans she couldn't pay back. After a couple of poor choices in her life, she ended up unemployable.

"It's the computers these days," I said. "It used to be a man showed up, did some work, and he got paid. Where'd he come from? What had he done last week? Nobody cared. That's just not how it is these days."

"I don't remember it ever being like that," Tessie answered.

"It was, once," I said. "Anyways, let me guess, the only place that would take you in was Legion Varus, right?"

She nodded her head. "Yeah, I was a bit sick about it when I first heard the responses from all the different legions rejecting me. All those credit-checks, aptitude scores, psych profiles..." She shook her head. "I didn't have a chance. It was like they had me marked down as a serial killer."

Thinking that over for a moment, I had to admit, Tessie had done a number on a lot of recruits in *Scorpio's* passageways. Maybe she really did have the bona fide brain of a serial killer. "Hell's bells, girl! You'll do fine in this legion. We're paid to be killers. You can stay as long as you like, and you'll probably end up staying a lot longer than that."

I smiled at her, and she smiled back. She was still befuddled, of course, but she was really taking her death rather well. There were no tears. Her glassy-eyed stare was fading away. She was eating, drinking, talking—performing more or less like a normal human being. That showed a high level of resilience in a young woman like her.

I was thinking about asking if she wanted me to show her around the big turrets up on top of *Scorpio* where they'd installed some seriously massive cannons—when her tapper buzzed.

She glanced down, reading the message automatically. She frowned at it, swiped a few times, and then looked up at me in surprise.

"Did you do this?" she asked.

"Uh... do what exactly?"

"You transferred me into your unit...?"

My mouth sagged low. My jaw was hanging open for a solid two seconds. That's a long, long time when a girl is looking at you and has just asked you a question.

Then, realizing I looked lame and clueless, I snapped my fool face shut. Then I smiled. It was a forced smile. It was an *utterly* false smile. Inside I was raging, but I smiled at Tessie. I sure as hell did.

"Why did you think I came down here?" I asked. "That's why I've been talking to you all this time."

"Why'd you look so surprised, then?"

"Well, I didn't think the request was going to come through so fast. Apparently, your old centurion decided it wasn't a big deal to let you go. That's a kind and thoughtful gesture."

Tessie blinked a few times. She was still confused, and I didn't blame her. Someone had just transferred her into my unit out of the blue. What's more, I knew exactly who had done it—and why.

"You know..." she said, "I don't want you to take this the wrong way Centurion, but I kind of thought you were going to ask me out or something—I mean, I got that vibe."

"What?" I laughed. "That's crazy-talk girl! I came down here because I was impressed by your performance in the exercise. You were putting down recruits like nobody's business. In fact, if you ask me, even though you didn't *technically* win the contest, you outperformed every recruit in the whole operation. That's why I'm here. That's why I transferred you into my unit—because I want the best in the 3rd."

That last lie was a big one, and it paid off like a charm. She smiled, and she smiled hugely. I didn't know right then if she would have said yes or no to my asking her out in a romantic way, but it didn't matter now, because Tessie was all mine—and I knew I couldn't touch her.

We broke up our friendly chat after that. I told her to move her stuff into my module and welcomed her to the 3rd. After a hearty handshake and a couple of texts sent to my adjuncts, we went our separate ways.

Fuming, I marched straight toward Gold Deck. I knew, of course, exactly what was going on. Somehow, Galina had found out about Tessie. It was the only explanation. No one just quickly shuffled a recruit from one unit to another without even talking to the centurions involved. Hell no.

Galina knew there was only a couple of different ways she could ditch Tessie and make sure I couldn't have any legitimate, within-regulations contact with her. One way was by shipping her ass back to Earth. The second way—and a very cagey way at that—was to put her close to me and under my wing. It would be considered flat out wrong and maybe illegal for me to fraternize with her after that.

Grim-faced and taking long strides, I marched down long, long passageways. I rode a couple of elevators, talked my way past some guards, and then banged on Galina's door.

She popped it open immediately and had the gall to look surprised. "Oh! There you are, James," she said. "I wanted to thank you for all the good words you put in for me today—all that covering-up you did concerning our little meeting with Abigail."

"Huh?" I asked.

"That's right," she said. "You remember? That business about how I wanted to teleport Abigail Claver in for a romantic tryst in the boiler room?"

"Oh... I don't know anything about that," I lied. "That must have been Winslade talking. I never said anything of the kind."

"You lying bastard," she spat suddenly. She turned around, her face transforming into a mask of rage, and she strutted away into her office.

I followed, closing the door behind me. As it was late, and no one else was on duty in her offices, I took a second to ponder the situation.

Galina had a good reason to be angry with me, after all. I *had* told some tall tales about her, or at least I'd suggested many strange things. Was this all her way of getting back at me? Or was she simply jealous and keeping Tessie out of reach? I supposed it didn't really matter. The results were the same either way.

My anger evaporated when she came back and handed me a drink. Then she took one herself and sat behind her desk. I sat in the chair in front of her, and we eyed one another.

"So, why are you here?" Galina asked me.

I jabbed a fat finger down at my tapper. "I got a notice that a certain recruit has been suddenly transferred into my unit. Why wasn't I consulted on this matter?"

Galina looked down and gave a little shrug. "Oh... that. It was a bureaucratic matter."

"Uh-huh. Sure, it was."

"Are you angry?" she asked.

I thought about that, and I sighed. "Nah, not really. How about you? About the Abigail thing?"

She stirred her drink with her finger and gulped it.

"I'm getting over it... We have more important things to worry about."

"Like what?"

"Like what the hell Abigail Claver was trying to tell us about this planet we're approaching right now."

"Now?" I asked.

"Yes. In less than a week, we'll make planetfall over 31 Orionis."

"We will, huh? Wow. These ships keep getting faster and faster. It's a technological marvel."

She rolled her eyes at me. "*Scorpio* is a Rigellian ship, McGill. The bears have a tech edge on us in many ways. This ship is faster than any of our other transports."

"That reminds me," I said. "Why is it we were able to push them off Sky World and Dark World so easily? They didn't send many ships out here to stop us, and it seems like they never made a counterattack. Weren't we expecting them to take that territory back?"

Galina nodded. "We absolutely were. It's weird that they didn't hit us back, and now we're threatening to take a third planet—one really close to their homeworld. Do you think what Abigail said could be true?"

I nodded. "It does fit, but then again, Abigail Claver is almost as big a liar as I am."

"Tell me about it. It's so hard to know what's true and what isn't. I suppose when we finally get to this jungle world, we'll know the truth."

We talked like that for a while, and we had a few drinks. We managed to patch things up a bit. Both of us had been pissed off, but each of us had been mollified, in a way.

Sure, I'd told a pack of embarrassing lies about Galina and chased another girl, but then she managed to turn things around so that the girl was my responsibility rather than a romantic partner. That left us more or less even.

I decided after my third beverage—quite possibly my eighth or so over the course of the day—to let bygones be bygones.

Galina had apparently chosen the same path. Eventually, she let me touch her. We did a lot more touching after that. Before we knew it, the night was gone.

-17-

Klaxons blasted us out of bed. I rolled out to the right side, grunting and groaning, while Galina did the same on the left.

"Oh shit," I said, "don't tell me they're having another exercise."

"This isn't an exercise," Galina said, and I knew she was right a moment later.

The ship rocked, then it lurched and rolled to the starboard side. I had trouble standing up straight, and it wasn't due to being half-asleep. The deck heaved under my bare feet, and I worked hard to pull my boots on.

"What the hell's going on?" I demanded.

"Defensive maneuvers, I think. Something is shooting at us. Dammit, it had better not be those frigging bears."

Before she even had her clothes all the way on, she began slapping at the wall next to her bed. The screen lit up, and an officer's face came into view.

Galina stuffed her bare breasts into her tunic top and let the smart straps do the rest of the work. "What the hell's going on?" she demanded.

The Navy puke who'd answered the call on the bridge looked stunned, but he recovered quickly. "Imperator, I'll transfer you to Captain Merton."

Ten seconds went by, during which I pulled my clothes on, and Galina managed to get her kit in order. I did my best to duck out of the range of the camera pickup. When it finally lit back up again, Captain Merton's craggy face looked out at us both. I could tell he was still able to see me. Damn these wide-angle, pinprick cameras.

"Imperator Turov..." he said, "so nice of you to contact me before breakfast."

"What is going on, Merton?" she demanded.

"We measured spatial anomalies in our region."

"What the heck does that mean?"

"A large mass passed by us in hyperspace. It appears, by our mathematical modeling, to have been traveling in an oblique angle with respect to *Scorpio*."

Galina blinked at him. "Passed us? Did it actually get close to our ship?"

"That's right. That's what I'm telling you. According to our instruments, a large gravitational mass nearly collided with *Scorpio*. Do I need to educate you on how rare a circumstance that should be?"

"No... no you do not," she said.

Even I knew what they were talking about in this case. Space is big—really, *really* big—especially interstellar space. It's also virtually empty except for a dust particle or two, maybe a puff of gas, or a frozen rock every trillion kilometers or so. We had deflector shields to brush aside such things.

But a large mass, especially something as big as *Scorpio* itself—that should be very rare. It was possible we'd whizzed by an asteroid or a comet, or something. There was stuff out here that a pilot couldn't even see since it was so dark in the emptiness between the stars.

But obstacles of real size were exceedingly rare. Hitting something like that would be like firing a harpoon into the Pacific Ocean at random and just happening to hit a blue whale. Sure, they were down there somewhere, but the odds of you actually nailing one, just with that random cast, were infinitesimally small.

Being a man who'd long ago given up believing in coincidences, I had to join in with the group opinion that someone had sent something out here. Someone had thrown something at us, trying to intercept us.

"Do the bears have tech that could detect us in hyperspace?" I asked.

Merton's eyes flicked at me, registering my presence for the first time. Then, he looked back at Turov, and he gave his lip a twisted sneer. He ignored my question completely.

"Imperator, following detection of the near-collision, I followed fleet regulations. I came out of warp, altered our course, then proceeded back into hyperspace. The key to avoiding interception is to be unpredictable. This means we'll arrive a bit late at 31 Orionis, as we're no longer taking the most direct route."

"Right..." Galina said, thinking about it. "The shortest distance between two points is a straight line. Now that they know we're coming, that's the one thing we can't follow."

"Exactly," Merton said nodding.

Galina ended the call, and we took a few minutes to wash-up. Apparently, we weren't in a full-blown emergency—at least, not yet. *Scorpio* was now gliding along on an oblique course toward our destination world.

I had to wonder who had detected us, and how had they'd done so? Were they going to throw anything else at us in the way of a welcome wagon?

Galina and I ate breakfast together at the officer's mess, but it wasn't a lazy and relaxed meal. She spent the whole time working on her tapper, talking to a dozen panicked officers.

"Hey," I said to her, "you know, I never did get a chance to ask exactly how things went with old Drusus and Winslade."

She eyed me. "I told them it was true," she said.

I blinked a few times, frowning in confusion. "You told them what was true?"

"All that bullshit you told them about you, me and Abigail getting together down on that steaming boiler deck for some lewd recreation. I stuck to the story."

All of a sudden, I got it. Howling with laughter, I slapped a big hand on the table twice.

Galina glared at me. "I'm glad you think it's so funny. Couldn't you have come up with something a little bit more dignified?"

I could barely talk, I was laughing so hard. She was pissed off all over again, but I didn't care. It was too funny.

"What did they say?" I asked her. "Did they ask to see pictures?"

"No. They asked me why I shot her at the end of it. I told them that I was too jealous and couldn't go through with it."

I thought that over while sobering up, and finally I nodded. "You know what? That's halfway believable—and weird. I bet they know it's not the truth, but they really couldn't get past that excuse, could they?"

"No, they couldn't. That's why I used it." She was glaring at me again, but we soon parted ways, and I didn't care anymore.

All in all, I'd say we were even now. Sure, she'd pulled a fast one by moving Tessie into my unit, but she'd had to embarrass herself publicly. In fact, I might even have to say I had a leg-up on her now.

The next several days went by with no warm beds offered to old Centurion McGill. All of the other women in my own unit—and even those from other units—all seemed to have heard about Tessie being transferred into my unit. They suspected the worst, and they shunned me.

Galina herself was just too busy with the possibility that someone was throwing rocks or spaceships or missiles or something at us as we approached 31 Orionis. She was in operational command of this mission, and she couldn't allow *Scorpio* to get blown up under her feet. After all, that would be two in a row, after *Dominus* had been destroyed less than a year ago.

Now, you might think that any reasonable member of the brass back at Central would realize it hadn't been her fault. But that's not how high-level brass thinks when something goes wrong—and by something going wrong, I mean when something very expensive happens.

When something went sideways that cost Hegemony trillions of credits, they immediately looked for a scapegoat to blame. And you could sure as hell bet that whoever had signed a budgetary line-item to refit *Scorpio* wasn't going to put down *his* name on a report as being the one responsible for the destruction of the new ship. No, sir.

Somebody like Captain Merton or Galina was sure to be tagged with responsibility for that nightmare. In Galina's case, because she'd so recently lost a command, she was for sure to be blackballed over the destruction of a second one.

Therefore, she was determined to keep her ship from blowing up, and it wasn't even due to any misplaced chickenry concerning her own pretty carcass. Nothing less than the death of her career was on the line—and that's what she feared more than anything.

-18-

After we'd switched directions and jumped back into hyperspace again, about a hundred tense hours passed by. During that time, Galina was no fun to be around. She was in a nail-biting mood.

Drusus had long since returned to Earth, having satisfied himself that there were no shenanigans going on aboard *Scorpio*—at least none that rose to the level of treachery. Graves, Winslade, Galina and I had all been reinstated and returned to duty.

Graves was still paranoid and suspicious, but that was Graves for you. He'd seen a lot in his day, and he didn't trust anybody—especially not me and Turov. When his mama knitted him a sweater for Christmas, he probably unraveled it looking for bugs, bombs, or poisoned threads.

But we finally arrived at our target planet without any serious incidents like our close-call in hyperspace. We came out dangerously near to the enemy world, dropping gravity waves and scanning everything around us for all we were worth.

Galina liked to arrive with a bang. Instead of popping in at the outskirts of the planetary system, scanning everything in detail, and then hopping to the target, she oftentimes preferred a bolder approach. Sure, it was dangerous, not just to our own ship, but to the inhabitants of the world that we were jumping close to, but she didn't care. Tactical surprise, that was her goal.

Whatever else you might say about her command choices, she achieved surprise this time. No defensive ships rose up to meet us. The entire star system seemed quiet, but it didn't take long after we came out of warp for klaxons to begin to sound. Now, that's all well and good when approaching a possibly hostile world, but this time was a little different. Everyone was ordered to quarters and told to wait there. I got my troops all suited-up, including helmets, gear and weapons—everything. We'd arrived in hostile alien star systems before and been immediately attacked. 3rd Unit wasn't going to be caught unawares this time.

After a half hour, during which there were a lot of maneuvers and a few random announcements, Winslade came onto the main viewing screen in our module to talk to all of us. His face was so big and so close to the camera pickup, that his nostrils were the size of manhole covers. It was more than disgusting.

We all winced and squinted and averted our eyes, but it didn't do any good. When I dared to look back at the screen again, he was still there, nostrils and all.

"Soldiers of Legion Varus," he said, "we appear to have stepped into an unexpected situation. Let me review the data."

His face disappeared and melted into a view of the planet. That was a sheer relief for me. Others sighed and dropped their hands from their faces. I think Leeson had even been watching through the laced-together fingers of his own gloves.

A beautiful large green world hung in the foreground, while a pinkish moon that had an atmosphere of its own, hung behind that. All in all, it was a lovely scene.

But then, as my eyes rolled over it, I saw something—something on the darker side of the planet. It was a reddish glow that shouldn't be there, like a hot coal in the bottom of a dying fire. It appeared to be a strange, pulsing red rock lodged in the planet's crust.

Winslade's giant finger tapped the spot. "You see this, right here?" he asked. "That's an anomaly—and it shouldn't be there. It is our current belief that a meteor of some sort has struck the planet and caused significant damage. Fortunately, this rock didn't land in an ocean. If it had, it probably would have caused a tidal wave and flooded much of the planet's surface—destroying forests, cities and everything else. Instead, it landed in a mountain range and embedded itself there."

"That's freaky…" Harris commented.

I glanced at him, then went back to listening to Winslade. For once, I wasn't bored by his briefing.

"Some of you may be thinking," Winslade continued, "that we've seen other similar rocks hitting our own planets. This one is different, however. It's much larger for one thing."

He showed some vids of smoking rocks on Blood World and Storm World. They were the size of an office building—not a mountain.

"Due to the sheer mass of this object, we're seeing some volcanic activity on the night-side of the planet. The meteor—if that's what it is—was so large and hit so hard, it actually broke through the crust of this world, leading to significant seismic activity."

"It all sounds good to me," Harris said, "these natives, whoever they are, aren't going to put up much of a fight if they just got slammed by a big rock from space."

"Here, here," Leeson said.

I didn't share in their enthusiasm. First off, countless local civilians had probably just been killed. Secondly, this all sounded far too familiar. I'd heard that our colonies had been struck out here in the Frontier Zone quite recently as well. Blood World, Dark World… they'd all been hit by rocks, even if they were a lot smaller than this one. What the hell was going on? Who was throwing these rocks at us?

Winslade offered no answers in that department. He continued the briefing, talking about our approach and how we were going to scan for enemy fortifications. Once he was satisfied there were no defensive gun batteries or missile bases taking potshots at us, we would proceed with an orderly invasion.

The briefing ended early, and we all began to slouch and lounge in our module. We were fully kitted and geared—all dressed-up with no place to go. That was how it was for ground-pounders aboard a starship. It was a random mix of dull tedium, followed by desperate terror and death. Oftentimes, there was no gradual transition between the two.

Not knowing when we would be ordered to deploy to Red Deck and drop on the planet, we had to assume the time would come at any moment. We stayed in a high state of readiness.

When the order did finally come, it was a total surprise. Buzzers, spinning yellow flashers—everything went crazy all at once, and the ship began lurching and heeling-over like a sailboat in a storm.

"Are we in evasive maneuvers?" Leeson asked.

"Looks like it," I said. "Everybody! Up, up, up! Move, move, move!"

Just as my men scrambled to their feet, they were dashed to the deck again. Groaning, they crawled back up again.

When you're aboard a starship under heavy maneuvers, sometimes the deck just jumps right up and slams you in the face. Fortunately, we were wearing helmets and armor. It didn't hurt as much as it could have. I could only imagine what kind of a fun time they were having down in the kitchens or working the revival machines on Blue Deck. Those poor bastards took these kinds of things much harder than we did.

The deck lit up under our boots, and arrows began to flash telling us where to go. We poured out into the corridors, along with thousands of other troops.

"Looks like 3rd Cohort is going straight to Red Deck and the drop-pods," Leeson said.

Moments later, Graves came onto our tactical chat to confirm this. "Every other legion cohort has been assigned to a different assault path," he said. "The odd-numbered cohorts are going to drop with drop-pods, 1st Cohort first, 3rd Cohort second, and so on. Even-numbered cohorts are going to board lifters and scramble for the planet's surface."

"What the hell's going on?" Harris demanded.

"Clane?" I yelled.

Adjunct Clane ran to my side. He was puffing more than he should be, probably due to being outright terrified. His face was as white as a sheet.

"Clane, scrape your lights off the deck, and get them ahead of us. They've got less gear, so they're going to be jumping first. The recruits are going to be scared. I want you to personally stuff each one of them into the drop-pods yourself. Understand?"

"Yes, sir!" He raced away, shouting for his troops, and soon his platoon of lights was in the lead and trotting by the rest of us.

The heavies and Leeson's specialists, the slowest of all of them, tagged along in the rear.

"Hell of a way to kick off a war," Leeson complained.

"It's better than being dead already," Harris answered.

The next few minutes were among the most terrifying of any legionnaire's existence. As we were mere ground troops, no one bothered to tell us what the hell was going on.

Clearly, something was wrong. Winslade had described a very orderly process, one that was more like a Danube waltz than this frenetic, mosh-pit chaos we were being treated to now.

"Visors down," I ordered. "Oxygen on. Pretend like this is real, people—because it is."

The troops fumbled with their equipment, and soon we reached Red Deck. This was simply a generic name that every legion gave to that region of their transport that was responsible for deploying troops.

Essentially, there were three different ways you could get a soldier's ass from a starship down onto a planet—well, four if you counted blowing up the ship and burning in the atmosphere.

The first, and by far the nicest method, was to board a lifter and ride all the way down to the surface in relative comfort. With a calm landing and an orderly deployment, there was nothing better for the peace of mind and wellbeing of the soldiers.

The second approach was through drop-pods. This amounted to loading every soldier into an individual capsule and firing it at the planet from high altitude. Each of the drop-pods were essentially tiny spaceships built to scream down into an atmosphere. They supplied just enough oxygen and fuel to keep the soldier inside breathing and not splatting down onto the surface.

The third option involved the use of Gray Deck instead of Red Deck. Gray Deck was the name given to the teleportation launch facility. Most transports had them these days, but as they didn't have the capacity for mass transmissions of troops to the battlefield, it was still technically the least often used method of deployment.

Judging among the three, I figured we'd probably gotten the rawest possible deal. We arrived on Red Deck with the 1st Cohort having melted away. They'd all been fired out of the belly of *Scorpio* by an array of some thirty-two launch cannons. It had only taken a few minutes for a thousand men to be deployed that way.

As we all shuffled closer and closer to the holes that led down into space itself, we gritted our teeth and squinted our eyes. The reason why this method was worse than the other possibilities wasn't simply because it was dangerous and somewhat terrifying—flying down to an enemy world in nothing but a small titanium capsule. A drop-pod was more like a tubular coffin than anything else.

No sir, worse than that was the inability to take down heavy gear with us. There was no room in the pods for luxury items like pigs to dig trenches for you, or light artillery pieces, or— most important of all—bio teams with their revival machines. All that stuff had to go down with the lifters.

Without the cargo in those lifters, any death my unit suffered was essentially a perming. Unless you could be revived back here on *Scorpio*, a man who died during a drop-pod incident stayed dead—possibly for a long time. Due to communications errors, or any of a dozen other possible mishaps, that didn't always work out.

Eventually, I stepped up behind Clane, who was stuffing one recruit after another into the firing shaft just as I'd ordered him to do. Each terrified recruit was encapsulated in a drop-pod and fired down toward the planet. I arrived just in time to see him march Tessie out into open space. She gave a little whoop and vanished.

Her form wasn't perfect. Her hands weren't down to her sides. She hadn't shaped herself like a perfect diving arrow the way she was supposed to. In fact, she was bending forward a bit, looking down with her helmet tilted.

That could be enough to splat a troop right there... If you were just a *little* bit off, the machine could kill you.

The two halves of the drop-pod were slammed together like two giant pieces of bread, smashing together the meat in between. If the meat wasn't perfectly placed, the two closing halves of the drop-pod would trim away anything that protruded. Arms, fingers, feet, faces—anything.

Frowning, I checked my tapper, and I took a look at her vitals...

Green! Tessie was all green.

I dared to smile. Sure, she'd messed up a little bit, but it hadn't been fatal. *Splat* wasn't going to be the joke term applied to her by all her platoon buddies. Not today, at least.

I took a deep breath and walked up behind Clane. As he shoved the last recruit through, I gave him a light kick in the rump. "Your turn, boy."

To his credit, he didn't hesitate or startle at my interference. He stepped out into open space, formed a perfect arrow with his body, and vanished.

A few moments later, I followed him.

-19-

No soldier of Earth has lived or died properly until they've plunged down into the atmosphere of an alien planet inside of a drop-pod. The scream of the wind, the roar of the jets, the way your balls crawled all the way up inside your guts—it was quite a rush.

Back in the old days, when I'd first started dropping onto unknown worlds with Legion Varus, I'd been a lowly, clueless recruit—like Tessie was today. We called such troops 'splats' and for good reason. Somehow, fresh recruits tended to find amazing ways to kill themselves—by either landing wrong, not getting into their drop-pod properly, or something.

If all else failed, they tended to jump out of their drop-pods too quickly and get themselves shot dead by the enemy before they'd experienced two pounding heartbeats of raw fear.

Originally—and I'm talking way back when I'd started—Earth's technology had left a lot to be desired. The drop-pods were relatively primitive things. They were little more than tin cans with loads of insulation encircling the hapless victim inside.

There was no feedback other than noises, jerks and sudden blind drops. As the pod terrifyingly plunged through the atmosphere, it just did whatever its little automated brain told it to do, without letting you know beans about what the overall situation was.

Things had changed significantly these days, and the pods had become much more advanced. Now, there was a screen of sorts to look at, right in front of your face. An external feed was essentially tapped into the HUD that was built into the helmet of every dropping soldier, and these screens displayed lots of interesting and, most importantly, *distracting* information.

There was a whole bunch of readouts about your vital signs. If you wanted to know your blood pressure, your heart rate, your breathing rate or the temperature inside the pod—well—it was all there. Of course, you couldn't really do anything with that information, but at least it gave your eyes something to do. Somehow it was comforting to go over these things—trying to figure out if you were dying or not.

In my case, everything looked pretty good. The external oxygen-mix was breathable, the external temperature was below freezing, but that was rising fast.

Thousands of pods punched down into the thick atmosphere of the planet and began the scorching process of reentry. Retros and steering jets fired automatically off and on—each time with a terrifying roar and no warning.

The one thing I wished they could provide was information about all the other troops in my unit. Were they all dying? Were they all making it? Was anything shooting at us right now? There was no telling. This was partly because of the data blackout that occurred when the external hull of any reentering space vehicle heated up by several thousand degrees.

Ever since the days of the Apollo moon-landings, troops in such capsules had been completely cut off during reentry. The people on the ground and the people in the sky were always cut off from one another. Neither one of them knew if the other was still breathing, and it was always suspenseful.

After about six enthralling minutes of watching my heart rate, my drop-pod came screaming down to land on an unknown planetary surface. I didn't pop the explosive bolts immediately, but rather waited for the external hull to cool just a bit and give me better information about the environment around me.

First of all, the pod's outer skin was cooling quickly—unusually quickly. In fact, I soon saw the word 'precipitation' on my displays.

"Raining…" I said to myself. "It's frigging raining."

"Sir? Sir? Centurion McGill?"

Now, who was that? I looked to see that it was Clane calling on tactical chat.

"Are you alive in there, sir?"

There was no data coming in that gave me any concern. I was encircled by green dots that represented troops coming to check on my drop-pod.

"Spread out and scatter!" I ordered. "Don't just cluster-hump my pod!"

When I saw the green dots reverse direction, I popped the explosive bolts and climbed out. I reviewed the situation closely. We'd only lost two troops on the way down. That was pretty damn good. Flicking at my tapper for a moment, I sure enough saw that two of the recruits hadn't made it, two of Clane's crew.

"Two down, huh Clane?" I asked.

"Yes, sir. Sorry, sir. They're really green."

"It's all right. Two is not bad, actually—three's average."

He nodded. I flicked at my tapper for a few seconds more and saw that yes, Tessie's name wasn't in the red. She'd made it down alive. For some reason, I found that made me a little bit happy.

Sucking in a deep breath and shouldering my morph-rifle, I ordered the group to gather up and take cover wherever they could, hugging trees.

Our drop-pods were programmed not to slam down into the trunks of trees. Instead, they found the open spots in between the largest clumps of vegetation and landed themselves there. Looking around, I gaped a bit.

"These trees are *big* suckers," I said.

"They sure are, sir," Clane agreed.

"It's almost like they're Wur or something… but no, I don't think that's the case. They're not *that* big."

The trees were overgrown with vines and other parasitic growths. They loomed up to a distant forest canopy, a vibrant green dome that had to be something like fifty to a hundred meters above us.

Yes, the trees were massive, but they weren't extreme. They weren't what we would call mega-growths such as we'd seen on planets like Death World. What's more, there was plenty of other life around besides just the trees—that was another good sign.

The forest was an absolute cacophony of noise. I'm not sure if they had what you would call "birds" here or not, but something was peeping and screaming up a storm. I could hear the noise right through my helmet, even without the external microphones turned on.

"What's the sitrep, Clane?" I demanded.

"I don't know, sir. Looks pretty clean, pretty clear. There doesn't seem to be anybody down here to greet us. There's no evidence that any of our pods were shot down during descent, either."

I grinned at him. "That's the best possible scenario. Looks like maybe Winslade panicked and wet himself. Wouldn't it be cool if there was nobody here to fight? What if they came out and welcomed us with open arms and maybe gave us a nice fruit basket, or something?"

Clane laughed and shook his head. "That sure would be great, sir."

"Yeah... don't count on it though." I laughed again, slamming him one on the shoulder which sent him staggering.

Within five minutes, everybody from my unit was down and out of their pods. There had been a few cases where the software had screwed up and somebody was in the bole of a tree, but we managed to get them down.

I gathered everybody together and hunkered down around the roots of what looked like a giant mangrove tree. There was one weird thing about these trees that I didn't really like. It seemed like their roots and big, long ropey sections of their trunks were *pulsating* a bit.

"You think these trees have a heartbeat?" Clane asked me.

"Could be..." I said. "I've seen it all. Anything's possible. If they start moving around and slapping people with their roots, let me know."

"McGill?" someone buzzed in my ear.

My tapper was flashing red. Whoever was calling me now—they were important.

"McGill? This is Tribune Winslade. Status, please."

"We're all good down here, sir," I said. "My unit made it to ground safely, with only two losses. We—"

"Shut up," he said, cutting me off. "We have much larger problems, McGill—with the lifters."

I frowned at that. Getting down onto the world with individual troops and drop-pods was one thing. Doing it with our supporting lifters, which were full of critical gear, was quite another.

"What do you mean? What kind of trouble are we having, Tribune?"

His face was on my tapper now. He didn't look happy. In fact, all I could see were teeth and a pointy nose. "Six out of ten," he said.

"Uh, how's that, sir?"

"You heard me. Six out of ten were destroyed on the way down."

"Oh, shit..." I said. "What did the Fleet boys do—slam them into these giant trees? Those pilots really should take an eye test every year, you know? I've always said it."

"Silence, you imbecile," Winslade said, huffing at me. "I'm calling because I want to know, McGill... I want to know what you know about this planet, and I want to know what Abigail Claver *really* told you."

"Uh... well sir, I already told you—she didn't say a whole lot. I mean like... you know... we were getting ready to smash and all that, so—"

"Damn you, man! You're really going to stick to that ridiculous story? The next time you get aboard *Scorpio*, I'm going to have you flogged. Six out of ten lifters lost! I can't believe this!" His big finger reached for the cut off button, but I tried to stop him.

"Wait, wait, sir. Come on, give me a hint. What blew up the lifters? How'd they go down?"

"It was that red, glowing thing—that wound in the side of this world. When the drop-pods fell, it ignored them. All your little troops landed like flying ants and were ignored—but not my precious lifters. That blasted red rock must have seen them as a threat. Maybe the troops were such small contacts it didn't activate... I have no idea."

"Um... what exactly are you talking about, sir?"

"That *thing*, McGill... That red abomination that's embedded itself in the side of this planet... It's unnatural. We were taking measurements of it. It's crystalline in structure, like a diamond—and impossibly large. Imagine a cut diamond the size of Mount Everest."

"Really, sir? That sounds kind of cool..."

"Well, it's definitely *not* cool. It's hot, very hot... red hot. What's more important is that it's capable of firing beams at passing ships."

"Beams, sir? What kind of beams?"

"The kind that can take out six of my ten lifters! They were shot down by an invisible force of some kind. They collapsed inward on themselves, almost as if a tiny singularity were formed in the middle of each lifter."

"Freaky..."

"I would use the term 'disastrous.' They were crushed like tin cans, McGill—spraying out their contents into space. Their very, very expensive contents of troops, revival machines and irreplaceable gear..."

I knew what he was whining about now. If there was one thing that was worse than losing a lifter, it was losing a lifter that was full of troops and gear. That kind of thing made the accountants back at Central bare their teeth in annoyance.

I opened my mouth to ask more questions, but Winslade was gone. Lowering my arm and looking up from my tapper, I gazed around myself at the relatively peaceful scene. So far, from what I'd seen of this world, it was all one massive primordial forest. There were vines, giant leaves, and unseen screaming beasts everywhere. I couldn't help but wonder what other hidden dangers were waiting to be found on any given side.

My troops were walking around, holding their rifles tensely, peering at every trunk like it might bite them. Some of them were poking at the tree trunks—at the ropey vines that encased them.

There were pulsations inside those roots and tubers that climbed up into the hazy emerald canopy above us. Just what was inside those strange plant-veins?

Was it just sap? Was it ichor, like inside of a bug? Or was it perhaps something weirder—like actual green blood?

-20-

Surprisingly, it was Adjunct Harris who was the first man to try opening his visor. Sure, we'd all tested the oxygen levels. In addition, Carlos, our bio-specialist—the man who was in charge of biochemical analyses when we got to a new planet—had given Jungle World the all-clear.

Naturally however, we were all a little mistrustful of that judgment. Sure, the numbers were good. The nitrogen was a little high, as was the oxygen, but that was expected on an overgrown planet. The carbon dioxide was actually a little low, but humans don't need carbon dioxide.

Our worries were really about toxins and things like alien spores—nasty stuff like that. You never knew, when you took a big deep breath for the first time on a new planet, if your lungs were filling with something that would start growing down there.

Oftentimes, the first guy to expose himself to such unknown dangers had to be volunteered by the unit commander. In this case, I didn't have to go that far. Harris volunteered himself.

"My frigging air conditioner..." he complained, "of all the things, out of all the troops this planetfall... It goes out on me!"

"I've got a solution for that," I told him. "We had two splats, right? Dig into their equipment and see if they've got anything usable. You can unplug your air conditioner and plug a new one onto your suit."

Harris shook his head vigorously. Sweat flew everywhere. He'd actually taken his entire helmet off—he was going whole-hog. "I already tried that. Been there, done that. Those two splats are pulped so bad, they look like road-pizza."

"That's a bad piece of luck," I agreed, looking him over. "Damn boy, just how hot is it? You're sweating like a pig."

"I always do when I get this kind of humidity. It's only about thirty-five degrees Celsius. What is that—ninety-five Fahrenheit?"

"Whatever," I said.

"Right. Well, it's enough to make any man sweat, but it must be like one hundred percent humidity as well."

"Aren't you from Alabama?" I asked him. "Anybody from that sector should be able to tolerate a little bit of humidity."

"You would think so," he said, "but it's just not true in my case. When I go back home to see my grandkids now and then…"

"You've got grandkids?"

"Sure as hell do. Of course, they're older than I am now… but that's just how it is for legionnaires."

"Right, right," I said, thinking about that. My daughter Etta was already older than me, at least in physical chronology. She hadn't been around for as long as I'd been, of course, but her body had aged further along than mine due to not dying all the time. It was, as Harris had mentioned, just one more of the strange things that happened to legionnaires.

"Anyways," Harris said, "even though I come from a hot muggy district, my body's never gotten used to it. I just sweat when I get into weather like this, and it never stops."

We spent the next hour setting up camp and watching all the rest of the drop-pods fall out of the sky. The remaining four lifters that survived came down to reach the surface intact.

All together, our legion was at about seventy percent strength, and we had enough revival machines to crank the rest back out over the next several days.

I sent my two ghost specialists, Cooper and Della, out to scout the area. I was glad that Primus Graves hadn't given us any critical missions yet. Long before it was time to camp and bed down for the night, however, my command chat channel lit up, and Graves began talking to me.

"Okay, listen up 3rd Cohort," he said. "Here's the deal. *Scorpio* has retreated several million kilometers into deep orbit."

My adjuncts, Harris and Leeson, both began muttering curses. As officers, they could hear Graves as well as I could.

We all knew what it meant when your transport flew away and left you on an unknown world. Galina had chickened, and she'd decided to steer clear of that obviously dangerous enemy base—or whatever it was.

I really couldn't fault her for that. Sure, she could have chosen to bring *Scorpio* around, fire her main guns, and maybe take out that ground-based fortification. If it had the range to reach out and nail *Scorpio* first, though… that could be bad.

After all, we'd never tangled with something like this before. The alien base—if it was a base—looked like a giant red glowing crystal stuck on the side of the planet. Who knew what kind of technological tricks it might possess? If that strange gravity-beam destroyed our only transportation out of here, we were all as good as dead—possibly permed.

Out of an abundance of caution, which she usually exhibited whenever her pretty posterior was in any kind of serious danger, she'd ordered Merton to fly the ship out of range. That essentially meant for us, down here on the ground, that our three-quarters strength legion wasn't going to get any help from above.

Graves was still talking, so I started paying attention again. "Yes, that's right—I said quit bitching. This means we're on our own, sure, but that shouldn't be anything unexpected to a real Varus man. I'm sending out one unit from each cohort, as per Tribune Winslade's orders, to go on a wide patrol to investigate the perimeter of our LZ. So far, we haven't seen anything more dangerous than a big ape that might throw some crap at us, but I figure there's got to be something down here of military value—and probably somebody is guarding it."

I had to agree with Graves on that point. We couldn't have come all the way out here from Earth for nothing—could we?

"Everyone is ordered to camp and prep today," Graves continued. "The entire legion will move out tomorrow night under cover of darkness to approach and investigate the unidentified enemy defense base. Graves out."

"Sounds like we've got nothing to do but camp until tomorrow night," I told my troops. "That's a pretty sweet deal, boys."

"Centurion…?" Harris said. "Maybe you should look at your tapper again. New instructions are coming in."

"What the hell?" I uttered, reading a command directive that had just flashed up on my tapper.

"Jumping Jesus," Leeson complained. "One unit out of each cohort on patrol and Graves, that bastard… he had to choose us. McGill, you simply have to stop shitting on his lawn in-between deployments."

"Don't I know it," I said, and I hauled myself wearily to my feet. "Break camp, troops," I said over my unit's tactical chat. "Everything you just unpacked, is going to get packed up again and shoved into your rucks. We'll leave the heavy stuff here, but it can't be just left lying around in the mud."

Adjunct Clane showed up at my elbow a few minutes later. He had a worried questioning look on his face. "Uh, sir… he said. I could tell that he'd been listening to chat and reading his tapper but not interrupting. That was a good practice for a new adjunct.

"What's up Clane? Don't tell me you got one of those big monkeys out there pregnant already."

There were, in fact, quite a number of large ape-like creatures in the trees of this jungle. So far, they hadn't really messed with us, but they were watching, and they hooted loudly now and then. Some of the men reported the aliens had actually thrown a little crap, too. My troops, being a rowdy bunch, had aimed snap-rifles up into the trees, but I'd sternly admonished them against nailing the wildlife out of spite.

"Who knows?" I asked. "They might be the local farmers. They don't look too bright, but then, neither do you…"

"But sir," Clane said, puzzling over his tapper and frowning, "Graves doesn't have a specific time associated with this order. I mean, it doesn't say we're supposed to scramble immediately or anything like that."

I smiled grimly, and I clamped a big, gloved hand down on his shoulder. "Look, Adjunct..." I told him, "I know you come from somewhere cleaner and fancier than Legion Varus, but now you're in the mud and the blood. Let me assure you that if Primus Graves gives an order for us to go on patrol, he means like yesterday. In fact, any minute now I expect a call from him, demanding to know why we're not already marching."

Clane walked away, shaking his head. He began clapping his hands together to get his lights hopping. They'd only just set up camp, dug trenches, and probably hung up their undies to dry, but all that had been a total waste. We dumped boiling pots on campfires, rolled up big sheets of plastic that were already wet with condensation, and twenty minutes later we moved out.

Graves called me again thirty minutes on the dot after his initial orders had been issued. He must have set a timer or something. "McGill? Why the hell...?" Then he trailed off. "Oh, I see you guys are on the move."

I smiled and cranked up my air conditioner another notch. I still hadn't opened my faceplate—not for more than a second or two. About half my troops had done so, but I'd noticed the more experienced soldiers were still operating with an abundance of caution. All of us were tossing frequent glances at Harris, just in case he began melting into some kind of foaming blob of fungus or something like that. So far, he'd shown little sign of toxicity, and he was already making a habit of calling everybody else a pack of pussies for not doing the same as he had.

We began a long, slow slog across the jungle-covered land. Graves had helpfully laid out a series of waypoints which appeared on my HUD and on everybody else's tapper maps to show us where our patrol was expected to go. Plenty of buzzers had already flown around the perimeter of our legion's encampment, and the spot Graves had indicated we should march to and investigate was marked vaguely as a point of interest.

"Point of interest, huh?" Carlos said. "What the hell does that mean?"

"It means you're doomed, boy," Harris told him, laughing.

It took us about forty minutes to hike two kilometers to the spot in question. On flat open ground we would have moved a lot faster, but the forest floor was a mishmash of bushes, ferns, pools of water, muddy bogs, and countless ropey green roots that pulsated grotesquely. Worst of all, nests of giant beetles were common. They seemed harmless, but we found them menacing if only because some of them were as big as a man's fist.

"These frigging things," Harris shouted, slapping at the bugs, which could crawl, swim, and even fly if they wanted to. "They're disgusting."

"Hey," Carlos said, grinning. "Since you're playing guinea pig Adjunct, maybe you'd like to toast one up tonight when we camp—it might taste just like lobster."

"What?"

"Just a suggestion, sir," Carlos said. "I mean, we never know when our rations are going to run out, and according to all my readings, these bugs are edible. Good protein. Just scrape all the guts out from inside of the shell, and you should be good."

"Are you freaking kidding me? Let me tell you, if you think I'm doing that, then you're crazy. You'll be the one eating one of these bugs, Ortiz."

Carlos smiled and went on his way taking measurements. He was poking sampler probes into the large, colorful, waxy flowers that were everywhere.

Harris sidled up near me during the march. He pointed a finger toward Carlos. "I say if it comes down to it," he said, "we make Ortiz be the first to eat one of these bugs. I mean, after all, he's the one saying they're good."

"He didn't exactly say they were tasty," I added.

"Yeah, yeah, but he said they're edible. Right there, that's almost a criminal offense. Graves or some other hoity-toity officer might go into a head-spin. They'll be thinking, 'we don't have to feed these guys out in the field anymore. Let them fend for themselves and eat bugs. It's good for them.'

That sort of thing only happens when a fool like Carlos mentions that it's a possibility in some bullshit report."

I nodded, knowing that Harris was probably right. "Okay," I said. "If we ever get an order to eat these beetles, Carlos has to eat the first one."

This verdict brought a big smile to Harris' face. I smiled in return. Sometimes, I thought, the fine art of raising the morale in a Varus unit was as easy as pie. All you had to do was make some promises. Of course, as the commanding officer, I didn't have to follow through. It was like being a politician or something.

Our relatively happy moment was cut short when we heard the sound of automatic fire up ahead.

"That's a snap-rifle!" Harris shouted. He waved a big arm directing his heavies to spread out and advance.

I splashed ahead, calling out for Adjunct Clane. "Clane! Clane, what have you got? Have you made contact with active hostiles?"

Clane, being the commander of our light platoon, didn't answer immediately. This concerned me, so I began charging forward, sloshing through a meter-deep pool of brackish water. I had a feeling the worst had happened, and I needed to know the truth.

-21-

After charging through a half-kilometer of soggy ground and big leafy plants, I came upon a squad of light troopers circling around what looked like a hump of fur on the ground. One of the troops toed it with a boot. The thing was clearly lifeless.

I knelt to examine the dead ape. "What the hell...?" I demanded. "This thing must have eighty rounds in it—maybe a hundred and eighty."

There was evidence of red explosions all over the creature. At least it had died almost immediately. I stood up again, and I glared at the circle of green recruits. One smiling nineteen-year-old dared to grin back at me.

"I'm the one that bagged it, sir—or at least I'm pretty sure I did."

I grabbed up a wad of spacer-suit fabric and almost lifted the young man off his feet. I gave him a good shaking.

"And why the hell did you do that?"

"Because... because, sir... It attacked us!"

I let go of him and glared around at the group.

"Let me guess, this thing threw some shit at you, so you all hammered away at it."

"No," said a soft voice.

I turned, and I saw Tessie. I hadn't noticed her before, but she was part of this squad. "It did more than that. It threw this at us. It almost nailed Walters," she said, pointing to the recruit who had proudly announced he'd killed the creature.

She offered me what seemed to be a primitive spear. It had an obsidian tip tied with leather strips to a stout shaft of carven wood. It was a weapon, I had to admit that much. Hurled with enough force, it would probably pierce a light trooper's suit and go straight on through him—through his ribcage and into his chest. Still, I was a bit angry with the wanton murder of the first local who had bothered to interact with us.

"Now look," I said, "I know you guys are green, and you're all a bit trigger-happy. That's only natural. But when you're dealing with new aliens—people who've never met you or anything like you—you have to go a bit easy on them. That goes double for cases like this. Look at this stone-age spear. These guys are going to be almost helpless against modern troops."

The squad looked kind of pouty, but I didn't care. I could tell they wanted to grumble and argue, but none of them dared to do it. That's when Adjunct Clane showed up, puffing and out of breath.

"Hey, sir, sorry about this. I was at the far end of my patrol and—"

"Clane," I said sternly, "just what orders are your men under? Is this a wide-patrol in unknown territory? Or is it a pack of murdering marauders?"

Clane seemed flustered, but he handled the question pretty well. He examined the dead creature and the spear, then he stood up.

"I think my men were in the right, Centurion," he said. "Their orders are, by default, to engage with deadly force any attacker which has the capacity to injure or kill them." He lifted the spear as evidence. "I'd say they did just that."

I nodded. "Standing on the rules of engagement, hmm? All right. You and your troops get a pass this time, but let's all walk ahead—up to that bluff over there."

The group followed me, and we soon stood on a rise in the land that looked down upon a large open region. This was, in fact, the spot that Graves had marked down as a place of interest.

In the middle of the valley, which hugged up to a river, was a cluster of huts perhaps a hundred in number. Strangely, there wasn't an alien to be seen. I pointed down into the valley.

"Maybe now that we've established how dangerous these ape-people are," I said, "we could just set up sniper rifles right here along this ridge and start nailing anyone who pokes a nose out of those huts. What do you guys say?"

They looked sheepish and ashamed. It was one thing to fight and defeat a determined threat. It was quite another to panic and blow away the first unfriendly ape-man that you met.

"That fella who came at you," I said. "He was probably just a lookout for his village. Now what do you see about this village? What do you notice? What's different about it?"

They stared. A couple of them scratched themselves.

Tessie finally spoke up. "I don't see any more of the aliens, sir."

"You think they've all run off?" I demanded.

"Either that, or they're hiding in their huts... Maybe they're underground? I don't know. What I'm sure of is that they're scared to death."

I slammed a big painful hand down on the shoulder of Walters, who had done the killing. "Maybe you should go back and cut the ears off that thing," I said. "You can take them home and hang them over your mantle."

Walters hung his head in shame, and I walked away. The rest of the unit was all coming up out of the forest by now. They examined the otherwise peaceful scene.

"What was all the shooting about?" Leeson demanded. "Have these gorilla-aliens got an army or something?"

"Nah," I said. I explained about the spear and the panicked recruit who'd gotten trigger-happy.

"Shit," Harris said. "I knew that new Clane fellow was green, but I didn't know *how* green."

There was no sympathy or second chances with my adjuncts. They'd been in the service too long and seen too much. They were hypercritical, as was I. But in the end, that's how you taught people things.

I ignored Adjunct Clane's apologies, and I thought about how I was going to handle the situation. Firstly, I reported back to Graves, but that didn't get me anywhere.

"Yes, of course we've got drone footage of the village," he said. "Your mission is to get in there, investigate it and give me a report. Something a camera can't see."

Reluctantly, I showed him the dead ape-alien and his pathetic spear.

"That's just grand, McGill. I shouldn't have sent you and your butchers out there. We aren't on the planet to exterminate the local populace. These people are probably nothing but farmers shipping food to Rigel. I'm sure I don't need to tell you that it's far easier to pacify a local populace if you don't start off day-one by murdering them."

"I'm mighty sorry about that, sir," I said. "My next move is to send in a couple of ghosts to walk around the village and get some close video. We'll see what the locals are up to. In the meantime, I'll just sit here on this ridge, and I won't fire a shot unless I absolutely have to."

"You should have thought of that before, McGill. Graves out."

There it was. Shit always runs downhill, and now it was flowing from Graves to me. Soon it would be heading to Clane and ending up on top of fresh-faced Walters.

I contacted Della and Cooper and sent them on their way. We lounged around on the top of the ridge for a good half hour or so, waiting for the report to come back.

Ghost specialists were equipped with some very specialized gear which we originally got from the Vulbites. This consisted of a thin suit of light-bending material. A naturally quiet and light-footed individual could walk with relative invisibility among the enemy.

Della was the first to whisper back her responses. "I've looked in about half the huts now, sir," she said, talking in a low tone. She had been a Dust World scout, and although the years and the missions had civilized her somewhat, she was still a born scout when it came right down to it—a huntress who had grown up living by her wits and her skills at stealth.

"Almost all of them seem to be civilians. They're mostly females huddled up with their young."

"What about their warriors?" I asked. "Have you seen any of them running around with spears? That kind of thing?"

"No, sir, not one."

I thought that over. We'd met up with one spearman, shot him down, and then within a few minutes every male in the village had disappeared. To my mind, that could only add up to one bad thing.

"All right, unit," I said, switching to tactical chat. "It might be time for us to reap what Recruit Walters has sown for us on this fine golden afternoon. Circle up, lights on the perimeter. We're going to hug up to this ridge, and we're going to aim our guns in every direction, at every tree in the vicinity—but not down into the village itself. Remember to look up, these guys can climb."

My troops rearranged themselves, but it was too little, too late. About seven minutes later, a shower of primitive projectiles came sailing down from the heights of the trees.

Somehow, they'd managed to sneak up on us. They'd climbed up the tall, vine-wrapped trees in utter stealth. At some unknown signal, they'd all attacked at once.

This time, they weren't just crapping in their hands and tossing it. They were throwing heavy darts which flew down into our midst. These objects were about a meter long, with a straight shaft and a black-bladed point.

To our surprise, the points weren't primitive obsidian tied onto the end of a stick, the kind of thing some stone-ager might have created back on Earth. No, these tips were metal, and they were sharper than razors.

What's more, the darts were hurled with incredible accuracy and power. On old Earth, there'd probably never been an Olympic javelin-thrower who could throw something as hard as a two-hundred-kilo gorilla-alien could—especially not when said alien had undoubtedly spent countless hours practicing the art.

I had, perhaps unwisely in retrospect, ordered Clane's recruits to form the outer circle. They were serving as pickets surrounding our tiny encampment. I hadn't really taken this foe seriously, and I was getting schooled on that point now.

The metal tips of the darts fell out of the sky like meteors. They struck home again and again. Darts sprouted from chests, eye-sockets, and thighs.

Several recruits fell screaming. Young Walters himself—the man who had started all this—ended up transfixed to a tree. He'd been run through the heart. After flopping around feebly for a moment, he stopped moving and slumped in death, still nailed into the wood of the trunk.

"Permission to return fire, sir!" Clane shouted in my ears.

"Yes, yes, permission granted. Open up."

Dozens of snap-rifles began to go off. A moment later, Harris joined in with his heavies using morph-rifles and firing power bolts wherever they saw a furred paw or a glinting, bloodshot eye.

The darts stopped falling amongst us almost immediately, and after perhaps ten more seconds of wild gunfire from my unit, I ordered them to stand down.

"Cease fire! Cease fire!" I shouted. "You're not hitting anything."

It was true. The alien warriors had retreated. I sent forward Clane's surviving lights, who carefully poked around among the trees but did not find a single body on the forest floor. The locals had managed to nail several of ours.

"That was total bullshit," Leeson said. "We were out of position, and we didn't return fire fast enough."

I walked over to where Walters was pinned to the tree and ripped the dart out of the trunk, allowing his body to slump down into the mud. I examined the tip.

"You see this? This isn't stone and leather. That's hard steel."

"Sure is," Leeson agreed.

I pointed with the tip of the dart at Walters' fallen shape. "Now this guy, you could say he deserved that. I could say that was on him—but not the rest of these troops. That was my fault. I didn't take the enemy seriously. I didn't position us to take on a serious threat. In fact, I didn't even have Kivi's buzzers out looking for them deep in the forest."

"Well, I'm on it now," Kivi said, coming up to me and showing me what was playing on her tapper. "You see this? I've got some video from the moment they attacked. They must have jumped from trees farther away to the nearer trees—way up high, so we didn't even notice them. Then, they all threw one nasty dart each and ran away. There were about twenty of them as best I can count. We fired back, but it was already too late. Five seconds after they threw that shower of darts, they were gone."

"Hit-and-run," Leeson said. "Classic hit and run—those big sneaky bastards."

I had to agree with him. Heaving a big sigh, I decided it was time to report back in to Graves again. We had certainly found the point of interest he'd marked on our maps, and we'd certainly learned a bit about this world and its inhabitants.

-22-

I had two techs in my unit. One was Kivi, and the other was Natasha. Kivi was a solid tech specialist, she'd learned to do all of her assigned tasks professionally—but Natasha was on a whole different level. Plainly speaking, the girl was gifted. She knew lots of science stuff that Kivi could only guess at—things that went above and beyond the normal specialist pay-grade.

I summoned Natasha to help me examine the alien-made spear tip and handed it to her. "What do you think about this?"

"Eew, it's got blood and stuff all over it."

"Yeah, I just pulled it out of Walters, over there." I pointed to the slumped body on the dirt.

She looked faintly disgusted, but soon the wrinkles in her face stretched out and smoothed away to nothing. She was intrigued. I also handed her the more primitive spear—the one we discovered earlier. She eyeballed them, comparing the two.

"The main difference is the tip," she said. "This metal point isn't anything that a culture on the level of that village we see below us could possibly have manufactured. The edge is razor sharp, and the alloy isn't simple iron or even steel..."

After running her instruments over it for a time, she looked up at me, startled. "James... You know, I think the edges on this spearhead are molecularly aligned."

"What? You mean like our combat daggers?" I asked.

She nodded. "Yeah, exactly. They're sharper than glass and harder than diamond. I wouldn't be surprised if one of these spears could plunge right through a breastplate like the one Harris is wearing over there."

"Oh, that's just great," Harris complained. "Not only does our new Adjunct Clane have to go and piss off these alien gorillas and get Graves breathing down our neck about it, but then it has to turn out that said aliens have a secret stash of high-tech spears to throw at us. This is our lucky day, isn't it?"

"Huh..." I said, looking over the weapons. "You think maybe Rigel made these spearheads?"

Natasha shrugged. "Could be that Rigel made them, or Earth could have made them—any advanced civilization could have made them."

I nodded, thinking it over. It made some sense. If you wanted to arm the local population with a fairly effective weapon, without having to train them to use something they were unfamiliar with, this fit the bill. They already knew how to make and use spears. All you needed to do was give them a better point, and the aliens would do the rest.

Still, I wasn't too worried. Sure, these locals were fast, and they knew the terrain. They were obviously tactically cunning, and they'd been given an advanced weapon that they knew how to use—but I still couldn't imagine that they were that much of a threat.

Legion Varus had all kinds of things to throw at these primitives that they couldn't stand up against. Long-ranged combat was one. A snap-rifle bullet didn't drop off for a couple of kilometers. Just a few pellets from a weapon like dead-man Walters was carrying could do as much damage or more than any spear tip ever made.

I handed the two weapons back to Natasha. "I want you to do some further work on the metallurgy. Get me whatever you can figure out—to see where that stuff came from."

She went to work while Kivi sent up a cloud of buzzers to recon the area properly. Next, I checked in with my two ghost specialists. The empty village was still empty. The warriors were still out there, somewhere, on the loose.

Eyeballing the huts and counting them carefully, I figured there was something like sixty of them. That sounded about right. I had to figure we were dealing with sixty warriors from the village, each armed with one or more spears.

Hmm... To change things up a bit, I had the heavies go out and hang around the perimeter, rather than lights. Without armor, my light troopers would be easily nailed by the stealthy hunters in the woods.

After making a full report back to Graves, I was given fresh orders.

"I want you to withdraw out of that position," he said. "All you're doing is provoking the locals with your hostile presence."

"But, sir," I said, "we only killed one of them. They killed a bunch of our troops."

"You think that matters to them? You're hanging out on a hill overlooking their entire village. You're an obvious threat, and you've already fired a thousand rounds at their warriors—probably more."

"Yeah..." I admitted. "We probably have."

"All right then," he said, "get out of there. I'm going to send in a team of xenologists to try to make contact."

This seemed unusually diplomatic on the part of Graves, but I was all for the suggestion. Marching in with troops first—that was never the way to a peaceful resolution.

Accordingly, we withdrew from our position and headed back toward the legion's main encampment. All my men were happy about that. They didn't want to spend the night out here, getting bitten by fist-sized bugs and possibly skewered in the middle of the night by angry ape-aliens. A recipe like that definitely wouldn't lead to restful slumber.

When we finally made it back to the main camp, I got a disturbing note. It was from Centurion Evelyn Thompson. Now, unlike most centurions in Legion Varus, she wasn't a member of any particular unit, or cohort. She headed up all the bio specialists who were in charge of reviving and oftentimes murdering soldiers that were wounded or killed in battle.

As a side note, she and I had been romantically involved long ago. We'd also killed one another and betrayed one another on a number of occasions. Despite all this, I considered her a friend.

What concerned me about her message was her role in the legion. When an officer-level bio sends you a special note, there's almost no chance it's for something good.

Still, I tapped on her name and called her, displaying a big grin. You never did know, after all, when a lady was feeling an unusual urge.

"Hey, Evelyn," I said, putting my face directly in the way of the camera.

Evelyn's image greeted me, and she looked a little worried. She was a girl who was a little on the small and thin side, but she still held enough womanly curves to interest the likes of me.

"McGill?" she said, "I've received all the reports from Kivi. She forwarded them to me for bio analysis. Carlos took some samples, too, and... this is strange. I'm getting some matchups on my computers. I'll need to see the specimen that you guys killed—personally."

"Uhh..." I said, thinking that over. "That might be kind of hard to do, Evelyn. Graves just ordered us to return to camp, and that corpse is several kilometers out in the bush."

"It doesn't matter. I need to confirm my findings. I need access to that body. I'm coming out to your unit's position right now."

Frowning at my tapper and cursing a little, I saw it had gone blank. To this very day, Evelyn still treated me as if we were not quite equal, like her rank was just a little superior to mine.

To my mind, that was the reverse of how things should be—especially when she went poking her fingers into something like direct legion security. That was my area, not hers.

Of course, that wasn't how she was seeing things, I'm sure. In her own thought-processes, she was doing sciencey stuff—biological sciency stuff in particular. That meant she was in charge.

Grumping about the situation for several long minutes, I waited until she showed up. I offered her a hot cup of fresh brewed coffee, but she passed.

"I need you or one of your men to lead me out there," she said.

It was about then I noticed she'd come alone. I was kind of surprised. I'd figured she'd probably bring along a couple of those bio-orderly, noncom goons her people so often kept in tow.

When I asked her about it, she shook her head vigorously. "No, that would never do. My people don't know the terrain. They don't know how to slog through a jungle with hostile primitives behind every tree, but your troops do. Now, how are we going to do this?"

Evelyn stared at me intently, waiting for an answer. She seemed kind of impatient.

"Well," I said, "wait just a second, here. Can you tell me exactly why you're so concerned about getting some hair and blood samples? Didn't you get enough of that stuff from Carlos?"

"There are some matches in the database, James—near-matches really. But I need confirmation. I also need to see the physiognomy. I need to see what we're dealing with."

I shrugged. "Well, okay. I'll tell you what. You can take either Della or Cooper with you. They've both got stealth suits. Then, you just put the other stealth suit on yourself. They won't like giving it up mind you, not even for a few minutes, but they won't have any choice."

Evelyn thought that over, and she nodded, but she still seemed troubled, and I noticed.

"What's up girl?" I asked. "You don't look happy."

"Well..." she said sighing, "it's really a matter of security, you know. I'll do it the way you suggest, but I'd rather that the other man in the stealth suit was you, James."

I blinked a couple times at that. Again, thoughts of romance struck through my dim brain. Could this be the weirdest pickup plan I'd ever heard of? I dared to hope.

"Why, exactly," I asked, "are you dissatisfied with going along with either Della or Cooper?"

She looked at me seriously. "Listen James, there's nothing wrong with either one of those two. Not when it comes to sneaking around. But these aliens have good senses, and I'm not an expert in a stealth suit. I'm sure to leave a print in some mud somewhere, right?"

"Yeah, yeah, probably."

"Well, that's just it. If it comes down to a fight with these creatures, who do you think would do better, Della, Cooper—or you?"

She fixed me with a straight stare, and I thought that over. The answer was obvious.

"Well, yeah… probably me. One ape does better when it comes to fighting another one, after all. At least I should hold up better than some scrawny weakling like my ghost specialists. They weren't picked for brawn."

"No, of course they weren't," she said. "Well, what do you say?"

I shook my head, and I knew I should say no—but I didn't.

After a bit of wrangling, I managed to get my two ghosts out of their stealth suits. You would have thought they were welded into them or something.

Evelyn and I slipped on the gear, and we effectively vanished. Once we were suited-up, I set off into the jungle.

"Wait!" Evelyn called after me in a hiss. "I can't see you. Where did you go?"

I led her more closely, but she kept getting lost and complaining every minute or so. She spoke with a stage whisper, but it was still way too loud.

"You can't go talking like that every few steps, girl," I told her. "Remember these aliens have good senses. They're also big, and frigging sneaky. They might be above us right now in these trees. We wouldn't even know."

After saying this, I felt something tapping at my arm. I almost lunged, but then I realized it must be Evelyn, although I couldn't see who was pecking at me.

Reaching out, I took her small hand, and I led her so she wouldn't get lost in the jungle.

The way out to the site of our initial deadly encounter with the aliens seemed to take longer than it had the first time. Possibly, that was because Evelyn was not a natural in the forest. She tended to get her boots stuck in every bog, or forked set of vines.

But also, in my opinion, the second time into this heavy brush was a lot scarier than the first one had been. After all, there were only two of us, and we now knew what we were facing. We knew there were aliens out here with effective weapons, creatures who might ambush us and plant a spear in our guts at any moment. At last, however, we found the body right where it had been left.

Evelyn knelt down. I could see her small knee-prints in the mud next to the dead alien.

"This creature is definitely similar to our own primates back on Earth," she said. "Primitive, yet somewhat more advanced than a gorilla. It's almost like a muscular homo habilis."

"A homo habilis?" I asked. "What's that like?"

"Some would say it's like you, James."

I frowned inside my stealth suit. I wasn't certain, but I thought, just possibly, that I'd been insulted.

Evelyn did her probing and made certain slices and dices, cutting a few pieces of flesh away from the palm of the creature. Then, she pried its mouth open and took part of its tongue. It was all kind of gross to watch, especially when you couldn't even see the person doing it. I looked away and watched the forest instead.

It seemed to me, after a time, that something was coming from the direction of the village.

"Hey…" I whispered. "Hey girl, we've got to go—right now!"

"I need to get more samples," she said, but I didn't listen to her.

"Come on." I took her by the hand again, and I pretty much lifted her into the air. She struggled lightly, but not with all her strength. Not that it would have mattered if she had.

Behind us, a whole group of alien primitives had appeared on the scene. These guys looked somewhat different than those we'd seen before, as they had a modicum of dress upon them—beads, furs, that kind of thing. They looked like ancient tribesmen to me, except with way more hair and much bigger, rounded shoulders than human Earthmen would have had.

Once we were at a safe distance, we watched as the group circled the fallen alien. They chanted and made certain gestures. After that, they picked him up as a group and walked back toward their village.

"That was some kind of burial procession," Evelyn told me. She sounded kind of excited. "These people are more advanced than I thought. They seem to have religion, ceremony and probably a lot more—definitely a whole culture of their own."

"Yeah, their weapons are pretty basic, though."

"That's not the way to look at it," she said. "Think about how we would have looked to an alien coming to Earth—let's say twenty thousand years ago. Sure, these guys have more hair than we do, but otherwise, they're essentially the same."

"Huh…" I said, thinking that over. I had to admit she had a point.

Once the ape-aliens had disappeared, I led Evelyn back to camp. We reached the safe perimeter and passed through undetected.

In the friendly light of our campfires, Evelyn pulled off her stealth suit, and I did the same. We stood next to each other, looking around and breathing hard due to our exertion and excitement. Mostly it was Evelyn who was excited. Running around out in the bush, that was something she didn't do every day.

I'd kind of expected her to walk away toward her bio bunker, which had been dug by drones that we called pigs and covered in puff-crete—but she didn't. She was just looking up at me for a moment, as if thinking something over, something deep and unknowable to one James McGill.

"Uhh…" I said, "you need something else?"

"I just wanted to thank you, James. For doing this—for babysitting me out there. I was really scared."

I nodded, and I smiled. "No problem. I owe you for old time's sake, if nothing else."

Her eyes kept on looking at me, and I got a certain feeling from her. Accordingly, I leaned down my big head, which was way too high for her to reach. She stepped closer and gave me a kiss.

"Thanks again," she said, whispering in my ear. "I'll share the results with you when I get them—whatever I find. Okay?"

"Sounds good," I said.

She scampered off then, and it took all my willpower not to slap her one on the butt as she turned away.

It was too early for that sort of thing I told myself—way too damned early. Before I knew it, she was gone.

-23-

Bright and early the next morning, I came awake with my tapper buzzing furiously. Bleary of mind and eye, I answered the call.

"McGill? Dammit, McGill!"

Graves was talking to me, and here I was, still scratching my ass in the green gloom of a jungle dawn. That was one trouble with modern conveniences like our tappers. A superior officer could just call you whenever they felt like it. You couldn't even turn the damned thing off without a major effort. People like Graves and Turov made a habit of interrupting my sleep and private moments like this on every deployment.

"Hey, Primus," I said. "Good morning to you. What's the trouble?"

Graves glowered at me. "Six tech specialists—all lost. Not just any specialists, but a rare, rare breed of technician. They're really a combination of bio-specialist and tech-specialist, and they're all dead as doornails—because of you."

"Huh?" I said, utterly baffled as to what he was talking about. I yawned and threw an arm wide.

Graves looked on sullenly. "It's that village you set on fire yesterday," he said.

"What? We didn't set anything on fire, sir. Not a single hut was burned down."

"All right, whatever. In any case, I sent six xenologists out there on a peaceful mission to make contact."

I grinned. I couldn't help it. "Oh, yeah? How'd that go?" I asked, but I already knew the answer. His poor attitude left little to the imagination.

He made some sweeping motions. I saw the camera angle change as his big finger moved across his tapper. "Just take a look."

A video began to play. The xenologists had all been killed. A small patrol of ghost specialists had located the bodies, and they were in an unhealthy state of repose. They had spears run through their guts the long way, with the gory tips poking out of eye sockets and mouths.

"Ooh…" I said. "That would hurt something awful."

"I bet it did, McGill. What are you not telling me about yesterday's events? What has got these apes so riled up? It can't just be that one murdered scout of theirs."

"Now look here," I said. "I didn't do anything to the locals, except what I told you. We didn't really have much contact with them. We ran into one while we were patrolling, and he threw a stick at us. My recruits put him down, so I reprimanded my men for it. Next, less than an hour later, they attacked us. This time they used those special spears."

"Yes, yes," he said, "the steel pointed ones."

"No, sir," I said. "They're not just steel. Those things are harder than diamond and sharper than glass. I had Natasha run a check on them."

"Whatever, McGill. I don't care. What I see is spear tips poking out of my xenologists. You were the first to have contact with this new species. You're also a master at telling tall tales. All this leads me to suspect you're hiding half a dozen baby aliens in your tent, or something."

I laughed. While Graves was talking to me, I was pulling on my boots and zipping up my gear. It was just after dawn, but I was pretty sure the time for sleeping had passed on by for one James McGill.

"The locals have gotten a little ornery. So what?" I asked in a reasonable tone. "That's nothing we haven't seen before. It's only to be expected, sir. Is one of those xeno-specialists your girlfriend, or something? You seem mighty upset about this."

Graves glowered at me without speaking for a few seconds longer. "The problem isn't the loss of some biochemicals. We can and will print out our xenologists again. But we can't so easily repair our diplomatic mistakes."

"I see what you mean, there, but I really don't think we ever had a chance of making friends with these aliens. They're flat-out hostile, and they've been armed by our enemies. The good Lord only knows what tall tales Rigel has been telling them about us."

Graves nodded. "All right," he said. "Let's say I buy all this. You're totally innocent. You haven't just started a new war with an alien species we only just met."

"That's the truth, sir. Now, if you don't mind, I'd like to go and have a bit of breakfast."

He laughed, and it wasn't a pleasant sound. "You've convinced me, McGill—but you still haven't convinced Winslade. He's blaming you for all this—all the way up to the top."

"The top?" I asked. "Isn't he the only officer of tribune rank on this entire planet?"

"You know what I mean," Graves said. "Turov and Merton—they're still up on *Scorpio*."

"Staying nice and safe up there, too, I bet..."

"I've prioritized your losses. Every recruit you lost yesterday should be returning to camp this morning."

I blinked in surprise. "That's mighty nice of you, Primus."

"No, it isn't. You're going on a wide patrol again today. In fact, every unit in this cohort is going on a wide patrol.

"Oh, come on, sir!" I said. "Hasn't Winslade got somebody else to pick on?"

"Apparently not. He pointed out at this morning's staff meeting that every trouble spot on his map has 3rd Cohort associated with it."

"Well, then..." I said, "maybe he should consider sending out a more diplomatic cohort into the jungle next time around. I've heard that 6th Cohort is full of pansies."

Graves shook his head slowly. "That's not how it works, McGill. Winslade's into punishments and blame."

I nodded tiredly. "Okay. Where are we going, and what are we doing?"

"I'm not putting you on the front lines this time. You're going to be the reserve force. We've got new points of interest. Our aerial surveillance has located large numbers of these aliens."

"Uh…" I said, "large numbers? Like, what kind of numbers are we talking about?"

Graves shrugged. "I don't know, thousands? Who cares? You're going to find out for me. I'm sending four units out there, with you hanging back in reserve. Their orders are to advance to contact, but not to engage. The other units will scout, and you'll cover their retreat if they get into trouble."

I blinked a couple of times, thinking that this plan sounded just as half-baked and provocative as the last one. "Hey, uh, Primus Graves, sir? Do you mind if I make a comment?"

"Yes, I do mind, McGill—but I'll allow it this one time."

"Well sir, whoever came up with this crazy plan is a card-carrying moron."

"And why is that, McGill?"

"Because we're sitting in their jungle. We killed one of them, and they killed a bunch of us. What do we do next? Do we sit back and act calm about it? Are we going to let them settle down a little? No! We're going to go in there and we're going to poke at the snake's hind quarters yet again. Sir, this situation is liable to turn into a full-on pig-fuck."

"Thanks for the academic input, McGill. You move out in forty-five minutes. Graves out." That was it. He was gone.

I was left kicking cans and cursing. By cans, I mean to say the lazy rumps of all my adjuncts and noncoms. In five minutes, I had them all up and humping around, gathering gear. Ten minutes after that, we were eating hot meals. Twenty minutes more, and we were moving out.

All told, we were about five minutes ahead of schedule. That was what Graves liked, and that was what he would actually expect. At forty-five minutes on the dot, he contacted me again.

"I see you're moving out, and you're not late, McGill. That's a nice change of pace. 3rd Unit is going to play rear guard in the formation behind the 4th, 5th and 6th."

"Not the 7th, sir?" I questioned.

He shook his head. "Nope. Your legion buddies are not involved. Manfred and Jenny Mills are not going to be in front of you—not this time. I've noticed that when you accompany friendly centurions, the whole mission tends to turn into a bigger mess than it might otherwise. Now remember, McGill. You're in a strictly supporting role on this mission. If some kind of firefight does break out, you will cover the retreat. That's it."

"I've got it, sir. That's crystal clear. There will be absolutely no shenanigans. Not this time, not on my watch."

Graves closed the channel sourly.

I contacted the centurions leading the 4th, 5th and 6th Units. They all seemed just as baffled by their orders as I was. During the night, however, they'd apparently read a number of action reports which I'd skipped over.

Once we moved out and began marching, the other officers paid little attention to me. When I made polite inquiries, their responses were things like… "Stay in position, McGill!", "You're not needed on the front line, McGill," or "3rd Unit is to stay in the rear at all times."

I soon stopped querying them and grumbled. Deciding to do my own recon, I ordered Kivi to send up a flock of buzzers. At least we could watch what was happening.

For about an hour all we did was march. At first, the jungle was hot, humid, bug-filled and kind of swampy. Then the early morning passed, and things got nasty.

Once it got to be about ten or eleven o'clock, the planet felt like Georgia swampland on the hottest day of the year. I suppose that's pretty much what jungles feel like anywhere you go, but I wasn't used to it.

The trees were full of leathery-looking bird-things. To me, they looked kind of like miniature flying dinosaurs. At least they weren't so large as to be dangerous, but they did resemble pterodactyls with two-meter wingspans—flying dinosaurs the size of turkey buzzards. Now and then, one of the recruits aimed a gun up at them, but some noncom or officer always slapped that muzzle back down again.

"No one shoots anything," Harris told them, "unless it shoots you first. Hear me?"

Cowed, the recruits nodded and behaved themselves. Just like always, our newest recruits were a rowdy bunch. Whereas the big-name legions such as Victrix, Germanica and the Iron Eagles tended to get college graduates, we got the high school dropouts or even the juvenile hall escapees. Only the fear of sudden, violent death could straighten out our hooligans.

During the second hour, we found that we had moved past the farthest point where any Earth patrol had gone before. For the first time, we came to an open area—I wouldn't call it a plain, but it was definitely a grassy plateau that rose up out of the jungle. Due to its dry, rocky nature, it was carpeted only with tall grasses and an occasional stubby tree.

4th, 5th and 6th Units all advanced before us, climbing the rocky walls of the table land and peeping over the top onto the grassy plain. This was apparently the point of interest that we were supposed to be investigating.

Watching the units advance on Kivi's buzzers, I frowned, and I questioned Natasha about the landscape. "Is this completely natural?" I said. "Doesn't look like it to me."

"No, sir," she said. "I don't think it is. I think it's an earthen mound—something built up artificially as a gathering point. You see, they've stacked up those black rocks around the outer wall and filled the top tablelands with dirt. In the center, I'm seeing another stone structure."

"Oh…" I said, checking out what our buzzers had spotted in the center of the wide plateau. "Look at that. These aliens built themselves some kind of stone city up there. These primitives are looking smarter all the time."

Natasha didn't share my enthusiasm. She looked concerned. "I don't know if we should be here, James," she said. "I mean, if these people are tribal, and they're gathering in large numbers at this spot, it might be sacred to them. It's best that we don't interfere before we understand the culture we're interacting with."

"Wiser words were never spoken, Natasha," I said, "but I'm only a centurion. I'm not in charge of this clusterfuck."

Still, taking heed of Natasha's warning, I ordered my troops to stop the moment we got close enough to spot the rock wall that the rest of the units were climbing. I tried to pass on the suggestion to give the aliens some breathing room to the other unit commanders, but the advice was rejected out of hand. All the other centurions on this mission were the snotty type.

I shrugged, and we waited. For a long while nothing much happened, but then some kind of ceremony began in the middle of the broad plateau. There on a squat, jagged pile of rocks that look like a ziggurat built by kindergarteners, a number of alien chieftains stood up on their hind legs and began to go through an elaborate ceremony of sorts.

"Hah!" I said. "It looks like they're summoning the great Jungle Spirit!" Natasha hushed me. She still had that worried frown on her face. I wasn't too concerned about that, because she always looked worried. She was what I'd always called an over-thinker. Then, however, something happened, that even set my eyebrows to furrowing.

In the center of the plateau, where the big structure of black rocks was, some blue flashes lit up the whole region. They were the kind of blue flashes that reminded me of an electrical arc, or maybe a strobe light. They were irregular and uneven in size and intensity. The effect was also somewhat violent. We witnessed the massive stones smoldering and shifting slightly.

"Huh..." I said, "hey guys... things are looking kind of weird out there."

"That's technological. That's technological!" Natasha repeated to herself with growing excitement.

"What are those frigging aliens doing out there?" I asked. "Is that lightning? Are they starting up some kind of a rain dance or something?"

Natasha glanced at me like I was an idiot, but I took no offense. It was the look I'd been getting from smarty-pants women like her since grade school.

"James," she said, "I don't know what's happening, but these aliens clearly have technology beyond what we suspected. What if they're in charge of that big, red crystal rammed into the side of this planet? What if they're controlling it? What if *they* directed it to fire at *Scorpio*?"

I looked at her, my mouth sagging open. "What are you talking about, girl? They've done nothing but sit around grunting in their huts."

She shook her head. "We don't know that. We don't know anything like that. We just made that assumption because their appearance and lifestyle seem very primitive. What if they choose to live this primitive life? What if they actually possess advanced technology, but haven't decided to utilize it for whatever reason?"

I gaped at her for a few more moments. This was something I'd never considered, mostly because it sounded like total foolishness.

I grinned at Natasha. "You've gone crazy, girl. Your mind is playing tricks on you. Just because these aliens have some pointy sticks, and they're setting off some sparklers out there in that field, doesn't make them tech wizards."

She shook her head, and we both went back to watching the video feed from our buzzers again. A big ring of furry shapes showed up and completely encircled the pile of rocks in the center. The electrical discharges continued as well. In fact, they seemed to increase in both frequency and intensity. Finally, I couldn't take the suspense any longer.

"Kivi," I said, "I want you to suicide a buzzer. Send it right into the middle of that rock-pile. Give me one clear snapshot of what the hell's going on in there."

"But, sir..." she said. "Centurion, we're not supposed to do that. We're not supposed to interfere with the aliens, and we aren't supposed to take the initiative on this mission."

"Kivi, you're my specialist. I'm your centurion. Send the frigging buzzer."

Natasha and Kivi gave each other knowing glances, and I found that annoying. I vowed to myself, not for the first time—probably not for the eightieth time, either—that I should request a new tech specialist who didn't know me. It should probably be some ugly dude who wouldn't care to spy on me, romance me, or second-guess all my orders.

Despite their misgivings, the two women worked together and sent in a buzzer on the killer run I'd demanded.

Natasha took over flying the buzzer in question, doing it manually from her own tiny computer screen. She was really good at this kind of thing.

Kivi didn't second guess Natasha at all. In fact, she sat silently next to her, just watching.

The target rock-pile was at the very limit of the buzzer's range, so they'd chosen a drone that was getting a little bit low on juice anyway. It would be no big loss if it went down in a tiny blaze of glory.

The buzzer zoomed from our lines to the bottom of the slope ahead of us. It climbed this rapidly to reach the plateau, then sailed over a long line of legionnaire helmets. After that, it dashed over open ground.

I hunkered close behind the two girls and stared over their shoulders. They were so intent on the scene on their tiny screens, they didn't even notice. Working a pair of tiny screen controls with her thumbs, Natasha glided the buzzer toward the center of the plateau where the aliens had gathered, flying low.

The drone was perhaps three meters off the ground now. It skimmed over the tall grasses with blurring speed. When it had crossed a few kilometers of grass, we could finally see the hulking forms of the aliens.

They were in some sort of a prayerful pose. All of them were on their hands and knees, with their heads down and their strange hands aimed toward the central rocky edifice. The buzzer whizzed over this vast, hairy circle and kept going.

Soon, it reached the crowd of priest-aliens that stood all over the rock-pile. I assumed the place was some kind of temple.

With a sickening motion, Natasha swooped the buzzer up and then down again, plunging into the center of the rock formation. At last, the tiny vehicle slowed down, and we took a good, long look at what was hidden in the center of what had to be a holy site.

There, to our utter surprise, we saw the last thing we'd imagined we'd ever see.

I'd honestly been expecting—maybe even with certainty in my heart—that there was going to be a stretched out and castrated goat. Maybe the priests would be in the process of gutting it alive, or eating it, or whatever—but no.

Instead, I saw more hunched figures inside the temple—a lot of them. These figures, unlike the aliens that were native to Jungle World, wore weapon harnesses and carried what could only be heavy rifles.

They were, in shape and dimension, somewhat similar to the ape-aliens that lived on this planet. But then again, they were also quite different—especially in the face.

They had perky ears, rather than tiny, almost invisible ears. Their fur was brown, rather than the jet black of the local primates. Most important of all, they had large snouts—faces that were more lupine or wolf-like than the faces of the locals.

"Dogmen!" I shouted out. "Those are freaking dogmen! The Clavers are involved in this somehow? Are you shitting me?"

The two women glanced back over their shoulders at me, but they didn't speak. They were too riveted by what we were seeing.

"Look, look," I said, jamming a huge arm, hand and finger between the two. I pointed at the tiny screen accusingly. "I'd bet my left nut that's some kind of a gateway post setup. See it? Right there!"

Natasha swooped lower, and I was vindicated. In the middle of the dogmen, a set of gateway posts flickered and ran with colored light.

As we watched, more dogmen came through the gateway, each of them armed and disciplined. You could tell by the way they walked, they were trained soldiers.

I'd dealt with these creatures several times before. Abigail Claver had told me that they were new hybrid troops they'd created to rent out as mercenaries. Even the Mogwa sometimes used them as cheap, obedient muscle.

I'd encountered them first on Green World, where I'd been an unhappy prisoner of theirs. Many a dogman had come up to my cell and pissed on the bars, which was my only window up into the world of light and sound and free open air.

Natasha let the buzzer hover there for several seconds, and some of the dogmen seemed to notice. A few thick fingers pointed up into the air, and a dozen power-bolts were fired at our camera pickup—but none of them struck home.

"Pull it out of there," I said. "They're starting to notice."

The drone buzzed, looped and began to fly higher.

At that moment, the gateway posts—which were now producing dogmen at a prodigious rate—seemed to short out, or something.

A bolt of lightning leaped up from the posts, frying a couple of the dogmen guards. These creatures were burned and blasted into humps of smoldering meat and fur. Apparently, the technology was not entirely stable.

"Looks like that last jolt fried their posts," I said.

Another bolt of lightning shot up high, and it fried the drone we were using to watch the bizarre scene. The feed went dark, and Natasha and Kivi both turned slowly to look at me.

Natasha looked stunned. She didn't say anything.

"What are we going to do, James?" Kivi asked.

"Uh..." I said. "Give me a minute. I've got to think."

As it turned out, I didn't have a minute. I don't even think I had ten seconds, because that's about how long it took for the aliens and their heavily armed dogmen friends to fly into a berserker rage and begin charging around in the grasses surrounding their sacred rock-pile. It looked like someone had stomped on a nest of giant ants.

-24-

When we saw a squalling horde of aliens blasting their way through the tall grass in our direction, I could only imagine the shock and dismay of the other unit centurions.

They had buzzers out there too, of course—but their scouts had been better behaved. They were just circling the perimeter of the crowd. Their tiny spies scouted and sniffed—but none of them had gone so far as to violate the sanctity of the rock-pile shrine. Only my buzzer had done that, and apparently, this had been seen as an affront to all that was decent and holy.

Judging by the precise direction and ferocity of their charge, it was obvious that the ape-aliens had known we were hiding out here all along.

"What are we going to do, James?" Natasha asked. She was panting a bit, and her eyes were a little wild. I think she was blaming herself for this disaster, although I myself knew I was at fault. She'd been following orders, nothing more.

Shrugging I recalled the operational orders I'd gotten from Graves before this entire fiasco had begun.

"Well," I said, "looks like we're going to have to move up and support our boys if they need it."

I stretched my men out into a line and led them, marching forward. When we were fifty meters from the base of the slope, I ordered them to halt and take cover. We crouched behind tree trunks, positioning ourselves so we could see up to the top of the plateau.

There, our brave legionnaire brothers were preparing to meet the alien charge. If any of the aliens broke through, we would take a shot. On the other hand, if the commanders of the 4th, 5th and 6th decided to stage a retreat, then we would cover that withdrawal.

At this point, I'd decided to studiously stick to the letter of what Graves had instructed me to do. Because after all, I had already lit this cat's tail on fire, and it wouldn't do at this point to step out of line any further. The weaponeers shouldered their belchers, and the light troopers set up on either flank of our group. Harris' heavy soldiers—armed and armored better than the rest—advanced an extra ten meters to stand near the base of the plateau's steep rise from the forest floor. Watching another buzzer feed, I saw the furious aliens charge in an unbroken wave toward our lines.

"Damnation," I said, "look at them run."

"Wow!" Leeson said, "they can really move!"

"A man's got no chance against them on foot," Harris added. "No chance at all."

"Why aren't our boys firing?" Leeson asked.

"Because they're chicken-shits," Harris said.

"No, that's not it," I said. "They're not chicken. They're trying to follow their orders. They're trying not to engage the locals."

Leeson hooted with laughter. "Good luck with that now!"

Watching the scene, I shook my head ruefully. I couldn't help but feel slightly responsible for this aggression on the part of the aliens.

The single happy thought I had caroming around in my brainpan was the realization that none of my adjuncts appeared to be aware of the small but critical role I'd played in this growing fiasco. That meant I only had two snitches to worry about, should events go tits-up completely.

When the charging mass of enemy troops was no more than a hundred meters away, the Varus soldiers finally opened fire. The characteristic snap, crack and whine of rifle-fire ripped through the air and the tall grasses.

Some of the hairy aliens fell. They rolled, tumbled and crashed into one another—but then those behind them simply leaped over the fallen and kept on coming.

So great was the vitality of these warriors that those we figured were dead leaped up again and continued limping toward our lines.

Leeson whistled. "These dudes are hard to put down," he said.

"They're a whole lot of trouble," Harris agreed. He addressed his determined heavy platoon. "Now, I don't want any of you boys holding back when they get down here," Harris admonished. "Sure, they're just primitive locals, but if they get in amongst us, we're going to be feeling some pain."

As if to reaffirm his point, the now ragged wave of primitives hurled a shower of darts. They'd reached a point where they were perhaps fifty meters away from the human lines, and they definitely could throw these deadly weapons that far.

The heavy projectiles lofted high and came hurtling down. They flew with great accuracy and power. The aliens even seemed to know how to give them a nice little spin for a perfect flight.

The darts chunked into the Varus troopers up on the ridge. A dozen were taken out within seconds, then two dozen more. Most of these were lights—men who screamed with agony and shock. As they were at the peak of the ridge, their bodies came flying and tumbling down to greet us. Sometimes, their helmets were transfixed with one of the heavy darts rammed right through their faceplate. On other occasions, they took the strike through the throat or through the chest.

In response, the Varus troopers stepped up their rate of fire. They blazed away on full-auto, holding nothing back. They tore up the grasses and shredded the aliens. The battle soon turned into a great, raging din. Men screamed with open throats, without even knowing they were doing it. In return, the deeper, hoarser voices of the aliens sounded like animals.

"Oh, boy…" Leeson said. "I recommend we pull out right now, McGill."

"I second the motion," Harris told me.

I didn't answer for about two seconds. My two adjuncts were highly experienced. They'd both been in this legion before I was. Between the three of us, we probably had damned near two centuries of experience in combat on dozens of worlds. With all that said and done, I didn't want to break and run for it—not yet.

For one thing, it would be deserting my comrades in arms at the very moment when they needed me most. For another, after witnessing the sheer speed and ferocity of these aliens, I knew if they wanted to, they would catch us no matter how far and how fast we ran.

"Hold your positions, men," I shouted. "If the line up on the ridge breaks, that's when we get involved, and not before."

Men grumbled, and they sweated, and they shifted their grips on their rifles. They cursed my mother, and they prayed to their gods, hoping against hope that we would be spared.

Although our Varus troops killed hundreds—perhaps even a thousand, they couldn't put them all down. Hurtling furry shapes leaped in the air, bounding that last ten meters directly into the lines of our Varus soldiers.

Their tactics were both unique and highly effective. Rather than coming straight on into our lines and leaping at the man they'd been charging toward the entire time, they instead launched themselves diagonally at the last moment.

Coming in from an oblique angle, they struck down their targets with ease. Our troops were firing straight into the charging masses—they never seemed to expect a two-hundred-kilo angry monster to tackle their flank.

The moment of impact alone often broke the lightly armored and the weak. Men and women tumbled down the rocky slope, ribs crushed, spines broken and skulls caved in.

Once on that line, wounded or not, the berserker troops flailed wildly and struck anyone they could reach.

When our losses reached around fifty percent, our lines folded. Hopeless though it might be, green recruits turned and desperately ran down the hill, many of them dropping their snap-rifles in the process. Some tripped or rolled. They tumbled and broke themselves on the boulders. Others were caught in the back by angry aliens, who were now hurling rocks down from the top of the ridge.

"That's our cue," I said. "Fire at will!"

A shower of snap-rifle fire and heavy bolts from Harris' crew struck the aliens who were screeching in victory on top of the ridge. Some of them were still chasing down survivors, but we shot them down.

The ragged enemy force was replaced by fresh aliens, but after we'd knocked down perhaps fifty more of their warriors, they retreated.

"Let's go after those pricks," Harris said.

"Nope," I responded. "We're going to hold our lines here, just like we were ordered to do."

Harris tossed me an evil, blood-eyed glance, but he didn't argue.

"Clane!" I shouted. "Advance upslope but stay off the ridgeline. Carlos, you take your bios to the dead and wounded. Touch the tapper of every fallen man—and grab every gun you can."

It was time to loot-and-scoot, a set of rules laid down long ago by the legions. When a man was down, dead or dying, what mattered most was to record his information, so he could be revived later on. After that, the next priority was to gather as much of his gear as you could.

The legion could replace bones, flesh and even the minds of these troops for the most part—but their guns cost real money.

The soldiers who had survived the attack staggered to our lines for protection. The last surviving centurion from the three units that had been defeated on the ridge approached me. He was bloody and sweating, and his helmet was gone. He had a glassy look in his eye and gore on his face. Fortunately, not all of it was his.

"Centurion McGill?" he called out to me.

"Hey, Pete," I said.

His real name was Petraki, or something like that, but most of us just called him Pete for short. He winced at the name because he didn't like it, but he didn't say anything.

He offered me a bloody glove to shake instead. I took that hand, and I shook it hard. I gave him a big grin as well.

"McGill," he said, "I can't believe it. I know everybody says you're an asshole and a loose cannon, but you saved our butts today. I think I would have lost my entire command if it wasn't for you guys backing us up."

"Just remember to tell Graves about that when we get back to camp," I told him. He nodded in agreement, shaking away the sweat and blood.

We picked up the pieces—quite literally in the case of some of our more heavily dismembered soldiers, and within ten minutes we were retreating back into the forest. We shot the wounded who were too far gone and dragged the rest.

While we headed toward the main encampment of the legion, Petraki reported the disaster to headquarters. That was a kindness, as I didn't want the grim duty of informing Graves concerning the battle. Petraki received an earful from the primus, and I overheard it on command chat.

"You mean to tell me," Graves said, "I sent in the 3rd, the 4th, the 5th and the 6th, but all I got back is the 3rd and half of the 6th?"

"That's not quite right, sir," Petraki assured Graves. "I've got at least a quarter of the 4th and the 5th with us as well. Their centurions, unfortunately, are dead and gone."

"Pick up the morph-rifles. Pick up the belchers," Graves steamed. "Don't make this more expensive than it's already become."

Petraki agreed, but before he could acknowledge the command, Graves' unhappy face was gone.

I was grinning inside my helmet. It was nice to hear someone else getting reamed besides just yours truly. I figured I was going to have to deliver an extra ration of booze to Kivi and Natasha tonight to buy their silence. I assumed convincing them to keep quiet wouldn't be that difficult as, after all, it had been their overzealous drone-piloting that had triggered the rage of the locals. Beyond a doubt, they were material participants.

Feeling fairly pleased with 3rd Unit's contribution to the last battle, I couldn't stop clapping soldiers on the back.

Nobody could deny the fact we'd killed triple the number of aliens compared to the men we'd lost. At least those bastards knew they'd been in a fight this time. We no longer looked like the giant wimps we'd resembled the first time we tangled with them.

"Um, Centurion?" Kivi said. "Sir?"

"What is it, Kivi?"

"The aliens—I think they're following us."

I stared at her. Then, I studied the buzzer feeds, and I had to agree. There were an alarming number of shapes that were now moving into the forests in our wake.

Pausing at the battleground, I watched as they picked through the corpses—either ripping apart human bodies in a rage or puzzling over our equipment. One alien tried out a snap-rifle, shooting his fellow in the leg and then hooting with laughter about it.

"Look at that," I said. "These guys can laugh!"

Kivi didn't look amused. "If they learn how to use snap-rifles, they're going to be really dangerous," she said.

"Then we shouldn't have left any snap-rifles behind," I said. "Come on, Varus! Let's pick it up! If you're wounded, ask for a shoulder to lean on. We're going to run for camp, and the devil take the hindmost."

The survivors didn't need any further urging. Everyone picked up their boots and plunged them down again, not stopping until we got home to the encampment and the rest of Legion Varus.

-25-

When we finally got back to camp, we were tired and beat up. I put my troops into recuperation mode, sending the worst injuries to Blue Bunker. Those sad-sacks limped away through the mud with heavy hearts. They knew as well as I did some of them would be executed and recycled. It always seemed like a rip-off when you escaped a bad death in battle—only to have some wicked bio specialist shiv you with a needle in the end.

Graves came out to meet me in person a few hours later. He reviewed my heavily edited and thoroughly redacted after-action report. Then he did a lot of frowning and nodding. At last, he heaved a sigh.

"Well... as best I can tell, you followed your orders perfectly. The role your unit was to play was needed and, in fact, it was critical. Do you see how things can go, McGill—I mean when you listen to your commander and avoid going off half-cocked?" He broke off then as another centurion walked up and interrupted him.

"Half-cocked?" Centurion Manfred said. "I won't have it said! In McGill's case, everything's always fully-cocked, Primus."

Manfred grinned at me, and I grinned back. He was probably the only centurion in this legion I could call a true friend.

Graves, however, didn't seem to be amused. "As I was saying," he continued, "you stuck to your mission parameters. You did your job, and you saved three units of men—more importantly, you saved their critical gear. Overall, the mission was a disaster, of course, with a near fifty percent loss rate. But as far as I can tell, you did your part to mitigate the losses."

"I surely did, sir," I agreed.

I smiled, and I beamed, and I happily accepted every compliment I could get. When Graves was done dishing them up, I couldn't resist asking one more question.

"Primus Graves, sir?" I said, "I was wondering if you might know who was so shit-off stupid as to set that avalanche of aliens into motion?"

Graves shook his head. "We haven't figured that out yet. I watched that whole front line too—tapping into one buzzer after another. I never saw anyone provoke the aliens."

"Oh…" I said, feeling slightly concerned. I was really glad he'd been watching through the buzzer feed of the other units—and he hadn't chosen to check into my units' drone fleet. If he had, he'd surely have seen incriminating video that would clearly implicate me and my techs.

Outwardly, of course, I showed no signs of these concerns. I just grinned and shook my fool head.

"Don't worry, sir," I said. "You'll figure it out. Somebody screwed that pooch. If I were you, I'd be inclined to carry out a personal grilling for the centurions leading the 4th, 5th and 6th."

Graves nodded thoughtfully. "I might have to do that…" he said, and then he left us.

Manfred studied me quizzically after Graves made his exit. "It was you that did it, wasn't it?" he asked.

As I said, he was my friend. He knew me well—and he wasn't a nice guy despite what his British accent might imply at first.

"Shh," I said, hushing him. "Shut the hell up."

Manfred hooted and guffawed and slapped his oversized knee. "I knew it! When a mission goes tits-up, it's always McGill's fault. *Always!*"

I shushed him again, until he finally stopped laughing and carrying on. To buy his silence, I bought him a row of beers at a makeshift bar the troops had set up in the forest.

"As it turns out," he told me, "Graves is pleased with me as well."

I look stunned. "How's that possible?"

"It's a rare day, I'll give you that. Essentially, when he sent us out to patrol with the other group…"

"What other group?"

He shook his head. "You never read the briefings, do you?"

"That's a damned-dirty lie."

"Sure it is, McGill. Anyway, if you'd read the briefings, you'd know that the other units in this cohort went off in the other direction. We ended up in a river valley. The aliens had some fishing boats down there. It was really quite quaint, actually."

"Let me guess," I said. "They ambushed you, too?"

"Nope," he said, shaking his head, "but the approach of so many troops to the fishing village terrified the locals. They stampeded out of their huts and ran away into the forest. This was seen as yet another diplomatic breach—even though I don't know what our troops could have done differently. I mean, if people run away when you approach them, it's not really your fault now, is it?"

I frowned. I didn't like the sound of this. The locals were both frightened and violently angry with us every time we attempted to make contact. What's more, they were definitely in league with the dogmen. I was now suspecting that the Clavers were involved in the arming of these primitive people. They might even be actively turning them against us.

"Well, if your group's mission was a failure as well," I said, "why is Graves happy with you?"

"Because he figured I would screw it up. Just like you, he put me in the rear of the formation." Manfred shrugged. "My unit had nothing to do with terrifying any of the locals. As soon as that happened, everybody retreated. The short version is that the only reputation besides yours that came out of this clusterfuck without damage was mine."

"Huh…" I said, thinking that over. "That is unusual, if not downright unprecedented. I don't think you and I have ever been the fair-haired boys before."

"It's frigging never happened before. Let's have another round."

Manfred and I had several more sour brews before we parted ways to go back to our individual unit camps. There, I found a posse of panicky women waiting for me.

Leading the pack was Kivi. At her side was Natasha, and they'd somehow recruited Della—my baby mama and ghost scout—to join them.

I'd lost track of Della during our retreat from the rocky plateau where the aliens had charged our lines. Apparently, judging by her wet hair and foul expressions, she hadn't survived the battle.

These women had known me for decades. In the past, I'd experienced certain questionable moments with all three of them. There's little that can strike more fear into a man's heart than facing a crowd of ex-girlfriends, but I put on a welcoming and innocent expression.

"Hey, ladies! Did I forget someone's birthday or something?"

"Hardly, James," Della said, leading the assault. "We have to talk."

"Aw geez…" I said. "Do we really?"

"Yes," Kivi said. "We do."

My eyes landed on Natasha next. She hadn't spoken yet. In fact, she was studying the dirt. To my eyes, she looked like she was feeling guilty.

That only made sense, mind you. First of all, that was the kind of emotional response that came naturally to Natasha, and secondly, there was the undeniable fact that she'd flown a drone into a hive full of aliens and lit them off like firecrackers earlier today.

Della noted my roving eyes. She followed my gaze and frowned at Natasha.

"Oh, come on, Elkin," she said. "You had plenty to say a minute ago."

Kivi was quick to support Della. Which made Natasha angry. She told them both to mind their own business.

After that, all three of them erupted into a fearsome squabble.

I'm no expert on expressions, voice tones or even appropriate responses, but I can always tell when there's trouble in the henhouse. "Ladies, ladies!" I said, "there's no reason to squawk and argue and carry on. There's enough of me to go around for all of you."

It was an unwise statement, and somewhere inside of me a glimmer of sense knew that, but I also was about six drinks in. I'd had a long day, and I didn't much care what any of these girls thought about my part in today's activities.

Today, Graves was calling me a star of virtue—and I kind of liked that. In fact, I planned to keep it that way.

They all glared at me. "That's an inappropriate comment, Centurion," Natasha dared to say.

"Aw, come on," I hooted. "I'm just joking with you. Let's step aside a little bit from the rest of this crowd."

By this time, many prying eyes had taken notice of our tense huddle, and I didn't want anyone who didn't already know the score to learn the truth. Accordingly, I marched them off some distance away from the campfires, the bug-zappers, and the plastic tents.

We squatted on a giant, fallen log with veins that were no longer green and pulsing but now flaccid and gray in death. I looked at Della first as she seemed to be the angriest of the three. I figured that was just sour grapes about having died in the mud earlier today.

"I know it was our unit that caused the disaster today," she said. "We all know it."

"Uh-huh," I said, unsurprised by the fact they all knew the truth. If there was one thing these women weren't good at, it was keeping secrets. "So what?"

"So what?" Della demanded. "So, what if Graves finds out? What if someone tells him it was Natasha's fault?"

Natasha looked up suddenly at that. She cast an acid glance in Della's direction. "My fault? Says who?"

Della looked back at her. "Yes, your fault. You two flew the buzzers, didn't you?"

"That's right," Natasha said, glancing at Kivi, "but Kivi is normally in charge of our buzzer squadron."

"What?" Kivi squawked. "You were flying that damned thing, Natasha, not me."

The girls fell to arguing again. I upraised two large hands and finally got them to pay attention.

"Ladies, ladies…" I said. "Look, here's the key to this whole thing. None of us here are going to tell anybody anything. Natasha, if you haven't already, you're going to delete that frigging video."

All three of them gaped at me.

"What?" Natasha said. "That's important intel, James."

"It's a flogging offense to delete any file without authorization," Kivi added.

"What kind of scout would I be?" Della asked, "if I went around deleting anything I didn't like from my scouting missions?"

"Okay. Okay," I said. "Let's just edit it a little bit—blur out the ending, or cut out the most important ten seconds… I don't care."

None of them seemed happy with that—but they were also unable to come up with a better solution.

"There's another issue," Della said finally. "It's the reason why I have joined this protest group."

I frowned at that. I didn't like the sound of it. "What's that?"

"Remember yesterday, James, when you borrowed both of our stealth suits? Both mine and Cooper's?"

"Yeah, yeah, sure."

"Well, what with my being a scout, and these two being tech specialists…" Della said, not meeting my eye. "We kind of found out where you went, and who you went with." All three of the women were looking at me now with accusatory eyes.

My mouth hung low for a moment. My brain was operating more slowly than usual tonight. That was probably due to fatigue and alcohol—but then I had it. "What… you girls spied on me?"

"I wouldn't call it that," Della said. "I wasn't even alive at the time." She glanced at the other two, who were studying the ground.

Obviously, they'd flown buzzers after me and bio-Centurion Evelyn Thompson during our little side mission.

"Okay," I said, "again, so what?"

"So, we were concerned that perhaps you and Centurion Thompson were secretly seeing each other, and we wanted to tell you that none of us approve."

"Oh, for crying out loud," I said. "First of all, it's none of your damned beeswax—not any one of the three of you."

They looked sullen, but they offered no arguments.

"Secondly, that's not what's happening—that's not what happened at all." Then, I explained to them how Centurion Thompson had requested that I escort her out into the forest to check out the corpse of the fallen alien.

This had them all puzzled—except for Natasha, who seemed intrigued. "She wanted to get some genetic material, you say?"

"That's right. You can go ask her yourself."

"I think I'll do just that. I've been wondering about these aliens ever since we saw the dogmen in their midst. Did you notice they look rather similar to one another?"

"Uh," I said, thinking that over "Yeah. Yeah, I guess that's probably true."

The witch-hunt broke up after that. I don't think any one of the four of us were satisfied with the results. The girls had gotten no promises, no admissions, and precious little fresh information. For my part, I was somewhat rankled that three noncoms saw fit to belabor their officer over both official and private matters.

This was just the sort of thing that happened after a unit fought together on dozens of campaigns for dozens of years. Your relationships tended to go far beyond ranks and formalities.

The situation was partly my fault, of course, as I'd been intimate with all three of them in the past. That sort of thing is always destructive to discipline, but it was an ongoing scourge in a mixed-sex military like ours.

Seeing their backsides was a sheer relief—and not just for my eyes. All in all, I considered the whole day to be a win.

Yawning, I retired early. I was blessed with a cot and a private tent to put over it, as I was the unit commander. As I dozed and reviewed the day, I had to admit, things had gone relatively well.

With the possible exception of my three nosy specialists, no one was really angry with me. Graves thought I was a rule-follower. Manfred was impressed with my style. I'd even made a bit of progress rekindling with Centurion Thompson. Yep—all in all, it was a stellar day.

Just as I began to pass out, however, something began irritating my forearm. Even when I silenced it, my damned tapper tended to buzz and carry on, vibrating the hairs and tickling the skin.

I finally sat up with a loud grunt of irritation. "Who's calling me now?" I demanded, thumbing the thing into life.

A small, pretty face looked up at me. It was Centurion Evelyn Thompson, and she looked concerned.

"James?" she said. "Did you send Natasha over to my lab to snoop around?"

"Uh," I said, thinking that over. "Nope, I most definitely did not."

I could tell by her expression that she didn't believe me, but I didn't much care.

"Well, when she comes back and tells you what I told her, just remember that none of this is confirmed yet."

"Huh?" I began to say, but she stabbed her own finger down at her tapper and shut off the channel.

Frowning and blinking away the sleep, I stared at my tapper for a moment. Then I stretched back out and began falling asleep again.

Next thing I knew, there was a rustling at my tent's flimsy door.

"What the hell is it now?" I demanded.

Natasha poked her way in. She looked around warily as if expecting that I wasn't alone.

"What is it specialist?" I asked.

"James, we have to talk about the findings."

"What findings?"

"From Centurion Thompson's lab… she's done a full genetic analysis."

"Yeah? So what?"

She looked at me patiently. "I know you're no biologist, James."

"You can say that again. My knowledge of biology is purely amateurish and practical in nature."

She twisted up her lips, but she didn't comment on my joke. "Whatever. Listen, James, this is important. Thompson has discovered a match in our database."

"A match for what?"

"The genotypes and the phenotypes."

I stared at her, and I blinked a couple times, then I cracked a wide smile. "That's just great. I'll tell you what—why don't you write this all up in a report? Then, come on back first thing in the morning, and we will circle back on it, okay?"

"No, no. Listen James," she said. "Just listen. I'm talking about the dogmen. The samples we have on record of their DNA, and the DNA samples she's been analyzing from the dead alien in the forest... You see, they actually have a similar physiognomy—that's what we call similar phenotypes. But that doesn't mean that much. Sometimes, two creatures can look similar, but actually be genetically quite diverse. Conversely, two creatures can be very close genetically, but not look like one another at all. Like with mice, for instance."

"Huh? What about mice?"

"Did you know that mice are actually quite close genetically to humans?"

"I sure as hell didn't."

"Well, they are. That's why they use them in lab experiments all the time. But anyway, Thompson discovered that the dogmen and the local aliens are related—too related for it to be a coincidence. In fact, we think that one is really an altered genetic offshoot of the other."

"You don't say... Well, I have to tell you Natasha, that's absolutely riveting. If you could just tell me about this over breakfast... Let's have a special meeting, shall we?"

She glared at me a bit. "James, you just aren't getting it. The Clavers created the dogmen, right?"

"That's what they told me."

"Well, the species they created them from are these aliens right here on this planet. What we're looking at is the primitive base stock for the dogmen—and maybe other synthetic species that they've been designing. They're not just cloning themselves with alterations anymore. They're cloning other species with alterations, too. That breaks all sorts of Galactic rules and Hegemony laws as well."

I thought that over, frowning. She was right. That sort of thing was far more than a flogging offense. It was more on the order of an extinction offense.

"Don't you see James?" Natasha was whispering urgently. "The Clavers must be involved here. They've got a stake in this planet, not just Rigel."

I nodded, thinking it over. "That stands to reason," I said. "Why don't you go and write it all up, make a report, and send it on to Primus Graves or even Winslade? Knock yourself out."

Natasha shook her head. "No, I'm not going to do that."

"Well, why the hell not?"

"Because I talked to Thompson, and I promised her I wouldn't. That's why she let me look at her data."

"Oh..." I said, thinking about the angry phone call I'd gotten from Evelyn. I'd almost forgotten about it already. "Why doesn't she want to tell the brass?"

"I don't know, but you've got to get her to do it. It's critical intel."

"I only just avoided taking the blame for a military disaster yesterday. Can't I enjoy that for a bit?"

"The information is in your hands," Natasha said, "I've sent you the reports and everything. You deal with it."

Then she staged a walkout, and I let her go.

On the screen of my tapper, I saw a huge text file. It was full of big words and boredom.

I sighed. It was just like Natasha to write up a big scientific paper and then throw it into my lap.

Stretching out onto my bunk one last time, I managed to go to sleep. It took me almost ten whole minutes to get there. That's a sure sign, in my case, that I was stressed and annoyed.

-26-

All my feelings of wellbeing and contentment ended early the next morning. It was the women who got me in trouble, and I should've seen it coming. I really should've.

At 0600, I was yawning awake and scratching myself in front of a fire with a hot cup of coffee in my hands.

Dawn, that was when the 31 Orionis was at its best. The mornings were cool and relatively bug-free, and today I dared to think the place was tolerable.

But then my tapper started going bananas on my arm. In fact, it started talking to me all by itself.

"James? James!" It was none other than Galina Turov.

"Hey there, Imperator," I said. "I thought you guys were off on *Scorpio* having a little sightseeing tour at the far end of the star system."

Galina gave me an unpleasant look. "I've been talking to Centurion Thompson."

I winced, and I grimaced. I tried to produce a smile and a nod, but it just wasn't in me. When there were secrets in the air, some of us just aren't built to contain them within our own skulls.

"I see by that guilty look on your face that you know this already," she said.

As a matter of fact, I hadn't known that Galina was speaking to Centurion Thompson, but it made good sense that she would. Years ago, Galina and Evelyn had an unholy pact together. The primary goal of which seemed to be prodding and spying upon one James McGill.

"Hey," I said. "That's a good thing, right? Catching up on old times with Evelyn...?"

"Hell no," Galina said. "There are no good times to catch up on between that woman and I, but she did tell me that you and she had gone on an investigatory mission and made critical discoveries. Why wasn't I informed of this?"

"Whoa, whoa, whoa," I said, lifting a big hand between me and my offending tapper. I managed to partly block out the glaring visage of the imperator. "That's not how things went at all. I helped her, yes. She asked for an escort, so I took her on a hike. I escorted her through the dangerous jungle, so she could get her samples. If she's done some fantastic scientific mumbo-jumbo that's got nothing to do with me. You know me, I barely got a C in high school biology, and the only reason I passed at all was because the girl sitting next to me—"

"Shut up, McGill," she said, interrupting me. "I'm not in the mood to listen to another one of your bullshit stories. You should have informed me about this. Evelyn should have informed me about this *immediately*. I can't believe I'm hearing about it a day late."

"Well, don't get mad at me," I said. "I can't make heads or tails of all these spectrographic genetic charts and stuff like that."

She continued to glare for a few moments, but then her face softened. "Yes, of course. Of course, you have no idea what she discovered—but you were there. You were out there, and we talked to Abigail Claver about this on *Scorpio*."

"No, we didn't," I said. "She told us not to come out here to Jungle World. She didn't say a damned thing about ape men and dog men being related, or the fact that apparently the Clavers have been raiding this planet to carry out genetic experiments for who knows how many years."

Galina frowned. I had succeeded in planting a seed of doubt in her mind. "Okay," she said, thinking it over. "Okay. I'm just upset. I don't like it when underlings know things I don't know and then keep it from me."

"That just didn't happen, sir. I don't think anybody knew this until yesterday."

"All right. All right. The main thing is—what are we going to do about it?"

I thought that over, and I gave myself a scratch while I was doing it. One finger slipped into my faceplate, which was flipped up. The finger worked on my chin, and there was plenty of scratching to do. When you're in a hot, sweaty environment and wearing a space helmet all the time, well sir, things could get kind of itchy…

"Aren't you going to say anything?" Galina demanded finally.

"Huh? Actually, I thought it was your turn to talk."

Galina rolled her eyes. "All right," she said. "All right, I've got an idea. What we'll do is set up another meeting with Abigail."

"We will?" I said, startled. "Uh… how are we going to do that?"

She kept on talking like she hadn't even heard me. "The problem is," she said, "she won't be very trusting—not after I murdered her to conclude our last meeting."

"I can't say as I would blame her for that, sir."

"So…" she said, looking up out of my tapper, "it's got to be you."

"Me, sir? What would I do, and how would I do it, exactly?"

"James, there's new technology that you don't know about. These days, we're able to trace the source of a deep-link transmission."

"Wow, really?" I said.

Of course, I knew about this. Natasha had, in fact, pioneered such an effort. It didn't surprise me that now, years later, Central was finally catching up with Natasha's amateur efforts.

"Yes, it's a big secret. Don't pass it on."

"It's in the vault, sir," I said. "You got my word. Cross my heart and—"

"Shut up," she said again. "I'm trying to think. What we'll do is run a backtrace on some of Abigail's latest deep-link transmissions. She contacted us that way when she set up our initial meeting on *Scorpio*. Then, we'll send you to her transmission point, wherever she is, to talk to her."

"Oh..." I was beginning to dislike the sound of this. "Imperator? This is starting to sound like a solid perming for one James McGill."

She shook her head. "It won't be. What we'll do is use the casting couch, and we'll watch you. Just make sure you die promptly after you're done talking to Abigail and get whatever you can out of her."

My face was beginning to itch and wince again all by itself. So far, I hadn't died a single time on Jungle World, and I was starting to like the feel of this body.

But here I was, just a couple of days into this deployment, and Galina had come up with a sure-fire way for me to suicide myself—just for the sake of satisfying her curiosity.

She talked on and on for a while, detailing various aspects of the plan, but I wasn't really interested. All I knew was I was going to have to go through the gateway posts that connected our legion's campsite to *Scorpio*. There, on Gray Deck, they had a casting couch. After strapping me in, they'd send me to my doom in style.

Eventually, she stopped talking and let me get started. Cursing and muttering, I packed a ruck, shouldered it, and then headed toward a row of bunkers with puff-crete roofs. Gold Bunker had been hastily constructed in the center of the camp.

I hadn't walked two hundred meters before I got a call from Graves. Apparently, he'd set a tracker on my whereabouts—or maybe someone else had, and they'd snitched on me.

Tracers, buzzers, deeplink backtraces... Hell, it was getting harder and harder every year for a man to get off on his own to do something fun.

"McGill?" Graves said, talking out of my arm before I'd even acknowledged the call.

"Yes, sir?" I sighed wearily.

"Where the hell do you think you're going? Why do you have a ruck under your arm?"

"Sorry sir, but I'm under orders from a higher source."

"I don't need a load of your bullshit right now, McGill," Graves fumed.

"It's God's honest truth, sir."

"If you're not the most maddening…" He busied himself while he muttered. "I'm putting you on hold for a second. Don't go anywhere."

I tried not to smirk. I knew there was nothing he could do about it.

"Well… I'll be damned…" he said at length. "I've questioned the imperator, and she's backing you up. At least this time, your cause appears to be legit, but it's still irritating. I'd already decided that you and Manfred were going to lead the march as we move out from this camp and advance to our next objective."

I stopped walking and stared at my tapper. "We're moving out? We're breaking camp?"

"That's what I said. We've managed to revive enough of our troops now and gather enough of our gear that we're ready to advance."

"Where are we headed, sir?" I asked.

"Toward that big, red crystal-thing—the thing that's embedded in the side of this godforsaken planet. If we can neutralize it from the ground, whatever the hell it is, then *Scorpio* can move in close, and we can get down to the business of conquering this planet once and for all."

I wasn't so sure about the "once and for all" part, but I did understand Graves and his sentiment. We'd been stuck here on the ground, organizing and scouting, but we really hadn't done much of anything since we'd landed.

In the meantime, it seemed that the locals had been gathering a force to oppose us. If we were going to actually go on the offensive and do something about that weird alien base, which had fired gravity-beams at *Scorpio* and destroyed several of our lifters, then we were going to have to get on the stick.

"How long of a march is it that we're talking about, sir?"

"Something like two hundred kilometers. A good three to four-day walk for a fit Varus man."

I bared my teeth. I couldn't imagine slogging two hundred kilometers through this jungle. The landscape was worse than anything I'd been through back on Earth—worse even than the Amazon. There were countless swamps, wide, slow-moving rivers and an infinite number of vine-covered trees. All the while, no doubt, we were going to be getting pelted by the locals with their helpful weapons. It didn't sound like fun to me. It almost made riding the casting couch sound positive.

"Why don't we just take the lifters, sir? Just load everybody up and take a couple of trips to get to a safer, closer location?"

Graves shook his head. "We can't really do that," he said. "The enemy base is too dangerous. Sure, we could probably cut off a hundred kilometers or so, but the brass isn't willing to do it. They don't want to take the chance of losing another pricey lifter. Keep in mind, each of those landing craft costs something north of a trillion credits."

I whistled long and low. "That is a big chunk of change," I admitted.

In fact, one lifter was probably worth all the infantry equipment it took to equip everybody in Legion Varus. The brass hated to lose snap-rifles, belchers or even spacesuits—but when you compared all that to just a single lifter...

The thing they cared about the least was flesh and blood. Soldiers on the march—guys like me—could be printed out like sheets of paper.

Graves cut the call short, and I contacted Leeson. I informed him he was in charge of the unit until I got back. I didn't tell him about having to move out and march within a few hours. Graves would be informing him on that score at any moment. I figured it would be better for Leeson's state of mind if he didn't know he was going to have to go on a two-hundred-kilometer hike starting real soon now.

After roaming around Gold Bunker for a bit, I found a set of gateway posts right where I expected they would be—in the middle of the place, which was right where the brass always hung out.

As I tramped down the puff-crete steps into the gloom of the bunker's lower level, I was greeted by primus-level officers with wrinkled noses and sneering glances of appraisal. No one seemed happy to see me, and they appeared to believe that I stank.

Now, in their defense, I probably did reek a bit. The mud on this world wasn't the freshest, and it was all over my boots.

Paying them no heed, I passed up all the fancy-pants officers, who although they called themselves centurions and adjuncts, were really no more than portable hogs. They were really glorified secretaries who serviced the legion's top-level commanders.

At last, I approached a set of standing, silvery posts. They were made of metal, but there was also a nimbus—a sort of an electrical field—that surrounded them.

The gateway was active, and it swirled with colors. Today, the color was gold with a hint of red in it. I didn't much care, and I wanted to get things over with.

As I never wanted to think about what I was actually doing, I ignored various questions and complaints from the hog wannabes who surrounded the gateway. Jostling them all aside, I walked between the posts.

I heard sort of a bug-zapper sound, and I was immediately transported to *Scorpio*. Only a wisp of vaporized smoke remained in my wake.

-27-

It didn't take me long to find Imperator Galina Turov. That's because she actually found me.

Galina was cute, if a little bit on the small side, with a near perfect body. Her attractiveness mainly came from the simple fact she'd discovered a fountain of youth. She'd refused to update her body scans for many decades—and she also made a point of getting herself killed occasionally, whenever she needed freshening-up.

To my way of thinking, it was a foolproof anti-aging plan. Sure, it was a bit unpleasant to be dying every couple of years—usually in a horrific and violent fashion. Her system of beauty treatments wasn't for the squeamish, that's true. But Galina was the kind of woman who would put up with damn-near anything to maintain her looks.

When I stepped out of the gateway posts and coalesced out of a swirl of vapor into a two-meter-tall man, I recoiled and almost stepped back through the posts.

Galina was right there, arms crossed, staring up at me. "There you are," she said.

I looked around at the techs to either side of the posts. They were supposed to keep people out of the area of immediate danger.

They shrugged helplessly and looked slightly regretful. I understood. Galina outranked them by a factor of a thousand, and worse, she had a bad temper.

"James?" she said. "Why do I get the feeling that every woman down on Jungle World is following you around?"

"Huh...?" I said. "I don't rightly know... Paranoia, maybe?"

She didn't appreciate my joke. She crooked one small finger and walked away. I followed her like a faithful pit bull until I realized she was leading me entirely off Gray Deck.

"Hey now," I said, "you don't have some special plans for old McGill, do you?"

"What do you mean, James?"

"What I mean is, I thought I was going to harness-up and fly off to find out where these dogmen are coming from."

"We know where they come from. The Clavers breed them—or manufacture them—whatever. What I want you to find out is what Abigail Claver is planning to do here on this planet. Did they trick us into coming here? Are they trying to protect something valuable we don't understand?"

"Uh..." I said, "I've got no clue."

She made a frustrated noise. "I know you don't know—and I also noticed you never answered my first question."

"Really...? Could you tell me what that was again?"

"About the women, James... I've been watching you through my tapper. My tracer apps are always with you. Always. I know where you've been. I know who you've been with."

I found this quite alarming. I didn't let on how much her words freaked me out, but I wasn't a man who could be called "innocent" by any sense of the word.

"Well then," I said, "I've got nothing to worry about. If you've been keeping tabs on me, you know that I've been utterly faithful. One hundred percent pure."

"Shut up," she said, and I did so.

I followed her off Gray Deck, wondering exactly how all this had started. I had to be up to something like a six-pack of women who were keeping tabs on me at this moment. That was unusual even for me, especially when I hadn't really done much of anything to deserve it—at least not on this campaign, and at least not so far.

Galina was talking as I followed along, of course, but I wasn't listening. While walking behind her, I'd always found myself captivated by the motions of her posterior. She wore tight, tight clothing. I was never quite sure if she did this out of a sense of vanity, or some sort of a need to show herself off. I was pretty certain she enjoyed hypnotizing any males in her vicinity.

Whatever the case was, it was very effective. In the end, when we finally halted and stood in front of a Gold Deck conference room, Galina looked up at me expectantly. Clearly, she was under the false impression I'd been paying rapt attention to her overly long speech. She really ought to have known me better by now.

"Well...?" she said. "You're supposed to go in first."

"Oh yeah—yeah, right," I said, and I pushed the door open, having no idea what I was going to see inside.

To my surprise and relief there was only one individual in the conference room. It was Consul Drusus. He was looking all metallic and shiny, like a golden robot—or maybe a statue.

"Here he is, sir," Galina said from behind me. "I've already briefed him. He's all yours."

"Just a moment, Imperator," Drusus said. "I thought you were going to join us."

Galina and Drusus had a short stare-down. I could tell that Galina was trying to exit the room as quickly as possible.

Since Drusus outranked pretty much everybody in the Heavens and on Earth, I could tell that wasn't going to happen. A suggestion from him was tantamount to a command from the Almighty.

Her mouth formed a tiny, pink, pouty rosebud for a moment, and then she forced a smile. "Of course, sir," she said, and she stepped into the conference room after me.

I clomped to the table in the middle of the room and sat myself down on the biggest, comfiest chair I could find. It was slightly larger and more padded than the rest of them, and I could tell it was special-made. I had to wonder if the one fat guy who ever attended such meetings, Praetor Wurtenberger, had ordered it to be constructed for him. As there was no way of telling, I just sat down, enjoyed the seat and smiled.

"Hey, Consul," I said, pointing at Drusus, "you're wearing one of those suits of stardust armor right now, aren't you?"

Drusus smiled. "Indeed I am. It's a pleasure to have some personal protection I have faith in."

"But uh... did you have some kind of an accident in the art department? It looks like you've colored-up your armor. Is that like... gold paint or something?"

Drusus shrugged. He was indeed as golden and shiny as a Las Vegas statue. "My support personnel thought that combat armor was perhaps a bit too militant for my appearance, so they did indeed disguise it," he said. "I've long admired the survivability that you've demonstrated over and over again in this kind of armor, McGill."

"That's right, sir. You can't go wrong with star-stuff."

Looking over Drusus and his new armor, I couldn't help but admire it. You could tell even though it was dipped in some kind of metallic coating, it was the same stardust that I was wearing. Its natural color was a deep, lightless black, the color of shadows in deep caves.

Belying its unusual color, the identifying characteristics were all there, giving it away. It was in the way the material folded, the way it moved. It was thick, but not so thick as to prevent free motion. It was rubbery and formfitting. The closest thing I could think of would be a scuba diver's diving suit.

What really mattered, though, was its impenetrability. I knew without asking why Drusus was wearing it. A man in his position couldn't be too careful. After all, only months ago I'd witnessed him standing up to the Ruling Council of Hegemony. He'd refused to step down from his leadership role.

That automatically meant he'd made some mighty big enemies in high places. Who knew when the assassin's bullet was coming for him?

Reflecting on it, I thought I was probably safer flirting with the dogmen and the ape-aliens back down on Jungle World.

"...are you listening to me, McGill?" Drusus asked.

I squirmed a bit in my nicely padded chair. "I certainly am, sir. I certainly am. I heard every word."

"Good," he said. "Now, when you meet with these individuals, I want you to be circumspect, but firm."

My mouth sagged open just a fraction. I wanted to say, "what individuals?" but I held that back. It was almost like holding back a sneeze.

"They're not Earth's friends," he continued, "but they're not our worst enemies. We've had good and bad dealings with all of them. They claim to have something critical to tell me and I, of course, cannot afford to go out there personally. Since all of them know you, and on previous occasions you've performed deep-dive missions like this, I felt you would be the perfect envoy."

Right about then, I got the first inkling that this entire mission-thing was not on the up-and-up. My eyes slid to the left, where Galina sat primly. She wasn't looking at me.

All of a sudden, I thought I knew why she'd tried to slip out and not be a party to this mission briefing. She'd set this whole thing up. She'd recommended me for a casting mission to God knew where, crossing an interstellar abyss via teleportation to somewhere dangerous. This mission was certain to end up with my death and possibly my perming. Everything had been arranged without my permission or foreknowledge.

That was Galina in a nutshell for you. She could be sweet, sexy and gregarious—but she could also be a conniving little witch. Apparently, on this occasion, she'd reverted to her worst nature.

"Well then," Drusus said, "if you don't have any more questions, let's…"

"Wait a second, sir," I said raising a hand. "What exactly should I be telling them?"

He blinked at me a few times. "It's all there in the mission briefing post. It's on your tapper, isn't it?"

I glanced down, and sure enough there were some blinking red texts. When the subject of any text came in with a blinking red flag on it, that meant it was coming from a superior officer.

The funny thing was, I was fairly certain none of that had been on my tapper before I'd stepped into this room.

I glanced at Galina again—and again, she avoided my eye.

Had she dared to surreptitiously send me this mission briefing? Even while I was sitting here in this meeting with Drusus? I figured that she'd done exactly that.

Galina was a wizard with a tapper. In fact, she could even tap messages while blindfolded, or tap behind her back. I'd seen her do it in handcuffs.

Looking down again at my inbox, I nodded. "Looks like I do have it, sir," I said. "But maybe you could just give me the gist of it, you know? What are we offering, what are we asking for?"

Drusus frowned. He was a busy man, and he didn't like repeating things that were already in print. But he sighed, because he knew me, and how I didn't like to read things. Sourly, he decided to give me the ten-second review that I was hoping for.

"All right," he said, "basically, it has to do with these crystals that have been crashing into so many worlds. This one is the largest and most dangerous to date, but it's by no means the only one of its kind."

"Yeah," I said. "I got that—but isn't it Rigel throwing them at us?"

"No," he said, "we don't think so. In fact, the people you're going to meet are in agreement on that point. They say they didn't throw these big, weird, red rocks at our worlds. They claim that we're all under attack from an outside enemy."

"Claims don't prove anything," Galina said suddenly.

Drusus eyed her harshly, and she immediately softened.

"I'm sorry, sir," she said. "What I meant to say was that the evidence they've presented isn't compelling. It could all be a grand trick."

Drusus nodded. "Yes, you're right—it could be a trick. That's one of the reasons why I'm not going in person, and I'm sending Centurion McGill as my messenger. He'll take in what information he can, and hopefully not offend anyone too much. Right, McGill?"

"Me? Offend an alien, sir? It will never happen. Absolutely never," I said all this with profound conviction—but we all knew I was lying. "But uh, sir… just why did you pick me?"

"Imperator Turov, here," he said, "she insisted on it. She made it very clear that you were the best man for this mission. She cited your long roster of similar duties in the past. When I asked her for a volunteer for this dangerous assignment, your name came up immediately."

My smile stayed on my face, but it tightened somewhat. Galina had "volunteered" me. That was an awful thing to happen to a man in any legion, but it was always the worst in Legion Varus.

The meeting broke up, and Drusus shooed us out of his office. Galina tried to skitter away, saying she was busy—but I didn't let her get away with that. It took two of her steps to match one of mine, and there was no way she was going to beat me to the elevator and be off.

"James, I'm very busy now," she said. "You'll have to talk to me about this later."

"No dice, sir," I said. "You set this all up. Was all that talk about me going out on some trace after Abigail Claver—was all that just horse hockey or what?"

"No, no, no," she said. "She'll be there, just as I said."

"Yeah… but there will be other participants, too? People I don't know who the hell they are?"

"You should have read the briefings."

"You didn't send me the frigging briefings until just now in the middle of the meeting!"

She looked a bit frustrated, but she finally sighed. "Yes, all right," she said, "I did volunteer you for this special operation. I thought you would be happy about it—unless perhaps you'd rather stay down on Jungle World fighting primitive aliens in the stinking mud."

Suddenly, I caught on. There was a hint of anger in her voice that told me the truth. I pointed a big finger at her. "Ah-ha!" I said. "You're jealous."

"What? What's this nonsense?"

"You heard me. You're jealous. You noticed a lot of women have been in my vicinity on Jungle World because you've been snoopy, and you've been tracing me and following me around."

She started walking again, and she was walking angrily. I stepped after her, matching her stride easily.

"So," I continued, "you thought to yourself, 'how can I put this poor bastard on ice?' When this mission came up, you put my name in the queue. Drusus probably thought you were crazy at first. Me? A diplomatic envoy? How did you convince him?"

Galina had reached the elevator by now, and she was rattling on the control panel. She slid her tapper over the security override, but it didn't work. Apparently, the elevator was between floors and couldn't be forced to come to this deck instantly.

Knowing that she was feeling somewhat jealous and that she had been given many reasons to feel that way in the past, I went ahead and began to explain things to her. I talked about the strange series of events that had led to me being tracked, prodded and lightly abused by several females down on Jungle World.

I don't think she quite believed me, but she was at least willing to listen.

By the time the elevator arrived, we stepped aboard together. She let me follow her to her quarters. I think what helped me out was the fact that she was feeling somewhat guilty for having misrepresented this mission, its purpose and its participants.

She helped me by going over the mission files. The details were quite startling in nature. She seemed to feel increasingly guilty as I expressed my utter dismay.

"James...?" she said, eyeing me strangely. "You really don't deserve this, but I'm going to give it to you anyway."

"Uh... deserve what, exactly?" I asked.

I was kind of thinking she was having second thoughts about airmailing my sad carcass into the unknown, but that wasn't what she had in mind at all. Instead, she jumped my bones, and we made furious love in her quarters.

That was pleasant enough, but it didn't last long. All too soon, I was mounted onto a casting couch for a quick disintegration and matter-transmission out into deep space.

Still, as I was preparing to be dismantled down to my component molecules, a smile appeared on my face. It was a real one this time.

Galina had gotten jealous, and she'd jumped to conclusions. Sure, she'd screwed me over by getting me assigned to a suicide mission. All that was undeniable.

But all the same, she'd relented in the end. We'd forgiven each other in our own unique way.

I had to admit, if a man has to be permed, her farewell was as fine of one as I could imagine. To hell with a last meal and a cigarette. I'd take a single moment of passion every time.

-28-

Galina left me in the cold-handed care of the Gray Deck tech people. When I was all settled-in on the casting couch, a tech approached me and made some odd gestures with her hands. After a moment, I figured out she was indicating I should strip down.

"What's the matter?" I asked looking around at my gear. "I thought these things could transmit a man without being naked now."

"Yes, yes, it works that way," she said, "but most people going to unknown, far-flung destinations don't want to take irreplaceable gear with them."

My eyes sprung wide. "My armor!"

"That's right. Do you really want to take it with you?"

"Nope," I said. "I've got to put it in a locker. You've got to keep it safe for me."

"Will do, Centurion."

I stripped down to just regular fatigues, then put on a spacer suit of thin, light material—something a spacer on maintenance duty or a hog might wear. Lastly, I grabbed my morph-rifle and got back onto the couch.

The girl kept gesturing.

"What is it now?"

"I understand this is going to be a diplomatic mission, sir." She pointed at my morph-rifle and the plasma grenades on my belt. "Maybe it would be better if you didn't go armed to the teeth."

I thought about that, and I grumbled a bit. Finally, I set aside my rifle. I wouldn't let her take my pistol, or my combat knife and last grenade. The grenade I cunningly stuffed into a belt pouch which was normally used for food rations. I figured that if I lived long enough to need food and water on this trip, well, I was pretty much permed anyway.

At last, the big machine began to hum. An anomalous ball of energy formed in the middle of my guts.

In my slice of technological history, there are three known ways to teleport a person across the cosmos. The first involved the use of gateway posts. The second was a teleportation harness. The third, easily the most heinous of them all, was the casting couch.

The benefit of this method is that no special gear was actually transmitted with the subject. There didn't have to be any equipment on the receiving end, either. Nothing like a second set of gateway posts, for example, which required power and prepositioning.

In the case of a teleportation harness, there was a device to deal with and a battery to worry about. If you wanted to get home, you had to use the battery, so you hoped that you could either recharge it or that it would have enough juice left to get you back safely. Many vanished teleportation adventurers had been permed in the past because they ran out of battery power.

The casting couch took a different approach. The benefit was that the individual could be flung practically anywhere. On top of that, a connection point was maintained between that individual and the people operating the couch back at the transmission point—which in this case was Gray Deck on *Scorpio*.

As long as that connection wasn't broken, the techs here could view, hear and even speak with the subject. This made the system superior for spying missions, as an agent could essentially act like a human buzzer. You could seek out and record whatever information was required.

The only bad part was the lack of an easy way to return home. You couldn't activate a teleportation harness with a battery and return to your point of departure. You couldn't just step through gateway posts going the other direction, either.

Your only recourse was to make sure you died before the connection broke—which it always did, eventually. That way, the techs at your departure point would know you'd died, and therefore they were allowed to legally revive you without making a copy by accident.

Of course, you could always get captured, or the connection could break early. That's when the specter of permadeath stepped into play once again. If no one could confirm your death, you were screwed.

That hadn't happened to me yet, obviously, but I did know others who'd enjoyed this particular form of demise.

Being a perennial optimist, I wasn't concerned. I stretched out on the curved circular couch which looked sort of like a hammock in shape but was made of metal with a bit of padding at the bottom. Like a man in an old painting who was sitting on the crescent of a moon, I waited for the techs to get their act together and send me on my way.

At long last, the glow and the sparkle began. There was a tickle in my belly, and before I knew it, I was gone and hurtling through hyperspace. Doing a slow count, I figured out that I'd crossed perhaps two or three hundred lightyears. It was hard to be sure.

When I arrived, I stumbled and looked around.

"Holy shit..." I said aloud, because I knew *exactly* where I was.

My first hint was the fact that I was surrounded by meter-tall fuzzy, bear-looking dudes. They were Rigellians, and they didn't look as cute as one might think by the description.

Their fur wasn't sleek and even in length, nor did it completely cover their nasty bodies. Don't get me wrong, the little bear men of Rigel *did* have fur, but it was organized more into tufts, and it was more uneven and curly in nature. Kind of like a darker, less-pleasant version of what you might find on the back of a sheep. Less charitable people might say it resembled a man's pubes.

"This has got to be Rigel," I said.

Hearing my speech, a few startled bears snarled in response.

It wasn't Rigel proper, mind you. I could tell that right away by the lack of gravity and the big view through the geodesic glass above me. It was apparently one of their orbital cities which were pocketed among the numerous space stations that made up their planetary defense shield.

Places like this were more than just powerful projectors for energy screens. They were small, inhabited planetoids. I knew from past visits that some of them were inhabited by a large number of the aliens from Rigel below.

Rigel... there everything was, just outside the glassy dome over my head. The planet and her big, fat red star were both visible above. The large burning star and the nearby planet were breathtaking, especially when seen together.

It took the nearest of the bears only about ten seconds to realize I didn't belong there. Snarling, any number of them came toward me.

Now, these were only civilian bears, you have to understand. They were unarmed, except for their nasty fangs and their black, shiny claws.

Their snouts opened up as they approached with caution. They pulled black lips back from their teeth. They were making snarling, growling sounds.

The Rigellians were a species of apex predator, and they'd never been all that friendly toward outsiders. If I'd been wearing my stardust suit of armor, I could have kicked some tail, as these specimens were untrained and mostly unarmed.

But today, circumstances were different. I was wearing the equivalent of crepe paper, and although I could have drawn my knife and my pistol to threaten them—I hesitated.

This was supposed to be, after all, a diplomatic mission. What was it that Galina had said to do? To be honest, I hadn't quite listened to everything she'd said during our private briefing, because I had been working on getting her into bed as hard as I'd been working on my homework—perhaps, if the truth were to be told, a little bit harder than that.

But finally, even as the Rigellians surrounded me, I remembered that my tapper contained a translation function. I engaged it and tried to sound as friendly as possible to the circle of angry little bears.

"Whoa, guys! Hey, I'm from Earth. I'm an agent. I'm… No, no, agent's the wrong word…"

They snarled and stepped another pace closer. Some of them were on my six. I was becoming a little concerned. After all, my buttocks and their nasty, fang-filled snouts were at about the same level.

"I'm an envoy," I said. "I'm an envoy from Earth, from Consul Drusus himself. I'm here to see Squanto. No wait—Squantus. I'm here to talk to Squantus."

It was that single name that finally broke the spell, I think. The truth was, it was the only name of a living bear that I knew.

Squantus was the son of Squanto. Since his dad had passed on, he'd kind of taken over the job of talking to Earthlings.

Rigellians were relatively short-lived when compared to humans. They also didn't indulge themselves with revival machines. They considered such things to be expensive, decadent—and somewhat shameful. To their minds, if a warrior fell in battle, then he deserved to be dead by definition.

Despite all their hostility, some of the Rigellians talked to the others which caused my tapper to beep and fart randomly. I thought this was probably because I hadn't bothered to adjust the settings so it would translate their language back into Earth standard. It was an oversight on my part.

They encircled me, and I did my best to nod and smile and to look harmless. All the while, I worked on my tapper. I managed to hold them off from eating me until some real officials arrived.

Unfortunately, long before Squantus showed up, a squad of no less than six hostile and well-armed bears appeared. They were wearing Rigellian armor, impenetrable dark stardust armor, and I knew immediately I had no chance against these boys. Just one of them could most likely have put me down. Diplomacy was my only path forward.

"Hey, hey!" I said, talking to the air, "are you techs listening in? Hey, *Scorpio*? Come in!"

"We are indeed listening, Centurion," a male voice responded.

I didn't know him. He didn't sound too friendly, but I didn't care, because he was my lifeline. If these bears tore me apart well, hell, at least he would witness it and get me a revive order.

"What am I supposed to say to these bears?"

"According to our records, all that information was in the mission briefing, McGill," said the unhelpful tech.

Cursing, I flipped through page after page of flowery, useless text. Why was it that I'd never been a man who was capable of doing his own homework? Even when I got some girl to do it for me, I tended to get bored before I could get the gist of it. When I explained the girl's answers, some of my teachers would inevitably declare that I was as dumb as a stump. Others had calculated that I was simply a fantastically lazy individual. They labeled me as a person both shiftless and shifty—with little personal integrity when it came to anything academic.

Privately, I figured that the truth was really somewhere in-between these two proclamations.

In the end, it was the civilian bears who saved my bacon. They explained to the patrol group that I didn't need immediate extermination, enslavement or general abuse. Instead, they claimed that I was an envoy who had invoked the name of Squantus.

Both confused and annoyed, the squad of Rigellian police led me away to a rock-walled holding cell. Everything was looking up for old McGill, until I realized this wasn't a *private* cell. The rest of the inhabitants seemed to be aliens of one sort or another. I was the only human interred in this hellish chamber, and my cellmates didn't look happy to see me.

There was nowhere to sit except for a few small steel stools, all of which were occupied. Trying to look cool and tough, I leaned up against the bars away from the group and near the exit.

An unsavory throng of aliens eyed me. Fortunately, most of them took little notice. There were a few cephalopods, a couple of Saurians—and in the back, a group of six dogmen.

It was this last group that approached. They had one among them who was different from the rest. She was a female, and she seemed to be the alpha. What's more, she could speak, after a fashion. "Human," she said pointing a claw at me.

"That's right," I said, "I'm from Earth. Nice to meet you."

The dog-woman snarled, showing an even larger snout full of teeth than the Rigellians had. Dogmen, like their apparent ape-cousins on Jungle World, had larger snouts and jaws than Rigellians did. They weren't, however, much stronger because they weren't from a world that had higher gravitational pull like the Rigellians were. Still, they were at least as strong as a man and a lot more naturally vicious.

"Human!" the dog-woman repeated, pointing at me again.

I wasn't quite sure what the appropriate response was, but I tried to figure it out. After working on my tapper for the precise translation, I told her she could sniff my butt.

Apparently, this was a diplomatic faux pas. They calculated—correctly—that my words were meant to be an insult. Then, all six of them attacked me.

Now, you might wonder if this was just another example of an insanely-stupid James McGill blunder—but it wasn't. You see, I'd already been at Rigel for at least twenty minutes. I hadn't seen any of the people I was supposed to meet and, in fact, I'd only been abused since I'd gotten here.

With a thirty-minute timer ticking away until the link back to Jungle World broke, I had to nudge things along. I'd been disarmed when I was arrested, so my biggest problem was how to get myself killed—and fast.

What can I say? The chief dog-bitch and her pack beat on me excessively. At first, it was just fists and claws, with a couple of nibbles around the soft spots. But then one of them realized he could pick up one of those little steel stools and use it as a club.

At that point bones, began to break. Unfortunately, I was not hit in the head, or at least not hard and often enough to put me out, so I got to enjoy the entire experience.

The whole time, I was thinking, *dammit, just let me die. Let me die!* I was also regretting the fact that I'd given up my knife and my laser pistol to the bears who'd arrested me. They'd even found my secret grenade.

I would have preferred to go out fighting. Maybe I could have gunned down a few of the locals just for good measure.

Right now, you have to understand, I was in the mood to heap hate upon all aliens. Just you try being beaten to death and mauled by a few of them. It starts to darken your outlook right-quick.

Bleeding from a dozen wounds and lying on my back, I had at least one broken arm and two broken legs. I gazed up at the roof of the prison cell trying to breathe.

Suddenly, the barred door opened. It shot up into the ceiling in fact, which was rocky, as we were on an asteroid.

Was the jailer coming at last? Had he finally finished his long piss-break and decided to check out what was happening in the aliens-only cellblock? I didn't know, but I was gratified to see a rush of angry, uniformed bears come in and beat the dogmen almost as mercilessly as they'd beaten me.

When the ruckus died down, a female human came into the cell behind them. She stood over me with her hands on her hips.

"What's this then?" Abigail Claver demanded. "James, can you even hear me?"

"You sound like singing angels," I managed to gargle out.

"I'm sorry about this." She put her hands on her knees, bent down, and peered at me. She did look honestly regretful. "This is a diplomatic breach, I know. I'm real sorry. Listen, something must have gotten crossed up when they transmitted you out here. I've got some better coordinates for next time."

She touched my tapper with hers. Then, she turned to the Rigellians, and she scolded them lightly. They didn't seem to understand what she was saying.

"You want this one?" said the chief of the guards. "He broken. You want him?"

I could tell my translation was less than perfect, but I got the gist of it. They wanted to get rid of me. I was just a mess on their floor.

"No, no," Abigail said, "you wrecked this man. You have to keep him."

The guard leader seemed angry. He walked near me, and I thought he was going to spit, but I was wrong. Instead, he urinated on my chest.

"He is of no value! I take scent-piss on him!"

Abigail bent over me again, and she sighed. "Sorry about this, James. Now, listen-up. I put the right coordinates into your tapper, so I'll bid you a fond farewell."

"Okay…" I grunted, hoping that she would do the deed soon.

"First off, tell me if you're still in communication with the people back at your Gray Deck."

I mumbled with broken teeth, and the techs back on *Scorpio* eventually answered in the affirmative.

"Good," she said. "I'll see you next time."

Then she shot me in the face, and I died with gratitude in my heart.

-29-

The first thing I did when I came back to life was cough and wheeze a bit. That was pretty much normal as revival often leaves your lungs full of fluids.

"What have we got?" asked a businesslike bio-woman.

"I don't know... His numbers look good. His heart is beating and his lungs are working, but he hasn't opened his eyes yet."

"His blood-gas looks a little off," complained the first one, "but I guess it'll do."

"I'm taking immediate custody of him," said another voice which I recognized immediately. It was Imperator Galina Turov, my sometimes girlfriend and sometimes nemesis.

Hearing that she was here, I decided just to squinch my eyes tight and play possum for a little while longer.

"He's not waking up," said the bio-woman.

"He's faking," Galina said with certainty. "Something must have gone wrong with the mission."

"I don't know about that, sir, but I've got to get him off my table. I don't care if he's ready or not."

They heaved me up into a sitting position, and I had a little bit of fun going limp and almost sprawling onto the floor. Then I realized that none of this was really working, so I staged a dramatic recovery and sprang up off the gurney. I almost slipped, as there was still a lot of amniotic goop on the floor.

Squinting and grinning I waved at Galina. "Hey Imperator," I said. "Nice of you to come down here and greet me. I like having a welcoming committee when I return to the living."

"I'm no such thing, James. The techs on Gray Deck informed me that nothing was learned, and that you got yourself killed early through random behavior. They claim you were about to make contact with the people you were supposed to meet."

"That's right," I said. "I guess I was just feeling lazy."

She reached out, pinched up a wad of my bare skin, and twisted it. Now, that may not sound like a big deal, but the truth is a man is naturally a bit sensitive after a revival. It was due to having skin that had never been touched by the sun before. It was easy to get burned.

"Hey," I said rubbing at the spot. "How come I am not the returning hero this time?"

"Because you didn't do anything you were supposed to do. Come with me." She walked out, and I pulled on some clothes while I stumbled after her.

"I kind of need a shower—and maybe some food," I complained.

"You're getting none of that. We're going back to Gray Deck right now."

"Aw, come on, Galina."

When we got to a private quiet spot in the corridor, she turned on me and put a finger in my face. "You tricked me into sleeping with you last night," she said, "telling me all about what a fantastic mission you were going to perform today—and now you've gone and screwed it up."

"I didn't do nothing!"

"Exactly," she said. "You did *nothing*. That's my point."

"Aw," I said, and I followed her again.

She began marching away at a rapid clip. By the time we reached Gray Deck I had hocked up a few big ones and spat the stuff on the deck. I'd also managed to snag a squeeze-bottle of water.

With nothing else in my belly and my hair still sticky-wet, I was shoved onto the casting couch again. I managed to give the new coordinates that Abigail had given me to the tech crew before they hit the launch button, but it was a close thing. A few moments later, I was fired into the unforgiving cosmos toward Rigel again.

Arriving some minutes later, I was met with a warmer reception this time around. Instead of a growling circle of civilian bears, followed by ornery dogmen, I was greeted by Abigail and two others.

I knew all three of them. One was Raash, an individual of dubious character. He was a Saurian, but a weird one. We'd never gotten along all that well since the first day we'd met, and we'd killed each other multiple times over the years. Essentially, he was a blue-scaled spy for Steel World—but right now, he appeared to be working for Rigel.

That made me wonder for just a bit. Was Raash actually spying on the Rigellians now? If he was, it was on behalf of Steel World, of course, and it stood to reason that he probably was. Maybe I'd underestimated the crazy lizard all along. After all, he'd managed to get into Earth's service, getting a job and working as a revival machine operator for years. Now, after that gig had been denied to him, he'd somehow turned up as a system operator here on Rigel.

I'd always considered Raash to be a ham-handed clown, in the sense that his spying efforts were never very subtle or all that successful. But the one thing he seemed to be *really* good at was worming his way into the capital of any enemy he wanted to.

I grinned upon seeing him. "Hey, Raash! How are you doing, my old lizard-buddy?"

Raash hissed at me. "This is the human we are here to greet?" he asked Abigail. "This must be an error."

"No, Raash," Abigail said. "Earth really did mean to send him as their envoy."

"Insanity," Raash said. "They will come to regret this failed selection—and so shall we."

Abigail shrugged, unable to deny that his prognostication might come true.

The third member of the group stood off to one side and back behind the other two a little bit. He was a Rigellian, a short little bear with nasty hair and fangs. His snout had black lips like a dog's, and those lips seemed to curl into a snarl most of the time.

He reminded me of the bear dude that I'd known the best, a guy named Squanto. I'd spent years tormenting that nasty little bear. This one was Squantus, Squanto's son. It just had to be. "Squantus?" I said. "Is that really you?"

"Yes, monstrous human," he said. "I am Squantus."

I walked over to him and offered him a fist to bump. Most aliens didn't get the whole "shaking hands" thing.

All Squantus did was sniff my knuckles curiously.

I nodded, as if he'd kiss my ring finger, and smiled at all three of them. "Okay," I said, "it's about time you all tell me what this is about."

"Essentially, James," Abigail said, "it's an appeal. An appeal to Earth from all of our species from different worlds. Drusus is making a huge mistake by invading 31 Orionis."

"I'm not surprised at their madness," Raash said. "Everything humans do turns into a giant mistake."

The one Rigellian present, Squantus, said nothing. He just watched our conversation. I thought about that, and I didn't like it. You couldn't trust any of these bears, not even as far as you could throw them—which is pretty far, actually.

"Okay, okay," I said. "So it sounds like you're asking for us to call a truce on Jungle World. But you're going to have to give me a little more information than that."

"Ah," Raash said, "here it comes. You see, he is a spy. He is duplicitous. He seems irrational and ignorant and extreme, and he is, in fact, a true ignoramus. Yes... but that is not the entire story. He possesses a certain low animal cunning. Even the dumbest of predatory apes are capable of trickery. He mustn't be trusted."

Abigail was trying to wave him back with her hand, getting him to settle down. "Now, now Raash. There's no need for insults."

"Hey," I said, "wait a minute. Before we go any further, can I ask exactly why this oversized blue lizard is even here at all in the first place?"

Abigail and Squantus glanced at one another. Before they could answer, Raash started talking gruffly.

"I do not have to explain myself, human," he said. "It is *you* who is unwanted in these halls. Humans have abused Rigel on countless occasions."

I crossed my big arms and frowned. "Well now, I'm not going to talk any further until someone tells me why this Saurian spy is here today. Either that, or you can kick his tail out of the meeting."

At this point, a buzzing began in my ear. The Gray Deck people back aboard *Scorpio* must have decided I was blowing the whole diplomacy thing again—or at least they thought so. They began offering up advice, but I tuned them out as easily as the buzzing of a mosquito at a picnic.

Abigail cleared her throat and thought over my demand. "I guess it's a reasonable request," she said. "Maybe we should have Raash excused from this meeting. Raash, what do you say?"

"No," Raash said. "My tail will not be lifted from this ground. If you want the aid of Cancri-9, then I must be present at all diplomatic negotiations."

Raash's words were starting to set off some serious alarm bells in my otherwise empty head. How had he suddenly gained enough clout to dictate terms to Rigel?

"Huh," I said. "So, Raash is the big cheese around here, huh? He's calling the shots? Does he order all these little bears around down on the planet, too? Maybe your capital city should build some new statues of him."

All of this talk finally lit up Squantus. He'd been staying quiet, but now he stepped forward, growling in his throat. "Not so, human. What you say is highly offensive. Raash and his people have offered us aid against a greater enemy. All Earth has done is attack us while we face a great threat from the deepest of stars."

I frowned at that. Rigel needed help? To me, Rigel and the bears had always seemed stronger than Earth and her people. The last time we'd engaged in a major fleet battle, they'd possessed a lot more ships, and their vessels had been more advanced in design. Sure, we were catching up, but I would never call Rigel weak.

On the other hand, they *had* shown weakness recently. During the Sky World campaign, they'd lost Dark World, Sky World and part of the defensive system that protects Rigel itself. They'd never really struck back with any strength.

"I must be missing something," I said. "What has brought Rigel so low that they would seek the protection of this blue-scaled freak over here?"

My words sent Raash into a fit of hissing, just as they were meant to. He complained, and he fumed, because for him, his blue scales were unnatural. He was, in fact, the only member of his particular species that possessed such scales.

That was due to happenstance, a bit of an accident which I'd participated in back on Dust World, some years ago. We'd lost his body scans, and in order to bring him back to life, the Investigator had had to do a little bit of guesswork. After a bit of genetic fuckery, we'd gotten Raash breathing again. But he'd never been entirely happy. He didn't like his unique appearance, and he was still sensitive about it.

To my mind he was just one big, ungrateful lizard. After all, we could have left him dead, and we certainly didn't have to go to all the effort we had done to get him breathing again. He was like many who'd lost a limb in an accident and forever hated the doctors for having taken away his appendage.

"James," Abigail admonished me. "Stop poking at Raash. His people have earned the right to be here at this meeting. They're offering help to us. Earth has done nothing but take advantage."

"Help… us?" I said. "What do you mean *us*? You're Clavers. You don't even have a planet anymore. You're just a trading group."

"That's sort of true," she said, "but sometimes, a threat arrives which supersedes everyone's baser interests."

I looked mildly intrigued. "What threat? Are you talking about those dogmen down there on Jungle World? You guys made those things, and we've figured out that you used the apelike aliens that live there to do it."

"I'm talking about the crystal, of course," she said. "Did you somehow miss the gigantic, mountain-sized red crystal stuck in the side of the planet?"

I shrugged. "Yeah, sure. We saw that. How did you guys get it to fire a big gravity-beam at us anyway? That was quite a trick, and it proves that Rigel was plenty-strong."

All three of them shook their heads in disbelief.

"You see," Raash said, "in addition to spouting mindless insults at unfortunates like myself, he fails to comprehend the most basic and obvious truths."

"James," Abigail said patiently, "what Raash is trying to say is that we don't control that crystal. It wasn't made by Rigel, or us Clavers, or the people on Jungle World."

My jaw sagged low. "It wasn't? Who made it, then?"

"We don't know, not really. It's from far beyond the frontier somewhere."

"Huh..." I said, "that's kind of weird."

"It's more than weird, ape creature," Squantus said stepping forward. "It is an invasion. It's a brutal attack. Strikes of this nature are occurring all over the frontier. First, a smaller structure arrives, presumably to probe a planet. These can be destroyed but with difficulty. Next, a larger and much more dangerous crystal arrives—slamming into the ground at the precise location where the first struck home."

"The same spot, huh?" I asked.

"Yes. Always. The world-wound on 31 Orionis is the second such strike. This one will consume the entire planet in the end. It's only a matter of time until such crystals fly out of deep space and embed themselves into the worlds of humanity as well."

For the first time I felt a sense of alarm. Squantus' claims triggered a few memories. I had heard-tell that something like this had happened already to Dark World and Blood World.

"Hmm..." I said, "so, you're telling me that you aren't the guys throwing these big red rocks around."

They all shook their heads.

"And, you don't know who's doing it?" I asked.

"Are your auditory organs impaired human?" Squantus asked.

"No," Raash said firmly, "it is his brain that does not function properly."

I nodded, and I gave my chin a scratch. "Okay…" I said, "I'm getting it now. Somebody from out toward the Galactic Rim is throwing dangerous red rocks at a lot of planets. But is it really that bad? Can't you guys destroy these things? After all, Rigel's got a fleet."

"It is too dangerous," Squantus said. "The crystals are more deadly than you realize at this moment. Each passing day, it is gaining strength. It is an injury that is festering, not healing. Eventually, the crystal will send out tendrils of itself until it destroys the entire planet."

"Wow," I said, "that does sound bad."

"Yes," Raash said, "and now you understand why humans must retreat from 31 Orionis. You must go back to your province and sit there and squat in your trees. You are attacking the sick and the dying at their weakest moments—exactly as might the most hated of scavengers."

I considered his words, and I began to understand them in a different light. I looked at Abigail next. "So, how do you fit into all this?"

"It's affecting us too, James," she said. "At first, we figured it was just another war. Wars are good for business. We'd planned to sell weapons to Rigel, which would make all the other planets buy from us as well, in order to defend themselves."

I tried not to look disgusted. I probably failed, but Abigail didn't seem to notice.

"So," she continued, "we became gunrunners—but that didn't last long. Nothing Rigel threw at these crystals had much effect. Next, we decided to offer them better troops. We introduced the dogmen and sold legions of them to multiple planets all around Rigel—we even tried to approach the crystals to see if a deal could be made."

None of this story surprised me much. The Clavers were nothing if not war-profiteers.

"But it still didn't work out," she said, shaking her head. "This new enemy is impossible to have a dialogue with. I don't know if they even have the capacity to use speech at all. We've been unable to communicate with them, no trades or bargains are possible. Worse, they're destroying every planet that we do enjoy a trading relationship with. Essentially, they're a scourge. There's no positive angle to be played."

"What are you going to do about it?" I asked.

"Recognizing a common threat, we Clavers have joined an alliance with Rigel and the Saurians to stop this menace from invading and taking over the frontier provinces—and eventually 921 itself."

I thought about that, and I began to understand. In the past we'd faced another plague like this one. "It sounds like the Wur," I said.

She nodded and pointed a finger at me. "Yes, it's similar to the Wur. Being a race of plants, those creatures are so alien they're very difficult to deal with. But even with them, we have a way to communicate and to make bargains. So far, we've failed to do the same with these crystalline creatures—if they are even alive in the way that we understand it."

"Huh," I said frowning in concern.

If the Clavers couldn't bargain with an entity, there was no room for negotiations at all. My mind moved ahead to thoughts of warring with such an exotic civilization. How would you even arrange a ceasefire? Was peace impossible short of the total destruction of this enemy? To my knowledge, Earth had never run into an alien species that could not communicate at all.

"Okay…" I said. "Okay, my dim bulb of a brain is finally seeing the light."

"It is a miracle," said Raash, "if it is true."

"So… what if I could arrange a ceasefire on Jungle World?"

"Are you in command of Legion Varus?" Squantus demanded.

"Nope."

Squantus waved curved, black claws at me. He shook his head. "Your people are somewhat primitive and always unable to see reason. Obviously, Earth should retreat from 31 Orionis at least, or help us destroy the crystal at best. Unfortunately, I doubt your leaders are capable of grasping the seriousness of the situation."

It was my turn to become a bit steamed. "How the hell are we supposed to start any kind of cooperation? Your boys on Jungle World keep throwing sticks at us."

"James," Abigail interrupted, "we're asking for just one thing. Ask your commanders to remove Legion Varus from Jungle World. Right now, we're busy gathering all the strength on the planet for one final assault against the crystalline base. The earlier we can destroy it, the more likely Jungle World is to survive as an ecosystem."

"You mean that thing's going to kill the whole planet, huh?"

"Yes, eventually. It's like a poison arrow slammed into the side of a massive, wounded animal. Eventually it will kill the host."

I thought it over, and I was actually feeling sympathetic for these three. All of them were somewhat offensive, mind you, and I was pretty sure they were equally disgusted by my existence—except possibly for Abigail herself.

The bad part was I didn't think the brass aboard *Scorpio* was going to be very receptive of the idea of pulling the legion out at this point. Galina and Winslade were both opportunists. They'd see this as a moment to pounce and seize more territory while Rigel was weak.

At last, I shrugged my massive shoulders, and I heaved a sigh. "Okay," I said. "I'll go back to *Scorpio*. I'll relay this message to Imperator Turov and Consul Drusus and anybody else who will listen to me. For what it's worth, if you guys are telling the truth, it seems like a reasonable request. After all, we can always go back to fighting once we get rid of the crystals, right?"

"Yes, yes," said Squantus. "Honor will be served in the end. Eventually, every human will be enslaved or slain by Rigel, but that does not have to happen today. That happy day might not come for generations. We from Rigel are willing to wait."

"That's mighty considerate of you," I said.

"Those of us from Cancri-9," Raash said, "have waited long enough for Earth's demise, but we can see the greater danger of these crystals. I would not want to have one fly out of the dark and slam into my homeworld. Better to fight these abominations out here on the frontier than in Province 921."

"That's an enlightened attitude," I told him. "You're downright reasonable today, Raash—a true credit to Steel World."

"I also find you less odious than usual, McGill."

We both nodded to one another. That kind of moment was as close as we ever came to exchanging compliments and pleasantries.

"All right then, James," Abigail said. She drew her pistol and checked to see if the charge was full. "Your time is about up, according to my tapper. Any last words before I send you on your way back?"

"Uh," I said. "How about a kiss for good luck?"

She twisted up her mouth and shook her head. Then, she raised the pistol. "Maybe next time, James," she said, "it was sweet of you to ask."

Then, she shot me in the head.

-30-

I expected to be promptly revived again back on *Scorpio*. As I was coming awake and going through that dreamy stage when you're gathering awareness of your surroundings, I considered the idea of asking Galina on another date. My troops down on Jungle World could wait, right?

Leeson could take care of 3rd Unit. He'd done it before. It had only been a day or two that I'd been gone. What was one more night?

But that wasn't how things turned out for old McGill. When I was revived, the first thing I noticed was how hot it was in the revival chamber—and it wasn't just hot, it was kind of muggy, too.

"Did somebody leave the heater on?" I muttered.

"He's talking," a bio said. "This one's talking!"

"That's good enough for me," said a second voice. "Get him off my table and out the door."

I was hustled into a standing position by strong arms. Orderlies stood me up like a ragdoll, shoved clothes over my head and just about kicked me in the butt to send me on my way.

Staggering and mumbling curses at the discourteous manner in which I'd been treated, I reached out to lean for support on the walls, but I found that my hand went right through the wall.

The walls of this revival chamber were, in fact, nothing but fabric. I was in a tent. I flat out fell on my face, crashing through the plastic walls and slapping nose down into a large mud puddle.

"Shit," I muttered to myself. I must be back on Jungle World.

It was true. It was hot, muggy and raining on top of all that. If you haven't ever been out in a rainforest that is so hot that the rain falling from the sky is actually as warm as bathwater, then you haven't been to Jungle World yet.

Climbing to my knees and then getting to my feet again, I wiped off the worst of the mud. I staggered outside, tilted my face up to the skies and let the blasting rainfall clear the mud from my face.

While I was doing this, I became aware that something else was wrong. I was hearing a lot of gunfire. There was the chatter of snap-rifles, plus the unmistakable hum and hiss of 88s. Even the sky lit up periodically, with the whoosh and flaring light caused by a star-fall warhead.

The heavy artillery brigades were launching a steady barrage toward the west. Each massive plasma-ball sailed into the sky and toward the frontlines.

"What the hell…?" I asked no one in particular.

Giving my head a shake, I wiped the last of the filthy mud from my eyes. I was able to look around and see what was happening now.

Troops were rushing back and forth in squads and fire-teams. They were fully armored and armed for battle. Boots splashed down in the muddy black puddles, sending sprays of gritty liquid exploding away in all directions.

"Holy hell… we must be under fire," I said. My big feet picked up speed and my brain unfogged. I managed to propel my new body on a staggering run through the rows of tents and bunkers. I soon found the 3rd Cohort, and then the 3rdUnit within it—my unit's home camp.

"Praise the Lord!" Lesson said when he saw me.

Harris seconded the motion. He rushed forward, grabbing my arm and giving my hand a vicious pumping. He grinned at me. "I'm so glad you're back, sir," he said, then he lowered his voice to a harsh whisper. "Leeson's really been screwing up."

I nodded, unsurprised. It was possible that Leeson really *was* screwing up. It was also equally possible that Harris just didn't like whatever Leeson had ordered him to do.

Whichever was the case, I did my best to turn my sorry excuse for a brain back on and assume command. I found my black stardust armor and pulled it on with numbed fingers. Those boys back on Gray Deck had sent the gear down from *Scorpio*, so I figured I owed them a beer.

It felt good to have excellent protective gear on again. If I was sent back to Rigel one more time, I might get the chance to teach those dogmen a thing or two with one of their steel stools...

With an effort, I pushed such ideas away. I was back in command 3rd Unit now, and I needed to act like it. When I was fully dressed and armored, I saw a circle of concerned faces surrounding me. Most of them were my adjunct's noncoms.

They didn't seem to know what to do next any more than I did. That's when I checked my tapper for the first time. There it was: red, blinking text. I had orders from on-high.

My instructions were clear and to the point. I was to follow the white rally points to the frontlines. My unit was needed at the front.

The last word was *HUSTLE* in all caps. That was all there was. Graves hadn't even signed it. He'd probably sent it to me as soon as he'd noticed I was undergoing the process of revival.

From the perspective of an officer like Graves, I was already ten minutes late. I began snapping my fingers and shouting, "Let's move out!"

We began to jog through the mud, passing and being passed by countless other groups of soldiers. I had a little time to ask my troops what the hell was going on. Leeson had been in command while I was out flying around the stars and being killed repeatedly, so he was the one to deliver my briefing, such as it was.

"Well sir," he said, "while you were up there on *Scorpio* banging Turov—and that comment wasn't meant to be disrespectful, sir," he said after I shot him a dark look. "All of us that stayed down here in the mud are both jealous and proud of your achievements."

That was a good cover, and it kept me from cuffing Leeson in the head. I was glad he'd made the effort, because such moments of discord among the officers might well lower unit morale.

I simply nodded, and I listened to the rest of his report.

Leeson cleared his throat before continuing. "Anyways," he said, "they started hitting us not long after you left. It was almost like it was coordinated. There's no chance you went off somewhere and, like, killed the ape queen or seduced her, or something like that, right sir?"

"None whatsoever, Adjunct. I wasn't even in this star system."

"Good, good," Leeson said. "Anyway, the locals seem to have gotten a bug up their collective puffy, red butts. Shitloads of ape-aliens and dogmen came whirling into camp. We had pickets out around the perimeter, mind you, but they must have killed five hundred troops out to the west of here. They came out of the jungle like a whirlwind."

"They attacked us?" I asked. "Without provocation?"

"That's what it looked like—just a disorganized mob, racing in from the trees. They used their classic hit-and-run tactics again. They just came out of the trees, throwing a few darts and firing a few plasma-bolts—depending on what they had—then ran off again. It's hard to believe how fast they can move through the jungle. I mean, all this mud and muck and vines and stuff doesn't seem to slow them down at all."

"If they ran off, what's going on right now?"

"It's something new, sir. Something none of us have seen before. The boys on the front lines say there are big shiny rocks coming out of the jungle. It's really weird."

I stopped trotting and looked at him. "Rocks?" I said. "Shiny rocks... is that what you just said?"

"That's right, sir. I know it's hard to believe. I mean, how do these rocks even move? I'd like to know that, but no one has told us squat."

I looked back toward the jungle we'd been plunging through. As crazy as it sounded, somewhere out there to the west, there were living rocks coming toward our lines.

Could it be that the invasion of Jungle World had moved into its final stage already?

What had Abigail said about this? It was hard for me to listen when someone talked for too long, but she'd mentioned something about how these big red crystals were the size of mountains. But then they'd start to—what was the word? Ah yes, to *fester*, to spread.

This business of moving rocks sure-as-shit sounded like an attack that was coming from the crystal itself.

"All right," I said beginning to stride forward again toward the frontlines. "Let's keep moving."

My troops jogged in my wake. They'd paused when I had, but now we pressed onward, toward the sound of gunfire in the distance.

The rain had been falling all along, but now it intensified, obscuring our vision. The problem wasn't just the rain itself, it was the mist—the steam that roiled up off of the jungle floor when the raindrops struck.

The falling water was hot, and the ground was even hotter. This generated a constant, hot, clinging cloud of water vapor that made it hard to see through your faceplate. Everything was visually dampened.

As we marched to the designated waypoint, I made repeated attempts to contact Graves. None of them were successful, so I stepped up the chain of command and reached out to Winslade.

"Damn you, McGill," Winslade said, "don't you know I have a battle on my hands? What is it?"

"I surely do know that, Tribune, sir," I said. "In fact, I'm right down here in the middle of it."

"Well then, go back to fighting. Kill whatever enemy you encounter. Winslade out."

"Hold on, sir!" I shouted. "Are you aware that I just got back from a big peace-pipe meeting out at Rigel?"

"Yes, yes, I heard about that. The techs have recorded everything that was said, and they plan to forward it to Drusus and Imperator Turov. Now, if you would mind getting off the line, please."

"Yes sir. Yes sir, I promise I will, but you have to listen to me for one second. This enemy—these red rock-things that I'm hearing about—that's exactly what Squantus and all those other bastards were talking about."

"It is?" he asked. "Hmm. They actually admitted they're aware of these threats?"

"That's right sir. They're red crystals. That's what they are, sir, as far as I understand it. They're some kind of silicon-based lifeform, and they're spreading. They're spreading from that big, central rock that struck the planet. They mean to kill all of us, sir—the dogmen, the ape-aliens and even us humans."

Winslade frowned up at me from my tapper. Finally, I seemed to have his full and undivided attention.

"All right," he said. "Thanks for the message and the warning. I'll look into it. With luck, I can find recordings of everything that was said during your recent visit to Rigel. For right now, I want you to fight and die well—or at least as effectively as you are able. Winslade out."

Then he was gone, and we reached our waypoint a few minutes later. The spot in question was a low hill in the forest. It wasn't much to look at, just a hump on the forest floor. We set up firing positions, squatting behind the numerous trees. At least we weren't standing in mudpuddles any longer.

Tense and not knowing what to expect, we spread out over a hundred-odd meters of ground and waited either for new instructions, or for this strange new enemy to engage us.

Eventually, the rain slowed and even stopped. The ground was slushy, and the skies were dark, billowing gray clouds which seemed to hang so low they were right above the treetops. The muddy ground steamed, especially when occasional shafts of sunlight burned through the clouds and struck the surface of the planet. It was when one of those golden beams reached all the way down from the tops of the trees and somehow found its way to the forest floor that I saw my first enemy crystal.

It was weird-looking. Even weirder than I'd thought it would be. For some reason, I'd expected something similar to a starfish, but maybe with pointier tips.

Instead, this alien creature was rounded, almost spherical in nature. Its sides were flat planes—a lot of them—which formed a set of even planes all the way around its surface. Each plane was a pentagon, and I knew in an instant how it was able to move.

"Sweet Jesus," Leeson breathed over tactical chat. "It's floating—no, it's flying. It seems to be riding some kind of gravity-repeller."

I nodded, thinking that over. To some degree, it made sense. After all, hadn't the big-daddy crystal attacked us by sending out gravity-beams? Those beams had caused things to collapse in upon themselves when struck. Perhaps, that was the core technology that these creatures—if they really were creatures—possessed. They seemed to have the ability to manipulate gravitational fields.

Natasha sidled close, and she knelt beside me, taking cover behind the same tree. "That's a dodecahedron," she whispered. She'd come slinking up to peer at the reddish, somewhat translucent crystal in fascination.

"Should we open fire, sir?" Leeson asked in my headset.

"No," I said, "hold your fire. Let them come in closer."

"Them?" Leeson asked. "We can only see one of them."

I turned to Natasha. "What'd you say it was? A dildo-what?" I asked.

"A dodecahedron, James. A twelve-sided object."

I turned back, and I looked at all those pentagons facing me. I figured that maybe she was right. Maybe there were twelve facets to this weird gem. "Is it alive?" I asked.

She shook her head. "I don't know. By our classifications, I would have to say it isn't alive, but it certainly is acting as if it's alive in some ways. I mean is a Skay alive? They have machine-intelligence, yes, but it's a composition of flesh, metals and electronics."

Natasha kept talking like that, but I'd long since stopped listening. A second one of the crystals had emerged. This one had a different shape. There were even more facets to it than the first one, and it seemed to be a little bit larger.

"Okay, that's good," I said. "Let's ambush this thing. Let's see if we can kill it."

Every combat soldier in my unit stepped out from behind a sheltering tree and opened up. Thousands of bolts and snap-rifle rounds sprayed at the two crystals.

I could tell we were hitting them. There were sparks, and chips of glass-like crystal flew everywhere. The one that we'd spotted first turned toward us, while the second one moved back into the trees.

We concentrated our fire on the first one, and it began to spin. It looked to me as if a shaft of glass like a spear was suddenly emitted from one of its many points. Like a lance, this crystalline shaft fired toward one of my men. It lanced through his body and put him down dead in an instant.

The crystal turned again and repeated the process, killing a light trooper from Clane's platoon a second or two later.

Damnation, if this thing could kill a man every two seconds, we weren't going to last five minutes in combat with it.

"Belchers!" I said, "focus beams. Sargon, destroy that thing!"

I'd held my weaponeers in reserve until this moment. As a group, seven of them revealed themselves and fired at once. The beams crisscrossed the steamy jungle and all seven of them struck the crystal at once. The effect was far more impressive this time. I could tell the crystal had felt the shock of those simultaneous strikes.

A chunk slagged off the right side, and instantly melted. Like a piece of glass or ice, it fell away from the main body and splashed down onto the muddy ground. There, it hissed and bubbled, sending up a gout of steam.

Two more such wounds opened up a moment later with similar results. We were wrecking that crystal. We were melting it down like a big chunk of ice hit by a blowtorch.

In return, the crystal reached out lancing one more man. This time, it was Sargon. It had struck him dead right through his chest plate.

Then, it began to retreat. Clearly, it was taking too much fire. Spinning, stuttering and slamming into trees, it ran for it. Every dozen paces it touched down to leave a sizzling spot in the mud. To me, it looked like a wounded soldier racing away for safety.

"Should we go after it sir?" Leeson asked.

I wasn't certain. Was this all a trick? Were there a hundred more of these things in the trees beyond? Pinching my lips together, I came to a sudden decision—one I knew I might regret later.

"Harris," I said. "Advance and bring that thing down. Weaponeers, go with him. The rest of you stay here, and provide covering fire if they need it."

Harris charged in pursuit, cursing my mother's name the whole way. But for all of that, he didn't slacken his pace.

He caught up with the crystal, and his troops did battle with it. Realizing it couldn't outrun the humans, the strange thing whirled around and began lancing my troops as best it could. It killed Harris and two other heavy troopers. Then, the weaponeers caught up, and together they beamed it until it went down, dying in a molten heap.

"Come back to me, troops," I shouted. "Grab your dicks and retreat to my position."

They hustled back to our lines without having to be urged to do so more than once. When all our survivors were once again hidden behind the trees on the hill we'd been assigned to guard, I had Kivi and Natasha send in buzzers to investigate these strange new enemies. They took video, they took samples and they exclaimed with excitement.

"It's definitely a new species," Natasha said. "In fact, I don't even know if we can classify it as a species at all."

Her eyes were lit-up with exhilaration. There was nothing that got Natasha out of bed in the morning faster than a new scientific discovery.

-31-

My troops were breathing hard and sweating after we drove away the crystal-creatures—or whatever the hell they were. After I reported the engagement, Primus Collins herself came out to review the battle scene. She brought along a few bios, a few techs and some of those weirdo xenology people that Hegemony liked to hire.

We covered the team with our rifles while they poked at the glass-like shards we'd blown off the monster. After a while, it looked like the jungle was calm again, so I strode down there under the cover of a hundred guns from the hilltop. I toed the strange remains with my boots.

"Do you mind, Centurion McGill?" Primus Collins asked. She seemed to be sour on me. Once upon a time, at the end of the City World campaign, she and I had gotten together and been close friends, so to speak.

All that was over and done with now, I could tell. But then again, a man like me was never satisfied with getting burned just once. It always took me two or three times to get the message.

"Say, Primus Collins…" I said, "have you and your techs learned much about these aliens? They sure are freaks, aren't they?"

"Yes," she said. "Very strange. We've never encountered anything like them."

I pointed out over the swampy ground underneath some ferns. "You see that over there? Those humps, those scraps of fur? That's a whole lot of dead locals."

She glanced that way. "Yes, I know. You engaged them and shot them from here, didn't you?"

"Nope," I said. "Not us."

She frowned at me. "What killed them then?"

"I don't know. Might be worth a look, though."

She met my eyes, nodded and led a couple of bios out there.

That was brave. I'd always liked Primus Collins. She wasn't really a frontline officer, but she was still willing to put her ass out there when the situation called for it. Speaking of her hindquarters, they weren't that bad looking, either.

I followed along while her team worked, remembering better days. "Say, uh…" I said, beginning a stumbling pitch, but she interrupted me.

"Look at this," she said. "There are bodies everywhere. Are you *sure* you didn't shoot these guys?"

"No sir, not us. All this must have happened before we even got to our post on the hill."

Collins frowned, and she bit her lip. She moved from one body to the next. She checked them all. She had her bio people inspect the dead as well.

"What killed these natives?" she demanded. "You have to know by now."

They shook their heads. "It looks like they were lanced. Stuck right through the guts, through the chest. It's like the kind of puncture wound that a spear would do. I'd say it was these crystal things, sir."

"Whoa, wait a minute," I said. "This is starting to make some sense."

Primus Collins looked at me. "How so?"

"Well sir, before I got out here our lines were hit by ape-aliens charging out of the dark coming right for Legion Varus."

"Yes, yes. So what?"

"Well, they hit us, and they ran off almost like we surprised them. It wasn't a very effective or long-term attack. In fact, if you review the vids, it looks like they were just trying to get away from something when they found us."

Collins thought that over, and she began nodding. "Maybe they actually *were* running. Maybe they were running from these freaks," she said pointing to the broken pieces of glass-like silicate. There were chunks of it here too, in amongst the fallen warriors. "There must be a hundred dead here," she said. "I don't think they managed to kill a single crystal."

"Nope," I said, "it doesn't look like it."

"We've got to record all this. We've got to get word back to headquarters. Gather up samples, team," she ordered the techs and the bios. "Scrape everything up, and bag it. I want to be out of here in five minutes flat."

I couldn't blame her for wanting to move fast, but it took more like fifteen minutes to complete the task. While we were waiting, I struck up a more personal conversation with old Primus Collins. "Hey, Cherish," I said, because I knew that was her first name.

She glanced up at me sharply. "Don't call me that, McGill. It's unprofessional in the field."

I shrugged, and I racked my brain to come up with another angle. I cast my mind back to City World—to those heady days when we'd finished a big campaign and were the heroes of the day.

Frowning, I seemed to remember something that was confusing to me now. "Hey, Cherish," I said, "wait a minute... Aren't you supposed to be in Victrix now? Or someplace else? I thought Legion Varus traded you and Barton away. Isn't that right?"

All of a sudden, her brusque attitude turned to straight-out anger. She gave me a venomous glare. "Your sense of humor is not appreciated, Centurion," she said.

I stared at her, and I blinked a couple of times. "Uh, if this is me being funny, well, that's by sheer accident."

"You know very well that things did not go as I'd planned. Perhaps they went the way *you* planned." Then she angrily tossed her head and looked away from me.

I stood there, slack-jawed and utterly dumbfounded for maybe three whole seconds. I couldn't figure out what was she talking about. But then, all of a sudden, that dim bulb in my fridge of a brain went on and the light shone out of my eyes. It was the light of understanding, with new knowledge.

"Wait a minute..." I said. "You're saying that you applied to Victrix with Barton—but they took her and not you? Is that it?"

She didn't look at me. She gave me an angry shrug. "They simply said they were going to pass this time. I haven't bothered to apply again. That's all."

"Wow," I said thinking that over. "Kind of weird that they didn't have room for two new officers in the end..."

She tossed me a glance full of hate. "Maybe that was all part of your grand scheme. In fact, I'm sure it was," she snapped, "and I'm fairly certain you're thoroughly enjoying this moment right now. I've heard from other women about this sort of thing. You cruelly pretend to be a forgetful ignoramus, even while—"

"Whoa, whoa, whoa! Wait a minute, girl," I said cutting her off. "First of all, if I seem like a forgetful ignoramus, I'm not pretending. Next, I assure you I didn't know what happened. Yeah sure, I knew you were supposed to leave… and then I guess you were still around during the Sky World campaign… and you're still around here now, but I honestly just didn't think about it."

Cherish finally turned around and faced me squarely. She turned her eyes up, and she stared with peering, narrow slits into my comparatively wide, goofy eyes.

Heaving a sigh at last, she shook her head and looked down again. "I can't believe this," she said. "I think I actually believe you. I just can't fathom it. All this time… how is it possible, James? How could you actually not have noticed that I've been stuck here in Legion Varus for years, even after I made a deal to escape this shitty outfit? Even after you managed to tack Barton onto the deal—which made the whole thing blow up in my face?"

I gaped, and I stood there in the mud. Finally, I nodded. "Yeah… that's pretty much what happened. I just didn't notice."

"Oh my god," she said whispering to herself more than to me. "I wasted so much time hating you for something you forgot about. James, I'm not sure if you're a genius, or you truly are an idiot."

I smiled and pointed a big finger at her. "That's what my grandma always said. She couldn't figure it out, either."

Primus Collins finally couldn't take it any longer. She threw up her hands and walked away in defeat. Shortly after that, the techs and the bios were done scraping up various chunks of glasslike material, along with innards and hair samples from the dead alien warriors.

We retreated back to the hill where my unit had been stationed. I was glad we hadn't been hit by anything during that short time out in the bush. By my estimation, there was no way that anyone could have gotten here fast enough to save us. Even covering fire and a rapid retreat probably wouldn't have done it.

I hadn't said anything about the level of danger we were in, mostly because I didn't care that much. After all, I'd already died twice in the last twenty-four hours. What was a third revival to a man like me?

But also, it would have freaked out poor Primus Collins too much, and she was already having a bad day. Before she left my tiny outpost, she extracted a promise from me.

"James," she said, "now listen. I'm going to go present this report to the higher-ups. But if they argue with me—if they give me a hard time on my findings—I want you to back me up, okay?"

"Uh…" I said chewing that over. "Is this about the, uh… the whole Barton and Victrix thing…?"

"No! No, you idiot! I'm talking about our conclusion that the local aliens were running away from these new crystalline aliens—or whatever the hell those flying rocks are."

"Oh yeah! Right, right. The crystals attacked the ape-guys and the dogmen, chasing them right into our lines. Got it."

Shaking her head, Cherish walked away, and I looked after her. I certainly had blown all my chances with her. Even I could tell that much.

Harris came up grinning after she'd left. "You still got it boy, don't you?" he said. "The ladies just love Old McGill."

"Shut up, Adjunct, or I'll send you on a deep patrol."

"Whoop! Sensitive today?" he said, but after I shot him an unfriendly glance, he scooted the hell out of my sight.

My unit stayed at that post for another ten hours. By then it was dark, and the men were getting hungry. I retreated the squad down the hill toward our frontlines and told them to sit there, squat in the mud and eat cold rations. They grumbled of course but not too much.

Just as night completely closed around us, a loud buzzing, crunching noise came from the direction of the main camp. It had the sound of a pig on the march.

Sure enough, while our camp lights glinted off of its skin, a large drone the size of a draft horse halted, and it quickly began tearing up the earth, forming trenches. Checking my tapper, I saw Primus Collins had sent it out from headquarters.

Leeson came up and put his hands on his hips. He shook his head ruefully. "Looks like we're spending the night right here in this garden spot. I thought we were on the march. I thought we were moving toward that crystal thing. We're not much more than halfway yet."

"I guess maybe our plans have changed," I said. "It seems like every alien on the planet has been coming at us. Maybe we don't need to move any closer to make contact with this enemy."

Shaking his head, Leeson found a spot in the freshly dug trench lines and sprawled out on the black earth. The walls of the trench oozed mud that was barely firm and dry enough to hold its shape. Probably, if we hadn't been on a hill, any trench we dug would have turned into an instant pond.

After darkness fell we had another grim meal made up entirely of field rations. Fortunately, they weren't cold but hot this time. The pouches heated themselves up when you poured some water in from your canteen and transformed into a halfway decent meal.

"The eggs always taste the worst," Harris complained. "I hate breakfast, but the dinners aren't that bad. What is this? Beef stew?"

"Something like that," Leeson said. "I usually like the red packs best."

"Well, I like the purple ones."

I tuned them out and worked on my tapper. All the while my jaws were slowly munching and chewing on nutritious but rather flavorless food, I couldn't help but imagine what kind of sumptuous repast Galina was enjoying up on *Scorpio* right now. I would hate to be the kind of officer that flew a desk and didn't know one end of his rifle from the other, but I did miss the good food.

I reviewed the various tactical reports that had been filed so far on this strange new enemy. My unit wasn't the only one to have encountered one of these crystals and shot at it. So far we hadn't destroyed many of them. We damaged quite a few, sure—running them off into the trees—but they were damnably tough to finish off.

Another thing that seemed clear was the fact they moved more slowly than flesh and blood creatures. They were way slower than the dogmen and ape-aliens, and slower than a man in power-armor as well. All that said, when they did run, they seemed to be hard to catch.

They moved at a steady pace, and they sort of glided over the surface of the earth. That meant they were more or less immune to terrain. A big root, a pond, even a rocky stream—all these obstacles might slow down a running man, but they had no effect on these crystal warriors. They simply glided along, probably manipulating gravity to achieve flight.

Given rough terrain and sufficient time, they outdistanced us and disappeared into the forests. So far however, according to all the reports, we'd yet to encounter a full army of these strange aberrations. We'd only encountered them in singles, or sometimes in pairs, and in form, the ones we'd seen were all many-faceted spheroids.

While I was puzzling out what these things were, exactly, and what we were going to do about them, my tapper began to buzz on its own. I only had a moment to read the name of the incoming call before the channel opened, and I was face-to-face with Primus Cherish Collins. Startled, I immediately broke into a grin.

"Say... you aren't feeling lonely tonight, are you Primus? I've got an excellent mudhole all warmed-up out here in the forest for you—if you're feeling bored."

Her face twisted in disgust. "As if, McGill," she said.

That was disgust, sure, but it wasn't outright anger. There were many subtle shades of refusal in a woman's response. Over time, I'd carefully worked-out a hierarchy of possible responses, and hers certainly wasn't the worst I'd been greeted with—not by a longshot.

In fact, I calculated she was just a little bit flustered and flattered by my suggestion. I could tell she might even be considering it, as her eyes slid to one side, not straight up in an expression of outright dismissal. If she'd looked downward, she would have been thinking hard about it, but when a girl glanced to the right or left... she wasn't sure what to do.

Encouraged, I grinned at her, and I let her stew for a moment. Finally, shaking her head, she turned back to me. She became all-business again. "James, remember what we said out in the forest when I came out to investigate your contact story?"

"I sure do sir," I said. "You wanted me to back you up on your ideas concerning the origins of these crystals."

"No, James. No," she said. "I wanted you to back me up on the idea that the local aliens were running away from the crystals and that's why they slammed into our forward lines."

"Oh yeah, yeah, right. I've got it."

"All right. Well now, I'm calling in that chip. I need your backup statement. Come to the headquarters bunker and remember to shake all the mud off your boots before you come down the steps, please."

"Will do, sir. I'll be there in a jiffy." When the call ended, I stood up, picked up my rifle, and looked around at the curious, grimy faces of my troops.

"Aw, hell," Leeson said. "Are you kidding me? Are you off somewhere for the night, sir? You're leaving me in command squatting in this mudhole, aren't you?"

"That's right, Adjunct," I told him. I heard footsteps on the other side of me, and I turned to see Harris and Kivi walking up. Both of them looked slightly upset.

Harris jerked a thumb at Kivi. "Your tech here says you just got a call from Primus Collins."

It was my turn to look disgusted. I turned on Kivi. "Girl," I told her, "you need to learn to keep your nose out of other people's business. Official or not."

Kivi looked angry, but she was looking at Harris, not me. "So quick to point the finger at me, huh? See if I tap into a feed for you again anytime soon." She turned away and walked off.

Adjunct Harris frowned after her but then turned back to me. He grinned. "It was a booty call, wasn't it?"

"If it was, I'm not telling the likes of you."

"Aw, come on sir. I've got a pool going. Ever since we saw the way you and Primus Collins were eyeing each other out there in the woods, half the unit wants in on the action."

Shaking my head, I refused to give a definitive answer. I began marching toward the center of the camp, away from the frontlines and toward what we all referred to as the "Gold Brick" bunker.

Gold Bunker was always a dry, cool, clean and pleasant place that the command folks squatted in during campaigns on nasty-ass worlds like this one.

Clane was the last one of my three adjuncts to accost me before I left the camp. "Centurion?" he said. "Are you really leaving Leeson in charge again, sir?"

"Looks like it."

"Well sir, I've got to say he's not the best. I mean he has his heart in the right place and everything, but the last time you took off for a day or two, things were a little rough."

I smiled, and I thumped a heavy hand on his shoulder. "That's why you're wearing that special armor boy. If I were you, I'd sleep in it."

With that said, I turned away and left my unit on their dark, muddy hill. The night-birds were just waking up now, and they were peeping and squawking away like there was no tomorrow.

-32-

When I reached Gold Bunker, I kind of enjoyed barging into the place. I caught some big frowns from a pair of hog-veteran-type guys who guarded the entrance. They objected to my uniform, which was dripping mud and sticks. More than that, they objected to me personally, as I was only a centurion-ranked individual.

Apparently, a lot of lower-ranked officers had been attempting to barge into the finest bunker in camp. It was, after all, the only clean, dry, air-conditioned place on the planet.

I showed the wannabe hogs my tapper with its legit orders, and they let me through. When they finally backed off and gave me the all-clear, I took a moment to do one of those dog-shake maneuvers. Mud splattered, with a little bit of extra jungle-juice in the mix, nailing both of them. They cursed and slapped at their clothes while I marched away with a grin.

Finding the conference room was pretty easy. It was always a big room near the end of the main passageway. When I say the room was big, I naturally mean big for being in a hole inside the ground. The ceiling was kind of low, and the floor was nothing but raw puff-crete.

In the center of the chamber was a big battle map, displayed on a table which was really a computer. The whole thing glowed. Three-dimensional holographic terrain showed the position of our various units with red arrows pointing down toward the hotspots.

I bellied up to the display and stood over it. Droplets of water fell off my helmet and my open faceplate, which caused the image on the table to waver a little.

"McGill?" Tribune Winslade said. At this point, he was the only man in the conference room other than a couple of those adjunct butt-kissers he always kept around. He shooed them out and then turned to me with a stern look and small fists on his small hips. "McGill? What are you doing here? I don't recall inviting you."

"That's probably right, sir. Primus Collins ordered me to be here."

"Oh, really? That's surprising... I thought she hated you."

I frowned at that. I hadn't realized until recently that Cherish was butt-hurt, but apparently everybody else in the legion was aware of it. "Huh..." I said, "that's odd. I always kind of thought she was sweet on me."

"Well, as long as you're here, you might as well give me your report.

I did so, detailing the action where my unit had fought against the crystals. Then I began going over the evidence we'd found in the forest.

In the middle of my speech, Primus Collins arrived. She threw open the doors, and she seemed to be slightly out of breath.

"James," she said, "you're here already?"

"Yes ma'am," I said. "You said to come in on the double."

She nodded and stepped up to take her place at the conference table. She stood at attention until Winslade noticed.

"At ease," he said, then he asked her to make her report. He listened politely enough, although I couldn't help but notice that his lips were twitching now and then. They even became tightly compressed during the presentation.

"So," he said when she'd finished, "we've got some kind of new and not well understood machines attacking our lines. That's in addition to the locals on this planet. That's simply wonderful news."

Primus Collins frowned. "Sir, I don't think that's what we've been encountering."

Winslade crossed his skinny arms across his skinny chest. "Oh no? How would you sum it all up?"

"First off, I don't think they're machines. I think these crystalline creatures are lifeforms. At least, they act like lifeforms."

Winslade shook his head. "I disagree. They don't bleed, and they don't breathe air. I doubt they reproduce. These things are definitely and decidedly strange and unique. I would even go so far as to call them unnatural, but then, so is an automated tank. I'd call them drones—semi-intelligent machines bent on our destruction."

I dared to lift a big hand. Winslade nodded to me. "But sir," I said, "if they're machines... then what's running them? Who's giving them their orders?"

He pointed a skinny finger at me and shook it in my direction. "Aha, a flash of insight from the muddy jungle. That is the very question we must find the answer to, McGill. I postulate that they're working for these locals just like the dogmen. They've brought in outside reinforcements to repel Legion Varus. They don't have the strength to do it on their own."

Primus Collins shook her head. "I don't know, Tribune. I don't think these natives are that sophisticated."

"Well, you're possibly correct about that, but someone is behind this resistance effort. Possibly, quite possibly, the Rigellians are involved. Why wouldn't they be? This is one of the last planets between Earth's territory and their own borders. Jungle World is the closest planet to Rigel that we've ever managed to invade. I believe they're pulling out all the stops in their own defense."

Primus Collins opened her mouth to object, but Winslade talked over her.

"Look at the evidence," he said. "They've summoned the Clavers, who provided them the dogmen. They've armed the locals with high-tech spears—not the most effective weapons, but at least they're able to use them better than something more complex, like a gun. And now, we see these strange crystalline automatons."

Primus Collins was shaking her head, and I couldn't help but interrupt. "That's just not how it is at all, sir," I said. "Leeson was in command at the time, he says these aliens came at us and hit us hard. I think they were running away from the crystals. In fact, look at this."

We showed him video of the aftermath which indeed showed many aliens had perished, killed by the crystals.

Winslade frowned at all this. "I admit the evidence is somewhat confusing," he said, "but for now, it doesn't even matter if they're allied or not. The mission of Legion Varus is to invade and secure this planet. All resistance is to be eliminated. I don't really care if they're an alliance or not. They must be pushed aside and conquered."

Next, I made an effort to present the discussions I'd had with Abigail Claver and Raash back at Rigel. "See?" I said. "Even Squantus wants us to stop fighting each other and to gang up on these crystal things."

"Maybe he does, and maybe he doesn't, McGill," Winslade said. "Perhaps it's all a ploy to gain time. Maybe they want to throw us against the crystals while they maneuver at our flanks and stab us in the rear."

"A favorite tactic of many, sir," I said. "I get that, but I think we should leave the locals out of this and attack the big crystal-thing."

Winslade nodded. "On that point, you and I are in agreement. Here are my orders, and I'm going to keep it simple. Legion Varus has sat here in this encampment for long enough. We're moving out, and we're advancing toward the crystalline base—whatever the hell it is. We'll reach the thing within a week."

Collins and I both blinked, startled. It was one thing to talk about moving the legion a hundred kilometers, but it was quite another to do the walking and the hauling of gear that far through an unforgiving jungle.

"We'll set up our base camp here," Winslade continued. An illusory arrow extended from his finger and pinpointed a spot on the scrolling landscape that glowed on the holotable. He tapped at a spot to the west of our current encampment. "I hate to have to leave these bunkers and all of these nice trenches we've built, but they're essentially useless. They aren't getting us any closer to our goals. When we get within artillery range of that alien structure, we'll set up star-falls and begin bombarding it continuously. Then we'll have a ground force—half the legion, I imagine—advance for a close-assault operation."

Right off, I knew what that meant. He was going to sit back with the half of the legion that protected the star-falls. He'd probably build himself an entirely new Gold Bunker. Maybe this time, he'd decorate it with cut gems, or something.

I scratched my head, leaned over the big table, and thought it over. "It's a fairly solid plan sir," I admitted. "I mean, I've got no idea if it's going to work or not, but it's worth a shot."

Cherish was still frowning at the map.

Winslade noticed that. "You still have objections, Collins?"

"I do, Tribune. I'm thinking about McGill's peace mission out to Rigel."

"What do you think of the appeals made by the Rigellians through McGill?" he asked.

Primus Collins looked up and stood straight. "I think they're reasonable, sir. I think the evidence on the battlefield shows that these crystals are killing humans and aliens alike. I think we should call a truce with them and possibly combine arms against this third-party invader."

"Hmm," Winslade said. He tapped at his chin with one finger and walked around the table slowly. He was pacing and thinking, as I'd seen him do before. "So… you're buying into this whole peaceful alliance? Is that it? Do you think they're in earnest with their requests for a truce?"

"I do, Tribune. Most of the primus-level individuals who've heard of this offer agree on that."

Winslade looked slightly more disgusted than before. It was as if he smelled an outhouse on a hot sunny day. Who knew? Perhaps he did.

He bared his teeth slightly. "I'm going to have to have a talk with our technical specialists," he said, "but again, let's set all that aside for now. Imperator Turov and I have discussed this. We reviewed all the pertinent data that McGill was able to gather. It is our joint belief that the Rigellians are simply stalling for time and that all of this is nothing but an elaborate ruse."

"But sir," I objected, "these big red crystals, came out of the sky from nowhere. They're hitting all over the place. I've heard they've already hit Blood World and Dark World."

"Yes, yes, yes," Winslade said, waving for me to shut up. "But you have to understand the desperate nature of the Rigellian situation. We're right here at the doorstep of Rigel itself. We've been island-hopping—going from planet to planet, getting closer and closer to their home world. They've started bringing in mercenaries to stop us. They've even been arming these apes with high-tech spears. All that smacks of desperation to me. I think they're willing to do anything, to *say* anything, to slow us down—but I'm not fooled, and neither is Turov."

Both Cherish and I opened our yaps to object, but Winslade stopped us with a small flat palm.

"We're going to advance," he continued, "and we're going to assail that crystal. If the locals sit back and don't interfere, so much the better. But after we've destroyed this crystalline aberration, we're going to apply similar techniques to every other military organization on this planet. We intend to conquer them all."

I shook my head slowly. "I sure hope you're right, sir. I surely do."

"Thank you for that vote of confidence," he said tightly. "Now, if you don't mind, I'm quite busy planning out the logistics of this march. I suggest both of you retire to your respective commands and do the same. We're going to pack up and move out at dawn's light."

I waved one of my hands in the air wanting to ask another question, but he ignored me.

"Dismissed, McGill," he said, turning his back and focusing on the planning table.

We walked out of the place, and a dozen other staffers scowled as they passed us by to surround Winslade and his table. They were like jealous courtiers. They didn't like lowlifes such as Cherish and I having any private chats with the big cheese.

When we were out in the passageway Cherish heaved a sigh. "Well," she said, "thanks for trying, McGill."

"You're welcome, sir. Say uh, I had one other thing I wanted to ask you about."

"What's that?"

"I've been hearing rumors that you're upset with me about something. Is that true?"

She stopped walking, and she slowly turned to face me. She peered straight up into my face. "Of course I'm upset," she said. "How could I not be?"

I stared at her, dumbfounded for a bit. Finally, I shook my head because my mind was still a blank even though I'd given it a hard think.

"I apologize profusely," I said, "but I've got no frigging idea what you're talking about. We've barely had contact with each other for a year or two now."

"That's it exactly," she said. Her lower jaw was jutting out at me, showing a fine line of white teeth. "You haven't said word-one to me. When I came back to this legion, I expected at least a courtesy call. And before that, when I sent you that text for help after I left Legion Varus, you didn't even answer!"

Unimpressed by my slack-jawed stare, she turned on her heels and walked quickly away.

My brow furrowed, and I began thinking hard. I gave myself a scratch thinking back to the City World campaign.

A text...?

Then, all of a sudden, a bolt of memory struck me out of the blue.

I had it! She *had* sent me a text after she'd left the legion. In fact, the very night she'd left, I'd gotten together again with Galina. I was lying there next to Galina with Cherish definitely gone out of my life, so I'd decided to ignore the text and, in fact, I'd deleted it.

To make sure Galina never saw it, I'd double-deleted it, digging down into the cloud trashcans to make sure it was gone for good.

That must be what she was talking about. She'd sent me a message, and I hadn't even read it.

Frowning, I felt just a pang, a tiny pang of regret. That was a rare thing for me, and it kickstarted me into action. I stepped after Primus Collins, who was walking pretty damned fast, but fortunately her legs were only maybe half as long as mine. I was able to catch up without even breaking into a trot.

Long before we'd reached the hogs I'd shaken mud onto at the entranceway, I caught up to her. "I know what you're talking about," I said.

She paused, but she didn't look at me. She just crossed her arms over her perky bosom and stared straight ahead. I could tell she was angry to the bone.

"You sent out a Christmas message last year. I think I saw it, but it seemed like a big group-thing you sent to everybody in the entire cohort. That was it wasn't it? Were you expecting like, you know, a present or something in return?"

Cherish turned around slowly. Her face was a combination of disbelief and rage. "No McGill, you idiot," she said. "I sent you a text shortly after I left the legion and was rejected by Victrix. You never answered, so I was transferred at random, and ended up stuck on some hellish planet."

"Uh," I said, "what planet?"

"L-347 I think they call it."

"Oh no..." I said. "That place... Death World?"

"Exactly."

"Did you get a chance to meet Helsa and Kattra?"

"Yes," she said between clenched teeth, "I did. I hated both of those witches, and they were hateful right back toward me. I did my best to get out of there as fast as I could and came back to Varus."

"Huh..." I said, pretending to be completely baffled. "What did you say in that text, anyways?"

She stared at me. "You know very well what it said. You just didn't want to answer."

I presented her with my best innocent and ignorant expressions. I widened my eyes, opened my mouth, shook my head, and even threw my hands up with my fingers splayed. "I didn't get any text, Cherish. I swear to it. If you want to check my tapper, I'll show you."

"That's not necessary," she said turning away again to pout.

Sensing that perhaps it was absolutely necessary, I pulled out my tapper and paged through the history section. Finding nothing from her with the search function, I dug deeper into the deleted bins, and then moved on into the *unrecoverable* deleted zone. That was a place they didn't even tell you about in the tutorial vids.

As I did all this, Cherish kept taking curious glances. She couldn't help herself.

Naturally, with me being a man who needed to delete evidence on a regular basis, I'd already hacked the applications on my tapper. I'd done things to it that other people didn't know how to do. One of those things was to absolutely and permanently erase a message with no trace that it had ever been there.

On the date in question, there was nothing from her or from anyone else using a deep-link system.

"You see?" I said. "These communication systems, they aren't perfect. Maybe you should have re-sent it, or something."

Frowning, even glaring, she grabbed my arm with firm small hands and began flicking through the menus. Just like so many other women who knew me well, she wanted to see the evidence for herself.

I let her tickle at my forearm all she wanted. At last, she pushed my arm away, and she put a hand up to her face. "I can't believe it…" she said. "The message really didn't get through."

"I guess not," I said. "It's probably the poor service coming out of Death World. It's not a high-rent place, you know. I'm awfully sorry about that."

"No, no…" she said, sounding haunted, "it's not your fault. It was something technical all along. You were, after all, deployed out on City World. That's a long way from Earth. That's all the way out in the Mid-Zone."

I pointed a big, fat finger at her. "That's it! I bet you, that's it! Messages to the Mid-Zone… How can they be as reliable as something that you would send just from Dust World to Earth, that sort of thing. It must have cost you a pretty penny, too. I sure am sorry I never did receive it."

Cherish stared down at the deck for a while. Her face was a tight set of lines. I could tell she was still upset and trying to let it go. At last, she heaved a sigh. She unwrapped her arms which were tightly hugging up against her breasts.

"All right," she said. "All right, okay. I've been hating you for a long time because of this, and I guess it just wasn't fair. The whole time..."

"That is a mighty big thing for a woman to admit," I told her. "I am impressed. My momma always said that a person's true character shines through when they find out they were wrong about something, and they're able to admit it."

Cherish glanced up at me, then down to the deck again. "Even if you didn't get my text, you never did try to reach out to me. You never even seemed to notice that I'd rejoined Legion Varus again. I was around all through the Sky World campaign, you know."

"Yeah, yeah," I said, "I remember getting some orders... That was a big fight out there, wasn't it?"

"Yes, it was," she said.

"Anyways... so... what exactly did that text say?"

She shook her head. "Forget about it. It was nothing. Nothing important, anyway."

"Okay, consider it forgotten. But say, how about you and I go do a little planning together?"

Cherish twisted up her lips. She knew exactly what I meant by "planning."

"I don't know, James," she said. "I don't think I'm ready for that yet."

"Okay, okay," I said. "I purely understand. How about we just go and have a drink over at the officer's pub, then? After all, we're in Gold Bunker with legit permission to be here. That means we can visit their high-class pub. It's the last day it'll be open."

She thought about that, and I could see by the set of her teeth I was tempting her something awful.

"Just think," I said, "by tomorrow, we're all going to be on the march. It's going to be nothing but mud and blood and pointy spears flying at you. This might be our last chance to have a drink that doesn't have dirt all over the rim."

This last line did the trick. She relented, and she nodded her head.

"Okay," she said.

Smiling, I led her to the pub. We barged in, ignoring every sneer we got from the higher-ups.

Primus Collins was, of course, accepted in this establishment. As a lowly centurion, I was a different story, and as far as the other officers were concerned, I was on the wrong side of the bar—I should be serving them, not drinking.

We ignored the looks and after a couple of excellent beverages, we were smiling at each other. The rest of the evening followed a predictable pattern. I found that Cherish, to my delight, had bunking rights inside Gold Bunker. I was thereby able to avoid returning to the stinking mudhole where my troops were stationed for the night.

It was the last gasp of civilized behavior that either one of us were going to see for a long time, and we enjoyed it to the fullest.

-33-

I woke up the next morning shortly before dawn—at least, that's what time my tapper said it was.

The damned thing was buzzing away at me, and the first thought that came into my head was the realization that the whole legion was supposed to be moving out of camp today. I hadn't even informed my adjuncts about it the night before.

"Oh shit," I said.

Cherish was snuggled up to me on the arm that I answer my tapper with, and I couldn't exactly reach a finger to the screen. I made a failed attempt to roll a little and swing my long tapper-arm into range of my longest digit—stretched out on the other side of the sleeping Primus Collins' head. That movement caused her head to bounce on my big biceps.

I'd also kind of forgotten that we'd fallen asleep together. While an officer's bunk was roomier than your typical grunt's bed, had still never been designed for two. As a consequence, when I made a sudden movement Cherish was tossed onto the deck in a tangle of limbs and bedsheets.

"What the hell?" she complained, climbing to her feet and glaring at me.

I opened the call on my tapper with the swipe of one finger and saw to my surprise it wasn't Graves or Tribune Winslade. Instead, it was my pretty tech specialist Natasha Elkin.

"Hey Natasha, what's this all about?" I asked. Cherish was standing there in the buff. She flipped me off and began pulling on her clothes. I gave her a friendly wave in return.

"Centurion?" Natasha said, "I waited as long as possible, but I have to tell you about a rumor flying through the cohort. Every tech I know online says that we're moving out in the next half hour. Is that true, sir? Were you aware of this?"

"Huh…" I said, "you know… I've heard-tell something about that. I just didn't know it was going to be quite so early…"

Both Primus Collins and Natasha gave me reproachful frowns. I shrugged that off as I'd shrugged off countless such looks all the way back to Sunday school.

Regretting the dismal fact that there wasn't enough time to make things right with Cherish, or to have a proper breakfast or a proper shower, I made the best of things. I pulled on some clothes, rammed some rations into my mouth, and marched out to my unit's encampment. I did pause long enough to give Cherish a kiss and a squeeze.

"You stole that," she said, pouting and glaring.

"Don't I always?"

She kicked me out of her quarters, and I was on my own in the relatively cool morning air of Jungle World in no time. Marching through the mud, I dared to whistle a lively tune. Things were looking up for old McGill, by my way of thinking.

I was greeted with a lot of sour looks when I reached my unit a few minutes later. Remembering that Natasha had contacted me and doubtlessly pinpointed my location, I realized that every noncom and officer in my unit probably knew by now where I'd spent the night.

Ignoring their poor attitudes, I chased the sour looks off everyone's face by giving them a long stream of orders. "Time to pack up and move out!" I shouted, slamming my oven-mitt palms together. "Let's go, let's go, let's go!" I clapped and stamped and shouted until they were all hopping. "Pack up your kits and fall in for the march!"

Scrambling troops shook their dicks, dumped coffeepots onto smokey fires and grabbed their rifles. Something like eight minutes later, every soldier in my unit was buried under a backpack and marching westward.

As we'd been near the front lines, 3rd Cohort naturally took a point position. We were to function as skirmishers—the tip of the spear—as we slogged west. I spread out my lights in front and put my heavies in the rear.

Our orders from Graves were to engage any enemy we met up with. My light troops were supposed to harass any enemy force while giving ground until the rest of the legion could meet up with us and overwhelm whatever we faced.

Ten thousand strong, Legion Varus slogged through the mud and the trees. Way back at the rear of the formation, the lifters drifted along hugging the treetops. The chicken pilots didn't dare to rise above the horizon as they feared being shot down by the red crystal's deadly gravity-beams.

A few long days passed, days that were filled with nothing but rain, sweat and misery. When we got close to our goal, the lifters stopped shadowing us. They weren't allowed to advance the last twenty kilometers or so. They would have to land and set up what defenses they could while the rest of us pressed forward.

We were only safe at this proximity because the enemy's big weapons were essentially beam cannons. Such tech could only strike a target that was within the line of sight. Although the big red crystal was tall, towering a hundred meters or more up into the air, even the tip of it couldn't sight us. We were far out into the hilly jungle enough to be heavily obstructed. The enemy base was well-positioned to shoot down vehicles coming down from space, but when facing attack from the ground it had serious limitations.

After leaving the lifters behind to set up camp, we slogged along all the way until noon the next day. We didn't meet a single enemy. The crystals, dogmen and ape-aliens had apparently taken the day off.

Pausing for lunch, we ate dismal rations. A slow, heavy, cool rain began. Each drop seemed larger than it might have been on Earth, something more like a squirt from a showerhead than what we would call a droplet. That had to be due to the gravity, the atmosphere or something else. I didn't know what, but I did know it was an unpleasant experience—being nailed by globules of water from above.

After a half-hour lunch, we continued marching. The days on Jungle World were long—almost twenty-nine hours long.

That may not seem much different than a twenty-four-hour day, but let me tell you, when you're trapped in a hot suit of armor marching in blood-warm rain, you were exhausted by the time the sun went down.

That afternoon our cohort was allowed to fall back. We were no longer marching ahead of the rest. 6th Cohort took on that dubious honor, and they led us into a rugged line of hills. It was when they mounted a ridge that was topped off by a rocky plateau that the entire legion was called to halt.

No one was interested in telling us why. I didn't think it was combat, because I didn't see any flashes or hear any bangs out at the front. A couple of kilometers away from my current position 6th Cohort had simply stopped dead.

I called together Kivi and Natasha to huddle-up and see what they could learn.

"We can't send buzzers out that far," Kivi complained, "not in this weather. These big raindrops will knock them right out of the sky."

"Okay," I said, "what else have we got?" I looked at Natasha expectantly.

She shrugged. "What do you think I can do?"

"You can start hacking, girl. Somebody must have eyes on the top of that ridge. What's the 6th doing up there?"

Frowning, she worked her backpack computer. That thing was bulkier and more capable than anyone's tapper. Finally, she tossed me a vid stream with the flick of her finger.

I watched as men topped the rise in question, and I immediately recognized the scene. It looked identical to the spot of worship that we discovered way back at Legion Varus' initial campsite.

"Another frigging sacred shrine?" I asked. "Aw damn, I hope these furry bastards aren't going to go berserk and charge us again."

This time, things were different. There wasn't a huge army of locals numbering in the thousands, nor was there a single oddly dressed priest standing on top of the rocks.

"Give me a better shot of the scene," I asked Natasha. "Something from up high, not just this feed from a helmet."

Natasha gritted her teeth. "I'll have to hack to get that video—the operators might notice."

I shrugged and gestured for her to get on with it.

Natasha worked at it, and I knew if she couldn't hack into the feed, it couldn't be done. She was a pro. Sure enough, less than a minute later she had it.

"Try this," she said, tossing a feed over to me. "It looks grim."

I eyed the scene, and I had to agree. It did look grim. All the native aliens who I'd expected to see when we got a good look at the top of this plateau were actually still there, but they weren't alive and worshipping their dubious gods. Instead, they were all dead. What looked to be thousands of them lay sprawled in the mud.

The buzzer—whoever's buzzer it was that we were leaching off of—flew to the central circle of rocks. The rocks formed an edifice in the middle of the bodies—a pyramid of sorts. There, I saw only more dead. No gateways, no dogmen. Just dead local aliens.

"Poor bastards," Natasha said. "Whatever hit them was thorough. They didn't have a chance."

That's when I got an idea, and it made me grit my teeth. I attempted to contact Tribune Winslade. He rejected my call and relayed it to Primus Graves instead. This was the appropriate chain of command, but he was a dick for doing it.

"Graves here. What do you want, McGill?"

"Sir, I don't like the looks of the death-party on top of the mountain."

He stared at me for a moment, then he became angry. "Tell Natasha to stop her hacking."

"I'm sorry, Primus. I've got no idea what you're talking about. But sir, I've heard a funny rumor. The story goes like this: We just got to the top of another one of those big plateaus. One of those funny places where the aliens like to worship whatever the hell they're worshipping?"

He stared at me flatly. "Go on."

"Well sir, it looks like the aliens up there got themselves skunked. I'd have to guesstimate that the crystal-thing did them dirty. I don't know if it nailed them all with a gravity-beam, or if it was a lot of those little crystalline flying geodes, or whatever the hell they are."

"McGill, so far this call is completely unhelpful. You've got ten seconds to regain my attention before I move on to more pressing matters."

"I hear you, Primus. I hear you." I then relayed to him the contents of the mission briefing I'd given to Winslade and his butt-kissers back on *Scorpio*.

This made him blink in surprise. "You mean to tell me they sent *you* out to Rigel to do diplomacy? Whose crazy idea was that?"

"Well sir… the meeting was requested by Abigail Claver."

"Abigail Claver?" he said. "Hardly a trustworthy source of information…"

"No sir, I suppose she isn't. But she did inform me that the primitive people of this world, plus the Rigellians and the Clavers, have all combined to try to fight against these crystal things we're seeing. They're deadly enemies to all of us."

Graves thought that over for a moment, and then he reached a big finger down as if to stab at his tapper and shut down the connection.

"Hold on, sir," I said, "before you move on, what do you think about all this?"

"I think that you should stay in your lane, McGill. I know I'm virtually asking the impossible, but if you were sent out on a mission and you performed that mission, you are now out of the loop. Your superior officers will make appropriate decisions based on the reports you gave them. You shouldn't second guess their choices or pass on clandestine information which I'm sure at the very least is classified to anyone not directly involved. That's what I think, McGill. Now, carry on following orders and killing the enemy when directed to do so."

With that Graves cut the channel.

"Useless," I said grunting in disappointment.

"What's that Centurion?" Natasha asked.

"He's as useless as a two-inch cock," I said. "At least that's what Galina would say."

Natasha smirked, and she shook her head and left me.

The day wore on, and the rain grew louder and heavier. Soon, you couldn't see a hundred meters away into the forest. The leaves above us were breaking up the raindrops sure, but there was a thick mist rolling up now. The ground itself was steaming hot.

When the rain really started pouring, gunfire broke out.

"Where are we getting hit?" Harris yelled. "Is anybody under fire?"

"No one in our unit has reported contact," I said, looking over my officer's displays. "Looks like they're hitting 6th Cohort up in front of us."

"It's probably those frigging apes," Harris said. "I bet they just love this kind of weather. They can sneak up close and shive you. It's like fighting in a steam bath."

Several minutes of confusion ensued, and it soon became evident that 6th Cohort was under attack. Graves came online, and he ordered 3rd Cohort to move forward to support the 6th.

"Oh, hell yeah," Leeson said. "This is what we signed up for huh, Clane? Jogging through a foot of mud and rain so thick we couldn't see our peckers if they were in our own hands. This is the perfect place and time to meet a committed enemy."

And meet them we did. At first, a wave of confused fellow legionnaires came streaming toward us. Some were wounded, others just looked panicked. Behind them, I saw a glint of reflected light. What was that? Did the enemy have beam weapons of some kind?

As we kept marching forward, getting jogged and jostled by the retreating troops from 6th Cohort, I called a halt. I had my troops formed up in a line and ordered my lights to retreat behind my heavies. I also ordered my weaponeers—those with belchers and other weapons like mini-missiles and drone-bombs—to advance and join the heavies.

"McGill?" Graves demanded a moment later speaking over command chat into my headset. "Why has your unit stopped advancing?"

"Because sir, it looks like the 6th is broken and fleeing. I've fought this enemy a few times before, sir. I recommend we hit them with mass firepower—everything we've got at close range."

Graves was quiet for a second, but then he seemed to decide he liked my idea. He liked it so much, in fact, he took it for his own. He ordered the entire cohort to form up lines, to let the 6th retreat through us, to allow them to reorganize back behind our protective line.

"Do you really think the primitives broke the 6th?" Graves asked in my headset.

"No sir," I said, "it was those crystal devils. Those giant floating geodes."

"And how do you know that?"

"Because, I think sir... I think I can see one right now."

And I could. That shine, that flickering I'd noticed before. It was getting brighter each time I saw it flash.

More flashes appeared every minute. They were spread out, indicating there was more than one crystal involved. There had to be dozens of them, maybe hundreds. It was like watching a little lightning storm. Silent and deadly, they were chasing our troops down and killing them as they ran through the mud.

"Harris?" I said. "Have we got any of those shotguns?"

"You mean the ones we keep for the Rigellians? To break through their armor?"

"Exactly."

He shrugged. "I've got one in my pack sir, and most of my heavies do as well."

I nodded. "All right, break them out. Hand them to Clane's light troopers. Have them distribute them around."

"What? We might need those things, sir!"

"For this battle, what we need is mass firepower at close range. You have your orders, Adjunct."

Cursing up a storm, Harris walked around his heavies, collecting shotguns and redistributing them to Clane's troops. The recruits slung their snap-rifles—which were going to be pretty much useless in the upcoming conflict. They took up the short-ranged but very hard-hitting shotguns.

"Tell them to stand firm and don't put it up against their shoulders," he told Clane. "If you do, these things will bust your clavicle when they kick."

Clane nodded, took a shotgun himself, and went back to his position standing behind the heavies.

When they were a few hundred meters away, my troops engaged them with heavy gunfire. We saw the crystals light up, struck by thousands of rounds. Some of them spun and many shed glittering chunks of themselves—but they didn't stop gliding closer.

These crystals were different. They were larger, and they had more facets. Twenty sides or more, if I had to guess. Some of them had points, too. Star-like points sticking out of various triangular planes.

The first gravity-beam strikes surprised me, because I'd kind of expected we'd be hit with spear-like spines as we'd seen from these creatures in our previous encounters.

The gravity-beams had considerable range, and they hit even harder than the spines had. Screaming for his men to duck low, Harris got our front line behind cover such as fallen logs, rocks—that sort of thing. What mostly stuck up and was visible consisted of helmets and gun muzzles.

The first gravity-beam struck a soldier in the head—going right through his helmet. It seemed to crush his skull inside the helmet where it was supposedly sheltered. The helmet offered no protection at all against such a physics-bending weapon in fact it was perfectly intact.

The man didn't even cry out. He just lurched and slumped, dead as a stone.

-34-

Seeing one of my armed and armored heavy soldiers get annihilated by a headshot sent a big jolt of concern through me and my other officers. It wasn't exactly fear, I wouldn't call it that, but we realized instantly that our armor wasn't an effective defense against this weapon.

That was especially disappointing to me and Clane. We were, after all, the only two men in the unit who wore stardust armor. I had the feeling that once we were hit by one of those gravity-beams from those weird crystal aliens, we were going to learn that our fancy suits did precisely diddly-squat to protect us.

This had to be due to the strange properties of the beam itself. It didn't operate as a projectile, which had to blast through whatever obstacle was in the way. Unlike a laser beam, or a particle beam, or even a bullet, the gravity-beams seemed to affect whatever matter was in the path of the beam. It affected that matter, such as a soldier's skull, by creating a strange physics-twisting anomaly.

Natasha was instantly fascinated. "Did you see that?" she hissed with excitement.

"Yeah, I saw blood gush out of his eye sockets."

"Yes, but... I'm just thinking about the technology. It's revolutionary. No armor can protect against it. I think it must work by temporarily changing the gravitational pull of the affected matter. For a millisecond, it causes whatever is struck to collapse in upon itself."

Her eyes were lit up like a kid at Christmas. I wasn't so happy.

Two more troopers had their heads pulped, and I shouted for people to hunker down lower. "Take your shot, then kiss the dirt! Drink that mud!"

From what I'd seen so far, when something very solid was hit such as a piece of metal or even a thick tree trunk, the warped gravity effect didn't do much. But when it struck something soft like human flesh, the effects were immediate and dramatic. People's brains were squeezed into pulp inside their skulls. Blood turned to jelly, and muscle became as hard as bone.

It took me only a few seconds to realize that this enemy was quite a different beast and that new tactics were needed. Our usual approach as human legionnaires essentially involved firepower. The goal was to send as much metal and energy as we could toward anything that threatened us. This was best done at a significant distance—the farther away the better.

But this enemy wasn't going to play by those old rules. They swept forward and closed with us. As my men were discovered, we sprang up into action. We were able to batter the crystals as they approached, and we did break chips off them. Our guns were like ice picks working on glaciers.

But more and more of the crystals kept appearing. We sent up showers of sparks off their strange rocky bodies, but we simply weren't putting them down. When they reached out with their beams, my troops melted and died instantly. What we needed was something that hit them very hard without exposing us to their strange gravity-beams.

I shouted new orders to my unit. "Everybody!" I said. "Cease fire! Hug the ground. Get down low. Find cover anywhere you can. Get behind something very solid and stay there."

Not everyone followed my commands immediately. A lot of the troops in my unit were young recruits. When a new soldier faces a hard battle, especially against a strange alien menace, he's not always fully listening to his commander. Such troops often either froze up and didn't fire at all, or they unloaded a continuous stream of fire in a near panic.

Clane and Moller squirmed towards troops who were disobeying my command and cuffed them, shoving them sometimes physically to get them to obey.

After perhaps ten to fifteen seconds, the firing died down to almost nothing. The enemy crystals, however, had already struck a dozen of my men dead.

As they approached at a relatively sedate pace—perhaps it was an all-out charge if you were a floating alien crystal—they kept firing those strange beams of theirs.

I think the only reason that you could actually see the beams as they passed through the air was largely to do with the significant amount of water vapor on Jungle World. The beams caused the raindrops and the mist-filled air between them to compress, transforming fog into miniature swirling cyclones.

A freaky sparkling effect was also released—some kind of electrical discharge. In any case, the beams were visible to us, and they were quite terrifying.

The deadly rays slashed over our heads. They struck obstacles, leaving trees and rocks scarred and smoking. Tree trunks didn't always stop them, either. I was a witness as some of my men kept to cover behind a thick trunk and still got struck down by this mysterious weaponry.

"Find a rock!" I shouted. "Find a shallow place in the ground! Get low people, get low. Let them come in close. When they get right on top of you, take the heaviest weapon you've got and carve up some crystal."

It was the only thing I could think of to do. The main objector was Harris himself.

"Sir?" he said, worming his way over the muddy ground to crouch next to me. "Don't you think we should get all of our weaponeers to concentrate fire on one of these crystals at a time? If we let them get in closer, they might just kill us all. Who knows if they've got some other trick up their sleeve? We've never been nose-to-nose with this kind of alien. What if they can radiate gravity waves or some freaky shit like that?"

I glanced at him, and I knew that he could be right. We were operating with very little information against a brand new and utterly alien enemy.

"In that case, Harris," I said, "we're fucked. But I haven't seen anything like that from these aliens yet. Until they demonstrate some such capabilities, I'm going to assume they've got nothing except their gravity-beams. Now, get back to your heavies and get ready to break these glass-like critters."

Muttering about his funeral and mine, Harris wormed away again. At twenty meters range, I shouted over tactical chat. "I want everybody with a plasma grenade on their belt to pull it out and throw it right under the closest enemy. Let's see if they like a little bit of gravity distortion from us."

The advancing crystals managed to kill a few more troops before they reached our lines. Off to my left and right flanks, I saw vicious firefights were underway, but it was all quiet on my little slice of rainy ground.

When the crystals came near, dozens of arms swept up and plasma grenades arced high. Two men howled in agony, their throwing arms having been sited, targeted and shot during the brief period they'd exposed them. These two unlucky troopers howled and hissed and writhed in the mud—the flesh of their arms having been crushed down to something that resembled strips of bacon clinging to the bone.

Flaring with blue-white light, the grenades splashed down into mudpuddles and simmered for a few seconds. We'd set them with very short fuses. They awaited the advancing enemy and quickly cooked-off.

When the odd, almost silent explosions glared, I was gratified to see they had a serious effect on the enemy. The crystals weren't shattered and destroyed outright, but they were decidedly affected.

Perhaps, as they were beings that naturally manipulated gravity for purposes of both motion and weaponry, they were disoriented and stunned by the effects of our plasma-grenades. These odd weapons had a wide area of effect. At first, they drew in and then threw away any small objects in the area with violent force.

Raindrops were turned into glass beads, exploding a thousand pellets in every direction. Stones, twigs, chunks of mud and everything were all weaponized. The shrapnel flew everywhere with terrific force. Chunks of the crystals were torn away. They shed these like pieces of glass from their bellies.

More importantly, the enemy crystals seemed to lose their sense of direction. Instead of gliding toward us at a steady speed with clear and sinister intent, they now reeled in random directions, confused. Some bounced high, while others sunk low, splashing down into the mud.

My eyes lit up when I saw this, and I recognized the opportunity. "They're shell-shocked!" I shouted. "Everyone with a serious weapon get in there and gut yourself a crystal. Move! Go, go, go!"

"Come on, before they recover!" Clane shouted. He launched himself at the staggering line of crystals.

So far, his troops hadn't done a whole lot during this difficult battle. That wasn't entirely their fault, since they were green recruits armed with ineffective weaponry, but now they truly proved their worth. Armed with shotguns built to kill Rigellians in stardust armor, they raced forward. They were light on their feet, and they carried what turned out to be the most effective weapon we had.

The shotguns shattered whole portions of the crystalline aliens. Some of them split apart outright. Others left behind as much as a sixth or a quarter of themselves, which fell like so much broken glass onto the soupy, muddy ground.

Harris's troops landed upon the enemy a few short seconds later. They used force-blades extended from their power-armor, rather than bothering with their slung morph-rifles, which hadn't done much to this enemy so far.

Leeson's weaponeers threw a few belcher blasts but soon stopped with orders to cease-fire. I knew Leeson was worried that he would hit friendlies who were in close-combat with the enemy.

In the end, of the twenty-odd aliens that had charged us, eleven were destroyed. The rest fled when they regained their senses. My men charged after them, eager for vengeance, but I called them back.

The trouble was the crystalline aliens seemed to be capable of firing backwards as they ran. They struck my troops down with accuracy and deadly effect even as they fled. It didn't seem to matter whether they were racing forward or running away, they were still able to fire their gravity-beams at us.

And so, after a few more deaths, my unit took cover again and dropped, panting into any muddy, rocky hole they could find.

"That was crazy," Harris said.

"How did you know it was going to work like that sir?" Adjunct Clane asked me.

Adjunct Leeson laughed. Harris grinned as well. Adjunct Clane looked from one of them to the next, not sure what the joke was.

"He's a magic man," Leeson told him. "Yep, old McGill—he's a sorcerer."

"That's right," Harris said taking up the joke. "He's only part human. He's more like one of those gifted nutjobs. An idiot-savant, that's what I'd call him."

Clane looked at me, and for just a moment, I thought the poor kid might believe them. I smiled ruefully and shook my head.

"Don't listen to these two, kid," I told him. "I'm a card-carrying moron. Just ask my daddy."

Then, as the danger seemed to have passed, I ordered my troops to withdraw. I passed on our tactical approaches and success to Primus Collins and Primus Graves. Soon, Winslade himself was on the line.

"McGill?" he said. "Barring the not unprecedented possibility that you've dealt with these aliens before, or were somehow tipped-off as to what the most effective means of resistance might be, can you tell me why your unit seems to have succeeded where so many others have failed?"

I was frowning at my tapper while Winslade kept yapping. He told me Legion Varus, especially 3rd Cohort, met up with the enemy crystals. The results had been a mixed bag. In some cases, especially where traditional tactics were employed, the crystals had broken the unit. They'd been routed from the field. In other cases, however, especially those which employed plasma grenades in a big way, the enemy had been repelled with losses on both sides.

When he was finally done making a speech, I explained to Winslade the particular tactics we'd employed.

"I see…" he said. "Typical McGill. Always looking for an advantage, always attempting to trick the enemy and apply force in a unique way…"

For my own part I considered myself complimented. "That's pretty much my job-description, Tribune."

"Right. Well, I'll pass on your tactics. They will be refined and repeated."

"I only wish we had a larger supply of plasma grenades and heavy shotguns. Both are in limited supply. What does the battle look like in the overall, sir?"

"6th Cohort was shattered. I think they were surprised by the appearance of the crystals and didn't know quite what to do. 3rd Cohort fared better. Your total losses are something like thirty percent, but at least a quarter of the aliens were destroyed as well."

"We gave them a whooping!"

"Next time, we'll be even better prepared."

"So… Tribune," I said, "are we going to keep advancing?"

"Negative," Winslade said. "I'm pulling back your entire cohort. We'll put the 8th on the front lines, with the 10th in full support. With these new tactics, we'll press our advantage, and we'll destroy that big, red, glowing bastard before this is over with."

I smiled, liking the smaller man's spirit. He still wanted some payback for all the lifters these guys had burned out of the sky when we'd first arrived. I was willing to entertain the possibility of victory as well. Really, however, it all was a matter of numbers and a lot depended on just how many of these crystalline warriors the other side had left.

-35-

My unit fell back. In fact, all of 3rd Cohort fell back. We licked our wounds and a few revived soldiers returned to us.

The rains slowed, then stopped. We were left with some purple-blue daylight and field rations to chew on. Everyone was spraying nu-skin, repairing their air conditioners and counting every plasma grenade and shotgun shell that we possessed.

Apparently, Winslade had either moved the lifters up to support us, or he'd set up some gateway posts to bring in more material from *Scorpio*. Perhaps the supplies were coming from Earth herself. Whatever the case, we were resupplied.

Slow at first, but then soon in a flood, we were rearmed with shotgun shells, plasma grenades for every soldier in the unit, and whatever else our higher-up commanders thought might help.

I rounded up my three adjuncts and discussed tactics. We talked about the strange nature of the battle we'd just fought. They all agreed that our tactics were far from perfect, but they had at least been reasonably effective. While we came up with ways to improve our odds the next time we met this enemy, the sky lit up overhead.

"Star-falls?" Harris said. "That's a star-fall barrage—it's got to be."

It was true. The big, slow-flying, blue-white spheres of energy and force were arcing up from behind our position. The projectiles moved like comets across the sky toward the west.

Some kilometers back, Winslade had set up an encampment and placed his heaviest artillery units. Now, at long last, they'd begun to bombard the enemy base.

"That's going to rip up these weird, ruby-red freaks," Harris said with excitement. "It's just got to."

"Let's hope," Leeson said.

Clane gaped at the sky. His eyes were wide, and his jaw hung low. He watched, as first dozens, and then hundreds of big plasma bolts went flying.

"They can't strike back at our artillery, can they?" he asked. "Their gravity-beams have incredible range, but they're totally line of sight, right?"

"That's right," I said. "We're something like ten kilometers out now from their big base. Even though it's up high, all our star-falls have to do is shelter behind a thick ridge of rock and mud, and I don't think those aliens can hit us."

We all smiled, and we marveled as the star-falls continued to rain destruction—at least we hoped it was destruction—upon the enemy's base.

Up at the front lines, two fresh cohorts were clearly engaging with the enemy. The skies flickered, and we could hear the rattle of heavy fire.

"Do they know about the plasma grenades and how they confuse the crystals?" Harris asked. "They've got to know that by now, right Centurion? They've *got* to know."

"I did my damnedest to report it," I assured him.

Harris was slamming one fist into his open palm. He showed his teeth, and he peered out to the west. "Those bastards are harder than diamonds," he said.

"But even diamonds can be split apart," I smiled.

All my officers smiled back. We felt like, just possibly, victory was soon to be had. Our legion had rarely met a planet we could not conquer. Our experience and tenacity combined with our flexibility of arms and tactics was a force to be reckoned with, even if we'd just met up with the freakiest damned aliens I'd ever heard of.

"I just thought of something, sir," Clane said to me. We all turned and looked at him. "What about the dogmen? What about all the natives of this planet? Do you think they might hit us in the flank while we're engaged with this dangerous enemy?"

I thought about it, and I shook my head. "I happen to know a bit about the other side, about their commanders and what they're thinking. They see the crystals as a bigger threat than Earth. I would expect at the very least they'll sit it out to see how it goes before they do anything. Now, they might just decide to finish off whoever comes in first in this contest—but I hope they won't."

Clane nodded, but he still looked worried. He tilted his head back and continued watching the show overhead, gaping up in the skies. The big, bright bolts of plasma continued to rise and fall.

An hour or two went by, during which we dared to set up camp. The men were hungry, tired, cold and wet. We did our best to make ourselves comfortable and to set up shelter wherever we could. We used puff-crete and drones to dig trenches and build a low wall above the trench line. It was about a meter high with loopholes in it all along. It was a minimal and primitive fortification, but it was better than nothing.

Night fell, and the battle slowed. We could no longer hear the crackle of gunfire and the strange whooping sound of plasma grenades in the distance.

Eventually, Winslade pulled back the cohorts he'd sent to the frontlines and replaced them with fresh troops. We sat in the middle, the secondary line of defense. All this time, the star-falls kept firing. Long, lobbing arcs fell onto the enemy base continuously.

Right about midnight, as troops were being exchanged at the front, something changed. The skies began lighting up, and the sounds of battle grew louder.

"Um, Centurion?" Natasha said coming close to me. She squatted down and showed me what was on her tapper.

I frowned, as my tactical displays weren't yet lighting up with any new data concerning the battle.

"What the hell is that?" I asked. I stared as dozens of—no hundreds or perhaps even a thousand or more—strange contacts approached our frontline.

It took me a moment to realize she'd tapped into *Scorpio's* overwatch data. It was the freshest and most unfiltered feed, and it was beaming straight down to Winslade's headquarters from our eyes in the sky. I stared at Natasha, and I blinked away sleep.

"What did you do, girl? Haven't you gotten into trouble for hacking at this level often enough?"

Natasha shrugged. "If they were going to court martial me for this kind of thing, they would've done it by now, right?"

I nodded. "I guess you're right. Okay, let's see what you've got."

She showed me what Winslade was getting almost before he himself had seen it. Apparently, a large number of crystals were advancing on our position. It was a much bigger mass than we'd ever faced before.

"They seem to know where we are," she said. "They seem to know what we're doing. You see how our fresh cohorts, our new troops moving up to the frontlines, haven't dug in yet? They've decided to attack the moment we did a shuffling of the guard on the front."

I nodded. Her conclusions were inescapable.

"What should we do sir?" she asked. "Should we wake up the troops?"

"Nah," I said, "let them sleep. It might be their last rest for the night. They've probably got another twenty minutes."

She nodded, and she slunk away.

In the end, I had less time to relax than I'd figured on. Apparently, this new attack was more serious than those that had come before.

The alert message came from headquarters, telling us to prepare for battle. The message told me what I already knew about the enemy crystals—that they were attacking in force. What I hadn't known was that our front lines, two cohorts deep, were already falling back under the onslaught.

"Harris!" I shouted, standing tall. "Clane, Leeson… Everybody up! Leeson, set up the 88s."

We'd been issued some powerful backup equipment during the night, namely two middleweight artillery pieces known as 88s. These were odd weapons that fired a long-lasting, wide-angled beam of particulate radiation. At medium range, these weapons were quite deadly to flesh and blood troops. As yet, however, they were untested against the crystals.

"The rest of you," I shouted, "get up off your asses. We're about to become the front line—right here. I want these trenches widened and deepened. Run the puff-crete walls out all the way over to the next unit on both sides of us."

"Sir?" Harris objected. "There's no point to that, is there? We've got enough room for all of us to stand and fight."

"That may be," I said, "but we've got incoming runners, and they're seeking shelter. When they come to us, I want them to have a place to stand and fight alongside us."

"Roger that."

The 3rd Unit jumped up and began working their tails off. They shook off sleep, opening their faceplates to allow errant raindrops to splash into their eyes and open mouths. This served to wake them up and get them moving again. Most of us had an hour or two of sleep by now, and that would have to be enough.

"Why are they attacking again now?" Leeson asked. "Do you think their first attack was just a scouting mission?"

"I don't know," I said, "but I bet our star-falls are beginning to piss them off."

Leeson clapped his hands together and pointed one finger at me. "That's it. That's got to be it. Maybe they're getting tired of our big guns, and they want to silence them."

I nodded. "You know what Winslade's going to say?" I told him. "He's going to say he wants to see every troop in this unit face down in the mud before one star-fall breaks—because we can't replace those."

"Yeah, that bastard…" Leeson said muttering and marching away to oversee his weaponeers.

I made sure that every soldier in my unit had at least one plasma grenade. I would have preferred two or three, but I'd take just the one if that's what I could get. We made ready to stand behind our puff-crete walls and lure the enemy in close.

It was Leeson who seemed to be working the hardest. His specialists, after all, were in charge of things like driving pig-drones to dig trenches and puff-crete machines to shovel out longer walls.

The man with the least to do or worry about was definitely Adjunct Clane. He came to me, and he had a worried look on his face. "Sir, I've just thought of something."

"Out with it, Clane."

"Well sir," he said frowning off to the west as if looking for the enemy crystals. He scanned the horizon, and I couldn't help but join him. "I don't think our tactics are going to work again.

Not the way this enemy is pouring out of that crater. Have you seen Natasha's tactical feeds?"

I nodded, because of course I had.

"You see," he said, replaying a snatch of video which he'd apparently stolen from the stream. "You see how they're all spread out now? They aren't coming at us in just one big, wide line. They're coming in staggered. They're coming in waves."

I thought about that, and then I realized what Clane was talking about. "If we throw our grenades and stun that first line," I said, "we can't just charge out there and shove a shotgun up the butt of every crystal we see."

"No sir, we can't, because the next line of crystals, the ones that are outside the range of our plasma grenades, they're going to press in and be all over us. They're going to be crushing skulls inside of helmets and turning every man's guts into a bowling ball."

"Yeah..." I said thinking it over.

We were going to have to change our tactics again. We were going to have to do something different.

The trouble was, I had no idea what that would be—at least not yet.

-36-

When the crystalline terrors came at us, they meant business. There were lots more of them this time, and they were spread out and staggered. Instead of a single line of perhaps twenty crystals, we saw a hundred or more. We humans still outnumbered them two or three to one, but it wasn't five or ten to one like it had been in the first battle.

The aliens came surging forward, gliding over the swampy ground and pushing through the thick foliage like it was nothing. Now and then, they fired spear-like shafts of force as if they were glass missiles. Others—the ones with more facets—sent sparkling beams at us that wilted the greenery and crushed everything they touched.

They clearly had some way of locating us, or sensing us. They also appeared to have the capacity to predict our direction of motion. They were able to fire with considerable accuracy, even as we dodged and dove for cover.

Exposed troops were struck dead, or they fell howling with horrible injuries. We returned fire, but sporadically this time rather than a crashing barrage. We pecked at them, shattering their forward-most facets and harassing them. I considered loading the plasma grenades we had onto the end of our morph-rifles when they got into range, but passed on the idea. What good would it do if the enemy was stunned and sent spinning far out across the field? We couldn't actually finish them. Not unless, I thought to myself…

"Leeson!" I shouted. "What's the status on those 88s?"

"I've got both of them online, sir. They're tucked into small puff-crete bunkers. I'm not sure if the bunkers are going to protect them or not, but we can try."

"All right. Hold your fire until they're in close. Let's try stunning them first and then beaming them while they spin in confusion."

Whether they were effective or not, the 88s were going to be big, bright torches of energy that the enemy could hardly miss. The crystals were bound to focus fire on them since there weren't many other targets. Those who were chosen to man the big guns knew they would probably die quickly.

Leeson had prepared his weaponeers, and he'd had them draw lots for the job of manning the 88s. This was done via their tapper, it was really a computer-automated randomization system. The losers of the lottery were already strapped into the driver's seat of the big guns, waiting grimly for the order to fire.

The rest of us were hiding down in our trenches, occasionally popping off shots. As the enemy drew closer, we wanted to lure them into a bunched-up mass. The numbers of troops in my trench swelled, as the men who had pulled back from the forward skirmish-lines joined us. Altogether, there were perhaps three hundred Varus legionnaires prepared to make a stand.

Centurion Jenny Mills, a decent woman I knew well, wormed close to me and threw her back against the mud wall of the trench. She had her morph-rifle in her hands and there was smeared blood on her armor, which was made of black stardust material.

"How's it going, Jenny?" I asked her.

"Not so good," she said. "I lost half my command out there on the front. I don't know, James—I don't know if we can break these guys this time."

"Well, we're going to find out in about a minute." I put out a gloved hand. "Let's say you and me make a pact?"

"What?" she asked, her eyes narrowing slightly.

She was suspicious right-off, as I did have something of a reputation with the ladies. For a girl like her, any and all dealings with one James McGill usually ended up being of a questionable nature.

I laughed. "Nothing like that. Let's make a deal that we're both going to make a stand right here in this trench. We're either going to stop those aliens, or we're going to die trying."

Jenny stared at me grimly. Her face softened, and she nodded.

"You've got that deal." She shook my hand, and we got up, galvanized. With a few hundred troops watching us, we lifted our rifles to our shoulders.

"What's your plan?" she asked. "You've got to have one."

"I do. We're going to fire grenades out of these morph-rifles, nailing the enemy at somewhere around two hundred meters out. Then we're going to open up with the 88s."

"You set up your 88s? Where the hell are they? Is Leeson asleep?"

I laughed. Usually, our light artillery engaged any approaching enemy as soon as that enemy was within range. But I'd held them back for the right moment. "They're well hidden. We didn't want the crystals knocking them out before they even get into the killing zone."

"Okay... I sure hope this works."

Seconds passed, then the approaching line of strange crystalline forms reached our magical point of no return. Me, Centurion Mills, and a few dozen heavies from Harris's platoon lobbed grenades from our morph-rifles.

As far as I could tell, every individual crystal on that frontline was struck. They began doing that weird spinning, dipping, bobbing, heaving up in the air thing and then I shouted the fateful command to Leeson.

"That's it," I said. "Open up with the big guns!"

Leeson didn't hesitate. He also didn't fire just the 88s, but everything else we had in our arsenal.

Flocks of mini-missiles, shoulder-mounted belchers and heavy bolts from a hundred rifles joined in the barrage. The 88s sang, releasing their sickly green radiation and sweeping over the jungle scene. The trees and foliage curled up and hissed when struck. The veins on those tree trunks exploded, transforming into nasty vapors.

In the middle of that mess, the crystals were hit by the wide beams of energy as they spun and wandered in confusion. I had to say, the 88s did a pretty good job of messing up these weird aliens. They didn't transform into ash the way normal biological lifeforms did, but they did melt and slag whole sections of the multi-faceted jewels.

A few of the crystals were split in two by the application of the intense heat. Perhaps some fissure inside had expanded and caused them to shatter. Several more cracked and sloughed off shards of themselves. It was like watching glaciers giving birth to icebergs that fell into the sea.

When the 88s swept back for a second pass, crumbling chunks of the crystals fell away. Some were molten and bubbling, others fell apart like brilliant glass-like shards.

We dared to whoop and slap each other on the back. I shouted orders for my troops to stay in the trenches, to reload, and to prepare for the next wave which was coming in right behind the first.

Our hopes were running high. Combining the 88s with the shock of the plasma grenades had been a more successful approach than hand-thrown grenades and shotguns—but the battle hadn't been won yet.

The trouble was the crystals had adjusted their tactics as well. They hadn't thrown all their strength into their initial charge. Plenty more crystals were still incoming, just emerging from the smoldering tree line behind the first shattered wave.

The first rush had been reduced to a glittering trash-heap of crippled forms, dragging themselves and drawing big furrows in the dirt, but the next wave didn't charge into our trap so eagerly. Instead, they paused behind the kill-zone and rose up higher, just a meter or two, to fire over their shattered first line.

The second line seemed to know exactly where our 88s were, even though we'd taken care to position them behind puff-crete barriers and even to hide the pillboxes with spiky palm fronds and the like. Without hesitation, the smarter, high-flying crystals began to snipe at our line.

"Uh-oh," Leeson said. "I think they're targeting our artillery."

"Pull back," I shouted. "Pull them back off the damned line!"

It was too late. Strange, gravity-warping beams leapt out. They ripped holes in our line and in our trench. The effects of the beam seemed to go right through puff-crete with little reduction of impact. Both of my unit's 88s were destroyed—their gunners physically melding with the big guns as if sucked into the guts of the machinery.

Once our artillery was silenced, the second wave of crystals lowered themselves and glided forward.

"These things are intelligent," Jenny said next to me. She sounded out of breath. "They recognized a threat, devised a plan, and they dealt with it."

"Sure seems that way to me," I agreed.

"The brass is insisting they're nothing but machines or automatons—some kind of robot made out of silicon."

I shrugged. To me it made little difference how the minds and the bodies of my enemies operated. All I needed to know was how to destroy them.

The second wave reached our trench less than a minute later. Without the 88s, we weren't able to stop them at range, so we waited until they swept right up close.

At the last moment, at point blank range, we launched our final volley of plasma grenades. The explosions were so close they were deadly to humans and crystals alike. We hugged the bottom of our trenches, splashing down in mud after throwing the grenades. Then, after the rippling explosions died down, we sprang back up again.

The confused enemy reeled and spun. We vaulted out of the trenches, roaring like animals. Using our most powerful close-range weapons, we broke them apart one at a time.

It was strange battling the crystals up-close and personal. They were like massive, jagged ice-sculptures. Some of them spun and fell right into the trench with us. All too soon, they awoke and gleamed with new light and purpose.

One of them managed to send a beam ripping right down the trench line. A dozen men were struck. Many of the victims howled and convulsed, dying in agony. Others simply flopped down, instantly struck dead. I realized then it was probably not smart to make a trench line that was perfectly straight. Not when preparing to meet with this alien threat.

If they had a line of sight, their weapons could effortlessly go right through men and armor, unlike any kinetic weapon. Flesh and bone couldn't stop it. The last thing you wanted to do when facing such a thing was line up straight.

In the end, it took maybe four minutes of exhausting battle to defeat the second wave. The count of the dead was getting high fast. Very few alien crystals had limped away, and my helmet display was full of red names.

At a glance, I could tell that half my command had been taken out already. I reported this up to Graves, but he told me to stand firm. He promised to send reinforcements. Another cohort was already on the way to the front.

It was about then that I noticed I'd dropped my morph-rifle. I couldn't recall having done so, and when I moved to retrieve it, I found that my left arm no longer functioned.

I must have taken a beam at some point along the way. I looked for Jenny to ask her about it, and I found her dead at the bottom of the trench.

"Ah, damn," I said.

Her wide, staring eyes regarded me from inside her closed, mud-smeared faceplate. Even her stardust armor hadn't protected her.

Checking through the rosters, I found that Leeson had died when his precious 88s had been torn apart. Harris had died as well. He and most of his heavies had dared to sally forth to meet the enemy on the muddy ground.

The only officer I had left was Clane.

"Clane?" I shouted. "Adjunct Clane, come to me."

I heard the splashing of boots. "Clane reporting, sir."

"I'm in a bad way," I told him. "I'm injured, but I'm still in the fight for now. If I go down, you're in command of this unit—or whatever's left of it."

"Shouldn't we pull out, sir? There's another wave coming."

I nodded. As far as I could tell from the tactical maps, there were at least three more waves on the way. Perhaps there were several more after that. I had no idea. There was no way of knowing our true tactical status, and I didn't much care.

"Our orders are to stand here and fight to the end," I told Clane. "Can I count on you?"

Clane's face was white, and his eyes were big. Then he sucked in a breath, and he nodded. "Yes, sir!"

I clapped him on the back with my good hand, and I sent him on his way.

The third wave hit us shortly after that, and I was never quite sure afterwards how I was taken out. I do recall that we were out of plasma grenades by that time, and that most of our remaining weaponry was essentially ineffective.

It was a slaughter.

-37-

I was revived an unknown time later. My tapper said it was the thirteenth, and it was morning. That information was useless, however, because I couldn't remember what the date had been when I'd died.

Curious as to the fate of my unit, my cohort and, in fact, the entire legion, I logged into the central database as soon as my eyes could focus. It was full of after-action reports, and I began browsing through them on my tapper.

The picture I soon gathered was chaotic and unhappy. When I read something about how the enemy crystals had managed to drive through our lines far enough to get to the star-falls, I began cursing.

"Holy shit…" I whispered to myself.

Brushing aside hand-flapping bios and orderlies who were giving me lame advice about how to recover from my umpteenth death, I shrugged on a uniform and staggered out into the crowded, dirty hallway of Blue Bunker.

Normally our field hospitals were placed to the rear of the entire formation in as safe a spot as you could possibly find. Only Gold Bunker was better protected.

Making my way on unsteady feet, I exited through the big, heavy steel doors and left the puff-crete bunker behind. The landscape outside was less muddy than it had been when I'd been fighting on the front lines. In fact, to me it looked like it was a little bit lusher and greener.

Looking up, I saw the trees, which formed a giant canopy of green overhead. Beyond that, there was no blue sky. Instead, there was a gray, misty shroud. Jungle World was often foggy for hours every morning, with blazing golden sunlight coming in the afternoons.

Everything looked a bit different than it had when I'd died on the frontlines. Using my tapper, I located my unit's post. I found that there were precious few members alive and breathing. I counted a grand total of twelve, of which I was the only officer.

Right then, a startling thought struck me.

"My armor!" I reached down to my chest, and my hands spread out. I was sad to feel the fabric I was wearing was quite unremarkable and papery thin. I began cursing up a blue streak all over again.

"Dammit! Where's my frigging armor?"

No one answered me.

The good Lord only knew where my irreplaceable suit of stardust armor was in this jungle—or what nefarious schemer had stolen it by now.

Shaking my head and growling, I turned and headed toward Gold Bunker. The guards at the entrance let me in because at least I was a centurion, and I looked like I was in a very bad mood. They glanced at one another, then gave each other a wise little nod and let me pass. They didn't even check my tapper for orders.

Stomping down the wet steps, I almost slipped to the muddy bottom but caught myself and walked on with greater care. My feet were becoming steady under me now.

Dying and being reborn again always left a man a little bit out of sorts in his new body. After all, nerve-endings had to report information back to a new brain, and all of it had only been grown minutes earlier.

Although my brain knew how to handle the incoming data, not every detail had been sorted out completely. It was like putting on a new pair of goggles with a different magnification, or driving a vehicle that was larger than the one you were used to. It took a while to get the hang of it.

All these sensations were nothing I hadn't felt dozens of times before, so my adjustment period was short. By the time I reached the end of the hallway in Gold Bunker I was walking straight and seeing straight, too.

Just as I reached the end of the main passageway, the big doors at the end swung wide. Winslade emerged and walked toward me with a small entourage in his wake.

Everybody in the group was a primus at least. I didn't see Graves, fortunately. He didn't like me doing things like this—stepping over his head and going up to the top. He wanted me to closely follow the designated chain of command.

Winslade was in a sour mood. There was nothing unusual about that. I'd rarely ever seen the man with a grin on his face, and if he was happy, that meant he was doing something very wrong.

"Ah," he said, "McGill? Graves must have sent you."

He stopped walking, and all the primus sycophants in his wake halted immediately. Frowning, he scratched at his tapper for a moment, and then he looked up. "But I don't see *how* Graves sent you," he said. "As he's still quite dead."

I shrugged, and I grinned. "Well sir, I like to think of myself as a prognosticator—a prophet of sorts."

Winslade frowned sourly. "I'm not sure if you're lying or making a joke, Centurion," he said. "But either way, I just don't care. Follow me."

He did a U-turn, and his three primus butt-kissers turned with him. They were all staffers, not combat officers. These were the sort of men who somehow achieved high rank while acting as mere secretaries. I even recognized one of them, Primus Gilbert. He was an undertaker-looking fellow, tall and spare with horrid eyes and a sarcastic wit. I figured perhaps Gilbert had learned long ago that in Legion Varus it was better to be a staffer than a frontline commander. I had to admit one thing: such men tended to die less often.

Following the group into a small conference room I was directed to a chair that didn't quite fit my oversized person. I cracked my knuckles, stretched and worked out a few kinks in my newly formed muscles. Sometimes after a revival, I cramped up a bit. It made me wonder if they were using the freshest of materials or something they'd recycled from the battlefields. Had I been constructed with old meat again? Ah well, such was the life of a Varus man.

"McGill? McGill!" Tribune Winslade was saying.

"Huh? What is it, sir?"

Winslade twisted up his lips and glared at me. "You never listen, man."

"But I do, sir. I truly do," I lied. "I just don't always know when people are talking to me in particular."

Winslade huffed and Primus Gilbert steepled his bony fingers. Apparently, he was the one who'd been talking to me. No wonder I'd ignored him. He was, after all, just another butt-sniffer.

"McGill?" the gaunt man said. "It has been brought to my attention that you were involved in a role that I would consider far beyond your station."

I was about to say "huh?" again, but instead I nodded as if I knew what he was talking about. Primuses tended to get upset if you misunderstood them too often.

The man looked at me expectantly, but when I said nothing, he continued. That gave me a much-needed second chance to figure out what the hell he was talking about.

"You were apparently playing the part of an envoy to Rigel…?"

"Oh yeah, that," I said.

"It was stated to you—and here I'm reading from transcripts, mind you, not full audio—that the Rigellians were in conflict with these crystals just as we are."

I nodded my head. "That's right, Primus. That's what they told me. They offered up a truce until we got rid of this larger, more dangerous enemy."

"And what did you do at that point?" Winslade interjected. "Did you perform one of your farcical speeches in which you presumed to speak for all Earth, nay all of humanity?"

"Uh…" I said. "No sir, not this time. I simply said I'd have to get back to them after I brought the message back home to you and Galina."

Winslade frowned. "Yes, well… regrets are always painful. Hindsight is forever 20/20, but under this circumstance, gentlemen, I think we have to admit we made a mistake. We misjudged the offer from Rigel. It is now painfully apparent that they were in earnest."

The three primus cucks all nodded solemnly in unison.

"Yes," Winslade continued. "Our mistake has become obvious. We sent the wrong negotiator, the wrong envoy, the wrong face for Legion Varus and Earth in general."

It was my turn to frown. I was a bit confused. I'd suspected—no, I'd been flat-out led to believe that Winslade was on the verge of admitting he should have taken the offer of a truce in the first place. But apparently, that wasn't exactly what he was saying.

A long, skinny finger rose high, and it waggled in my direction. "This man… This man performed his mission, as we'd instructed him to do. But because he's an individual of such low character, of such poor reputation, we didn't take his message seriously. Our error was made, therefore, at the moment we chose him to do the job."

I sputtered a bit, and I half stood up. "What?" I said. "Are you guys saying it was my fault you didn't take Rigel's offer of a truce?"

"Not exactly," Winslade said. "Our error was in choosing the wrong go-between to begin with. Make a note of that."

Winslade flicked a finger toward the nearest of his sidekicks. The man dutifully scribbled on his tapper with one claw-like finger.

I sat down again, and I began to frown. Somehow, I was getting the feeling that this meeting was a big cover-your-ass party. That's how things oftentimes went with the big brass, especially the less self-confident members of that celebrated group.

When something—pretty much anything—went wrong, their top priority was always to find a way to blame someone besides themselves. Barring that, they would seek to find some way to lessen the charges they were clearly guilty of.

Shrugging, I heaved a sigh and put my fingers back behind my head, lacing them together. I decided it didn't matter. As long as I wasn't going to be executed for this, what did I care what Winslade put in his report back to Central?

"Hey, Primus Gilbert," I said, talking to the man who was scribbling on his tapper. He eyed me with an unwelcoming stare. A lot of the staffers were like that. When a subordinate spoke to them out of turn, they tended to eye them as if we were dogs begging under the table. "Who are you sending that report to?" I asked him. "Drusus?"

The man only frowned and turned back to his work. He made no response.

"McGill," Winslade said. "Listen to me. You were there. You were out there at Rigel. Do you think the situation is repairable?"

"Huh? Do you mean, like, will they honor the agreement after we've had several skirmishes with them? After we shot their troops as they retreated from the crystals and ran right into our lines? Adjunct Leeson caught me all up to date on those shenanigans that happened while I was away on Rigel."

"Poorly stated," Winslade said, "but essentially, yes. That is what I'm asking."

I shrugged. "I'm not really sure, sir. I mean… we did pretty much blow them off. We can hardly expect that all these dogmen and ape-aliens will suddenly jump up and sing hallelujah. Of course we want to be friends now—we just got our butts kicked trying to take the crystals on solo."

The men twisted up their faces into sour expressions. Winslade made rapid, irritable motions over the battle table between us. The computer lit up and projected a glowing scene of the Jungle World terrain in our vicinity.

"The crystals have retreated for the moment," he said, "as have we."

"What?" I said, "we weren't driven all the way back to our main encampment, were we?"

"No, no. It's not that bad. They punched through our frontlines, and some elements managed to drive all the way to the star-fall artillery brigades. There, they did woeful damage."

Winslade turned to Primus Gilbert. "Show him the battle," he said, "the *real* battle."

The gaunt man frowned. "But sir, he doesn't really have the rank or the expertise to comprehend—"

"Show him the data, damn you."

Immediately cowed, Gilbert began to poke at the holo table we sat around. I was glad to see this, as the brass oftentimes candied-up or outright hid the actual damages the legion had suffered after a bad frontline action. But I knew that in secret little cubbyholes like this one, when staffers huddled around some desk deep inside Gold Bunker, the truth always came out. As a centurion, a fighting man from the frontlines, I was rarely privy to this sort of information.

The battle computer went into replay mode and displayed the battle. The table glowed, showing terrain and then unit positions.

"Here," Gilbert said, displaying various labeled blocks with lines and arrows. The contacts glowed and some of them crept along. "The enemy formations are the red, we're the green. Every two seconds represent a minute of real time."

"What are all those yellow dots and boxes?" I asked.

"Those are structural fortifications and equipment—or the dead."

"Ah right, I get it. This line over here to the east is where they're pressing forward." As I watched, the animation glided slowly. "Over here, back behind the front lines, this must be our star-fall brigade, right?"

"Yes."

The battle began to play out. The swarming crystals reached our lines, and the fighting began in earnest. I was gratified to see that along my portion of the front, the enemy advance halted for a while. But all too quickly, we were overwhelmed.

"Your men fought hard," Winslade commented. "3rd Unit held up fairly well—better than most."

"We only held out for ten minutes…" I said. I whistled long and low. "But let me tell you guys, that ten minutes was longer than it looked."

Winslade waved his fingers at me, urging me to be quiet. The battle took several minutes to play out. That covered more than an hour of real time. We all watched as the crystals broke through here and there, and then, pretty soon, it was an avalanche. A flood that overwhelmed all resistance, rushed onto our second line, then our third, and finally to the star-falls themselves.

I whistled as it ended with the enemy crystals reaching our star-falls. After doing serious damage there, they retreated back to their base. Once that long, yellow rectangle of equipment went dark and was therefore marked destroyed, the crystals turned around and rolled away back into the mists. They went back toward their big red mothership, or base, or whatever the hell it was.

"They're running home to mama," I said, "slinking away to lick their wounds."

Winslade looked at me sharply. "Do you think they can heal? Do you think they can repair damaged patches of their own—for the lack of a better word—bodies?"

I thought about that, and I nodded. "I don't see why not. I mean, we can certainly patch together a human. We can also grow a whole new one. Why couldn't crystalline lifeforms melt themselves back together again, too?"

Winslade thought about that, and he nodded, looking concerned. "Maybe that's what they're doing now," he said. "Licking their wounds, just the way we are. It's been nearly two days now, and they haven't come at us again."

"Yeah," I said. "That's probably because we stopped bombarding them."

All the officers looked at me sharply. "You think that's what initiated this all-out attack on their part?" Primus Gilbert asked.

"Yep," I said. "They sure as hell didn't like that artillery hammering at them. I think the star-falls were having a pretty big effect. They took big losses just to press through our lines, wreck our star-falls, and then retreat again. In fact, if I had to guess, I'd say they did this whole thing just to silence those guns."

Winslade bared his teeth. "Great. If you're right, McGill, we've lost our only effective long-range weapon."

"They destroyed all of them?" I asked.

"That's what I said. They destroyed every single star-fall, and then they turned around and retreated. They didn't care about our troops, they didn't care about our bunkers—nothing.

They left everything else intact and raced back to their base where they reside until this day, this very hour."

I thought that over, frowning. "Then sirs," I said, "it seems to me this is a good time to attack."

Two of the three primus cucks tut-tutted and shook their heads at me. They seemed bemused rather than annoyed.

"Insanity," said one.

"Our troop levels are at seventy percent, if that," said the second man.

But the third man, the undertaker-looking Primus Gilbert, took a different tack. After thinking it over, he spoke seriously. "McGill might have something. If the enemy is reviving their own troops, or creating new ones—or whatever the hell they do to send these crystals out to attack our lines—they might be in a weakened state. We've yet to press an attack against them the way they have against us. Maybe we could wreck some of their gear—like whatever it is they use to make more of their soldiers."

"That's the spirit!" I said, waving a finger at Gilbert. "You should promote this man to top butt-sniffer," I told Winslade. "He's the only one here who still has a single lonely ball left in his pants."

That statement earned me several disgusted glances, but Winslade looked thoughtful. Finally, he shook his head. "I understand the tactical advantage we may possess, but it's so hard to know the truth. We're simply not ready."

"Well then," I said throwing my arms high, "we do have one other option that no one's mentioned."

"What's that, McGill?"

"Why, we could patch things up with the dogmen. We could get them to march with us."

They all looked at me with suspicion. "You just said that was an impossibility," Winslade pointed out.

"I sure as hell didn't. I said I didn't *know* if it could be done. I said that we've behaved badly during this entire campaign. That they may not be in the mood to join us at this point—but I didn't say it was impossible."

"Yes, well…" Winslade said, "there is more information on that front. Primus?" He turned to the undertaker dude again.

Gilbert dutifully worked the battle screen between us. He expanded the outlook. Another large contact appeared, a big blob. This third blob was a light blue.

"What's that?" I asked.

"Neutral forces," Primus Gilbert said. "At least, they're neutral for now. This is where a large mass of primitives has gathered."

I frowned at that. "You mean those apes with the techno-spears?"

"Exactly. They also have two brigades of well-equipped dogmen at the core of the formation."

"Huh…" I said looking at that. "So, they're just sitting on our flank?"

"About ten kilometers away, yes."

"And when the crystals hit us hard, they didn't do anything?"

They all three shook their heads, and Winslade snarled. "That's exactly right. We've got a huge alien formation off to our south. They're just sitting out there and grunting in their huts. They're totally useless."

The four of them all continued talking and poking at the screen, discussing various options.

I, however, kept staring down at that blue blob. Inside my dim-lit, overly thick skull, an idea was beginning to form.

-38-

Winslade and his three hoity-toity wisemen soon moved on to discuss boring stuff. The rest of the meeting was all about troop positioning, the digging of new trenches, and how they should fill out request forms begging for fresh star-falls from Earth.

To my mind, all of that was total horseshit. The enemy crystals had retreated after taking serious losses. That had to mean something. To me, it meant that the time for drastic action was *right now*.

But since the three of them had already decided I'd been the wrong man to even talk to Rigel, they weren't too interested in my opinions. On top of that, they planned to blame me for everything that had gone wrong with the negotiations. That meant they'd never choose me to make a second appeal to the neutral army on our flank.

Naturally, I had no idea if it was even possible to get back into the good graces of the Clavers and the Rigellians at this point, but it certainly couldn't be done by squatting in Gold Bunker and squabbling over maps and numbers.

At the earliest moment I could, I got to my feet and excused myself from the meeting. Winslade dismissed me with a wave of a disinterested hand, and I headed out into the hallways again.

I soon found the quartermaster's office, and after politely waiting my turn, I made my case to retrieve my stardust armor. The quartermaster, a character of ill-repute, frowned at me. His moustache moved around on his upper lip like it was a thing alive.

I wondered if, just maybe, he was remembering me from previous run-ins we'd had in the past. I dearly hoped not.

"Centurion McGill..." he said. "Legion Varus, 3rd Cohort, 3rd Unit... Yes, yes, I have you right here. One morph-rifle in serviceable condition, one..."

A big hand lifted high to stop him. "Quartermaster," I said, "you know why I'm really here. Is there any chance that my specially fitted suit of armor has come in from the field?"

He glanced up at me and then worked his screens. At last, he sat back, and he looked up at me in surprise. "Actually," he said, "there is one suit of armor which doesn't fit any of the countless officers I've had coming in here to request one."

"Any of the who...?" I asked.

He smirked at me. "You would be quite surprised how many men like you have come in from the field demanding their armor be returned."

I frowned. "Are you sure these men had been issued this gear in the first place?"

The quartermaster shrugged. "Normally, it's not a big issue. It's not my job to give back the same piece of equipment to one soldier that he remembers fondly from a past life. Armor is armor, rifles are rifles."

My big mouth opened to object, but he waved for me to calm myself, so I did. "You know how the legions work as well as I do. We get surplus gear handed down from the Galactics. When you die, and you're reissued a new uniform, a new rank insignia, a new weapon—these are rarely or never the same ones you had before. It's a pool system, and it's always served the legions quite well."

I stopped him right there. "Okay, okay," I said. "I get it, and I stand in awe of your efficiency, sir," I said. I'd called him 'sir' although we were the same rank. To my mind, this was practically butt-kissing, but I really wanted that armor back today. "But you said something about a really *large* suit? One, I assume, that didn't fit anyone else that came in poaching gear?"

He nodded, and he finally stood himself up. To me, it looked like he hadn't done that in a while. His backside was plump—even wider than his shoulders. I managed to keep from making any remarks as he waddled into the back of a rather large storage compartment and dug out one grimy, blood-crusted suit of black armor. He draped it over the countertop, and it was so large it spilled over the side. The boot sections dragged on the puff-crete floor.

"That's it!" I said, as happy as could be. I signed, initialed, voice-scanned and thumb-printed everything he threw at me. It took a few minutes to spray my own guts out of the middle of the thing. Apparently, a couple of parts of me had been compressed into tight wads of flesh that were as stiff and gnarled as an oak branch.

All the while I was doing this disgusting work, I was smiling. I had my baby back again. Proud as punch, I marched out of that quartermaster's office. I even thanked him and offered to buy him a beer someday. Bemused, he went back to work, and I marched to the very edge of the Legion Varus encampment zone.

At the perimeter, I was warned to go no farther by a few pickets. They were soggy-looking recruits who'd been stuck out here on watch. "If you pass this line Centurion, even just to take a piss, it doesn't matter why you do it, we can't let you back in."

Nodding, I touched my helmet to them. Then I kept right on walking. I made my way out into the forest a full kilometer before anyone important noticed. At that point, my tapper lit up with a couple of red messages.

Damn it all, what foul luck. They must have just revived Graves, and here he was already checking up on me. My response was immediate and automatic—I sped up my pace and began to jog.

Part of my plan had been to move immediately into the forest before Primus Graves was revived. He, of everyone in Legion Varus, was always the first to notice when I'd strayed from the straight and narrow. The only other officer who was really good at keeping tabs on me was Galina, but she normally did so only when she thought I was looking at another woman.

Today, she was up on *Scorpio* and keeping busy—so it had to be Graves.

My tapper beeped and vibrated with greater enthusiasm. It was making the hairs on my arm tickle, but I ignored the irritation. Finally, a voice began to speak.

Cursing and slowing my pace, which had now taken on the looks of a dead-run, I walked calmly and lifted my arm up to my face. I flipped open my faceplate and forced a smile. "Hello there, Primus Graves," I said. "So good to see you up and alive again."

"McGill," he said, "you're outside the camp perimeter. *Way* outside of it. I'm hereby ordering you to do a U-turn and—"

"I will sir," I said. "I surely will."

"What the hell are you doing out there, anyway? You're a good three kilometers from your post."

"Well sir, you know what? It's the funniest thing. Did you ever line up with a whole bunch of other men at the urinal—and find that you just couldn't take a piss? Sometimes, I have that problem. Now, back on Earth, I usually just go and find a stall, see. A private place where I can focus and squeeze it out. But today, out here in the field, there aren't any—"

"Shut up, McGill," Graves said. "I don't want to hear another damned word of your horseshit story. Whatever you're doing, whatever female dog-woman you're going to meet, that's all canceled now. You're hereby ordered to return to your unit and report from there in ten minutes time. Graves out."

Our call ended, and I was left staring at my own blank arm. Damnation, Graves was a hard man to crack. Why'd they have to go and wake his ass up right after mine? If I didn't know better, I'd say the good Lord had it in for me on some days.

Heaving a sigh, I chewed on my lower lip for a few moments. I had a decision to make, and it was going to be a fairly big one as they went.

With the distinct suspicion that I was making a bad choice, I pulled back the sleeve of my armor, drew my combat knife, and stabbed my tapper until it went dark.

I jogged deeper into the jungle. I was off the grid now, with no buzzers on my tail, no way for an eye in the sky to see through all those clouds and that canopy of thick green leaves overhead. Without the electronic tracking-devices built into my tapper, no one could find me without making a serious effort.

Without a map app to guide me, I ran through the jungle using dead reckoning. As it turned out, I almost overshot my goal. Fortunately, the ape-aliens with their spears made sure I didn't run past their camp and deeper into the jungle for an all-night jog.

My first clue I wasn't alone came as a hard jab in the back. Fortunately, the spear tip couldn't penetrate my armor. Even as I slowed down and glanced back over my shoulder, two more long, pointy objects slammed into my spine. They'd been thrown like bullets.

I went sprawling in the mud but bounced back up. A dozen furred aliens charged at me. Three more threw their spears. I took one in the arm, one I in the leg and one in the belly. None of these strikes felt good, but none of them penetrated.

I was glad the crystals hadn't given these guys gravity-weapons. They had the old-fashioned kind of killing tools, stuff that I was pretty much immune to.

When they got in close on me, I was just getting back to my feet. I managed to grab one brute by the wrist, and with a twist, I threw him down on his face. The next of them caught my boot in his ugly mug, and he backed off howling. I didn't think you could break a gorilla's nose—but apparently you can.

Then the rest of them were on me, and they took me down. They reminded me that I wasn't immune to big, thumping fists and brute strength. Fortunately, these primitives were not a sophisticated group. They made no actual attempt to remove my helmet, which would have been difficult, but not impossible for creatures of such great physical power. Instead, they flailed and thumped on me with fists and attempted to bite me.

Some stabbed at me with their spears, really leaning into it. They shouted in rage when they looked at their spears and saw the tips were bent.

Finally, however, before I could be beaten to a pulp and die from my broken ribs and other internal injuries, there was a loud grunting roar from behind them. The brutes backed away, a few taking a moment to deliver a final kick—or, in one case, splatter my faceplate with a load of excrement.

While I lay there, working to breathe, a new figure came into view. This was a different sort of beastie. It was a dogman, rather than an ape. They were related, of course, but I knew that the dogmen were much more sophisticated and had a better grasp of technology. I'd seen them fly airships around and man artillery guns—that sort of thing.

Their fur was different, too, much as a wolf's fur was different from that of a primate. The snouts and ears were all wrong as well. Rather than a flat face, they had a much more lengthened and elongated look to them. It was more predatory and full of fangs.

The ears did not quite stand up on their own, but they did partway, like a dog that was partway between a German Shepherd and a pit bull.

The dogman looked me over curiously. His nostrils quivered, and although I wasn't capable of recognizing a frown on a face such as his, I sensed that he found me curious. Finally, he signaled his squad of primitives, and I was lifted high. They carried me over the jungle floor at an alarming rate. I was whipped by ferns and palm fronds.

Soon, I found I was in the encampment of this local alien army. They shoved me into a bamboo cage with a vine rope around my neck. I thought this was amusing at first. I figured I could easily cut my way free—but alas, they'd taken my knife.

I tried exerting my strength on the cage, but without an exoskeletal power-frame I was unable to bust it open. I supposed it only made sense. The cage had been made to contain creatures with the strength of an ape, which had to be greater than that of a man.

Over the next few hours, a parade of dogmen came to peer at me in my cage. Some of them prodded at me, a few of them lifted their legs, peeing on the bars. I'd never been sure if this particular ritual was an insult or an honor, but I rather suspected the former.

Eventually, someone showed up who wasn't like the rest. She was a female—a human female. She looked me over, and she shook her head in disgust. I grinned back through my smeared faceplate.

"You look and smell pretty bad, James," Abigail Claver said.

"That's funny," I answered. "I'm feeling fine."

Nodding, she opened my cage. Instantly, several of the guardian ape-aliens rushed forward. They rammed me back into the enclosure with their strong, unyielding hands.

Abigail urged them back by making clicking noises. I realized then that she wore one of those strange snake-bone necklaces that went diagonally across the body. Pretty much all Rigellians carried those, and I knew that they used them for purposes of translation in addition to many other functions. In this case, it seemed to me that she was speaking in the natural Rigellian language. Presumably, this was something that the natives of 31 Orionis knew how to understand. The aliens retreated reluctantly.

"It seems like you've really pissed off the locals," she said.

"It's a gift," I answered.

She let me out of the cage, and I stretched out on the floor of the jungle. I was given some water and invited to sit at a campfire. Abigail sat on the other side of the fire from me but no one else came to join us.

The aliens encircled us, and all I could see was their shining eyes reflecting in the darkness. "James?" Abigail said. "To what do I owe the honor of this visit?"

"Well, Lady Claver, the plain truth is I haven't been able to get you out of my mind since we met out on Rigel."

She rolled her eyes, but I kept right on going.

"You and I have had some good times together," I said.

"Oh really? Like when you rammed my face down into the sand on Green World? Or when I blew you up with that grenade—or maybe you're thinking of the dozen or so times we've shot each other?"

I lifted my hands, which caused a half-dozen hulking figures to step forward, grunting in alarm. I got the feeling I was one second from getting another beatdown, so I lowered my hands again, and they all backed off.

"No, no, no," I said, "nothing like that. I'm talking about the good times." I then proceeded to recount some of the times we'd spent together that were intimate and memorable.

She folded up her lips and shook her head. "That was a long, long time ago," she said. "Now, you listen to me. I might—just maybe—be able to get the chief to let you go and send you limping back to your encampment. I think that's the best I can do."

Then, since the moment was right, I spilled my guts to her. I didn't do so literally, as I might have with my combat knife, but rather by explaining the massive error that Winslade and Galina had made by rebuffing the generous offers from Rigel.

"They just didn't get it," I told her. "They didn't understand how dangerous these crystals are. Now that we've tangled with them, we've realized they're pretty damned tough."

"That they are..."

"Well, what do you say? Are you still willing to honor a truce?"

She narrowed her eyes and stared at me. "Is that why they really sent you out here? As their envoy again? Why didn't they just teleport you out to Rigel? I had to come all the way out here with this harness." She flicked a teleport harness which she had strapped over her coveralls.

"The dogmen alerted you that I'd arrived, huh?"

"Yes," she said. "We had orders that if any envoys from Earth came to talk to us, they were to at least tell us about it. We'd hoped your leaders would come to their senses, but I didn't expect to see you again."

"Well, ma'am," I said. "As you know, I speak with the authority of Earth behind me."

"Are they watching you right now?" she asked. "Is this some kind of a casting couch trick?"

I shook my head. "Not this time. It's been too long."

"Oh, right. That breaks in half an hour or so, doesn't it? How do they know you're here, then? How do you plan to catch a revive?"

I spread my hands wide and gave her a knowing smile and a shrug. I knew that would disturb her. She would assume there was some kind of new technology afoot, something she wasn't aware of.

She would never figure out the truth—that I'd run off into the jungle, killed my own tapper, and then thrown myself into enemy hands. No Claver would ever have done something so shit-off stupid without a secret way to escape the situation, so she figured I wouldn't have done so, either. People often underestimated my pig-ignorance in these situations.

"All right," she said, "keep your secrets. But as to fixing the truce, some of the local chieftains aren't happy with Earthers. After all, when they tried to retreat into your lines you shot them all dead."

"Yeah," I said. "That was just a simple misunderstanding."

"A misunderstanding that cost us damn-near a thousand troops. Here we are, out in this jungle killing each other for nothing, while the real enemy lies just a dozen kilometers to the west. Doesn't that seem crazy to you, James?"

"It surely does," I said, "but you know Earthmen, and officers like Winslade and Galina. They don't always see things clearly when you first talk to them."

She frowned, and she nodded. "All right," she said, heaving a sigh. "I'll give it a shot. I'll talk to Squantus about it. If everyone agrees, Legion Varus will have reinforcements by tomorrow."

"Uh..." I said thinking that over. "Tomorrow noon?"

"No, tomorrow at dawn. Nobody marches an army at noon."

"Even better!" I said, thinking about how much work I had to do in the very short number of hours left tonight. "But listen," I said, "I have to get back to camp, and I have to relay all this information. We've got to establish some real connections."

She thought that over, and she nodded. She took the rattling snake-bones device from around her neck, and she handed it to me. When I raised my hand to take the necklace, the aliens surrounding us surged forward, but she shooed them back again. "You can use that to communicate with us at any time," she said.

"That's real good," I said, "but… you know… I think I might have a busted hip or something. It's going to be kind of hard for me to hike back through the terrain in the dark."

"Oh geez, are you kidding me? Are you trying to ask me for a ride or something?"

"That would be wonderful."

She groaned, and she fussed, but she finally gave me her teleport harness. After making a few adjustments to the coordinates, it was good to go.

I took this second gift gratefully, and I put it around my chest after letting the straps out as far as they would go. I checked the battery and then ported out. As I transformed into a wavering, blue-white light and flashed away into nonexistence, I blew her a kiss.

I never saw if she returned it or not.

-39-

Abigail Claver hadn't been fooling around. She popped me right into the middle of Gold Bunker. Now, that right there was a security violation on many levels. I knew the brass hated that kind of thing, if only because it made them feel vulnerable. After all, if a Claver could pop me into their inner sanctum like that, why couldn't she have sent a big bomb to wipe them all out?

Normally, critical infrastructure like Central itself was protected from teleport attacks by various fields and tricks of physics. But here out in the field—in the mud and blood of Jungle World—we didn't have that kind of gear.

The long and the short of it was, I appeared in the central hall of Gold Bunker in the middle of the night. I looked like hell, but that didn't stop a half dozen guards from rushing me. They snarled, and they beat on me, and they landed a few shock rods on my aching belly.

Fortunately, my armor absorbed almost all of it. I just staggered a bit. I was lucky I didn't pull a facer—after all, I'd just taken some serious blunt-force trauma from the aliens in the jungle.

"Is that all you hogs have got?" I asked. "Remind me to give you some personal combat training tomorrow morning. Hold on a second... make that the day after tomorrow. We've got a big day coming at dawn."

Irritated and bemused, the pack snarled a bit and circled me. They reminded me of the apes at Abigail's encampment.

Finally, the hog team contacted Primus Graves, who then contacted Tribune Winslade. They both showed up half-asleep and in a terrible mood.

I relayed to them what Abigail Claver had offered while they stood there with their hands on their hips, glowering at me. "And just what authority was given to you McGill," Graves asked sternly, "to undertake a *second* diplomatic mission?"

I sucked in a breath, and for a long second or two my mind was a blank. My ribs were burning like they were on fire, making it hard to think straight.

But then my head cleared, and I had it. I pointed a finger in Winslade's direction. "He gave me permission, sir. Tribune Winslade did it. We talked about this at length."

"What are you talking about, McGill—?" Winslade began to sputter, but I cut him off.

"This was all your idea, sir. You're the one who initiated the diplomatic effort this time. You're a rising star, a junior tribune who's going to be famous for saving Legion Varus and 31 Orionis at the same time."

Tribune Winslade opened his mouth to shout at me. His finger was up, his teeth were exposed—but then he suddenly caught on to what I as saying. After all, I'd thrown him a most excellent-tasting bone.

Slowly, his finger drifted down to his side, and his teeth went back behind his lips. His jaw slid around a little, and his eyes—which were always shifty—traveled from me, to Graves, and then back again.

"That's right, as a matter of fact," he said. "If Abigail Claver has agreed to help us, then yes, I did condone your actions."

Graves frowned, looking at the two of us, and he shook his head in disgust. "All right," he said throwing his hands up. "What's our next move, Tribune?"

Everyone looked at Winslade. I could tell he was half-asleep and trying to think. Fortunately, he was a ferret of a man, the kind of creature who could bounce up snarling and ready for action when he had to.

His mind sped up as we watched. He pushed away sleep, and he realized he had to move quickly to take advantage of this opportunity. "Action is required…" he said. "Impressive action…"

His hands clasped together, and he rubbed them against one another like a raccoon washing a slug. "So McGill, you say they told you they'd bring an entire grunting horde of apes to our door by dawn tomorrow? They'll march with us against that crystalline monstrosity?"

"That's what they said, sir. Just the way you wanted it."

Winslade bared his teeth at me again, but just for a moment. If he was going to take credit for this whole thing—if he was going to play the hero—then he was going to have to pretend that it was all his idea from the get-go.

"Right," he said, "very well. This is how things are going to go… Graves, you alert all the cohorts. Wake up every primus and every centurion immediately. Let them know they have to be ready to march before dawn. That's… let's see… two-and-a-half hours?"

"It'll be tight, sir," Graves said, "but Legion Varus will get it done."

"On your way, Graves. Dismissed."

Graves thumped away, and Winslade eyed his trio of primus suck-ups, who had shown up by this time to hover around and look useful. I wondered if they had some kind of an alert built into their tappers to awaken them whenever Winslade dared to step out of his quarters.

Primus Gilbert, the bony guy with the bald head, yawned and spoke up first. "We've got a lot of work to do, sir, if we're going to coordinate an assault by morning."

"Yes, yes. Hop to it. All of you."

They marched away, and that left just me and Winslade standing in the hallway. Winslade lowered his voice and sidled a step closer. "We're going to have to talk to Turov," he said. "I can't pull off a joint-forces operation with an alien horde purely on my own."

"That's right, sir. That's a good idea. You'd better contact the imperator."

"No," he said, "*you* do it." He stabbed a finger in my direction. "You're the one who invented this entire fiasco in the first place."

Thinking it over, I nodded. "All right, Tribune. I'll do it. Turov will be in on this deal, and she'll give it her personal blessing. Don't give it another thought."

Winslade shook his head, but then he turned away and went off to make more arrangements. It was about three in the morning, but he knew as well as I did that sleep was over with for the night as far as he was concerned.

Contacting Galina Turov up on *Scorpio* turned out to be the most difficult mission of the night. It was easier to locate an army of primitives in the jungle than it was to get her out of her quarters in the middle of the night. What made it even harder was that I wasn't able to use my tapper. After all, I had destroyed it.

Instead, I fondled that tangle of snake-bones that hung around my neck and down my side. Fortunately, the thing understood human standard speech and could take verbal commands from me. Experimentally, I used it to tap into the local grid. It was smart enough to do that at least.

I think it was this last effort that did the trick. Instead of her software interpreting my calls as a tapper to tapper contact to her personally, the communications system aboard *Scorpio* interpreted the call as coming from the Rigellians. In less than five minutes, I had her in voice contact at least.

"Who is this?" she demanded. "Is this Squantus? If so, you'd better explain yourself."

Her voice sounded rough with sleep. I was glad to hear that, as it indicated she was probably alone in her quarters.

"Nope, not Squantus," I said. "Guess who?"

"Oh my god."

"That's right," I said. "This is your lucky day, Imperator. Old McGill has arrived to save your bacon."

I explained the situation, making sure to give Winslade the credit for having sent me out into the jungle to perform the mission which had ultimately been successful.

Galina seemed somewhat confused by this detail. "But if he sent you on a diplomatic mission into the jungle... why isn't he calling me to take credit for it?"

"Well sir," I said, deciding to depend on her devious mind to fill in the blanks for me. "If you think about it for a minute, I'm sure you'll come up with the reason."

Galina was silent for perhaps three seconds. Finally, she spoke again. "Oh, I get it. That weasel. He went off the rails with this, and he doesn't want it to look like he's upstaging me, right? Well, I'll accept his gift. Remember McGill, from now on, *I'm* the one who sent you out into the jungle. I ordered you to reinstate the pact with the Rigellians. I accepted their original offer, and we're going to win the 31 Orionis campaign because of it."

"That's exactly how I remember it, sir."

After that, we were off to the races. I soon grew bored of the whole thing, yawning, limping and wheezing a bit from a few broken ribs that were poking at me. I decided to take the long walk over to Blue Bunker to see if they could patch me up for the morning. When I arrived, I was surprised to find Galina waiting for me just inside the doors.

"That's right," she said. Her arms were crossed over her breasts, and she was glaring at me. "I did a little thinking after our conversation. I asked Winslade's staffers where they thought you might be going, because for some reason, your tapper seems to be dead, McGill."

"Uhhh... that's right, sir. It got busted... or something," I said.

Galina eyes squinched even tighter. "So... let me get this straight. You wandered off into the jungle, destroyed your tapper, and spent the night in the ape encampment talking to Abigail Claver. Am I right?"

"Pretty much, yeah—but hold on a second. I wasn't a celebrated guest at their camp. I was beat up and shoved into a cage. There was even some dog piss and ape shit involved."

"Shut up," she said. "I know you, James." She stepped close and looked me in the eye. "I know what you're like. You went out there on your own. The real reason you did it wasn't to negotiate a deal with the apes, but to visit that woman, that Claver-freak. The clone you like so much."

"That's just crazy-talk, sir."

Her eyes went dark, and I realized I'd made a fatal error. If there was one thing you never did with crazy ladies, it was call them crazy.

Galina whipped her hand up, and I saw she had a slim, long-barreled laser pistol in her grip. She aimed it at my face.

"James," she said, "I've come to a critical command decision. I need you on the frontlines in a few hours, but you're in no shape to march with Legion Varus. Therefore, you're being recycled."

Then, she shot me down.

-40-

Dammit all if I wasn't waking up from another revival only thirty minutes later. Somebody must have put me in the priority queue and pushed the "go" button.

"How's he doing?"

"He seems okay," said the second biotechnician, "but his sides are hitching oddly."

In fact, I was trying to laugh. That can be pretty difficult when your lungs are full of fluid. Just try it sometime.

I coughed, and I spat. I rolled onto my side on the gurney. I wanted to throw up, but I couldn't, so I got off the cold, thinly padded table instead.

"What time is it?" I asked the nearest of the two technicians.

"It's about thirty minutes after you died, sir," one of them said.

Squinting, I reached out and tried to grab ahold of him. "No," I said sternly. "I want to know what *time* it is." I was vaguely aware that in my uncoordinated grabbing motion I'd managed to poke my big thumb into something soft. It was probably a cheek and eyeball, or maybe a boob, I don't know. I could hardly see anything.

The bio slapped my hands away angrily. She managed to do it because I was only at about half-strength right now, with maybe one-quarter of my normal coordination. "It's 0400 hours, *sir*," the technician answered. "Now, get the hell out of my revival chamber."

I staggered around the room, gathering my things. Fortunately, in this rare case my armor and my gear were present. That was one of the few benefits to being executed by a superior, rather than dying in some crap-hole of a battlefield. The bio goons could simply take your body straight to Blue Deck and revive you on the spot. That meant your gear was handy, giving you no easy excuses about not returning to duty.

While I was putting on my armor, I heard a strange buzzing sound. It was really more of a rattle. "What the hell is that?"

"I don't know, Centurion. It's something in your gear. I think it's that weird-looking bone necklace of yours. Is that something from back home?"

"That's right," I said. "My momma strung these together with catgut. This here is a big king snake from the swamps of Georgia."

"That's real nice, Centurion." I got the feeling I wasn't their favorite officer. "We felt like recycling that damn thing over the last few minutes. It keeps on rattling and buzzing weirdly like that."

"Good thing you didn't," I said. "Because, really, this is the Rigellian equivalent of a tapper. These things are radioactive. What's more, I think they've got a tiny hint of antimatter in the core of each of these bones. Throw that in the recycler and boom! All Blue Bunker is gone."

They cast me disbelieving looks which my eyes were just good enough to see by now, and they kicked me out of the revival chamber. I left without further fuss and headed for the exit. Right about then, the damn bones started doing that buzzing thing again.

"Crap," I said. "What's wrong with this thing?" I commanded the bones to tell me what was wrong with them.

They answered in Terran Standard. "All systems are operating optimally. You have a call incoming from a remote location."

"Who is it?" I asked.

"Caller unknown."

I muttered curses and poked at the thing a few times but, of course, it didn't respond. "Answer the call dammit," I said aloud.

"James? James, this is Abigail."

My bleary eyes widened a fraction. Naturally, I should have expected Abigail to be calling me. Nobody else even knew I had this thing much less how to call it.

"Oh, hey," I said. "What's happening? We've got a couple of hours until dawn, so maybe you'd like to get together and have a coffee?"

"No James, that's not happening. Not today. Listen, I wanted to tell you that all the native levies and the dogmen under my command are approaching Legion Varus. I wanted to make sure your boys weren't going to start taking potshots at us like last time."

"Uh..." I said thinking that over. "I'd better check on that just to be sure."

"Yes, you'd better. Oh, and James, there's one more thing."

"What's that?"

"Squantus has promised some aid, too. He's willing to help us get rid of these crystalline invaders once and for all."

I frowned. "Well, he damn-sure ought to be willing," I said. "After all, this is a Rigellian colony, isn't it?"

"Pretty much, yeah. The local primates send all their extra foodstuffs and trade goods back to Rigel. I'd call 31 Orionis a protectorate under Rigel's benevolent rule."

"Yeah, sure. Whatever. What kind of aid is Squantus sending?"

"He wasn't specific, but he promised he'll help us defeat the enemy base."

I shrugged and closed the channel. Soon, my mind was working better, and I had all my clothes on. Then I contacted Galina.

"Hey Imperator," I said. "I've got some good news."

"I could use some good news. What is it?"

"Well, first-off all the ape-aliens are nosing their way through the jungle in our direction. They should be coming close to Legion Varus right now."

"That isn't good news, James. Tell them to push off. Tell them to stay at least a kilometer away from our southern flank. I want our two forces to attack from separate angles. That will make it less likely we'll accidentally shoot each other."

I thought it over, and I figured she probably had a point, so I didn't argue. After all, if some of these crazy aliens came rushing toward our lines, our boys were going to be trigger-happy and shoot them. Probably the same would go in the opposite case.

"Wait a minute," Galina said suspiciously. "Who are you talking to?"

"I was using those snake bone things, you know. One of those Rigellian tappers."

"Yes, yes, I figured that out, but that's not—"

"Oh hey, did I mention that Rigel's promising material aid? They're going to provide direct support for this attack."

"That's great, but you still haven't answered my question."

"Uh... I don't rightly remember what that was, now," I lied.

"I want to know who you've been talking to. It'd better not be that little bitch, Abigail."

I gave the bones a shake and managed to hang up on the call. I smiled when she found she couldn't call me back. That was one nice feature about using this Rigellian tech hooked into our grid instead of my own tapper. It was kind of like I'd hacked a tapper and had full control of it. I could get used to this new-found freedom.

I even considered stabbing my own tapper again to put it out of my misery. The bones didn't seem to have as much functionality, though. There was no screen at all, and—

All of a sudden, Galina began talking to me again. This time her voice was coming out of my arm. She'd figured out that that the call-back feature wasn't working and contacted my tapper directly.

"James...?" she said, "if I find out that you've been banging that nasty clone-woman, do you know what I'm going to do?"

"You already killed me once this morning," I pointed out. "Do you think you could wait for round two until I can at least see straight?"

Galina sighed, and she made an effort to control her jealousy and irritation. "All right, all right," she said. "Get to your unit. They're mostly revived and ready to fight again. I'm putting you on the flank closest to the enemy formation."

"Enemy? You mean the crystals, or…?"

"No, no, no. I mean these weird monkey-people."

"They aren't enemies anymore, sir. We have to kind of stop thinking that way."

"I'll believe that when I see them fight the crystals instead of throwing their fancy spears at our backs. In fact, James… I have specific orders for 3rd Cohort. When you make contact with the crystals, I want you to hold back."

"How's that?" I said.

"You heard me. Let the apes go in first. Let them absorb the first shock."

"Aw now," I said, "that doesn't sound fair at all, sir. After all, I don't think they have plasma grenades or anything."

"They're strong, they're fast, and they're expendable," she said. "Think about them as being light troopers on steroids. They'll distract the crystals while you get your own troops into position to destroy them."

As I thought about that, I realized she had a point. After all, I didn't think these furry dudes with their pointy spears were going to do a whole lot of damage to crystals that were two meters in diameter. It would have been better if the Clavers had made them heavy sledgehammers to swing, or something.

"Turov out," Galina said, and that was that. There had been no warm, fuzzy rekindling with her. Not today, at least.

The next hour or so was spent gathering my troops and getting into motion. We ate, we broke camp, and we began to march. We weren't carrying our full kits of course, just our combat gear. The rest of it we left behind for later. I wasn't sure if there would be a later for this lifetime, but I hoped there would be.

About a kilometer out on our flank, I spotted Abigail's horde of aliens. She had been true to her word. There were tens of thousands of primates with a few brigades of trained, disciplined dogman troops in the center.

The alien army appeared as a blob of blue on my tapper—a big blob. The estimated numbers kept swelling as I watched. I was impressed. There had to be about thirty thousand of them now. Too bad their performance was going to be hobbled by inadequate weaponry.

When we had about an hour left to go before dawn, I contacted Graves with an idea. He wanted to ignore my suggestion, but he couldn't quite, so he kicked the idea up to Winslade.

After discussing it for a while, the tribune reluctantly agreed.

"All right," he said. "We'll do it your way, McGill. It's a stupid idea, but I'm willing to try just about anything at this point."

As dawn began to break, we hustled toward a rupture in the planet's crust. The red crystal had made a massive crater when it slammed into 31 Orionis. The jungle was burnt here, and the land had heaved up into a jagged ridge.

I'd come up with an idea I thought would make our native troops more effective. When Leeson caught sight of an entire air-sled loaded down with the fruits of my labor, he hooted with laughter.

"Puff-crete bricks?" he said. "What the hell are those things for?"

"Not just bricks," I told him. "These are hammer heads. Each brick weighs about five kilos. The nice thing about puff-crete bricks is they're nearly indestructible."

Leeson looked over the bricks curiously. He tapped a few with the butt of his rifle. "You think these gorilla-aliens are going to be able to hit hard enough with these to crack some chunks off the crystals?"

"That's what I'm hoping," I said.

"How are they going to swing them?"

"Well, see—I asked for there to be a hole drilled in the center. I figured they could just put the butt of one of their spears…"

Leeson shook his head. "Nah," he said. "That's never going to work. This is shit-engineering, McGill. These heads are going to fly right the hell off those spear shafts of theirs."

I was kind of angry that he was full of objections and sneers, instead of answers. "All right," I said, putting two fat fists on my hips. "What do you suggest we do to solve the problem?"

He thought that over carefully. "Here's what you've got to do. Take some puff-crete resin—you know, that softer, gushier stuff that's quick-drying and all? You ram their sticks into one end, then you pour in some of the puff-crete resin at the other end. After it all hardens, you've got yourself a pretty good hammer."

Clane walked up to poke at the bricks next. "The handles will break," he complained. He'd apparently decided to join the bitching brigade Leeson had started. "All they've got is a hardwood shaft made for a spear. That's going to snap right off when they give this hammer its first solid swing."

I thought that over, and I figured they were both probably right—but it was all we had. After communicating with Abigail Claver again, I delivered loads of the bricks to her. We had literally thousands of them left over from the construction of our bunkers. All we'd done was drill some holes down the middle.

Fortunately, the big attack was postponed for a few hours. The various units—alien and otherwise—hadn't all gotten to their assigned positions yet. That gave us the time to make some adjustments.

We provided Claver's native troops with gallons of the resin which was stored in a liquid state to serve as mortar between the bricks. She thanked us, and she put her dogmen onto the task of constructing and distributing these new weapons.

I had no idea how effective it was all going to be, but if nothing else, I figured I'd bought us some good will.

The sun came up slowly, and the attack was finally ordered. I hustled back to my unit, and I joined Harris's heavy platoon. We moved toward the enemy crystals at a steady pace.

This battle was about to start, and I had a feeling it was going to be bloody.

-41-

The legion advanced at a steady pace, and we met little resistance. Everyone was tense, however, remembering some of our disastrous encounters with the alien crystals we'd recently experienced.

We spread out five cohorts wide and two deep. It was a classic formation, similar to what the Romans had used thousands of years ago. As the 1st and the 5th Cohorts were made up almost entirely of light troops, they were placed on the flanks. They naturally moved ahead of my own 3rd Cohort, which was in the center of the first wave.

The poor bastards on our flanks were like the cavalry of old. I didn't give much for their chances in this kind of a fight, even though every one of them had been issued a plasma grenade and a few special explosives. These were sticky-bombs, rarely used weapons we employed to destroy enemy armor or to blow holes in doors.

In this situation, their use was rather obvious. The light troops were supposed to get in close, first using plasma grenades to stun the enemy, and then rush into contact to paste a sticky-bomb onto the surface of an alien crystal.

The devices supposedly had a ten second fuse on them, allowing the soldier to get away. But knowing Legion Varus, I figured they may not give a soldier that long before they went off.

Every light trooper in the entire legion was all out of smiles today. They knew they were facing an enemy that was nearly impervious to anything they could dish out. Most of them hadn't even been issued a shotgun, unlike the men in my unit. The recruits felt like they were pretty much cannon-fodder—or gravity-beam fodder.

I did my best to put a good face on the whole thing. "It's not going to be pretty," I assured them, "but we're going to kick their butts. Can you believe how many of those crystals we cracked the last time they came at us? Notice how they haven't come near us since? That's because they're chicken."

I kept on talking like that, and I was happy to see that some of them seemed to be buying it. Pep-talks always seemed to work, which was why we used them. I think the talks worked because the troops *wanted* to believe what I was saying. They didn't want to believe they were about to die again. They didn't want to think this enemy might be invincible—immune to our weapons and able to burn through our best armor with their strange attacks.

Once I was done pumping them full of sunshine and jelly beans, I used the snake-bone thing to communicate with Abigail Claver. I was kind of surprised the brass hadn't taken the device away from me. Apparently, they figured as long as they could see where the native army was, that was good enough.

Using my tapper, I was able to see Abigail's army was mounting the crater wall on our left flank, out to the south. The big blue blob that represented her unruly horde was moving faster than we were. That was only natural, as they carried less gear and they were native to this terrain.

"James?" Abigail said, between puffing breaths. "Your boys are lagging behind. This isn't some kind of trick, is it?"

"No ma'am," I lied. "Not at all. Just think about it this way: We aren't in any kind of coordination with your troops. Most of our weaponry is long-ranged rifle fire. If we race into the crater at the same time your guys do, there's bound to be some confusion and blue-on-blue death."

"Yeah... all right," she said, "but if this is all bullshit, I'm going to haunt you in your dreams."

"You do already, Abigail," I said, and she laughed.

My tapper was blinking red again, so I answered another call. This time it was Galina. "James?" she said. "My techs tell me you're in communication with that awful woman leading all those apes."

"Yeah," I said, "sort of. Isn't that what I'm supposed to do?"

"Yes—but don't distract her. She's moving into position, and she's way ahead of us. The situation is perfect. With any luck, her zoo-escapees will do all the work for us. Maybe I can sneak in with *Scorpio* after that and throw one big blast with every gun I've got. A volley of fusion shells might solve all my problems at once."

"Hold on, now," I said. "I don't want to hear that kind of talk. Legion Varus is way too close for any of that kind of nonsense. If you use heavy nukes, you're going to paste everybody."

Galina was quiet for a moment, and I figured she was doing some calculations. Finally, she did a little bit of cursing, "Dammit, you're right. I don't think we can do it at this point. How disappointing… Maybe I should order Winslade to retreat with Legion Varus."

"If you do that sir," I said, "Abigail will pull back, too. She'll know something is up."

"All right, all right. Keep advancing. I'm going to tell Tribune Winslade to stall just a little bit—but without making it obvious."

"Are we seriously going to screw the Clavers now? After they pushed everything they have onto the battlefield? That's just plain dirty." As I finished my little tirade, I noticed my tapper had stopped blinking red. Galina had closed the channel, and she was gone.

"That double-crossing witch," I muttered to myself as I worked my tapper some more.

I almost called Abigail to warn her—but after thinking it over for a moment, I knew I couldn't. If I spooked her, and she pulled her support out of this fight, the whole campaign was going to fail.

I didn't think we could do this without her. Hell, we may not be able to win even *with* her troops.

325

The land was beginning to rise now as we marched forward. I realized, looking up, that the jungle had broken open and exposed a vast, ragged ridge of open black dirt. The ground smoked and was coated with a crust of glass.

The glass wasn't manufactured, it was natural. It had been created by the original impact of the crystal. The mountain-sized object had struck with such force and such heat, it had melted much of the ground around it. Trees were burned, and the ridge itself was blackened. It was all rocks, dirty chunks of melted sand, and broken tree stumps.

Graves called the cohort to halt at the base of the final crater wall. All along our lines, troops halted as well. Winslade had apparently ordered the entire legion to stop.

We circled up against the base of the crater, and we could feel the heat of it right through our suits. The great crystal had struck Jungle World like a hot, burning bullet. Now, it was lodged in the side of the planet, and the lands around the impact site were still sizzling.

Tribune Winslade took the stage personally then, and he began to speak to all of us. "Legionnaires," he said, "this is another fine moment for Legion Varus. We will all recall this day with pride in our hearts."

"Yeah, sure," Harris said, muttering off to my left. "That sounds just like a man who's huddling in a bunker ten kilometers behind us."

"Spoken like a true hero," Leeson said.

Clane looked from Harris, then to Leeson, then to me. He had a questioning expression on his face. I think he wanted to figure out if I was going to reprimand my officers for talking badly about the tribune—but I did nothing. I didn't even meet his eye.

Clane nodded at last. "Winslade really is a douche, isn't he?" he asked. "I'd heard that before I joined Varus Legion, but I had no idea..."

"You haven't seen anything yet," Harris said. "Just wait until he gets up to some of his weird shit, torturing people and whatnot."

I frowned at Harris and waved for him to shut up. Adjunct Clane looked a bit alarmed, but he read the room and decided to quiet down himself.

Obviously, my wiser officers were infecting my newest man with their particularly bitter form of griping. I supposed that was sort of inevitable, but at the same time, I was unhappy to see it.

Winslade continued to talk. After a while, he put up a display of the tactical situation. All of our tappers and helmets lit up. We saw a massive crater encircling what looked like a giant red egg that glowed in the center.

"Once we climb this ridge," he said, "we'll go over the top in a rush. At that point, we'll be exposed to the enemy's main armament, a massive gravity-beam. That reality is what's been holding us back from employing close-assault tactics like this in the past. But notice here…"

Off to the south side of the massive crater, a big blue blob lit up. I knew in an instant what it was. It had to be Abigail Claver's avalanche of primitives.

"You see this ragtag army of local aliens? They're going to perform the function of the ultimate light-trooper brigade. They shall rush the enemy, thousands strong, swinging their absurd puff-crete hammers at whatever crystals come their way. Hopefully, it will take the crystalline fortress a long time to kill all of them, because we're going to use that time to advance. We'll strike them from the flank, and when we do, it will probably be difficult to sort out one alien menace from the other."

Winslade paused for dramatic effect. I showed my teeth, as I'd already figured what was coming next.

"If it comes down to a question as to whether to fire a grenade or a belcher into a mixed melee at the bottom of this crater, I don't want any of you to hesitate. Remember, these aliens are doing their best to protect their own land. They're more than willing to give their lives to help us defeat this enemy. If the crystal does win—and according to our intel it probably will—every being on this planet will perish in the end, anyway. Therefore, the only emotion any Legion Varus trooper should have in the fateful hours to follow is an unquenchable thirst for victory. Don't let any misplaced sense of pity slow your hand, Legionnaires! If you do, you'll only be dishonoring the dead who are about to give their lives."

With his speech finished, he cut the signal. I looked around to see how the troops were taking it. Overall, they seemed to accept Winslade's argument. They were hard of eye, and I knew that when it came right down to it, they were also hard of heart. Varus men were forged out of the worst fire—hellfire, some said.

"Is he telling us to just shoot right into the middle of those poor bastards and kill everyone?" Natasha asked. She seemed scandalized, but she was one of the few.

Most of my troops were staring upward and straight ahead, eyeing the ashen ridge above us. They gripped and re-gripped their weapons. Trickles of sweat ran down their faces. I knew when the time came, they would perform exactly as Winslade wanted them to. It was a shameful thing, but there it was.

Watching my tapper, I saw from the tactical feeds that Abigail and her horde of locals had reached the top of the ridge. Fully a quarter of the rim, all along the southern flank of the enemy base, was packed with her army.

We waited for a minute or two, expecting an earth-shaking charge—but it didn't come.

"What are they waiting for?" Leeson demanded.

"Looks like they fell asleep," Harris said.

"No…" I said. "They're just spreading out and getting themselves into position. They're going to rush all at once from a wide angle of attack."

"Maybe…" Harris said, "or maybe they just turned chicken."

"I've got a worse idea," Leeson said. "That Abigail Claver, she's no dummy. I bet she hacked into our tactical chat, and she probably just heard Winslade's speech. He was an idiot to broadcast that talk before they were committed."

I frowned, and I wondered about that, and I even considered calling up Abigail to ask what the holdup was. But before I could do anything, my tapper lit up red.

"McGill?" Winslade said. His sharp, angular face pointed up at me from my tapper. "What the hell is going on? You didn't tip off those grunting savages, did you?"

"Certainly not, sir. But then... maybe you did."

He scowled at me, not liking the idea at all. "Well listen," he said, "you know that woman better than any of us. Contact her on a private channel and talk her into attacking. Short of that, find out what the hell the holdup is."

Using the Rigellian communication device, I did exactly as Winslade had suggested. I attempted to contact Abigail Claver.

There was no answer, so I tried it again. Then I tried it a third and a fourth time. She wasn't responding.

Something had gone wrong.

-42-

Finally, on about the sixth try, Abigail Claver answered my call. "What the hell is it, James? Stop buzzing me."

"Hey, uh... Abigail? Miss Claver? People are kind of wondering, you know... what the hell is happening up there on that ridge. Are your boys getting cold feet, or something?"

"No, no. Not at all. They're itching to go. In fact, it's all I can do to hold them back."

I blinked a few times. *She* was stopping them? This indeed sounded like she'd gotten word of Winslade's planned treachery.

"Well," I said, thinking that over. "What exactly are you waiting for, if you don't mind my asking?"

"Tell your legion commanders that it's not quite time to strike yet."

"Why not?"

"James, do you remember when we all met together—Squantus, you and me?"

"Uh, sure. I guess so."

"Do you remember what he said?"

I blinked a few times, and I thought that over. It did seem to me the midget bear had said something important... Something about sending reinforcements from Rigel itself.

Suddenly, I caught on. "Are you saying the bears are coming to help us?"

"I'm not sure, exactly," she said, "but Squantus has signaled me to wait. He said reinforcements are on the way and should be arriving in-system shortly."

I began to smile. This was the best possible news—better news than I'd ever expected to hear today. Far from learning that Abigail and her apes were going to screw us—either by holding back or staging a retreat—we were about to get more support than we thought was possible.

"Hell, girl," I said. "That's fantastic news! I'll pass it on."

"You do that, James. Over and out."

I talked to Winslade, Graves, and eventually even Galina herself. She demanded that I contact her in person when she got wind of the hopeful news.

Of course, they were all suspicious and grumbling, but they also dared to hope I wasn't full of shit this time.

"Rigel lifting a finger to aid Earth?" Galina scoffed. "That's crazy-talk. It's all bullshit. She's pulling something."

"Why do you say that, Imperator?"

"Because I know her. She's a Claver. She's as devious as you or I are —worse maybe."

"Yeah…" I said, unable to argue the point, "but she's cut a deal, ma'am. She won't break that."

"No, no. She won't *break* it. She'll just *twist* it. She'll reinterpret our arrangements. She'll screw us somehow, in the end. Don't you know that by now, McGill? She knows Winslade made that stupid speech about how we should fire indiscriminately into the middle of her army. He as much as said kill them all and let God sort them out."

"Oh, yeah," I admitted, "he did pretty much say that. You think she overheard?"

"Obviously, James. She's sitting up on that ridge, and not a single hair from one of her monkey-friends has poked over the rim of the crater in nearly an hour."

"You don't think help is coming in from Rigel?"

"I'm up here in space, James. We're scanning everything. Every minute. There's nothing in the star system. Nothing but us."

I shrugged my big shoulders, then I sat down in the dirt and made myself comfortable. This entire situation wasn't all that unusual to me. Any long-term military man knows that war wasn't a continuous camera-shaking orgy of excitement. No, far from it. For the most part, it consisted of long, boring waits followed by frenzied desperation. The deadly stuff oftentimes came with no warning at all.

Any man who's spent as many years in this trade as I have knows the best time to catch a nap was whenever you can. Accordingly, I stretched out up against that steaming mass of crunchy, smoldering dirt and made myself as comfortable as possible.

The rest of my troops soon began to do the same. It was a good time to take a piss, grab some extra rations, or talk to your friends.

Some men worked on their rifles, cleaning, checking and rechecking them. Everything had to be charged to the max, fully loaded with explosive rounds and ready to go.

But the real veterans did none of these things. They were more like me. They stretched out on the ground, and they tried to go to sleep. Only the good Lord knew how long it would be before we were allowed to rest again.

An hour passed, and soon that moved on into a second hour. Winslade, Graves and even Galina herself all sent me notes demanding that I contact Abigail again—or even better, put them into a direct channel with her.

I knew better than to do that. I told them I was too technically incompetent to do it—not a stretch of the imagination. The trouble was none of my three superior officers possessed a single diplomatic bone in their bodies. They would only demand things, complain, and generally piss-off Ms. Claver.

So, I invented technical difficulties and left it at that. This answer was met with snarls, disbelief and abrupt channel disconnections.

Another hour passed. Hell, pretty soon it was going to be high noon—which is not saying a whole lot in the jungle. The main problem was the increasing heat. I could hear the sound of fans beginning to whir inside our suits. Automatic air conditioners were tripping inside my troop's combat suits all up and down the line. Naturally, the light troopers didn't have air conditioning, so they just suffered quietly.

It was around about four hours after we'd reached the base of the ridge that something finally happened. When that something did occur—it was quite a big surprise.

"What in the nine hells is that!?" Leeson shouted, pointing straight up.

I gazed into the sky between the blackened bone-like branches of burnt trees. We all looked up, and it seemed like a big glowing region had appeared overhead. It was as if Jungle World had sprouted another sun.

A huge sphere had materialized above 31 Orionis—and it appeared to be hot with radiation.

"Hit the deck!" I shouted, and almost before my faceplate splashed down into the crusted-up mud under my feet, gravity-waves and blasting winds swept over the entire legion.

When the atmospheric reaction faded, we dared peep overhead again. The mists and the rains had retreated enough to see Jungle World's sky in all her blue glory. There, smack-dab in the middle of it, was a massive, haunting image.

It was an unnaturally smooth sphere. It appeared in the shape of a white crescent, because only part of it was reflecting the light of the local star. But the rest of it was up there, I knew, hidden by the blackness of space.

"Holy shit!" Harris said. "That's got to be a frigging Skay!"

I nodded, because I knew in my heart, he was right.

"It's a big bastard, too," Leeson added.

Someone was tugging at my sleeve. I looked down and saw it was Natasha. Her face was an ashen white. "James," she said. "That *is* a Skay, and it's a massive one. All the readings coming in from the various techs all over the legion agree, even those coming from *Scorpio*. They say it's the biggest Skay they've ever seen."

I blinked a few times, thinking that over, and then I squinted. "Is it bigger even than the one that followed us to Earth a year or so back?"

She pondered that. She went to work on her tapper and within less than a minute she had an answer. She shook her head. "No, it isn't bigger than that one. It's the exact same size as the monster that visited Earth."

I was finally catching on. "That's the same Skay that has been orbiting Rigel, protecting the bears for years, right? That's the watchdog Skay from Rigel itself."

"It's got to be, James. It's too similar in size, and it's pretty smooth, too. I think it's young, not that well-versed in combat."

I thought that over, and I had to agree with her. It had, after all, run from our combined fleets when we'd threatened it at the end of the Sky World campaign. It also made sense that if any Skay was going to be seen out here at Jungle World it would have to be this one.

This big bastard had been in charge of patrolling space around Rigel for quite some time now. In fact, it was the primary reason that our fleet had never dared stray into Rigellian space.

My mouth hung open, and I stared wide-eyed up at the monster. "Look, its mass is stirring up the local clouds. How far out is that thing? It can't be very far away."

"It actually is," Natasha said. "About a hundred thousand kilometers at least—but that's close enough to create tides down here, and to reshape weather patterns. It might even start a massive hurricane with its gravity well at the eye of the whole thing."

"Weird…" I said. "What do you think that old boy is doing up there?"

Natasha shook her head. "I don't know, but it's getting closer."

It was true. Just since we'd been watching, it seemed to me that the Skay had grown fractionally larger.

What was it going to do? Come right down into a low, close orbit? I frowned as I considered the tactical repercussions of the situation. I began to realize just exactly what I was seeing.

"That thing is attacking," I said. "It's attacking the crystal base. It's coming in right now to divebomb this crater right on top of us."

I attempted to relay these thoughts to my superior officers, but they ignored me. It had apparently occurred to them long ago.

We were ordered to withdraw from the crater wall and make a hasty retreat back into the jungle. That was an order you didn't have to give Legion Varus troops twice. We promptly did a U-turn and began to flee.

Checking my tapper, I saw the big blue blob that represented the primitive native levies working for Abigail Claver was doing the exact same thing.

After five minutes passed, I began to think we were going to escape. We had run out of the ground-zero zone, and every step carried us closer to something approximating a safe distance.

Maybe with luck, we weren't going to have to fight this crystal base at all. That would be great. It would be *awesome*.

If this big-daddy Skay just rolled in, whacked the crystal, then patted us on the head and sent us on our way... well sir, there couldn't have been a happier solution as far as I was concerned.

-43-

We ran for our lives into the forest. Instead of cursing at the big, thick trunks, fallen logs and tangly vines, we were wishing they were thicker and tougher. That way, they might provide us more protection.

We were running from the titanic battle that was about to begin. If the big Skay and the crystalline base were about to throw-down... well sir, that was all good if you were up on *Scorpio* watching from a million kilometers out—but that wasn't our situation. We were more like fleas riding on the backs of two vicious dogs.

The first shot was fired by the crystal. A big red beam appeared, punching through the atmosphere and momentarily connecting the two alien monstrosities.

We'd witnessed the power of this alien super-weapon when we'd first arrived at 31 Orionis. *Scorpio* had turned around and run in fear when it slashed the heavens, destroying our lifters.

The air itself roiled with the passage of that raw power. Crushing gases in upon themselves, it created a massive thunderclap. Clouds formed and spun in an unnatural spiraling pattern. It was like looking into the aftermath of a tiny black hole.

The looming white sphere was struck. The Skay, being a Galactic of unprecedented size and strength, wasn't destroyed outright, but it was affected.

Although my men and I were all scrambling for our lives, we couldn't help but toss horrified glances up and over our shoulders. I saw the beam strike home. It drew a line across the face of the Skay, a fresh dark scar.

The artificial beings known as the Skay are encased in thick, stardust hulls. Armored by a hundred meters or more of compressed matter, they're very tough, very difficult to damage—but somehow, this big, red, glowing crystal-thing was managing it.

Seeing that, I began to wonder at our wild hubris. We were mere tiny mortals in spacesuits, backed up by a bunch of ridiculous ape-aliens with puff-crete hammers. How had we imagined we were going to destroy something of such incredible power on foot?

The scar started about the midpoint of the big sphere, and it slashed upward to the right. To me, it looked like a half-smile carved into the face of a pumpkin—a bone-white pumpkin.

"Holy shit," Leeson yelled. "Keep running!"

"That Skay is about to unleash hell," Harris added.

"Run faster," Clane shouted, pushing and urging those of his men who'd paused to gape up at the sky to greater speed.

I noticed that his lights were actually pulling ahead of us while our weaponeers lagged to the rear. This was one of the few situations when it wasn't good to be in heavy armor or to be carrying a belcher that thumped on your back.

Harris and his heavies took the midpoint as we moved farther into the trees. The jungle was green again now, at least. We had partial coverage from the impending battle overhead, but I knew leaves would offer no protection against fallout from these warring titans.

"Hold onto your weapons, boys," I shouted. "Run, but don't throw everything away. We still might need it."

A few men turned around and went back to pick up their rifles. I didn't execute them or berate them. I knew in the end I might need every man here—even the cowards.

"What's that thing doing up there?" Leeson demanded.

"It's scanning us," Natasha said. "It's scanning the jungle, Legion Varus—everything."

To me, that sounded like good news. We needed the time to escape.

Around us, every cohort was in full retreat. Checking my tapper, I saw the blue blob which represented the horde of local native troops was outdistancing us. Not even our light troops could keep up with them as they raced away into the jungle. Abigail was doubtlessly planning to hide far from ground zero, hoping to survive.

When there was an open spot in the forest canopy again, I dared a glance upward. I expected to witness a vast amount of ordnance coming down from the Skay, something like missiles or vicious beams slashing against the giant red crystal embedded in the ground.

But instead, I received an earsplitting interruptive transmission. Everyone heard it. The overpowering voice broke into our headsets, broadcasting across every channel. Somehow despite encryption, signal-blocking, and all of our modern technology, the Skay was able to speak to us directly from the sky above.

Like a huge interstellar god, it began to berate the tiny fleas that ran from it. "I have been damaged," the Skay said. Its voice rolled through our helmets, and each word was painful to hear. "This cannot be tolerated. I came here to render aid to allies, but I was immediately attacked. I've scanned this planet, and I now see the source of your weaponry, although you've sought to hide it."

"What the fuck?" Leeson said in my ear on tactical.

"Does that thing think we're shooting at it?" Harris demanded. "Oh, God. I knew I should have quit this year. I knew it!"

I realized then that they were right. The Skay thought we'd taken a shot at it. No doubt, everyone on *Scorpio* was trying to communicate with the monster, to assure it we meant no harm. But I knew from long experience such monstrous beings rarely listened to tiny mortals—especially when they were pissed off.

Even without my urging, 3rd Unit began picking up their heels. We raced even faster over a mudflat. We vaulted vines and plunged through ferns. Palm fronds whipped and beat at our legs, our chests, and our faceplates.

Where were we going? Where were we retreating to? None of us knew. Probably, in the back of our minds, we planned to plunge all the way back to the legion's encampment. All the way to where Winslade and his staff officers squatted in Gold Bunker. Perhaps there, we'd find some protection in our trenches.

It was a faint hope, really, as there was no way to outrun deadly beams of radiation from a Mars-sized alien bent on your destruction. But we ran on anyway, not knowing what else to do.

"It's pulsing," Leeson said. "Look at it! Looks like it's frigging swelling up or something!"

"That's the atmosphere," Natasha said. "The atmosphere is pulsing—not the Skay."

"It's going to do something," Leeson insisted, "something bad!"

"All right," I said, "everybody go to ground. Get behind something, get under something, crawl into a hole or under a rock."

My men obeyed, their sides heaving, their faces glistening with sweat. They flung themselves onto the muddy ground. They crawled over one another in desperation to find shelter, to find cover of any kind.

"Your treachery has been duly noted, humans," the Skay boomed into our eardrums. "I have located the power source for your weapon. It will be eradicated—as you will be afterward."

The Skay seemed even larger in the sky than before. The very air between us, the very clouds seemed to pulsate. It was like watching heat waves coming off a puff-crete highway in the distance. Looking up, I saw a strange shimmer, a distortion. Then the massive alien from the Core Worlds struck. A gushing beam of radiation tore down through space puncturing the atmosphere of Jungle World and bathing the entire crater that the crystalline invader was hiding in, and everything went blinding white. Our faceplates automatically reacted to the released radiation and blackened to protect our eyes.

"Put your faces down in the dirt," Leeson was shouting. "Put your faces down in the dirt. Don't look at it!"

Most of the men complied. Some, however, remained gaping up at the awe-inspiring celestial contest going on above us. Their eyes were met with such a burst of radiation, they hardened and steamed like boiled eggs in their heads.

Screaming and crawling, some of these unfortunates killed themselves. Others were finished off by officers and noncoms with a shower of power-bolts from rifles.

"Behold," the Skay said. "You see my power. You have witnessed it. The technology you worked so hard to build—the great weapon you dared to turn upon my person—has been destroyed. It now lies smoldering in its bed. Know, however, that your punishment is not yet at an end. Your treachery has doomed the worthless existence of every microbe on this miserable planet!"

It went on like that for a bit, but I managed to squelch out its voice. Our techs had finally figured out how to block the transmission, or at least to dampen it.

"McGill? McGill!" Leeson was saying.

I got to my knees, looked off to the west and saw Leeson there, waving at me. He was pointing—pointing up toward the rim of the crater.

I turned, and I stared. There was a pulsing red light coming from the crater. Something brighter than we'd ever seen from it before.

"The crystal isn't out of the fight yet," Leeson said. "It's doing something!"

The Skay went on speeching. It talked about how it would hunt us all down. It told us humanoids were only valuable as sources of entertainment, and that the process of our destruction would bring great joy.

To the Skay, we were ants. In fact, we were less than ants. We were more like noisy amoebas. Beings unworthy of note. A trillion of us could have fit inside of its massive hull, and it thought no more of us than we thought of the microflora in our guts.

"You are all nothing but particles of waste," it continued.

"Jeez," Harris complained. "Why doesn't it just burn us and get it over with?"

It was a reasonable question. To me, it seemed like the Skay was offended and maybe a little scared. It probably wanted to terrorize us first because it was angry.

Naturally, every officer and tech in the legion was trying to signal the monster, to tell it that we weren't behind the attack. The arrogant alien ignored our tiny voices. It had turned a deaf ear to all of us. It had already decided our fates in its cold, alien, artificially intelligent heart.

"What's this?" the Skay said suddenly, interrupting a paragraph about how worthless we all were for having to eat and excrete, "you dare attempt to strike me again? For this fresh insult, I shall lengthen your torment. Your expungement shall take years—no, centuries!"

Right then, it broke off because the great red light was glowing in the crater behind us again. This time it lit up the skies more brightly than ever.

Roiling like a volcano of steam and flame, the red crystal released another massive gravity-beam upward into space. The crystal had summoned up its strength and fired again.

This time, the strike was much stronger than before.

Some of us watched, me included. We knew we shouldn't. We knew it might be the end of our lives—or at least, the end of our eyes—but we were drawn to it. This was a battle between immortal gods played out in the heavens for all to see.

The second, great, reddish beam struck the Skay. This time, it hit a little above and closer to the dead center of the facing side. Instead of slashing across the hull of the great sphere, it bored deep. The beam lasted longer this time as well. The crystal had chosen to focus on one small portion of the Skay's hull, and to keep burning into it.

The beam was actually digging into the Skay's face. Chunks of debris flew from the spot. Layer after layer, the beam blasted a growing hole in the Skay's shell. Burning, spinning shards of compressed matter exploded out into space.

The massive alien had stopped talking to us. It forgot about trying to terrify tiny beings with god-like words and instead fought back. It launched a fresh attack on the alien crystal.

We hugged the mud. Our voices were hoarse from roaring and wailing in terror—but we couldn't hear ourselves or even think.

It seemed to me that the battle went on for a long time, but it might have been less than a minute. During that time, I saw on my helmet's internal display that the Skay was attempting to break off. It had begun to rotate toward the local sun. The hole being drilled into its face was widening as a result.

Judging by its behavior, I could only surmise one thing: The Skay was turning away to run. Simultaneously, it fired back a massive burst of radiation toward its tormenter.

But then suddenly, the Skay's beam was cut off. It was as if a light switch had been flipped from on to off. Daring to lift our heads, we stared into the heavens, and we watched the monster from the Core Worlds die.

The red crystal had fired its beam with such persistence and accuracy upon a single focused point, it had punched through the Skay's thick hull. I could only imagine that the beam had lanced deep into of the guts of the great sphere causing great destruction.

The Skay stopped talking. It stopped threatening us. All its words of bravado, rage and arrogance ceased.

A moment later, the red beam from the crystal inside the crater died away as well. Everything fell quiet, except for the hissing of hot, irradiated mud around us.

"Is it over?" Natasha asked, lifting her face out of the muck and scraping at the mud that covered her faceplate.

"Yeah," I said, "I think it's over."

"Who won?"

I shook my head. "I'm not certain, but I'll tell you one thing… I don't think it was us."

We mortals who'd survived crawled out of our holes. We stared up from the steaming jungle at the great Skay overhead.

It was spinning, faster than any moon I'd ever seen. Black streaks crossed its face like claw marks drawn with soot.

When it had spun long enough, we could see the opposite side of the monster, which was clean and unscathed. Then as it came back around again, we could see into the guts of the monster through the hole that had been viciously drilled through its outer shell.

The opening was a hundred kilometers across, perhaps wider. Deep inside, fires raged. Gases were escaping—venting out into the void through that horrible wound.

The great Skay was now silent, and we knew in our hearts that it would never speak again.

-44-

We climbed to our feet, gathered our gear and tended to our wounded. We tried to brush off the worst of the mud and the shame. After all, we'd run like hens when it had come right down to it.

When the skies above had shaken, and the great gods of the heavens had done battle in our midst, we'd done nothing but run away. That was what any tiny mammal on primeval Earth would have done when one Tyrannosaurus rex met another and fought until one fell dead in the mud.

Attempting to alleviate the general feeling of gloom and shock that all of us were experiencing, I clapped together my big, gloved palms. Then, I gave a couple of whoops.

"Did you *see* that?" I demanded. "Those two aliens just kicked the shit out of each other! I've never witnessed such a stroke of luck! Not in all my years with Legion Varus."

The surviving light trooper recruits, and even Harris' seasoned heavies looked at me in disbelief—but they were listening, so I pressed on ahead.

I pointed up at the dead Skay that was still slowly rotating in the heavens above. At least it was in a stable orbit. Otherwise, it might have crashed directly into Jungle World, possibly demolishing the planet and all of us on it.

"Don't you guys get it?" I asked. "That big white bastard up there just took the heat for us. We could have gone down into that crater an hour ago. We were just about to do it—don't say we weren't! We would have faced all that firepower, everything that crystal had to throw at any enemy. But now it lies half-dead, wounded and smoldering... just on the other side of this here ridge."

I pointed dramatically toward the blackened crater walls. A vast column of smoke and steam was rising out of the crater, as if a volcano had just shot its wad into the sky.

"We're frigging *lucky*," I insisted. "That's right, *lucky*. That's the only thing I can call it. It's like we're all crapping golden horseshoes and four-leaf clovers!"

They seemed baffled, and many of them cast a squinting or questioning look toward the crater.

"If we'd gone in there, we would have gotten nailed. That big Skay fellow... sure he was a little bit of an asshole—I'm willing to admit that—but he gave his life for us. He gave his all to soften up the enemy for us. Talk about an artillery barrage! That tremendous exchange of heavy beams made our star-falls look like sparklers."

A few of the troops seemed to be buying it. For the most part, these were the least experienced of my men.

I continued clapping my hands, and a few others joined in. Clane, in particular, made an effort to encourage his surviving light troops.

After that pep-talk, I inspected the tattered remains of my unit. I had to shoot a few of them, of course—those who were flagged as incapacitated.

Ordering that extra water rations be released, I let the able-bodied survivors splash toxic grit out of their eyes.

That process woke everybody up, and we all focused on locating a serviceable weapon and a fresh battery pack for everyone. We cannibalized equipment, stripping the dead. After wiping some mud and blood off the best of our gear, we gathered together. 3rd Unit was now about seventy strong. Sure, we'd lost fifty or so troops, but we could still fight.

After frequent urging from our commanders, we began slogging toward the crater again. This time, we didn't advance quickly or with high spirits. There was no bravado left in us, but we still had grim-faced determination. It was better than nothing.

When Graves ordered us to begin the march up to the top of the crater, we did so. We didn't race up to meet our doom with enthusiasm, mind you—but we marched.

When we reached the smoky rim, I'm not ashamed to say that we crawled on our hands and knees. Lying flat on our bellies, we peeped up over a sharp, hot edge of melted stone. We gazed down into the crater to see what was left of the great crystal at the bottom.

At first, there seemed to be nothing but a blackened pit with white mist rising up in a thick column.

"You see that?" I said. "That rock is as dead as a doornail. We've already won this fight."

Daring to hope, my troops wormed their way up, and they took a look for themselves. We sent buzzers into the crater, and nothing shot them down. This was very encouraging.

But then, just as we were about to stand and march into the great hole, something began to glimmer down there. At the bottom of the crater, under that white mist, a deep red glow became visible. It wasn't the continuous gleam the crystal had emanated before, but it was clear the thing wasn't completely dead.

Some men panicked. It was shameful. Far off to our left and right, other unit commanders had chosen to advance more quickly than I had. These men turned in fear and tried to scramble back up to the ridge of the crater. They were desperate to get on the far side of those walls again, hoping for safety. I could imagine their squalls and shouts of fear.

My own men halted, and they wavered in their tracks—but they didn't run.

After a minute or so, the great deep red glow died down again.

I dared to laugh. "Hey, Harris! Did you take a shit in your suit? You sure look like you did!"

"Almost..." he admitted. "What do you think that was? Just a last gasp?"

"Yeah, sure. You and I have seen a thousand bodies if we've seen one. Sometimes they do a little kicking and twitching hours after they're dead."

"That's true..."

Despite our brave words, everyone looked worried now. A moment later, Graves began to squawk in my ear. "McGill? Your unit has stopped advancing. What the hell are you doing? Stop playing with yourselves and advance to the bottom of that crater. That's an order."

"We're just checking out the enemy, sir. We're looking for some of those little crystals. You know the ones—"

"Yeah, yeah, I know," he interrupted. "Now look, the Skay just put a big whammy down on top of this alien base. The time to hit them is now while the enemy is still shellshocked and trying to recover."

"Uh…" I said. "Do you think the crystals are still kicking down there, sir?"

"Something is. We can see with our orbital probes. All the sensor data beaming down from *Scorpio* indicates there's heavy radiation in the pit—and some movement, too. Your orders are to get in there and hit the enemy—hit them now."

"Got it, sir. You can count on 3rd Unit." I would have said more, but the channel had already been closed.

I grinned at my troops with a completely false expression of self-assurance.

"Guys," I said, "the word from on-high is this thing's as dead as can be—but it's our job to go down there and make sure. Just a little cleanup mission, that's all it is. We're mopping-up."

The troops grumbled, and they shot me distrustful glances, but I ignored it all. Marching in the lead, I took big steps downhill. Loose dirt and rocks followed my boots and soon showered down around me.

"James?" I heard a voice. "James?" It was Abigail.

"Hey, Miss Claver," I said. I was surprised to see the snake-bone equipment was still functional, despite all the punishment I'd put it through. This Rigellian piece of tech was as tough as nails. I probably should have stuffed it under my armor rather than on the outside, but what was done, was done.

"Are you guys actually going down there?" she asked me.

"That we are," I said.

"Are you frigging crazy? That thing's not dead yet, you know."

"That's right," I said, "but it's not getting any deader while we fondle ourselves and hide in the forest. Legion Varus will destroy this thing once and for all. We would highly appreciate it if you brought in your surviving troops to help out."

She thought about that for several long seconds. Abigail Claver was a fighter, but she wasn't really a soldier. She was more akin to a pirate than a naval officer. She was willing to fight if she had to, yeah—but she was also willing to run away when the running was good. I figured she was sensing in her heart-of-hearts that this might be one of the latter occasions.

After a minute or so had passed, perhaps shamed by our example, she ordered her primitive horde to advance. Eyeing the blue blob that represented her army on my tapper, I couldn't help but notice that the blob seemed somewhat smaller than it had been before. No doubt many of the native levies had already lost their lives. In my judgment, she had maybe half her forces left.

They came in behind us, and they came in faster than we did. The apelike creatures could run along the ground on all fours at a pace no human could match. Two legs could never outrun two legs and two arms.

When it came to climbing the ridge and then coming down again their ground-eating pace brought them even with us. They were decidedly more surefooted than humans on steep ground. Clutching their somewhat pathetic-looking puff-crete hammers, I saw them through the steamy distance. Whatever you might say about these simple warriors, they didn't lack for bravery.

Together we advanced toward the center of the great crater on two flanks. When we got near the bottom, the crystal gleamed again. It had been silent, except for that single pulse of light that had been emitted as we reached the top of the ridge.

Now, as we sank into the white mists, the crater lit up with a ghostly glow. Could this be a signal of some kind? Perhaps it had laid dormant, trying to recover like a wounded man gasping for breath. I wasn't sure, until the moment that second red glow shone bright and—the enemy counterattacked.

At first, dozens of crystals appeared, gliding silently toward us from the very bottom of the crystal. Then hundreds appeared.

They were strange, multifaceted, almost spherical formations. We'd seen this kind before. One to two meters in diameter, they came at us without any apparent organization or plan, and we rushed to meet them in battle.

Some of them were already damaged. Some of them spun off-center, drifting to either the left or the right as they advanced. Now and then, they even crashed into one another drunkenly—but still they came on.

In response we hurled a hail of plasma grenades. This shocked the crystal defenders as it had before. Our light troops rushed in with sticky bombs, gluing them to the side of any confused enemy they could catch. Within seconds, these bombs went off.

Sometimes, the light trooper in question was lucky enough to scramble away—and sometimes he wasn't. In either case, the crystal was usually destroyed.

More crystals came forth from the bottom of the crater. I figured they must be emerging from below the giant red crystal monster that was their parent, or their mothership—whatever.

When the battle was in full swing, I heard a wild grunting to my side. I turned, raised my rifle, and almost fired. It was a close thing, but the furry alien never seemed to know it. He rushed on by with his crudely constructed hammer lifted high over his head. The warrior wasn't looking at me at all. Instead, he leapt atop the nearest crystal and began banging away on it, chipping pieces from the strange spinning chunk of living rock.

Some of the crystals were waking up now. They'd gotten their bearings again, and they began to beam indiscriminately. Their gravity weapons tore apart humans, ape-aliens and dogmen at random. The beams seemed to go right through their own kind, doing no damage. Hundreds of organic soldiers were killed or left flopping and crushed.

For several minutes, a wild dance of violence ensued. I was dashed to the ground, and some of my fingers caught a few crushing rays. They ached in my glove, unable to move. The bones had been fused together.

In the end, the crystals stopped pouring out from under their parent, and they found themselves overwhelmed. There were just too many of us, and we were determined to finish this foe. We destroyed every crystal, shattering it down to its core.

Their corpses, strangely enough, were almost beautiful to look upon. Like frozen chunks of colored ice, their broken dead resembled shattered icicles that reflected Christmas lights. Hundreds upon hundreds of the crystalline soldiers, perhaps even a thousand or more, had been destroyed.

When they stopped coming at last, we slowly advanced to the center of the crater. There, we saw a curious thing. The central crystal itself seemed to be riddled with holes. There were gaping cracks all over its surface, fissures that ran deep.

We figured out this is where the crystal soldiers had been coming from. A single great crystal had been fired from deep space and had embedded itself like a bullet in the side of Jungle World. It had then spawned many jewel-like offspring. These minions, tiny by comparison, then rushed off to do the bidding of their creator.

Now, however, the great crystal seemed to be fully exhausted. Whatever power source had enabled this thing to fight so hard and so long was dying now. She could no longer give birth to her warriors, shedding them out of her own gut to fight us.

Legion Varus and the natives of 31 Orionis had won the day.

-45-

As one might imagine, there was a great deal of death and destruction left behind in the wake of the struggle between the Skay from the Core Worlds and the strange alien crystal. A lot of my troops had to be recycled, even those who'd survived the battle. They were too burned by radiation, or too seriously injured by the crystalline soldiers to be salvaged.

Coming out of the revival machines in a long, marching line, we were in a celebratory mood. One of the recruits, in particular, came to seek me out.

Now, you have to keep in mind at this point that I'd consumed six or seven mugs of bootleg hooch by this time. The biotechs were making it, as usual, but today it was quite a bit more potent than it had been on other campaigns. I thought this must be due to the high sugar-content of the local fruits in the jungle. I'd often said that the bio people of Legion Varus could make an alcoholic drink out of battery acid and alien dirt mixed together in an old boot. Fortunately, they hadn't needed to go to such extremes on this occasion.

The person who came to seek me out was one that caused my eyebrows to ride high in speculation.

"Oh… uh…" I said, "Tessie? Isn't that the name?"

"That's right," she said. She was young and fresh-looking. She'd obviously stepped out of the revival machines with her new skin and matted hair just minutes earlier. Despite the fact she'd experienced a hard death fighting the crystals, Tessie was all smiles.

"What are you grinning about, girl?" I asked her, and I found myself giving her a smile of my own. I couldn't help it. She was cute, after all, and we were having a victory celebration. On top of that, the Jungle World hooch in my cup was really starting to kick in.

Tessie looked down at the mud of Jungle World shyly. "Two things," she said. "Number one, I was able to secure the rank of a regular."

"Already?" I said questioning. "That's excellent."

She smiled. "I wanted to thank you for the recommendation, sir."

I nodded, and I told her how much she deserved it—and she did deserve it. Naturally, I left out the part that it was standard procedure for any half-functional recruit to be elevated to the rank of regular at the end of a successful campaign. You never wanted to tell a girl she wasn't special. Never.

"Uh..." I said, "what's the second thing?"

Tessie seemed a little more shy than before, but she finally looked up and answered. "I've been transferred out of 3rd Unit," she said. "I made the request, and I was accepted into Manfred's unit."

"Oh... is that right? Good for you. Any special reason for leaving?"

She didn't answer for a few moments. She just kind of moved her boots around on the mud. "Well," she said, "there are certain legion policies that no longer apply now that I've transferred."

All of a sudden, like a bolt of lightning, it hit me right between the eyes. This girl knew that as her commanding officer I could not fraternize with her in any way without violating Legion Varus policy.

Now mind you, I'd never been a man who was much of a stickler for such rules—no matter who had written them. But I'd happened to follow them this time around, with Tessie in particular.

My foggy brain continued to slowly connect more dots. I realized the girl had done quite a bit of work to both get herself to a higher rank, and to get herself transferred out of my unit.

I blinked once, then twice. Then, I slugged down a big gulp of hooch. I offered her one for herself. After a moment of sniffing at it delicately, she wrinkled her nose, but then accepted the beverage and consumed it rapidly.

Somehow, over the next ten minutes or so, I managed to slip my arm around Tessie's shoulders. This spectacle was met with outright disgust and possibly even outrage. Several of the women in my unit were now sneering in my direction. This included Kivi, Natasha and others too.

I didn't care. It was legal. We'd just won a war, and hell, if a girl like Tessie was going to go to all this effort just to get a date with me, who was I to crush her dreams?

I was, in fact, about to consummate our newfound friendship when something or someone arrived at the camp. A lot of my unit legionnaires squawked and raised their rifles.

Seeing that it was a dogman, I waved my troops back and shoved the muzzles of their guns down, aiming them at the dirt.

"Hey doggie," I said. "Nice doggie. What have you got there for me?"

Upon seeing me, the dogman approached. He seemed harmless, so I allowed him to come close. When he stood in front of me, his lips trembled a bit as if he wished to lift them and show me his white fangs, but he didn't. Instead, he handed me something.

It was a tangle of black wires with a black brick in the middle of it. I frowned and eyeballed the mess, picking it up like a dead rat. I held it aloft. It was a teleport harness.

"Is this for me? I asked.

The dogman made a few pantomime gestures, suggesting that I put the harness on and push the button.

"You're damned crazy if you do it, McGill," Leeson said.

"Don't tell him that," Harris argued. "If he disappears forever, he's as good as permed. That'll make you our new centurion."

Leeson looked a bit alarmed. He never really liked playing the part of centurion. He put his hands on his hips and frowned at me and the dogman. "Do whatever you want," he said. "It's your funeral."

Following his advice, I took the harness, and I put it on.

A small, fine-boned hand laid itself upon my gauntlet. I looked down and saw Tessie. She looked both alarmed and disappointed.

"Centurion, sir?" she said. "Do you really think this is a good idea?"

I looked into her eyes, and I knew exactly what she meant. At the very least, I was blowing the evening with her.

Frowning, I reconsidered the harness. Maybe Leeson and Tessie were right. Who knew what kind of bullshit trickery was behind this harness and this visit from out of the blue? Right about then, a blue glimmer began to shine.

It was the dogman. He was wearing a harness of his own, and he'd pushed his button. He was quickly retrieved home and vanished.

"Well," Harris said, "aren't you going to at least call Abigail and see if she's the one who sent this—and why?"

I thought that over. Of course, the harness had come from Abigail. She was the one in charge of the dogmen.

My mind must be foggy with alcohol and good cheer. "Yeah, of course," I said. "I was about to do that."

Reaching down to the snake-bone device, I tapped at it and thumbed it. The bones rattled and came to life. Every time I died and retrieved this strange alien technology, it seemed to take a while to wake up again. I used the thing to contact Abigail and she peered up at me through my tapper.

"McGill, what are you doing?" she said. "What's the delay?"

"So… this is an invite from you?" I asked.

"Of course, it is. The chiefs of all the local tribes are celebrating now. You're considered to be something of a hero as you negotiated the truce between our peoples. Don't you want to come and talk to them?"

A small face came near my elbow and peered down at my tapper. I realized it was Tessie. We'd gotten rather close over the last hour or so, while we drank and chatted. She frowned at Abigail's face. "Are you going off to see her?" she asked me.

A loud bark of laughter came from behind us. We both turned and noticed that Carlos had appeared from somewhere—probably the revival chambers. He looked a bit drunk already, and more than a bit evil.

"Hey lady," he said. "If you're applying for the job of James McGill's sidepiece, you'd better learn to take a number and get in line."

I gave him the stink-eye, and he wandered off, but the damage was already done. Little Tessie had her fists on her hips.

I ignored both of them and turned back to Abigail. It was hard to think clearly. "What's this all about?" I asked. "The battle is over, isn't it?"

"Yes, it is—at least the battle here at 31 Orionis. But there are a lot more worlds under attack by this same enemy, and we don't have a giant Skay to save us on all of them."

I thought that over, and I realized she was right. All by itself, Legion Varus—even with help from a local army—hadn't shattered this crystal base. We could never have done it without the raw power of the Skay. The trouble was, as far as I knew, there was only one Skay in the province, and it was dead now.

"Hey Tessie?" I said. "You wouldn't mind waiting until morning, would you?"

Instead of answering she turned away and frumped off.

I shrugged and turned back to Abigail. She smirked at me.

"I'm dearly sorry," she said, "for having blown your evening's plans, but this is important. Are you coming out or not?"

"All right," I said, and I pushed the button.

Now, don't go thinking that I didn't know I was blowing things with Tessie. But now and then a man like me has to make a moral decision. Sure, I could have chased some tail and probably had a good time during the big victory celebration, but Abigail Claver represented something much more important. She had helped me arrange a temporary truce with Rigel. I owed it to all humanity and to Legion Varus in particular to hear what she had to say.

The jump was a very short one as we were all on the same planet. I arrived with a popping sound in the middle of one of those rock-piles the native aliens used for their ceremonial gatherings.

This time, however, instead of having ten thousand or so primitive warriors surrounding the location, the entire plateau was quiet. It was dark outside and relatively dry with a few misty clouds overhead obscuring what was now Jungle World's new moon. The giant dead Skay loomed overhead orbiting the planet forever. The big black hole in its face could be seen quite clearly.

Abigail stepped close, and I gaped up at the dead, monstrous hulk. "Looks like Earth's Moon riding up there," I said, "except for, you know, that black eye."

Abigail didn't seem happy. She gazed at the same dead alien, and I could tell it brought her no joy. "That's a terrible sight, McGill," she said.

"Why's that?"

"Because that's not just one more boastful Galactic from the Core who came out to the provinces and got himself killed. That Skay was the only thing keeping Rigel and Earth from destroying each other."

I stared up alongside her, and I began to frown. I supposed she was right. Sure, we'd been squabbling with Rigel, snapping up a planet or two, but we'd never dared to throw our fleet against Rigel itself. The big reason why was hanging right there above us in space.

"Huh…" I said. "Do you think we're going to start the war up again, seeing as how that Skay's gone and got itself killed?"

"What do you think, James? You've been around the big government officials on Earth more than I have lately. Do they want war, or do they want peace?"

"Well, there is that little matter of ninety-odd million people dying on Earth after the destruction of the Big Sky Project."

She looked at me. "Who do you think did that?"

"Did what?"

"Destroyed the Big Sky Project. Who made it fall out of Earth orbit and kill all those people?"

I stared at her for a moment as if she was the dummy. "Rigel, of course," I said.

Abigail shook her head slowly. "That's not what our intel says. We think it was an inside job."

I considered her words, and even though I was riding a brain that was fogged with alcohol, I didn't totally disbelieve her. There had been signs from the beginning. For one thing, the various official investigations had never concluded who was at fault. Before Big Sky had fallen, one of our own missiles had crashed into it. That had wrecked the shielding system before it was fully operational.

The fact was this single incident had kicked off the entire Sky World campaign. It had led us to invade a number of worlds, including the one I was standing on right now.

If Rigel had been having trouble with these crystals all that time… what sense did it make for them to choose this moment to attack us? With a dirty trick, no less?

Today, we'd pulled together and forged a truce that had allowed us to stop these weird crystalline entities. But was that about to end? I wasn't really sure.

"Well," I said, "there are definitely people on Earth who don't want to stop the war."

"That's right," she said aiming a finger at me. "They don't want to end the war. The war has been great for Earth. You've made multiple strides, you've taken several planets. Only this new greater threat has gotten in the way. But I want to tell you a secret, James."

"A secret? I love secrets."

"Yes, and this is a good one. The secret is that Squantus doesn't want this war. He never wanted this war. It's the people back on Earth who wanted it all along. They're the ones who blew up the Big Sky Project. Knowing he was going to get blamed, Squantus ran from Earth soon after he met you."

I made a mental effort to shake off my alcoholic fog and think about that distant day. It was a year-and-a-half ago now when I'd first met Squantus. We'd talked quite a bit. He'd told me that his father had told him he'd made a mistake going to all-out war with humanity. In his old age, he'd begun to wish things had gone differently between Rigel and Earth.

"James? James!" Abigail was talking to me again, but I hadn't been listening. "Did you hear me?"

"I certainly did."

"I was saying that it doesn't even matter who destroyed the Sky World Project, who struck the first blow in this decades-long war between two young empires on the edge of the galaxy. What matters is that it needs to end right now. This new enemy is greater than any of us. If Rigel falls, then Earth will be next. Even now, it might be too late."

Blinking at her. I managed to get out an intelligent sentence. "Too late for what?"

"To stop the crystals, that's what. Even combined, Earth and Rigel may not be strong enough to fight these creatures. They come from a strange world, far out past this frontier province we're in now. They come from the deepest, wildest fringes of the galaxy. They don't know about the Galactic Empire at the Core, and they don't care. They're here to take us all out. It's their kind of life against ours, and nothing will stop them short of destruction. You need to take these words and thoughts to Drusus."

"Who? Me?" I asked, and I laughed. "You're talking to the wrong ambassador. I'm not a man of fancy words. I've got no influence or power."

"Not officially," Abigail said, "but you are one of those go-betweens, one of those little men who are always at the right place at the right time. Anyway, you're not the only man we're talking to tonight. There are others. We…"

"Who's we?" I asked. I'd only seen Abigail. There wasn't so much as a dogman in the vicinity besides her.

Then, as if he'd been listening—which he probably had been—a figure stepped out of the dark from the stones off to my left.

I spun around, drew my pistol, and almost fired. Fortunately, I managed to stop myself before I killed him. It was Squantus.

"You, human," he said, "you I trust. Not in all things, but in matters of honor and promises."

"That's mighty nice of you, Squantus," I said. "Your daddy and I, we made a few deals back in our day."

"That's right. I now understand my father's wisdom in telling me that you were a human that could be dealt with."

"So…" I said, "what exactly do you want me to do? What do you want me to say, and who do you want me to say it to?"

"Drusus," he said. "Go to Drusus. He is one of the few human leaders who isn't lusting for war."

I nodded, knowing what he said was true. Drusus had always tried to reason things out and come to a reasonable conclusion. He was rarely hotheaded or stubborn. "What should I tell him?"

"Tell him that Rigel wishes to continue the truce. That we must combine our forces to defeat this enemy. That these crystals are greater than Earth or Rigel, and our only hope lies in working together against these alien monstrosities."

I thought it over, and I finally nodded. "I'll give it a try," I told him.

The two of them thanked me, and Abigail even gave me a little kiss on the cheek.

Then, she secretly reached a finger to my chest and pushed the button on my harness again. I'd been wearing it the entire time.

Apparently, it'd been programmed to return me to my encampment. A few moments later, I was gone.

-46-

Legion Varus left the 31 Orionis system about a week later. With our mission accomplished, we headed back home to Earth. No, we hadn't conquered Jungle World, but our orders had shifted in the middle of this campaign, and we'd successfully defended that planet against another alien entity from beyond the horizons of known galactic space.

I'd often heard whispered tales of unknown monstrosities out past Rigel. The outer rim of the galaxy was a chaotic wilderness. There were plenty of species of aliens, whole civilizations, and creatures that knew nothing about the Empire and couldn't care less.

Apparently, such beings had existed and flourished all throughout the galaxy many eons ago. But once the Galactics from the Core Worlds had gotten themselves together and established their dominance, they'd managed to eradicate the wildest types—at least in their own neighborhood. They'd tamed the center of the Milky Way, providing some level of civilization and order to what otherwise was a nightmarish hellscape.

Farther out along the rim, however, things were still unknown and terrifying. Perhaps the crystals were beings from that ancient time when evolution and fate had created a great bounty of organized, intelligent lifeforms. Not all of us were based on water and carbon. Some weren't organic at all.

The return trips to Earth tended to be dull and uneventful—but this trip was different. The second week out from Jungle

World, a message came for me over the deep-link. It glowed on my tapper, and I was reluctant to read it.

Finally, I succumbed to curiosity and took a peek. It was a summons to Earth. It told me I was to be transmitted home in the fastest manner possible.

Frowning, I hoped this didn't mean I was to be executed. I was really getting to be attached to the current version of James McGill. He was healthy and happy, and I considered him to be a winner.

With a grunt and a sigh, I left my module and my unit behind and trudged to Gray Deck. There I was met by a squad of unsmiling tech specialists. A crowd of doubting fleet types mulled over my summons, and they decided at last it was legit.

As they began to suit me up with a harness, another familiar face showed up to join me.

"What are you doing here, McGill?" Galina asked.

I glanced at her, and she squinted in suspicion. Almost immediately, we realized the truth. We had both been summoned.

"Oh, hell," she said, "don't tell me this has something to do with all that investigation nonsense from last year. I don't want to even hear that."

I shrugged my big shoulders. "I'm clueless, sir."

While we were suited-up, she kept giving me sour glances. I could tell she was upset about something, but I couldn't think of what it might be for the life of me. As I thought about it more, it struck me that she'd made no attempts to communicate with me at all after the campaign had ended. She'd been on *Scorpio* the same as I had, and normally Galina had made a point of sharing her bed with me on return trips like this one—but not this time.

"Hey," I said, "if this is all just a quick meeting at Central, maybe you and I could hit the town tonight. What do you say?"

"Forget it," she snapped. It was as if she had been waiting for me to request a date with her.

"Huh..." I said. "Is something wrong?"

"Ask the enlisted girls," she said. "As I understand it, that's more your speed these days."

All of a sudden, I got it. Somehow, she'd gotten wind of Tessie. Now, how the hell had that happened? Couldn't a man like me go out with one undersized, rambunctious regular trooper—from a different unit mind you—without every female on this battleship buzzing about it?

"I've got no earthly idea what you're talking about, Imperator," I lied.

"I'm sure you don't." Her tone was still sour.

After we were trussed-up and shipped to Earth, Galina and I arrived in close proximity. Without even looking at me, she began striding on ahead toward the exit.

I followed along, hulking after her. No matter how fast she walked, there was no way she was going to lose me. I made sure I didn't catch up too quickly, as I was enjoying the view.

Now and then, she tossed a sour glance over her shoulder, but I didn't say anything to her. She entered an elevator for the upper floors, and I reached out a big hand to stop the doors from closing. That's when she pointed a finger up into my face.

"No, you don't," she said, "you take the next elevator up."

"What? I'll be late."

"I don't care."

My mouth hung open a bit. "What'd I do?"

"I don't even want to know what you've been doing."

That baffled and annoyed me, but I smiled anyway. "Ah, come on. Galina, you're going up to see Drusus, aren't you?"

"Yes," she said.

"Well, so am I. What the hell's the point of us going up in separate elevators? Besides, this is our chance to get our stories straight."

Her eyes shifted and her brow furrowed. "We don't have any stories to get straight."

"You're the one who brought up last year's investigations. Remember how hot these hogs were on finding unification rebels? That witch-hunt can't be entirely forgotten."

My words made her reach up and slap me one in the face. Startled, I lifted my chin up out of her range. I thought for a second she might go for my balls next, but she didn't.

"All right," she huffed. "Get into the elevator."

I stepped inside. She pushed the buttons, and we began a long ride up to the top of Central.

"What are you going to say to Drusus?" she asked me after about a minute of silence.

"Nothing much. I was just going to ask about his day, and if he's seen any good feelies lately. That kind of thing."

"You lying bastard," she said crossing her arms. "You're always lie about everything."

"That's just not true, sir. Anyone who tells you that is slurring my good name."

Galina fell silent again, and I did the same. She was fidgeting, however, while I stood there unconcerned. Finally, she couldn't take it any longer. She stepped close to me, raised an acrylic-dipped fingernail into my face and waved it under my nose. "Have you really been sleeping with an enlisted girl? Really? It's disgusting."

I gaped for a moment. "No, sir! Where'd you even get that idea?"

"From every female in your unit."

"What? Do you ladies talk online, or something?"

She shrugged. "Once in a while…"

"I'm not sure if I should be flattered or pissed," I said. "But no, I blew the whole thing with Tessie a long time ago. She's just not interested."

"That is a flat lie."

Galina was correct, of course. But it *was* true that I hadn't managed to get my hands on Tessie since we'd left Jungle World.

I continued giving her my heartfelt denials and talking about how important this meeting was with Drusus. Galina fretted for a few moments, thinking things over. Finally she sighed, and her shoulders slumped a bit.

"Okay, I'll forget about your tomcat behavior for today," she said. "You're right. This is more important. I'm going to tell Drusus it's time for him to step aside."

"Huh?" I said, somewhat confused.

"He's being asked to step down as the consul of Earth, James."

"Oh…" I said, "yeah, that's probably so…"

"You agree, then?" she asked me.

I shrugged my shoulders, completely unconcerned. I didn't really think Drusus was going to listen to me on the matter anyway, but if it made Galina happy, I was willing to follow her down this particular path to pointlessness.

After gaining my tepid support, she relaxed a bit and even warmed up to me. About fifteen seconds later, the elevator stopped and dinged. The doors opened, and what I saw in the lobby surprised me.

Usually, the hallways on top of Central were pretty much empty with a few hog guards placed here and there for show. Today was different. Instead of fat-boys with pistols on their hips, there were two long lines of fully armed and armored troops. There were ten on the left side and ten on the right.

Each man carried a morph-rifle and a sealed helmet. They looked like heavy troopers, but they weren't wearing real legionnaire uniforms. I figured they must be hogs in fancy gear. Even when pitted against a real fighter like me, I had to admit they might be dangerous if they all ganged-up at once.

There wasn't a smile or a nod from any of them as we marched down the corridor towards Drusus' overly flamboyant office. I'd noted over many years that Drusus had slowly expanded both the size and quality of his office. Today, for instance, there was a row of live orchids in glass terrariums lining one wall of the lobby. They all looked unique and expensive.

Primus Bob still worked here, but it seemed to me that his uniform was a little more crisp and dressy than it used to be. He was also somewhat more stiff and formal. He greeted the two of us and requested that we wait outside while Drusus held another audience with someone else.

"Hey, Bob?" I said. "What's with all the fancy-pants hogs with morph-rifles standing in lines outside?"

"Increased security, McGill," he said.

"Why is that? Have there been assassination attempts or something since I was last up here?"

"No," he said, "not exactly…"

"Oh wait," I said, pointing a thick finger at him. "I remember you getting killed by men just like this a year or so back. You know, when you walked in with all that coffee and—"

"Yes, yes, I know," he said angrily. "It was very amusing, I'm sure. Now, would you please shut up? I'm going to let Consul Drusus know that you're here."

"Is he really in there with someone else, Bob?"

"Yes, of course. He's always in a meeting. Always." Primus Bob seemed harried and a little upset, so I let him go.

He signaled Drusus somehow, and then the door suddenly popped open. Instead of Drusus himself opening the doors, however, yet more hog-like guards did the deed. Again, they were heavily armed and armored, and none of them smiled. None of them even made eye contact.

They held the two doors open and Primus Bob shooed Galina and I inside, but he made no move to follow.

The big doors clanged shut, and we were in the consul's giant office.

-47-

Drusus' office was, if anything, more impressive than it had ever been before. Today there were rich, red velvet curtains hanging here and there. They all had thick, gold tassels dangling from them.

I immediately walked over to one of these curtains and fondled the golden threads. I whistled long and low.

"Real gold?" I said. "Is this *really* spun gold? I've never seen the like!"

"McGill? Come over here, please," Drusus said.

I left the entrance guards and the sumptuous curtains behind with reluctance. Giving the ropelike golden threads a final tug of curiosity, I turned and walked to the middle of the gigantic office. There, I stood tall and confronted the man who was essentially the ruler of all Earth.

Drusus stood at one end of the main conference table. At the far end of the table was another individual, and I recognized him in an instant. It was none other than Galina's father, Alexander Turov.

I'd always called him Old Alexander in my own mind—but today he didn't look so old. I recalled that he'd died not that long ago on the Big Sky station. Since he'd been revived, he now looked more like a middle-aged, balding man—rather than an elderly coot. He was still thin and had a naturally sallow complexion. The sour expression on his hollow-cheeked face matched the rest of him.

Approaching the group with Galina at my side, I nodded to Alex and saluted Drusus.

"May I question," Alexander said, "the presence of this centurion at such an important, high-level meeting?"

"I value his opinion," Drusus said. "In fact, my sources tell me that he was present when the natives of Jungle World helped destroy the crystal that is at the crux of this discussion."

Turov's lips squirmed a bit, but he said nothing.

For my part, I stood still and smiled like an idiot. This had the usual effect of causing everyone else to stop staring at me. They glanced at one another distrustfully instead until Servant Turov finally spoke up. "Very well. Let's continue the discussion we were having. The Ruling Council believes we're at a major turning point in this conflict with Rigel."

Drusus faced him. "I agree. In fact, now that we've declared a truce with Rigel, I believe we've legitimately ended that conflict."

Turov didn't look happy, but he nodded to suggest that Drusus should continue.

"Defeating Rigel was my initial charge as the consul of Earth," Drusus said. "At this time, although we haven't defeated them, we've come to peaceful terms. The initial reason for my appointment has passed."

Old Alexander's lips were squirming again, but he still didn't say anything. I could tell that he wanted to, but he was controlling the urge.

"So," Drusus continued, "here's what I would ask the Council... Should I continue to hold high office now that we've discovered an even greater evil? The crystalline enemy represents a threat that is possibly even more serious than Rigel itself. Shall I continue to serve in the role of Earth's consul, or should I step down from my post? No matter what the Council decides, someone must lead Earth against the crystals until this new rival has been defeated."

"Let us be perfectly clear," Turov said, "you admit your original charge has been completed?"

"Yes, I said as much."

Alexander nodded. "Good," he said. "Excellent..." He seemed to be all but salivating for Drusus to leave his lofty post.

I recalled that this was a point of contention between the Ruling Council and Drusus. He'd originally been appointed to the rank of consul, which was an old Roman office. In Old Rome, whenever the entire state was deemed to be under the threat of possible destruction, a consul was essentially a dictator.

At the end of the Sky World campaign, the Ruling Council had expected Drusus to retire and give up his powers. He'd refused, as Rigel had not yet been defeated. Now that Rigel and Earth were at peace, I could logically see how he felt his mission had finally been accomplished.

To be honest, it would make me happy if we had a few peaceful years in our near future. I dared to hope that my fondest wishes would come true.

"I must summon the Ruling Council to make this decision," Alexander said. He then performed some acts of prestidigitation with his hands. The big table projected the other eight members of the Ruling Council. Soon, they all stepped into view in their hooded robes of jet black. They encircled the table and looked on, listening in silence.

Old Alexander turned to address the quiet group of holograms.

"To reiterate," Alexander said, "Drusus, you have agreed to step down as consul of Earth, as was requested a year or so ago?"

"Yes," Drusus said, "but what I'm really asking is if the Ruling Council wishes me to continue in my role to defend Earth against this even greater enemy we've now come into contact with."

Alexander shook his head. He folded up his lips and made a dismissive gesture. "Let us do one thing at a time, Drusus. Fellow public servants. Drusus has summoned us here to witness an event of momentous import. Drusus, please continue and address the Council."

Drusus faced the Nine. All of them were holograms except for Alexander himself. "Esteemed officials," he said. "I am hereby resigning my post because as far as I can tell my mission has been accomplished. Earth and Rigel are no longer at war at this time. Since the threat has passed, the need for my position has passed as well."

Alexander looked like he was going to jump in, but Drusus stopped him with an upraised hand. "One more thing, council members," he said, looking at each of their cowled faces, "the threat from Rigel has passed, but the threat from these new aliens—these crystalline entities—is still here and perhaps greater than ever. Left unchecked, I believe these crystals will invade every world in this province. I must point out that it took the combined might of Rigel, Earth and a Skay of great size to defeat just one of them."

The heads of the eight holograms swiveled to face Old Alexander.

"I believe," Alexander said, "that Drusus has served us well and competently. We should thank him for his service and offer him a commendation."

I clapped my hands loudly at this, but no one seemed to appreciate my enthusiasm. When I finally stopped interrupting, they all went back to ignoring me again.

Alexander smiled. To my eyes, it was a thin, wicked smile. "Consul Drusus," he said, "let it be known that Earth will be forever in your debt for your service. You are hereby deposed as consul of Earth and restored to your previous rank of praetor. May your deeds and triumphs be remembered forever."

"Thank you, sirs," Drusus said, and he opened his mouth as if to begin a new speech, but Old Alexander cut him off.

"Now, Council Members," he said, "we have a further matter to discuss."

Suddenly, Drusus was a nobody. I could see in his eyes that he realized this, and it wasn't a comfortable feeling for him.

He was no longer consul of Earth. He was no longer above the Ruling Council. Now, he was kissing their butts instead of them kissing his. It must have come as a shock after long years of serving in the highest office.

Old Alexander seemed to take notice of all this. He looked from one member to another of the Ruling Council.

"We must, as Praetor Drusus has so graciously and repeatedly pointed out, deal with a new threat. Perhaps we need a new consul of Earth."

I blinked at this, and so did everybody else in the room—except for the counselors and the hog guards at the entrance. None of them moved a muscle or said a damned thing.

"Let us have a show of hands," Alexander said. "Who here thinks that we need to appoint a new consul of Earth?"

He raised his own hand, and only after he'd done so, with his hand clearly lifted high into a position of the affirmation, did the rest of the eight Council Members raise their hands in the same manner.

"Excellent," Alexander said. "The motion has passed unanimously. Now, I have a recommendation for this appointment. She is currently here in this room."

I heard a small gasp.

Up until this moment, Galina had stayed dead-silent. I figured she was somewhat overawed by all these scary-looking, ultra-powerful government officials in their intimidating robes. Such things had never impressed me much, but for some people, these old spooks seemed to be downright terrifying.

"Galina?" Alexander said. "Step forward, please."

On stiff legs, she walked toward the table.

Drusus must have realized she was moving to his spot at the head of the conference table. Frowning, he backed away. He was surprised and a little upset. He hadn't thought things were going to go this way. He'd asked to continue in his role with a new charge, but instead—he was being replaced.

Galina, for her part, looked like she'd been sent to the principal's office for her first spanking.

"Imperator Galina Turov," Alexander said, "I hereby appoint you to be Consul of Earth. Will you accept this duty?"

"What would be my charge, Servant?" Galina asked.

"You will be appointed to the highest office until Rigel has been destroyed, and this new threat from the Galactic Rim has been eliminated."

At that, Drusus made a small choking sound. Alexander's eyes flicked toward him, then back to Galina. He opened his mouth to continue, but Drusus interrupted him.

"Esteemed servants?" Drusus said suddenly. "May I speak?"

Alexander looked at him coldly. "Must I remind you, Drusus, that you are now a praetor? That is a significant rank, but the rank of consul is infinitely superior—as is the rank of every member of the Ruling Council in this room today."

"I understand that, sirs. I truly do, but I thought it was understood we were going to continue the truce with Rigel until such time as the crystalline enemy has been defeated. In fact, I think we should maintain the truce permanently, turning it into a longstanding peace between our two great nations."

"Your opinions are appreciated and duly noted," Alexander said. "Under these circumstances, however, they're both impertinent and immaterial." He turned his eyes back toward Galina. "Now, as we were saying…"

Drusus had a sour look on his face now. He'd been shunted aside and slapped down, just like that. He was a nobody in his own office. The only creature that was less important was me—or possibly the hog guards that stood around the doorway.

As a man who'd been told to shut up and sit down countless times, I understood how poor old Drusus felt—but even I winced when he started talking again.

"Esteemed Servants—" he said.

At this, Alexander made an angry gesture. He banged a skinny fist on the conference table.

"Guards!" Alexander said loudly.

Every guard hanging around the entrance—all six of them—stepped forward alertly.

"Arrest Praetor Drusus," Alexander ordered, pointing toward the shocked ex-consul.

Drusus was swarmed by hog guards. This angered me. After all, he was a man I respected almost more than any other officer on all of Earth.

My hand moved to my laser pistol, but I realized that was a mistake. If I was going to do something, I would have to get in close and be sneakier than that.

371

"Servant Turov, your overlordship, sir?" I said. "Can I volunteer to take this disruptive man to the brig?"

Alexander looked at me, and Galina did as well.

"Request denied," Galina said. "You're going to stay here with me, McGill."

I shrugged, but as Drusus was hustled past me, I whispered a quick question. "Do you want me to do anything, sir?" I asked him.

His eyes were wide. I could see the whites all the way around. He seemed stunned, as if he couldn't believe what was happening.

"No, McGill," he whispered back, "bide your time."

Then he was hustled away, and the door slammed behind him. At that point just the three of us were left in the room—plus, of course, the eight holograms who were all as silent as ghosts.

Alexander faced his daughter across the long, long table. "You have not yet answered my query," he said. "Will you accept the post of consul of Earth?"

Galina opened her mouth, but then she shut it again. She was his daughter, of course, and she was as ambitious as anyone I'd ever met—but I think at this moment she was as stunned as Drusus himself about the recent turn of events.

It was one thing, after all, to watch Drusus fall from dictator to prisoner within a matter of seconds—but it was quite another to be offered his job.

Galina hadn't gotten this far in life by recklessly taking on new responsibilities she knew nothing about.

"This comes as a total surprise to me," she said at last. "Please, Council Members, allow me some time to consider your kind offer. I must decide if I'm worthy of this fantastic responsibility."

Old Alexander didn't look happy with that statement. He looked, in fact, somewhat pissed off. "How much time will this decision take?"

"A week," she said. "No wait—a month at least. In fact, make it two. I will have to commission a study."

"A study?"

"Yes, I must also assemble a staff."

"What are you talking about?" her father demanded.

She waved a hand toward the outer office where people like Primus Bob and a dozen other sycophants bustled and simpered.

"Drusus has a much higher rank than I do. I don't have a large staff. What should I do? Promote Gary to be my second in command?"

Alexander showed his teeth momentarily. I guess it was a grin of amusement.

"All right," he said. "We shall expect an answer after you have performed your... study."

With that, the holograms faded out. Alexander himself marched out of the oversized, echoing office.

I was left alone with Galina. I walked close to her while she leaned on Drusus' massive desk with her hands spread and her head down low.

"What the fuck was all that about?" I asked her. "That was just plain crazy."

She didn't lift her head, and she didn't answer me.

I stepped closer still until I stood at the table beside her.

"Uh... Galina?" I said. "Are you going to take this job? Are you actually going to become consul of all Earth? Those seem like some mighty big shoes to fill."

Finally, she raised her head slowly, and she looked at me. "A year or two ago," she said, "I might have told you I've never desired anything more in all my life—but now I'm not so sure."

"Say... did you know this mess was going down today? Did you know your dad was going to try to appoint you to running the entire planet?"

She shook her head slowly. "I knew something was up—something big—but I didn't expect this."

I chewed that over for a moment, and I decided I believed her. She didn't look like a woman who was calmly enjoying the fruits of her own scheming. This mess was all caught up in her dad's schemes now. She was trapped in a spider's web.

"So, like... what are you going to do?"

"I don't frigging know, James. That's why I put them off for as long as I possibly could."

"Yeah, yeah, right," I said, "but there's another thing... Why did you keep me here, exactly? I could have been with Drusus right now."

She looked at me, and her expression softened a bit for the first time. "Let me ask you something, James. Did you notice the six hogs in here, the men who were ready to kill at my father's slightest command? Or the twenty more men positioned outside in the hallway?"

"Yeah, sure. I couldn't help but notice them."

"Right," she said. "If Drusus or I had needed you to kill them, would you have done it?"

I didn't think about it for a second. "You know I would have—I would have tried, at least."

She nodded, and she smiled. "Now you know why you're here."

"I've been playing the part of bodyguard without even knowing it?"

"That's right. Drusus probably requested you attend this event for that purpose. After today's startling revelations, I wanted you to stay for the same reasons."

I gave my neck a scratch. Whenever I got caught up in a bunch of cloak and dagger politics, I felt kind of itchy.

"Well, uh..." I said, "you want to like, go out on the town maybe, or...?"

She shook her head. "No... I would, but I've got too much on my mind tonight. I'm supposed to make a momentous decision about my future—about everyone's future."

"Well..." I said, "maybe I could relax you? I could help take some of that hard thinking off your shoulders."

She looked at me, and I figured she was seriously considering my offer. She knew what I was really saying, and she was tempted. But then, she shook her head.

"No," she said, "why don't you head on home to Georgia? Relax with your family for the short while you have left to do so."

I thought that was kind of a cryptic comment. It was, in fact, downright fraught with negativity. I might have questioned her about it, but my advances had been clearly rebuffed, and I'd been given an invitation to escape an office meeting that had gone on for far too long already. Under such circumstances, I was always late for the door.

On the way out, I fingered a few of those gold tassels one last time. They rattled and hung heavily against my hand. I had a powerful feeling that by the time I came back here, all the décor in this office would have dramatically changed.

At the door, I glanced back one more time. Galina was still standing there at the head of that massive table. She looked small, alone and a little bit lost. I had to wonder what she would decide to do next.

-48-

After leaving poor Galina in that lofty office, I thought about doing what she said. I thought about going home to Georgia and enjoying myself—but I just couldn't do it. The honest truth was, after I'd watched poor Drusus getting himself unfairly arrested, I felt unsettled.

Drusus had always exhibited fine judgment, law-abiding self-control, and above all a sense of duty. Despite all his good work, his final reward had been arrest and probably execution at the hands of a bunch of assholes in robes. It just didn't seem right to me.

I also didn't like the idea that Galina was clearly fearing for her future as well. On the surface, her reaction seemed hard to understand. After all, her own daddy had just clearly engineered her into a rulership position over all Earth.

But I had to remind myself that being the head of Earth's military and having extreme powers on a temporary basis may not be all it was cracked up to be. I mean, just look at Drusus himself. He'd done his damnedest, and he'd actually *deserved* the post. Despite all that, in the end, he'd been tossed aside by the true powers that were behind his throne.

I'd never seen a clearer demonstration of what people often whispered—that except for the Galactics themselves, Earth was ruled by its public servants. Not the people on the frontlines, not the people you saw, not the people you cheered for—but instead these unknown, faceless individuals who had wielded power in secret for many, many years.

I happen to know that Old Alexander Turov himself was of extreme age. I suspected all his kind were the same. They hadn't put Drusus into power to save Earth, but rather to serve their own needs—whatever they were.

Now he'd installed his own daughter—or at least he was trying to. Galina was resisting. The temptation and the pressure on her had to be tremendous. I knew she was a worrier and an over-thinker, so she was naturally having a hard time with it. She seemed terrified of the very post that Drusus had accepted as an honor.

Even I was worried by these events. It was a strange situation, and I knew that if I went home to Georgia tonight and tried to sleep in my own bed, it would probably take me half an hour or more to get to where I was sawing wood. I'd probably even wake up once or twice during the night to pee or something. For me, that was an astounding level of disquiet.

So, instead of heading home, I went to seek out the one who I thought might be able to shed some light on the situation. Heading down to Gray Deck, the very place where I'd arrived not more than an hour ago, I walked toward the least busy set of gateway posts in the entire chamber.

Various night-watchmen-type hogs tried to stop me, saying operational hours were over. They told me I had to come back and buy a ticket in the morning. But when I told them where I wanted to go, they let me pass.

There were two worlds on the very long list of planets that Earth now claimed dominion over that were easy to travel to. One was Death World—because freaking nobody wanted to go out there—and the second was Dust World, because *almost* nobody wanted to go there.

I took care to cover up the teleportation harness I'd been wearing all this time. It was still programmed to take me to Central. I knew with a good recharge and a little bit of luck it would return me back to Earth whenever I felt like it.

Some hog, who was yawning because it was late at night by now, mulled over my "papers." These were nothing but computer scrolls I used now and then to play porn-feelies when I was deployed on various planets.

While he perused these dubious documents in confusion, I stepped in a spritely manner toward the gateway posts.

"Hey—hey, wait a second," the hog called after me.

With a simple wave of my hand over my shoulder, I disappeared.

Dust World was hot and dry. It felt like I'd opened an oven door.

No one followed me out from Central. I knew no one would. Anybody who wanted to subject themselves to one of the worst planets humanity had yet to overpopulate and exploit was welcome to it.

The hog guards on the far side squinted at me and spat in the dirt. They sullenly made a few notes on their tappers, but they didn't say a word. Guarding the gateway posts on Dust World was a punishment duty, and these two didn't seem like they were enjoying it.

The good news was it was a bright, sunny day on Dust World. In fact, it was almost too bright—and too sunny.

I was at the bottom of a deep canyon. Everyone who lived on Dust World lived in such toad-holes in the vast desert that covered the planet's surface.

Shafts of harsh light from the brilliant star known as Zeta Herculis struck the high walls of the canyons above us. Even that reflected light was enough to make any man squint.

After touching my cap to the surly hogs, I walked calmly down a dusty road toward the only village in this part of the world. I never reached the village, as I'd no intention of doing so. Instead, I struck out into the wilds on the far side of the central lake.

Like all such valleys on Dust World, this puncture-wound in the side of the planet was really a sunken volcanic crater. There was a deep lake in the center of it that bubbled like an evil swamp. Past the reeds and the pond-like water, I discovered the broken walls that had once hidden colonists who'd survived down here for over seventy years without any influence from Earth.

In these ancient stone warrens I wandered, and I called out. I thought I was in the right passageways, but no one answered me for nearly an hour.

Eventually, a single, tall, thin figure appeared. She was feminine and lovely... but aging now.

"Floramel?" I asked. "Where is everybody?"

"James?" she said. "You shouldn't have come here."

"Why the hell not?"

Floramel cast a wary look over her shoulder and then looked back to me. "She won't like it," she said.

"She? She who? Are you talking about Etta?"

"No, not Etta. Just go on home now, James. Etta will come visit you someday in the future. Maybe for that Thanksgiving-thing that your people like to do every November."

I thought that over, and I found her answers unacceptable. I walked toward her. "Floramel, is something wrong?"

She showed me her teeth as I got closer. "James," she hissed, "you just can't be here. The people from the town, they all listen to her. They all believe everything she says."

"Who says?" I asked whispering back. "Who the hell are we talking about?"

"Boudica," she said. "At least, that's what she calls herself."

"Boudica?" I said. "What the hell kind of a name is that?"

"I've investigated the name. It's actually from an ancient source on Earth. There was a rebel Druidic queen in a place called Britannia..."

"What the...?" I began, but she cut me off.

"The point is that Boudica was a famous rebel queen. She led a tribe of primitives against ancient Rome. She was quite successful—and vengeful, from what I could learn of the incident."

"A rebel queen, huh?" Then, all of a sudden, I began to get an idea. "Say now," I said, "we aren't talking about the loudmouth brain in a jar that I brought out here a year or so back, are we?"

Floramel showed me her teeth again. She looked like she was going to hiss, but she didn't.

"If you meet her, you must call her Boudica," she said.

"Okay, sure. What's she look like? A brainstem? Can she even see? The last time I saw her, her eyeballs were drooping down to the bottom of that tank, and—"

"Don't talk like that. Come on—and remember that I warned you."

I followed her, and she led me deeper into the warrens under the mountain. The endless dark tunnels under these cliffs were holes the original colonists had dug to avoid their enemies. Eventually, we found a region where the Investigator had set up new labs.

The last time I was out here, I'd counted maybe ten bubbling cauldrons of varying sizes. Each of these were experiments, attempts to breathe life into what amounted to muck, mud, flesh, bone—the most basic organic rudiments.

Unlike the revival machines, which worked in about a half hour's time, the Investigator's illegal and rather primitive methods could grow a corpse to fruition in a period of something like six weeks. Now however, instead of ten such tanks there were a hundred. They weren't in various shapes and sizes anymore, but instead all of uniform dimensions.

"Would you look at that?" I said. "The old Investigator's been busy, hasn't he?"

"Yes, he has," Floramel said, "and I'm afraid my husband has fallen under Boudica's spell."

I almost laughed aloud at that. The Investigator was one of the weirdest, hardest-headed men I'd ever met in my life. The very idea he was under the spell of any woman, no matter what weird name she'd chosen for herself, seemed ludicrous.

I walked into the room, but Floramel stayed at the entrance. I began to mosey around between the various tanks. I poked, I prodded, I took a glimpse. There were bodies in every one of the tanks. They all appeared to be human. Some were half-formed, but others were almost ready to come out of the oven.

Then, all at once, figures stepped out from the corners of the room. I realized that the darkened corners were tunnels leading off to God-knew-where. There had to be at least twenty strangers converging on me. They were human, fortunately. Men who wore nothing but leather pants. They had bare feet and bare chests, and each of them had a gleaming blade in his hands.

I stopped poking around in the various stewpots and stood tall. I didn't run. I didn't even retreat a step, or cry for my mama. Instead, I grinned at them.

"Well now," I said. "Look at you boys! What are you, a bunch of illegal clones or something? Why don't one of you guys head on out and find Boudica for me? I've got an appointment with her. She and the Investigator both."

For some reason, these words stopped the advancing pack of knife-wielding bandits. They stood there tensely. Each of them stood on the balls of his feet with his knife in his hand, aiming it in my direction.

I did my best to look unconcerned. So far, I hadn't drawn the pistol on my belt, or the knife strapped to my leg. I wasn't going to be the first one to draw blood in this low-rent revival chamber—but if things went badly, I wasn't going to be the only one dying here, either.

Taking a moment to glance back over my shoulder, I saw that Floramel was no longer in the doorway. She had, in fact, disappeared. I frowned at that. She'd been my girlfriend once upon a time, and now she was the wife of the Investigator. That made her, what? Etta's step-grandma? I didn't know for sure, but it did seem rude in any case for her to take off and leave me with this bunch.

Preparing mentally to do battle, I watched as the large group of silent and aggressive young men encircled me. They stayed three or four meters away, but they certainly didn't look friendly.

"What's the meaning of this?" said a loud sonorous voice.

It was the Investigator, a man I knew well. The creepy old fossil had appeared in the doorway where Floramel had vanished. Perhaps she'd gone to get him rather than abandon me. At least I could hope that was the case.

"Back children, back," he shouted to the crowd that approached me.

They milled for a moment, then quietly crept away. The whole time they backpedaled between the numerous bubbling tanks, they kept their blades up and aimed in my direction.

I took no notice of this, but instead turned to warmly greet the Investigator. I acted as if nothing weird was happening down here in this stone pit that served him for a laboratory.

"Hey, Investigator," I said. "I've returned for a visit. I've been looking forward to some Dust World hospitality."

The Investigator walked in, and he looked at me sternly. I couldn't recall him ever having looked at anyone any other way.

"James McGill..." he said. "I must apologize for your poor reception. These fools don't know you. They don't know yet that they owe you a great debt."

"They do...? Well... yeah, sure. Damn straight, they do."

The Investigator turned away and beckoned. I followed him out of the stinking revival chamber. When we were walking together, I sent a harsh whisper in his direction. "You aren't trying to tell me those boys are all my genetic offspring or something, are you?"

"No," he said, "certainly not."

"Good, good. Just checking, mind you."

"Come, you must meet Boudica."

"Uh, okay..."

I followed the Investigator. Floramel was still nowhere to be seen. Neither was Etta, who was the one I really would like to meet on this trip out to Dust World. She was, after all, my one and only daughter. I was starting to think I was going to have to have a certain conversation with her about her choices in life, and the people she'd chosen to hang out with.

After what seemed like a long walk into ever darker passageways and galleries of carven stone caverns, we reached a chamber with two women in it. One of them was Etta, who gave me a welcoming smile.

The second girl I'd never met before. She was a striking woman. She was tall, with long auburn hair that hung to her hips. But it was when she turned to face me that I was outright stunned.

She wore leather pants, just like the guys back in the room with the bubbling cauldrons. But that wasn't the weird thing. The weird thing was she wasn't wearing anything else.

My widened eyes were immediately caught, trapped and entranced by a very prominent pair of milk-white breasts. To me, she looked like a woman who rarely went out in the sun.

"Uh…" I said staring at her.

"I am Boudica," she said.

"That much I gathered, ma'am," I said. "Do I know you?"

"After a fashion, you do, McGill," she said. "You're the one who freed me from the rebel bunker in that dreadful swamp.

"Oh…" I said. "So, you're the lady in the jar. The… uh… brain-thing."

"That's right. The Investigator here was kind enough to grow a new body to my specifications."

I lifted a hand, and I pointed in the general direction of her chest. "So, like, this is what you used to look like before you were put in that jar?"

"No, not at all. I chose this appearance for its historical significance. The original Boudica was infamous, you see."

"Oh yeah, right… somebody told me you were a rebel queen, or something like that."

"Yes. Boudica—the original—was a Druidic queen who resisted the Romans fiercely. They feared her. She made a powerful empire tremble!"

"Huh…" I said, chewing that over in my big, slow brain. "That's cool. So… are you a scientist doing a little work down here with the Investigator?"

"Far from it. I'm a revolutionary, James."

"Whoa," I said. "Whoa! That's not a good thing. That's not a good word in our time."

"No," she said. "I daresay it's not a good word in any time."

Finally, I was able to tear my eyes away from Boudica long enough to look at my daughter. I noticed she seemed to be slightly annoyed and a little bit worried.

"Hey girl," I said, throwing my arms wide for a hug.

She came to me reluctantly and allowed me to give her that hug, but it seemed like she was uncomfortable the entire time. I got the feeling from both her body language and her facial expressions she wasn't completely comfortable around

Boudica. Even more importantly, she wasn't talking at all. That was a bad sign with Etta. She normally dominated the conversation whether you wanted her to or not.

"To what do we owe the honor of this visit, James?" the Investigator asked.

"Well, first off, I'm came out here to check up on you guys. I haven't seen you for a long time."

"That's very kind," the Investigator said. His tone indicated he didn't care at all. "This is not really a good time for social pleasantries. We're quite busy and engaged in a large project."

"I can see that," I said, eyeing Boudica again. "Are you guys out here planning a big revolution or something?"

To me, the whole idea was ludicrous. What I'd seen was a couple of dozen strange guys in pants who didn't seem to have a brain between the lot of them, all wielding knives like they were scary weapons. Their blades didn't even look like they had molecularly aligned edges. Even pitted against the two hogs with morph-rifles at the gateway posts, these jokers were doomed.

"You scoff at us?" Boudica said suddenly. "You do so at your own peril."

"What?"

"Revolutions, McGill," she said, walking forward. "They don't begin with the weapons in your hand. They begin with the thoughts in your mind."

"Uh-huh," I said. "That's some deep-thinking, lady. Well, I figure I should be heading back to town for some dinner. Etta? Maybe you would like to come with me for a bit?"

Boudica seemed to ignore all this. Etta didn't move, and neither did the Investigator.

Instead, Boudica walked around me in a slow circle. I kind of felt like I was being snake-charmed what with her long hair and those perfect breasts.

Had she planned all this out? Had she decided to have the Investigator sculpt her body into such a formation just so she could influence fools like me? I was beginning to think that she had.

"Tell us why you *really* came here, McGill," she said.

"Well, uh... you see, things have gone a little strangely back home on Earth, and I was kind of wanting to talk to some of you guys about it—to the Investigator in particular."

"Talk then, James," the Investigator said. "We're all friends here."

I nodded, and I turned toward him. I tried my best—my damnedest—to avoid looking at that strange woman at all.

I told him in brief what had happened back on Earth. That Drusus had been deposed, and we now had a truce with Rigel—but the Ruling Council of Hegemony didn't seem to want to keep it.

Then, I spilled my guts concerning the new, even greater threat. The weird crystalline life forms we'd discovered on Jungle World.

Lastly, I talked about Galina Turov and how she was strongly considering the throne that Drusus had just vacated. That's when the Investigator's face lit up.

"Ah-ha," he said. "The final piece of the puzzle is now in place."

"It is?" I asked.

"Yes. Have you ever seen a spider web, James McGill?"

I stared at him for a moment. "Yeah, I sure have."

"What is in the center of such a web?"

"Uh," I said puzzling for a moment. "A spider, I suppose."

"Correct. So and therefore, when you identify a complex weave, a plan, an unnatural structure with deadly intent behind it, do you believe that such a thing was created by happenstance, or by carefully thought out machinations?"

"Macha-what?" I asked.

"What I'm trying to ask is, who do you think is at the center of this plot to drive Rigel and Earth into a grinding war?"

I thought about that, and I gave my head a scratch. This took so long that the Investigator decided to give me another hint.

"Who, James, is the spider at the center of this web? Who do you think ordered a real warhead to be loaded onto the test missile that destroyed the Big Sky Project?"

"Oh..." I said. "Do you think somebody ordered it?"

"Of course."

"And that guy… is the spider… right?" I asked, getting a bit confused.

"Yes James, but the web is much more complex than that."

"Oh yeah…?"

"The web involves not just kickstarting a new war, but also the effort it takes to install a leader who is under the spider's control."

I was feeling itchy all over again. I tried to think. In my mind, I pictured a web. There were strands everywhere. They gleamed white in the sun. One spiraling strand was that missile that had destroyed Big Sky and killed millions of people on Earth. Another strand was the one that had put Drusus into office to run the war. Then there was Galina. She'd stumbled into this weave, and she knew she'd been captured by it. She was a strand too…

All of a sudden, I knew who the spider was.

"Alexander Turov…?" I said.

The Investigator smiled. "You see?" he said, turning to Boudica. "His mind is not that of a helpless child. He simply needs a modicum of guidance."

"You're wrong," she said. "He's a fool with huge arms. That said… I have use for such men."

I nodded to them, knowing in my heart of hearts they were both right.

* * *

After spending about a week out at Dust World, I decided it was time to head home. I tried to get Etta to come home with me, but she refused. She said there was too much good work to be done at Dust World. She wanted to help her grandfather, and his wife—and this strange new woman, Boudica. I couldn't talk her into leaving and coming back home to safe, friendly Georgia Sector.

I'd spent enough time visiting my oh-so-strange relatives, so I charged the teleport harness I'd brought with me.

Activating the big, single button on the rig, I air-mailed myself back to Central.

Searching for hours, I was unable to find Galina. I sent her various messages which she ignored. As far as I could tell she wasn't dead, but she'd apparently returned home to Eastern Europe. Maybe she had some kind of family function to attend.

Not knowing what else to do, I flew home on the sky-train to Georgia. Shortly after I arrived, *Scorpio* loomed in orbit over Earth. The regular rank-and-file members of Legion Varus disembarked, and they mustered-out.

After *Scorpio* docked, Carlos sent me a carefully drawn picture of a finger. He was angry that I'd managed to escape the return voyage home. A dozen other messages flittered in. Some were well wishes, others were complaints. I pretty much ignored them all.

A few weeks later, I'd already settled into civilian life again on my parent's farm. As was normally the case, I did everything I could to forget about the stars and the adventures I'd experienced under their grim light.

During the first cool night of early Fall, something came scratching at my door. I bounced awake, armed myself and moved to glance out the window.

I saw a small silhouette on my porch. It appeared to be female. Immediately, my mind leapt to one conclusion—it was Galina.

I turned on the light and threw the door wide. There stood a startled woman, but it wasn't Galina after all. It was Tessie.

"Did you expect me?" she asked. Then she glanced at the weapon in my hand. "Oh… I guess you didn't."

"I surely did!" I lied.

"I sent you six tapper messages. You never responded."

"I read every one of them," I told her.

"Well then…" she said. "What do you think?"

I blinked a couple of times. "…about which one? I mean, uh… there were six."

She twisted up her lips. I knew I was disappointing her somehow.

"I've been asking for your advice, Centurion," she said. "You know, about which specialty to pursue? I mean… do you think I'd make a better tech, or a bio? I'm certainly not a weaponeer."

"No, no, not that," I said. "In fact... you know what? I think you'd make a good ghost."

And I meant it. She was, after all, kind of sneaky. She was also a bit mean and an assassin at heart. The way she'd ambushed a dozen losers back on *Scorpio* during the exercises... yes, she was a natural ghost.

Tessie thought that over, and she smiled. She nodded. "That's actually good advice," she said. "I'm glad I came to get it."

We stared at each other for another long moment.

"Is that all you were thinking about...?" I asked finally. "About asking me, I mean?"

She smiled shyly, and she studied my shitty wooden porch swing.

I opened my screen door wide. It creaked loudly on rusted hinges.

Tessie looked a little wary as she walked inside, which was wise of her—but she did come in.

The rest of the night was preordained. After we made love, Tessie fell asleep on my old couch.

Strangely, I was a bit troubled. Somehow, my surge of false recognition had me thinking. I'd truly believed, just for a moment, that it was Galina outside. I'd been certain of it, in fact—and yet it wasn't her.

Where was she? What was she doing right now? Why hadn't she answered any of the text messages I'd sent her?

Then I thought about Tessie. When I hadn't responded, she'd come to seek me out. Perhaps, soon, I was going to have to do the same and go looking for Galina.

THE END

Books by B. V. Larson:

UNDYING MERCENARIES
Steel World
Dust World
Tech World
Machine World
Death World
Home World
Rogue World
Blood World
Dark World
Storm World
Armor World
Clone World
Glass World
Edge World
Green World
Ice World
City World
Sky World
Jungle World

Visit BVLarson.com for more information.

Printed in Great Britain
by Amazon